The Mafia Trilogy

by

Jonas Saul

PUBLISHED BY:
Imagine Press Inc.
Ebook ISBN: 978-1-927404-23-2
Amazon Print ISBN: 979-8-387256-67-7
Paperback ISBN: 978-1-998047-94-9

The Mafia Trilogy
Copyright © 2013 by Jonas Saul

The Sarah Roberts Series

Dark Visions (One)
The Warning (Two)
The Crypt (Three)
The Hostage (Four)
The Victim (Five)
The Enigma (Six)
The Vigilante (Seven)
The Rogue (Eight)
Killing Sarah (Nine)
The Antagonist (Ten)
The Redeemed (Eleven)
The Haunted (Twelve)
The Unlucky (Thirteen)
The Abandoned (Fourteen)
The Cartel (Fifteen)
Losing Sarah (Sixteen)
The Pact (Seventeen)
The Terror (Eighteen)
The Chase (Nineteen)
The Betrayal (Twenty)
Sarah's Return (Twenty-One)
The Hunt (Twenty-Two)
The Delivery (Twenty-Three)
The Trap (Twenty-Four)
The Ultimatum (Twenty-Five)
The Depraved (Twenty-Six)
The Condemned (Twenty-Seven)
Payback (Twenty-Eight)
The Unknown (Twenty-Nine)
Wrath (Thirty)
The Damned (Thirty-One)
The Game (Thirty-Two)
The Decoy (Thirty-Three)
The Disappearance (Thirty-Four)
The Whole Truth (Thirty-Five)
Alex (Thirty-Six)
Parkman (Thirty-Seven)

Darwin (Thirty-Eight)
Aaron (Thirty-Nine)
Remains To Be Seen (Forty)

The Jake Wood Novels

The Immortal Gene (Book One)
The Immortal Target (Book Two)

Standalone Novels

'Til Death Do Us Part
The Drowning
The Woman in the Woods
The Threat
The Specter
The Mafia Trilogy
A Murder in Time
Frequency of the Dead

Co-Authored Novels

Collision Course (Written with Gary Ponzo)
There Will Be Blood (Written with Rania Stone)
The Soulless (Written with Rania Stone)

Short Story Collections

Twisted Fate (Tales of Horror)
Twists of Fate (Tales of Hope)

Part One

The Kill

Prolog

Vincenzo Fuccini reached inside his Armani jacket and gripped the butt of his weapon, which hung suspended in his shoulder holster. He turned in his seat and looked back at Ronnie and Frankie. Both men sat ramrod straight in the back seat, staring out at the passing countryside as the sun dropped below the warm July sky.

"Ronnie, Frankie, you know what you're supposed to do?"

Ronnie turned to face Vincenzo. "Yeah, boss. We got it. Take out anybody who is not supposed to be there. Any sign of trouble toward you, we take them out."

Frankie nodded his understanding and said, "We got this, boss."

"Good. Don't let it get fucked up because if it does, we won't be going home; even if we walk away tonight, we're still dead men. There are powerful men at this meeting."

"Awww, boss," the driver said. "Don't talk like that. Your dad would kill us in the worst possible way if anything happened to you."

Vincenzo turned back in his seat, let go of the weapon he'd been holding, and placed his hand on the door's armrest. He could never remember the driver's name. They changed so often that he stopped caring who they were.

"Nothing is going to happen tonight," Vincenzo said. "Believe that. We make our deal, and we leave."

They continued in silence, racing along the back-country road, heading to an abandoned airplane hangar in their brand new black Cadillac, each man lost in his thoughts.

Lights in the distance alerted Vincenzo they were close.

"Slow down and cut the headlights. Here is good."

The driver slowed the Cadillac and pulled over to the side. He flipped off the lights.

"Okay, Ronnie, do this and do it right. When the deal is over, we can't pick you up. It'll be too obvious. Just do what you gotta do, and when everyone leaves, fall back and wait. We'll come for both of you an hour later. Got it?"

Ronnie nodded and looked at Frankie. He nodded, too.

"I want to hear it. Got it?"

"Yeah, boss. Got it."

"Frankie?"

"Got it."

"Wait for my okay, and then go," Vincenzo ordered.

Vincenzo opened his door and slowly stepped out of the car. He stood by his door, placed both hands near his crotch, and pretended to take a piss as he scanned the woods on each side.

After a moment, he tapped the vehicle's roof and whispered, "*Go.*"

The back door on the passenger side opened, and Ronnie jumped out, followed by Frankie, who shut the door softly enough that Vincenzo heard the click as the lock snapped in place. Then, both men, staying low, hustled off into the woods.

Perfect.

In case he had eyes on him, Vincenzo shook his hands near his dick for effect. Then he leaned back in, sat on the front seat, and closed the door hard.

"Go."

The driver flipped the headlights back on and pulled away. They covered the last mile in moments and pulled up to a makeshift checkpoint.

Two men holding assault rifles stood on either side of the road.

They had been hard to see as they had stood behind a pair of black vans parked on either side of the gravel road.

The one on the driver's side motioned with the tip of his gun —what looked like an M16—for the driver to slow up and open his window. Vincenzo's driver came to a stop and rolled his window down two inches. "What's this?"

"Open the trunk," the guard said.

The driver flipped a button, and the trunk popped open. The guard on the passenger side scanned the back seat with a flashlight. After a minute, the man at the back of the Cadillac slammed the trunk shut and returned to the window.

"Names." It wasn't a question as much as an order.

The driver looked at Vincenzo. "Is that okay, boss?"

Vincenzo nodded.

"This is Vincenzo Fuccini," the driver told the guard. "I'm Alex."

The guard leaned down and looked in at Vincenzo. "I'm sorry, sir. Precautionary measures. Pull in and stay to the right."

The guard stepped back. Vincenzo's driver eased the car down the lane and pulled in behind a line of three other Cadillacs. He cut the engine.

Vincenzo collected himself and stepped out of the car. The driver would wait in the vehicle; the windows rolled up. The guards would allow all the drivers to lower their windows an inch for air in rotating shifts after the meeting started. Vincenzo wasn't comfortable with all the details, but he was here and had two men hiding, watching his back. If anything went down, he would walk away, and the bosses of the other families wouldn't.

Vincenzo stepped around the Caddy and stopped as two guards approached him.

"What's going on?" he asked.

"Everyone gets patted down before entering the building."

"You're fucking kidding, right? I'm Vincenzo Fuccini."

Neither guard said a word as one stepped back to give room for the other to do the pat down.

"Get on with it then," Vincenzo said.

He raised his arms level with the ground. The guard started at his shoulders and worked his way down, pausing when his hand touched the gun in Vincenzo's holster.

The guard eased it out by the butt end and handed it to his colleague, who emptied the ammunition and dropped the weapon in a leather satchel.

When the frisk was completed, the guard said, "You'll get your gun back when the meeting is complete."

Vincenzo grunted and started for the open door. He knew the pat down was more about hidden wires than weapons. In this business, there wasn't any trust. He smiled, knowing they had allowed him to keep his keychain. On it was a Kubaton with a hidden surprise should he need it.

Three Canadian crime bosses in one building were exactly why his father said he wouldn't attend. Too much power in one room. If any of them lost their temper or one of their guards got trigger-happy, a major war would be on everyone's hands, and no one wanted that.

Vincenzo had argued that he shouldn't go either. But his father said this was a peace deal. It was a long time coming, and since Vincenzo would be taking over as Captain in the coming year, he needed to be there. The other bosses had reluctantly agreed that Vincenzo could stand in for his father.

He reached the door and stepped into the bright interior of a remodeled airplane hangar. Guards were interspersed around the perimeter, standing by every door, each with an M16 in his hands. They were armed for war with thick Kevlar vests, spare bullet belts, and radios, along with other junk strapped to their belts. A large rifle-like gun leaned against the wall beside each guard. The huge weapon reminded Vincenzo of the elephant gun he'd fired a year ago at an African Safari. It had enough stopping power to kill a charging pachyderm.

What the fuck is all this for? I thought this was a peaceful meeting.

"Vinny, come join us," Phil, the boss for the Montreal area, called out.

The three family leaders sat in leather armchairs around a circular coffee table in the middle of the hangar. One chair remained empty. A bottle of booze sat on the little table, an empty glass in front of the unoccupied chair.

Vincenzo walked over, leaned down on the table, and grabbed the bottle of Johnnie Walker to pour himself a shot. In all his years of running errands for his father, he had only met two of the men sitting at the table. The third man was hardly seen by anybody.

The last thing he wanted was for them to see his hands shaking. He poured fast, set the bottle down, and with the ease borne among men of stature, he sat down, arms stretched out and legs open.

"It's Vincenzo, not Vinny. Don't ever call me Vinny again. Only my mother got to call me that; God rest her soul."

The three men exchanged glances as Vincenzo took a large swig of the whiskey.

"Now that we're all here, let's get started—"

A gunshot in the distance cut him off.

Vincenzo jerked and leaned forward. "What the fuck was that? Weapons firing at a peaceful meeting?"

All three men turned to him. Another gunshot rang out through the night.

He studied their faces, one by one.

What the hell is going on?

Phil, the man who called him Vinny, spoke first. "Does your father know about the two men you brought?"

"What men?" Vincenzo asked.

Phil looked at his colleagues and then fixed his attention back on Vincenzo. "Is this how we're to conduct a meeting? One that is supposed to be based on trust? Your family was asked to be here out of respect. Your family has ties to the old country. The Fuccinis are one of the strongest families in Sicily today. But you come here and lie to us. How do you expect us to respond?"

Vincenzo was stumped. He held the lowest rank. He knew it, and they knew it. It should be his father sitting here. Was this an ambush? Would they try to take out a boss's son? Was that the purpose from the beginning?

Whether it was or not, he couldn't come to them from a place of weakness. He had to show strength. One day, he would run the Fuccini Family Organization, and these men would have to respect that.

"I brought my own security. That is how a Fuccini Family member handles things. If you have a problem with that, talk to my father."

There was a moment of silence before Phil responded. Vincenzo lifted his glass and sipped the whiskey. As soon as he did it, he judged the sip weak and feminine. He needed to hold their stare, not back down, and especially not sip his beverage as it smacked of nervousness, which equated to weakness to these men.

Shit, I wish I could walk in the fucking door again and do this all over.

"We have no issue with security. Look around you." Phil gestured with a wave of his arm. "I have security everywhere. We have an issue with you defying the terms of our meeting. We made sure every family knew the terms. This meeting was to broker peace among us. We hire a joint security force, unbiased to any family. Our drivers wait in their cars. The location was announced hours ago and distributed through your Mississauga store. That's it. Any other guns or security detail would be considered hostile, and the family member who brought them would be expelled from the meeting."

Okay, now you're talking to me like I'm a baby.

"Look, Phil, my men were here to watch my back; that's it. They weren't hostile." Vincenzo pointed his finger at Phil.

"Killing them was a mistake. That was hostile. You will have to make good to my father."

Phil laughed.

"What the *fuck* is so funny?"

"We won't have to make good to anyone. Your father knew the terms, and he agreed to them. You will have to make good, and you'll have to do it to every person in this room."

Vincenzo had no idea what to say. Losing his temper right now would go a long way to kill any deal for the Fuccini Family, which would go against his father's wishes.

"We watched," Phil said, "as you slowed your car and pretended to piss on the road, your headlights turned off so that your two guys could run and hide. What do you take us for, amateurs? We have men posted ten kilometers in every direction. A fucking Cessna couldn't get within a hundred meters of this building without being blown back into the last century. Maybe you're not ready for this. Is it possible your daddy sent the wrong man?"

Vincenzo had heard enough. Two good men were dead. He needed this deal because if peace could be brokered, the families were supposed to work together in a more financially connected way. Within a year, his father had told him, they would be three times richer than they already were. But he wouldn't be talked down to by some asshole who just had two of his men clipped for the crime of protecting him.

He got to his feet, swallowed the last of his whiskey, and slammed the glass down.

"We're done here."

"I don't think so," Phil said. "The meeting hasn't even started. But it won't start until you tell us how you will make good on your disrespect."

Vincenzo scanned the faces of the other men present. He looked up and examined the faces of the security detail closest to the foursome. What were they thinking, challenging him like this? He had done nothing wrong, nor would he bow down to these men like he was a pussy. No way. They will always remember this night. If he caved, years from now, the word on the street would affirm that anyone could push the Fuccini Family around.

But he couldn't leave without the peace deal in hand.

There had to be another way.

He reached into his jacket, pulled out his pack of cigarettes, flipped one out, placed it on his lips, and started patting himself down for a lighter. He came up empty. The nearest guard watched him. Vincenzo stepped around his chair and walked up to the guard.

"Got a light?" he asked.

The guard shook his head in the negative.

Vincenzo turned back to the three men, their eyes on him. He reached into his pocket and touched his keychain. "Ahh, here it is."

He yanked the keychain out and grabbed the guard's hand at the same time. The Kubaton was about the size of a regular Bic pen but was made of steel and twice as thick. Vincenzo slapped the Kubaton on the guard's wrist and twisted up with force, snapping the wrist bone.

The guard screamed and dropped to one knee in front of Vincenzo. At that moment, he flipped the catch on the Kubaton and slid the hidden knife out. Knowing another guard might attack him at any second, he spun on his heels and, in the same motion, sliced the knife along the exposed neck of the guard, deep enough for a killing blow.

He was still turning back to the men in the leather chairs as the guard gagged on his own blood and fell to the hangar floor.

Vincenzo grabbed the huge elephant gun resting against the wall and aimed it at the nearest guard.

"Everyone, be cool. Stay calm, or more people will die." He aimed the weapon at Phil, hoping a guard wouldn't use his M16 to redecorate his face. "There will be no *making good* from me. You three will make good *to* me and my family."

The men standing along the perimeter of the building edged closer. Phil raised a hand, and the men stopped.

"Enlighten us," Phil said, his tone tighter, clipped. "Why do we have to make good to you?"

They seemed all too calm. "For killing the men I brought with me."

The man at Vincenzo's feet had stopped making gurgling sounds, his arms splayed out at his sides now, eyes wide and staring at nothing.

Phil grinned and looked around at the other two bosses, who smiled along with him.

At that moment, the urge to use the first bullet to erase that fucking cocky smile off the man's ass of a face overwhelmed Vincenzo.

"Put that weapon away and sit down before you get yourself killed," Phil said.

"Are you threatening me?"

Cars pulled up out front. For the briefest moment, Vincenzo looked at the open door and saw headlights pass across it.

Who else was invited?

He looked back at the three bosses in the middle of the room.

Phil's face had hardened.

"Put that fucking gun down now," Phil said. "Or bear the consequences."

"You motherfucker. How dare you—"

Rapid-fire gunshots from outside cut him off. Vincenzo dove to the floor as more shots rang out around him. He raised his gun and searched frantically for who was shooting. The portable lights flickered and went out, plunging the windowless hangar into pitch black.

He covered his head with his hands. Gunshots popped off like firecrackers at a Canada Day celebration. Flashes of light interspersed with gunfire as the guards stood in their fortified positions and shot at whoever was attacking them.

Things quieted for several seconds. Vincenzo patted himself down to look for wounds but found none. Moving blindly in the darkness, he flipped onto his back and listened. He detected movement to his left, about where that cocky bastard Phil had been. He closed his eyes and lifted his weapon. Listening as best he could, he moved his weapon toward the movement and fired.

A grunt told him he had hit his mark. The thump of dead weight confirmed it.

He thrust himself forward with his feet, sliding along the hangar floor on his back, trying to get some room between him and the four chairs that circled the coffee table.

After another bout of heavy machine-gun fire from outside, Vincenzo made it to the outer wall unscathed.

"You in there," someone shouted on a bullhorn. "We have the hangar surrounded. Come out, or we'll storm the building. I repeat, you are surrounded. You have one minute to come out."

Shit, shit, shit.

Someone grabbed him from behind. He couldn't help the gasp that escaped his lips.

"Shhh," a man whispered. "Take this."

A cold metal object landed in his palm.

"Put them on. You'll see better."

Vincenzo felt around the object's surface in his hands and found the cloth backing strip. Goggles of some kind. He pulled the elastic-like cloth out and placed it on his head, the goggles over his eyes. Instantly, the blackened hangar came to light in a green haze.

"There are a lot of men out there, and we need everyone here to do their part," the guard said.

"Their part?"

The guard with the M16 looked down at him. "Our orders were if the meeting is interrupted for any reason, all enemies die. That includes the Gambino Family members who are out there right now. The cops had guaranteed we wouldn't be interrupted."

"Why is the Gambino Family attacking us? On second thought, why weren't they invited?"

"Those are questions I can't answer."

Through the green lens, Vincenzo watched as the guard stood, aimed through a small hole in the corrugated metal wall, and carefully adjusted his weapon. Vincenzo searched the wall and found a similar hole. He stared out at the men lined up in pairs behind the cars and vans.

The guard beside him began firing. *Boom, boom, boom.* Just like that, men dropped one by one. A few lucky assholes ducked in time, but then the guard switched guns. Vincenzo saw that it was another elephant gun. As the guard fired, each round was like a cannon, the vehicles taking most of the hits.

Then, a van exploded.

Vincenzo dropped to the floor and ripped off his goggles, blinded by the fireball. After his eyes cleared, he placed the goggles back on and surveyed the hangar. Two other guards pumped bullet after bullet out of their respective holes in the walls. He saw three bodies sprawled out on the floor by the coffee table.

The bosses of the other families are all dead.

The Fuccini Family was the only surviving member of the peace accord, with the Gambino Family making a major power play outside.

What the hell had happened? How did it get so bad, so fast? Now, the four top crime families would be at war after all, and the Gambinos had started it.

He stopped the pity party, turned around, and began firing his gun out through the hole in the wall. What a waste of bullets. He hit nothing and saw no one outside anymore.

He pulled his weapon back in. The guard, three feet to his left, was reloading.

Vincenzo aimed his weapon at the open area on the guard's neck. As he pulled the trigger, he closed his eyes to avoid the blinding flash. He opened his eyes again as the guard fell to his knees and then the ground, dark liquid shooting from his neck.

Vincenzo looked back at the two remaining guards. They still stared through their holes.

He crawled over to unstrap the hand cannon from the fallen guard, then chambered a round. With the resolve of a Fuccini Family man, he stood, wiped the sweat off his forehead, and aimed at the guard on his right, at least twenty feet away.

Vincenzo fired and then fired again, the recoil knocking him back a step each time.

The second shot wasn't necessary. The first knocked into the man high in the chest area, throwing him at least five feet in the air before he fell, now a clump of human waste.

He turned to the other guard who watched him now, his weapon leveled at Vincenzo.

"Don't make me fire, Vinny," the guard pleaded. "I have orders to keep you four safe. You are not the enemy. They are." He pointed to the outside wall. "I will fire to save my life, but I don't want to. Let's walk out of here together."

He needed to wipe sweat from his forehead again but resisted, letting it slide down, tickling him as it went.

"Okay, you're right. Let's leave. Can you drive?" Vincenzo dropped his aim.

The guard lowered his weapon. "Yeah. I'll drive."

In that second, Vincenzo lifted his gun back in place and fired round after round into the guard. The man had no chance and no time to respond.

Now alone inside the hangar, Vincenzo walked over to the guard and looked down at him as he gasped for breath. Blood pooled around the man's mouth.

"Next time, don't call me Vinny."

He chambered a round, aimed at the guard's face, and fired from one foot away. The man's head exploded and disappeared in a wet mush of skin and bone. Vincenzo looked back down at the body and the dent in the hangar floor where the head had been.

A shame. A fucking shame.

He headed for the only open door in the hangar. No one remained alive in the building, and it didn't sound like anyone was alive outside, either. Not a single bullet had been fired outside or inside since he'd killed the guard who had given him the goggles. Nothing else came from the bullhorn. Only the crackling fire from the fully engulfed van.

As he neared the door, he removed the goggles and stepped up to the edge of the door frame. He dropped the guard's gun. In all his thirty-eight years, he had never seen this many dead men. A major battle occurred, and he was the only man left standing. His father would be so proud. Not a scratch on him. That was what family bosses were made of.

He realized the peace accord had been handed to him on a platter. Now, with all three crime bosses dead and many Gambino Family members' bodies strewn about, Vincenzo's father, and by extension, himself, would garner the respect due to an original family. The fact that Vincenzo would walk away from this carnage was enough to make him a hero. His name would go down in the mafia history books for years to come.

He looked out and scanned the territory surrounding the hangar. Nothing moved.

"I surrender," he shouted in case anyone could hear him. "I'm coming out."

Vincenzo stepped into the open, his hands raised.

Two feet from the door, and no one had taken a shot at him. No one popped a head up or said anything. He took a few more steps. Still nothing.

His stomach couldn't handle the tension. At any moment, he was convinced that someone would sit up, like a fucking Jack-in-the-Box, and fire a round into his eye.

But no one did.

The moon sat high, the fire crackled to his left, the night's insects remained quiet, and no one shot at him.

He walked farther, feeling more secure. His Cadillac was shot up pretty badly. It was also boxed in by two of Gambino's vehicles, one of which was the van on fire.

A police siren wailed in the distance.

Not a single vehicle was available to use. They were either on fire or shot to shit. He knew he had to hustle. In minutes, the area would be littered with cops, and dogs would search every square inch. At least a ten-kilometer radius would be shut down.

He looked up at the sound of a car approaching. Not a cop car. No flashing lights. He walked up to the shoulder of the road. The car was coming fast but slowed as it approached the flames. A Ford Mustang with the interior light on.

When the Mustang was fifty paces out, Vincenzo stepped from hiding and, with his legs spread, aimed the gun two-handed at the driver of the vehicle.

It didn't slow. It sped up in the last few seconds before the vehicle was upon Vincenzo.

Vincenzo fired a bullet into the windshield as a warning.

"Pull over," he shouted. "I need your car."

Vincenzo didn't have time to jump. He'd waited too long. He'd just walked out of a hangar full of dead men, surrounded by dead men, the only survivor. Surely, a car would stop for him or at least veer away from an invincible mafia leader. When he shot a warning at the vehicle, he thought the driver would lose control. All it caused the driver to do was hit the gas pedal.

The Mustang connected with Vincenzo at the knees, knocking him onto the car's hood at fifty-five kilometers per hour. Vincenzo rolled up and smashed into the windshield and then tumbled over the car, clearing the trunk on his way to the ground.

The driver slammed on his brakes and pulled to a stop on the side of the road.

The pain was intense and all-encompassing. He lay at an odd angle. His hips weren't meant to twist that way. Only his right eye still worked. In his peripheral vision, the back of his left foot rested near his shoulder.

He couldn't move. He couldn't speak. He lay there, breathing slower and slower.

A young man ran up and stood over him.

"I'm sorry, I'm sorry, I'm so sorry. I didn't see you. I was watching the fire over there. Then something hit my windshield. I panicked, and then you jumped in front of me. Oh, man, I'm in so much trouble. I'm sorry, mister. I'll call an ambulance."

The young man moved away from Vincenzo's vision, crying, whispering crazy things. Then he was talking on the phone to someone.

"Rosina, it's Darwin. I'm sorry. I couldn't see him in the dark, honey," he paused, then, "I don't have to call the cops … I see a ton of them coming now. I'm sorry, Rosina. I'll call you when this is over."

The man didn't hang up. He sounded angry *and* distraught. The guy asked whoever he was talking to how things could get messed up so bad and what her parents would think of him since they were now engaged to be married.

Hey, kid, I'm dying here. Can you worry about that shit later? Call a fucking ambulance.

Vincenzo closed his one good eye. He was tired. Breathing became a serious chore. A tiredness swept over him. He felt lighter. When his heart stopped, the blood oozing from his open wounds ceased flowing.

1

DARWIN KOSTAS HANDED THE key to the man at the hotel's front desk, then wrapped an arm around his wife's shoulders.

"How was your stay?" the clerk asked in his accented English.

"Great," Rosina answered him. "We had a fabulous time in Rome. Loved the Coliseum."

Darwin grabbed his backpack, slipped both arms through the straps, and lifted the handle on their suitcase.

"Let's go, hun. We don't want to miss the bus to the airport."

She shot him a glance that said, *don't rush me.* He raised his eyebrows and smiled to avoid revealing how nervous he was.

They bid farewell and promised to return, then went down the stairs and out of Hotel Luigi. It was a block from where the bus was to take them to Fiumicino Airport, where they had tickets to fly to Athens, Greece, to continue their honeymoon.

Darwin surveyed the area, scanning the faces of everyone who moved too close to them. They were too exposed out in public. He watched his back, paid attention to the street ahead, and waited for the sky to fall. At any moment, they would be attacked.

He knew it. But his wife didn't.

He had wrestled with telling her but hadn't brought himself to it yet. It was their honeymoon—he didn't want to ruin it. He would come clean on the flight back to Toronto. That would allow him a chance to give her all the details about the death threats, the two attempts on his life, and the new way they were going to have to live. Stuck on a plane together, she couldn't just run away from him. She wouldn't yell at him or hit him on a plane, either.

The situation they were in wasn't entirely his fault, though. Fate did this, but they had to live with it. Or die because of it.

They made it to the bus stop unscathed. Darwin placed their luggage under the bus compartment and handed their tickets to the driver. Other people were dumping their luggage and scampering onto the bus as well. After a long line, Rosina walked on first. Darwin waited until it looked like no one else was coming. As he stepped on, something stopped him. Two well-dressed men had just exited Rome's Termini train station. Both of them were on cell phones. One locked eyes with Darwin and pointed at him.

Darwin leaped up the bus stairs. The driver shut the door behind him.

"How long before we go?" Darwin asked.

"Right now," the driver said. "You were the last."

He started down the aisle, looking for Rosina. He saw her halfway down, near the middle exit door. The bus pulled away from the curb. Just as he sat down, one of the two men had made it to the side of the bus.

The man jumped up and banged on the window beside Rosina, who leaned away from the glass.

"Wow, crazy people," she said. "They really should try to get here on time."

"Yeah," Darwin agreed. "Insane."

His stomach clenched. That was too close. One minute either way, and they would've had to deal with his pursuers. He had to be more proactive. He had to fix the situation. They couldn't run forever.

He stared at the ceiling of the bus. They would never go away. That was just it. These kinds of men were too powerful. When they put you in their sights, there really was no negotiating with them. It was over, and there was nothing anyone could do about it. Not even the police.

"You okay?" Rosina asked. "You're pale."

"Yeah, I'm okay," he said. "Continental breakfast didn't really sit well with me."

"Could it be your fear of flying?"

Darwin met her eyes and wished he could explain everything. "No. Really, I'm fine. Don't worry about it."

She leaned closer and snuck an arm inside his. "But you're my husband now, and I love you. Tell me what's bothering you so I can make it all disappear."

I wish it were that simple.

"It's nothing, really. I'll be fine once we're on that plane to Athens. This is going to be awesome. I cannot wait to see the Acropolis."

"Me, too." Rosina glanced out the window.

Darwin looked over his shoulder on a couple of wide turns to see if he could spot anyone following them. As far as he could tell, no one tailed them.

Within twenty minutes, the bus descended a ramp and merged onto a highway. They said the ride from Termini Station was an hour to Fiumicino Airport. Darwin settled back, closed his eyes, and prayed. They had to get to the airport, check-in, and pass through security. Once that was accomplished, they would be in the clear. The men hunting him wouldn't get through security with a gun. They'd also have to buy airline tickets and obtain boarding passes. That was too tall an order for those assholes.

Bumps in the highway woke him. He'd almost fallen asleep, the stress of the last few days adding up.

One of the reasons he chose Hotel Luigi was because they accepted cash. Sure, the hotel staff took their passports and wrote the information down, but that information wasn't handed to the Italian officials promptly, giving Darwin and his wife a few days in Rome before they were detected.

The same would happen in Athens. He had a nice hotel picked out that offered the same kind of anonymity.

Rosina had nodded off beside him. At the front of the bus, a red digital clock told him they were fifteen minutes away.

A late model Crown Vic raced by the bus on his side. A moment later, another one did. He watched as both vehicles lined up in front of the bus. Then they slowed down, slowing the bus, too, the driver applying the brakes.

They can't do this. Not in public. Not like this.

He'd almost gotten his wife to safety.

Instead of feeling defeated, he had to think. What could he do? He had no weapon, no way to escape. Open fields were on both sides of the bus, which had slowed to half its speed. The bus driver hit his horn and shouted something in Italian. The two Crown Vics drove side by side, blocking all exits for the bus and the traffic piling up behind them.

The speed couldn't be any more than twenty miles per hour

now. The bus driver jerked on the steering wheel, turning left and right in a futile attempt to get around the two vehicles. Passengers were getting anxious. They had planes to catch. One man stood in the aisle and shouted in Italian.

Rosina woke and lifted her head. "What's going on?" she asked.

He turned to her. "Looks like a couple of idiots playing a game on the highway. They're blocking the bus, not allowing us to get around them."

Rosina leaned forward. "That's ridiculous."

The bus came to a complete stop. The driver spoke on his phone.

Then, a siren sounded in the distance.

A moment later, a police cruiser raced by their window just as the Crown Vic's driver's side doors opened. Darwin leaned up to look out the front window as four men stood on the highway beside their car, all dressed in suits, two with their hands up to ward off the sun's glare.

The police officers who had jumped from their cars yelled something. Horns blared behind the bus, yet none of the four men moved.

One of the men lifted his hand and made a gun symbol with his hand. He dropped his thumb and lifted his finger as if it recoiled.

"That's rude," Rosina said. "They stop us and then get mad at the bus driver. Unbelievable."

If she only knew.

"I know, eh," was all Darwin could say.

The police convinced one of the men to move his vehicle. After a few minutes' delay, the bus got underway again. The passengers cheered in unison.

At that moment, Darwin made a decision that would get Rosina to safety.

Ten minutes later, the bus entered the terminal and stopped alongside a row of travel and tour buses.

Darwin and his new bride got off via the middle door, collected their luggage, and headed to the airport.

He kept his eyes peeled for anything, but every second that passed, he felt safer and safer. No one would try anything with all the airport security. Policemen and security guards roamed the corridors on the check-in side.

"Are you sure you're okay?" Rosina asked. "You look even whiter."

"Really, I'm fine. I'm just not feeling so hot. We'll have a blast when we land in Athens."

They lined up to walk through security. A smattering of people had lined up ahead of them, but the line moved well. People began to converge behind them, too. In a matter of minutes, a sea of travelers swallowed Rosina and Darwin, all heading to different destinations, all leading different lives, not knowing that a man in line with them was one of the most wanted men by the mafia in recent history.

Darwin and his new wife were about to begin their life together. What a wedding present this was. When Rosina finally learned what was going on, she would probably ask for a divorce. They'd only been married four days, and she would want out. He was sure of it.

As they stood in line, he thought about what his father would say when he told him about their marriage. Her parents were going to freak out. Both their parents had objected to them being together in the first place. Rosina's mom and dad were from the old country in Italy. Darwin's mother had died when he was born, and his father was from Athens. They had chosen Rome as the city to elope to, in honor of her parents, and Athens as the city to finish their honeymoon in as a respectful gesture to his dad.

When they were done touring, they'd go home and announce to everyone that they'd gotten engaged. Set some ridiculous date two years away and let their families work it all out. Ultimately, if the parents refused to sign off on the wedding, Rosina and Darwin would drop the bomb that they were already married and had been for a long time.

The line moved. People ahead removed their shoes, pulled off belts, and took laptops from carry-ons.

Darwin took a final glance over his shoulder. Nonchalant, bored, tired, and impatient faces looked back. No one stared in anger. No one aimed ill intent at him.

Bringing Rosina to the airport was the smartest thing he could've done. Sure, they'd know where he was, but it would be difficult for them to find him. It would take time. If his plan worked out, at least Rosina would remain safe.

It was their turn now. Darwin watched as the woman ahead of him took off at least ten pieces of jewelry. Then she undid her earrings, removed her boots, and started working on her pockets.

He couldn't believe it. If you knew you were coming to the airport and security would require you to remove all that junk, why would you cover yourself in jewelry and fill your pockets before coming?

After several moments, she turned back and whispered an apology to Rosina. The woman didn't look at Darwin.

Those men on the highway and the organization they

belonged to were trying to kill him. It was time to get angry. It was time to deal with the issue at hand. In fact, the time was past due. He'd let things go on too long, and now Rosina was at risk.

"Are you sure we should be doing this?" Rosina asked.

Darwin snapped out of his reverie. "What? Doing what?"

"This. Flying to Greece. Maybe we should just go home."

"What? Why?"

She took off her shoes and set them on the conveyor belt. "You haven't been yourself lately. Even now, you're pale, and at the same time, you look angry. I just don't know that side of you."

Darwin undid his belt and then set his backpack on the belt.

"I'm sorry. I've got a lot on my mind."

A security guard gestured at Darwin. "Step forward."

He didn't like leaving Rosina with so many strangers so close to her, but he took a chance that no one would try anything in a crowded terminal with this much security.

He walked through the metal detector without incident. Rosina followed.

In silence, they grabbed their belongings and stepped away from the area.

"Since you're unclear on what's bothering you, I'm starting to feel it's the marriage. Are you sure you didn't rush into this?"

Darwin stopped, grabbed both her shoulders, and turned her to face him. "Don't ever think that. This was *my* idea. I bought the tickets to Rome and drove to your job at Yonge and Bloor to pick you up. It was my idea to do it before anyone could stop us. I love you and will always love you, Rosina. It's an honor to be your husband. I can't pinpoint anything in particular that's bothering me, but maybe it's just me formulating a new story idea. I have to always be thinking, formulating, ruminating. You know I write three novels a year. That's been the secret to my success. To come here, this week off doesn't stop my brain."

I hate myself for lying to you, but I have no choice. Your life hangs on this decision.

Rosina glanced down at her fingers as she twiddled with them. "I'm sorry, I just haven't connected with you since the accident." She looked back up at him and stared into his eyes.

The accident. The one where I killed a man in the street, and the police ruled it an accident? That one? The one that resulted in us running for our lives because I killed a made man in the Toronto mafia?

"I think that accident has affected you more than you know," Rosina continued. "I think it's killing you on the inside, and you aren't talking to me about it. I just want you to include me. I'm your wife now. Don't deny me."

Darwin released her shoulders. "I'm sorry. You're right."

Together, they turned and started toward their gate.

"I'm right about what?"

With all that had been happening, he'd had a hard time enjoying himself in Rome. The entire time they toured the Coliseum, he'd been watching over his shoulder, wondering when a bullet would enter his head. They were almost run over by a car two streets from their hotel. A gun went off somewhere in the street and took a chunk of concrete out of the wall by them as they left a pizzeria the night before. Two attempts on their life since they'd been in Rome wasn't a coincidence.

It was his idea to leave the hotel two days early. He had to get her out of there. His assailants had found them.

"You're right. The accident has affected me."

They reached their gate as the attendants prepared for

boarding.

Rosina chose a seat in the lounge by the large windows so she could look at the planes. After Darwin sat, she said, "Remember, it was determined an accident after the re-constructionists did their magic. And anyway, that guy was a criminal. You did the world a favor by running into him. Not just that, he fired a bullet at you. He could've killed you."

Her voice raised on her final words. Two women across the row of seats looked up at them.

"Keep your voice down," Darwin said.

"Okay, I know, I'm sorry."

"Sure, it was ruled an accident, but do you ever wonder, even if I'd aimed at that guy with the intent to kill him, that it would've been classified an accident anyway?"

She frowned. "Why would you say something like that?"

"That man at the airport hangar in Toronto killed a lot of people. There were bodies littered all over that place. He was part of a criminal family responsible for many illegal activities. When the cops saw that I'd mangled the guy with my car, they patted me on the shoulder, said I did a good thing, and that I'd be taken care of. Well, I got taken care of all right. I got notoriety. My name was printed in the papers all over the world." He lifted his hands to portray a marquee. "Darwin Athios Kostas is an average Canadian guy and writer of thriller novels like *The Mafia Killer*."

"Well, the notoriety sure helped sales of your books, didn't it? The guy's dead. He can't come after you."

But the family he was connected to can, he almost said out loud. Instead, he nodded. "I know, you're right. Also, I've got those bikers to deal with."

"Has anything new happened with them?"

"Ever since I wrote that part in my novel, *The Biker*, about their Port Dover adventures and Ride For Sight and how bad I portrayed them, they've been out for blood. Richard H. has contacted me three different times. You remember when we were having dinner at Red Lobster?"

Rosina nodded.

"He told me to take that stuff out of the book, or there would be consequences. I said that I couldn't because it was already selling on Amazon. It was too late. It was out there. And you remember what he said next?"

Rosina patted his leg. "I know, but they aren't going to hurt you. If they were, they'd have done it already."

"He said that I had to make good. This guy is scary. I mean, that's fucked up."

"I know." Rosina started as the attendant announced the flight to Athens would commence boarding people with disabilities and children first.

"No one is celebrating a man's death," she said. "Just don't let it kill you."

I'm trying. Oh, how I'm trying. If you only knew.

"Look, honey." Darwin got to his feet. "Before we board, I have to go to the bathroom. Will you wait here?"

"But, Darwin, they're already boarding. Can't it wait? Use the one on the plane."

Darwin shook his head. "No, I hate how small and confined those toilets are. If I wait much longer, I'll piss in my shorts. Boarding takes time, too. I'll be back in less than five."

"Okay, but hurry."

Darwin walked three steps, stopped, and turned back. "I almost forgot. I've got something for you."

"Can't it wait? Go to the bathroom."

"In light of what we just talked about, I'd like to give it to you now."

The attendant announced the boarding of the back half of the plane.

"You're running out of time."

"I have at least ten minutes and only need three." He pulled a white envelope out of his backpack.

"What's this?" Rosina asked, a smile playing across her lips.

"It's a surprise. But there's a condition."

Darwin hopped from one foot to the other, implying his desire for a bathroom. In reality, he was building the courage to do what had to be done.

"What's the condition?"

"You cannot open it without me present."

"That's fine. Go to the bathroom and come back. We'll board the plane, and I'll open the envelope. Deal?"

"Sure," Darwin said as he stepped away. At ten paces, before he turned around and lost eye contact with her, he said, "Get on without me. I've got my boarding pass right here." He slapped his pocket. "Save me a seat. Keep it warm. I'll be with you sooner than you think."

Rosina stood and grabbed his backpack. "Okay, but hurry. You have me seriously curious now about this envelope."

Darwin averted his face before she saw his tears and hurried away, wondering if he'd ever see his wife again.

****

Rosina got to the attendant and presented her passport and

boarding pass. The attendant scanned her boarding pass and told her to have a nice flight.

"My husband is coming. He's been delayed a few minutes but is already through security. He still has time, right?"

The attendant looked at her watch. "Oh, yes. We start boarding early enough so people like your husband can make it. He still has at least fifteen minutes."

"Okay, thank you. His name is Darwin Kostas."

The attendant nodded and reached for the documents of the traveler standing behind Rosina.

She moved along the boarding ramp until she slowed behind people gathering near the plane. After a small wait at the plane's door, two more attendants stood there to greet people. She showed her ticket and was told to go to her seat nine rows up. The aisle was jammed with people placing luggage in the overhead bins. She politely waited and then squeezed by to take her seat.

Darwin would be coming at any moment. She couldn't wait to see what was in the envelope. It was just like him. He'd been surprising her during their whole relationship, and this was just another surprise in a long line of them. She tried, but couldn't figure out what was in the envelope.

Rosina glanced around at all the people seated close by. Then she looked up the aisle. Darwin still hadn't boarded. She lifted the envelope and tried to peek through it. It was one of those security types with the crisscrosses on the inside, obscuring anything legible from the outside.

She thought maybe it could be tickets for a cruise. Or perhaps tickets to the theater or an opera. Maybe he would fly her to New York next so they could tour Broadway or Las Vegas for a little gambling.

The suspense was driving her nuts. But then, that was why Darwin did his surprises.

She flipped the envelope over and noticed that it actually wasn't sealed. The lip was pushed inside the back, like with a birthday card.

Darwin didn't lick envelopes.

Throughout their relationship, Darwin had opened up to her about his phobias, of which he had a couple. He was afraid of the dark, which many people are, but his was an actual phobia. He had an irrational fear of it like the dark was a living thing. They always slept with lights on. He also had a fear of sharp or pointy things. He couldn't get a needle at the doctor. He would get too angry. They had to put him out to administer a needle. It was that bad. At a restaurant, he'd only use spoons or plastic utensils to eat with. No fork, no knife. And he didn't lick envelopes because the paper could cut him.

Darwin was sure his stepmother had caused his phobias. She always had needles in the house, and as punishment, she would leave him in a dark room for hours on end, waking him with a jab of a fork in his side when dinner was ready. He'd end up being awake most of the night, languishing in the dark as the house slept, crying, waiting to be poked. By the time he was twelve, his fear of sharp and pointy things had grown to where he wouldn't enter the kitchen anymore.

His stepmother had died a horrible death. It was some freak accident, he'd told her, impaled on a pitchfork in a farmer's barn. No one knew what she'd been doing there. No one was charged with any crime related to her death.

The flight attendants announced that the plane would be getting underway shortly. Rosina snapped up and sat rigid in her seat.

Darwin hadn't returned yet.

She looked down at the envelope. A flight attendant walked by, counting the heads of the passengers, no doubt looking for the missing person.

Against better judgment, Rosina slipped her thumb under the lip of the envelope and flipped it open. She looked one more time to make sure Darwin wasn't walking up right then, catching her in the act of sneaking a peek.

She pulled the paper out and opened it. A note. After scanning the beginning, her eyes raced to the bottom.

It said he was sorry and that this was for the better. Stay on the plane. Do not get off. He would handle this on his own.

Baby, I love you, but they aim to kill me, and I can't lead them to you anymore. Go to Athens. I'll meet you there in a few days.

If you don't, you could be hurt or, worse, killed.

DO NOT get off the plane!

Rosina's eyes watered. The attendants were shutting the plane's doors.

"Wait!" she yelled.

Heads turned toward her. She got up, opened the overhead compartment, grabbed her backpack, and ran for the exit door.

"Wait. Let me off."

"But, ma'am, they're getting ready to taxi out."

"My husband is supposed to join me. He's not here. I'm not leaving without him."

She pushed past the woman to the door as the entry ramp pulled away. Rosina looked down and saw how far the ground was. She stepped back and then ran and leaped over the open space, landing solidly on the ramp, where she ran after her husband, having no idea where he was or where to start looking.

***

Darwin had stood off in the distance to watch the gate. He'd seen his wife processed and boarded just like everyone else. And yet he waited. The final boarding call had been announced. Then he heard his name over the loudspeakers, asking him to come to gate C36 for immediate boarding. After several attempts to reach him, the attendants closed the gate's doors and dispersed.

He saw the ramp slide away from the plane through the large windows.

Unable to watch further, he turned and walked away, happy that Rosina was finally out of danger. She would be in Athens soon. She had her purse, a credit card, and a debit card attached to his bank account where over fifty-thousand dollars sat. Every month, Amazon deposited his royalties into his account. She would never want for money again. They were married. What was his was hers now.

They would reunite and share the rest of their lives if he made it out of this alive.

He walked back to security and told a guard he had only aided in boarding his child, and he needed to be let out now. The guard showed him to an exit, and Darwin walked back into the main part of the airport.

Travelers ran this way and that without a single care in the world. At least not the kind he had. They moved to and fro without fear of death—except for the people who feared flying— which he was glad wasn't one of his phobias.

He had no idea what his next move was. Calling the police

was out of the question. What could they do? Protection? Some of the police were on the Fuccini payroll. That's probably how they knew about the meeting in the hangar. The same hangar Darwin happened upon late that night while looking for a group therapy session.

No, contacting the police wouldn't work. He had to solve this on his own. Maybe an apology would suffice? Or maybe doing something for the family? Would that make things right?

He'd be willing to steal from someone, maybe pick a few pockets. But he suspected the mafia wasn't interested in small amounts of cash or minor criminal activities to repay the debt of a lost member of their family.

Dejected about his options, Darwin made his way through the throng of travelers. It had only been twenty minutes, and he already missed his wife. The idea that he'd been deceitful to her early in their marriage made him feel about one inch tall. He loved Rosina with everything he had but couldn't include her in his problem. More specifically, *this* problem.

Darwin hit the doors that led outside and decided to take the bus back to Termini Station and hang around there until they caught up with him. They had located the hotel to avoid trouble finding him at the station.

He didn't get ten paces before two men came out of nowhere and grabbed both arms.

"Don't protest," the man on his left said into his ear. "Don't say a word."

The man on his right opened his jacket and showed him the butt of a gun.

Darwin nodded. "I was hoping to find you guys. I want you to take me to your boss. We need to talk."

They hustled him to a waiting van. The side door sat open.

"Oh, don't worry. We'll take you to our boss, but I don't think he'll be in the talking mood."

They shoved Darwin inside the van so hard that he slid along the floor and slammed into the wall on the other side.

***

Rosina had made it through security and was searching everyone's face. Darwin was nowhere in sight.

She started for the doors that would take her to the bus she and Darwin had taken to the airport not an hour before.

Then she saw him through the airport's glass windows. Two men, one on either side of Darwin, appeared to force him along.

She ran for the large revolving doors but was too late. The men threw her husband inside a van, slammed the side door shut, and hopped in.

The van raced away when she got outside, oblivious to her screams.

Rosina stood in the departures section, where families hugged and cried as they said goodbye to their loved ones. She cried for another reason altogether. She should call the police, but what would she tell them? Her husband had deserted her. He left the airport with two other men in a van. Of course, it was forceful, but she didn't have a plate number. He wouldn't be a missing person yet. There was nothing they would do.

After a few minutes, she collected herself, righted the backpack on her shoulders, and walked toward the busses. Darwin would know where to find her. She would never leave her husband. She wouldn't abandon him in his time of need.

She didn't recognize the men, and she didn't know what they wanted. She had nowhere to turn and nowhere to start.

All she could think of was the police. Maybe it was time to bring them in after all. She determined to show them the note and get them involved.

She had to do something.

2

THEY BOUND DARWIN'S HANDS with tight-fitting metal cuffs. One of the men jumped in the driver's seat and got the van rolling. The bigger man in the passenger seat made Darwin think of Andre the Giant. His hands looked like meat hooks. He had flipped Darwin around and slapped the cuffs on him with ease. Then he'd righted Darwin and shoved him back down.

He came to *them*. He could've gotten on that plane. He could've been miles away by now, but he stayed behind to clear things up, and they were acting like he had wronged them somehow.

The van turned onto the highway, heading back toward Rome.

"Hey, do you know Andre the Giant?" Darwin asked.

The large man turned around. "Hey, kid, you got some balls. Shut your fucking mouth. This ride ain't a social one." He spun back in his seat.

"Take it easy. I came to you guys, remember? I could've stayed on that flight."

Andre kept staring forward, not baited into the conversation.

The van was a normal utility unit with metal walls, two back doors, and two front seats. Large pieces of plywood had been laid down on the van's bed.

There were broken, splintered parts. Dark stains circled those areas. He leaned in closer. The wood smelled terrible.

"What the hell is that smell?" he muttered.

Andre spun around fast, leaned out of his seat, and brought his meat hook hand across Darwin's face.

The contact was so fast that he only had time to shut his eyes. He fell to the plywood and rolled to the back door, banging into it with his knees.

His face lit up with pins and needles, flaring pain and heat. It reminded him of the consequences of speaking when he wasn't supposed to.

It also pissed him off.

He hated pain ever since he was a kid, which was something else he blamed on his stepmother. Everyone hated pain, but Darwin reacted in anger to it. Nothing fired him up more than pain.

They aimed to kill him. It was the mafia, after all, and he had killed one of their men. Accident or not, a made man was dead because Darwin was behind the wheel that night. He knew this on some level last week but wasn't ready to acknowledge it.

With nothing left to lose, Darwin said, "It was an accident."

He rolled over and looked up at Andre.

"Did you speak? You're joking, right? Is this a fucking joke? After a slap like that, do you want to risk talking again?"

"I'm just saying, it was an accident. I didn't *try* to kill anybody."

Darwin braced himself. At any second, Andre would come.

"Tell the boss your theories about it being an accident," the driver said.

Andre laughed. "Yeah, see what the boss says about you killing his only son and successor. It'll go over just fine, I'm sure."

His son? His successor?

"Is he a reasonable man?" Darwin asked, his voice betraying him. His decision to stay behind at the airport had been wrong. But what was right when dealing with these kinds of people?

"Oh sure," Andre said, infusing a smile into the sound of the words. "He'll make sure you're reasonably dead." Andre glanced over his shoulder at Darwin. "Seriously, man, what did you think? That he'd just walk away? Let it go? Man, do you believe in Santa Claus, too?"

He needed out. At all costs. Two men in a van or an entire crew of mafia tough guys back at the boss's lair.

Decision made.

"Tell me, Andre, do you have a knife on you?"

Andre looked over at the driver and then back to Darwin.

"What's it to you?"

"I need to see one. Anything pointy. That kind of thing really pisses me off."

Andre laughed, a deep, guttural laugh. He held his stomach and leaned into the back of the passenger seat. After he finished his burst of laughter, he wiped his eyes and looked over at the driver.

"Hey, Joe, we got a knife so we can piss this guy off?"

The driver laughed, but not as long or hard.

"You are a piece of work." Andre's face hardened again. "You want a knife? You wanna be pissed off, is that it? Then what you gonna do? Hurt us? Steal the van, huh? Take us out? Fuck you and your little fantasy world. I'll show you a knife."

Here we go.

Andre leaned over and lifted his pant leg, revealing a brown sheath with a hilt sticking out. Andre wrapped his finger around the hilt and slid out a four-inch knife.

"Here, here's your knife. Nice, huh?"

Andre left his seat and edged closer on his knees, staying low, the knife extended in front of him.

Darwin felt something akin to a chemical change take place. A dark shade of red blurred his vision. Death became an answer, not a question. Choices left him, options died. Nothing remained but anger so vile that an absolute rage coursed through him. Fear for his own safety fled in the face of his rage.

He spun in place, landed on his knees, placed a foot on the plywood floor, and lunged with every ounce of his one-hundred-eight-pound frame. His shoulder hit Andre in the stomach and propelled him toward the front of the van.

Odds couldn't have played a better role in that moment. As he connected with Andre, the driver who'd been watching in the rearview mirror applied the brakes at the same exact second, propelling them toward the backs of the front seats with greater speed.

Andre had been in the center. He continued forward through the seats, his back smashing into the dashboard. Andre's considerable bulk halted Darwin's short flight from the back of the van. In an intense fury, he opened his mouth and clamped down on the driver's right ear. He bit so hard and so fast that his teeth severed the floppy top, cartilage and all, blood splattering his face.

Darwin screamed like a bleeding pig as he dove for the driver's cheek but missed. The driver jerked away from him, shouted in pain, and then promptly lost control of the van. The vehicle veered to the right with such force that Darwin shot forward across the driver's lap.

Then, the van swerved sideways and lifted into the air. As it flipped over the highway several times, the sound of the wheels ceased. Darwin was momentarily suspended, weightless, and then the van crashed onto the unforgiving concrete highway.

Darwin's back was braced against the steering wheel, his stomach across the driver's stomach. When the van landed, he was thrust sideways out of the front seat and toward the back, away from the breaking windshield. When they hit the back door, the driver's body connected first, snapping something in his back. As the van stopped sliding on the road, Darwin saw the driver's body was broken in the middle like a twig.

With his hands still cuffed behind him and his shoulder on fire from something hitting it, Darwin got up and crawled along the side of the van, which was now the floor.

Andre was dead. When the windshield broke inward, a chunk of it had cut into Andre. The oozing blood formed one big splotch of red across most of his body. Andre stared with open eyes, his jaw slack, and his neck broken so violently even the skin had snapped open, like a large, human Pez dispenser.

Darwin spotted the keys in the ignition, the engine still running. A small handcuff key dangled from the keyring.

With his hands cuffed behind him, he backed up and felt his way to the keys. His hands found the steering column. He felt his way up until his wrist bumped into the ring. He latched on and twisted, but they didn't budge. He twisted the other way, and the keys turned. The engine shut off with a small protest. He leaned forward and yanked the keys from their slot.

He had to get out of the van. People would be coming. Cops would show up. He'd have too much explaining to do. The police would want to know how he came to be their prisoner. Too many questions without any good answers.

But what if people witnessed him running from the scene of an accident in handcuffs?

That was a risk he would have to take.

Darwin stepped through the broken windshield and onto the hot pavement of the highway.

Cars slowed on the other side of the median to look at the accident. He glanced behind the van. A long line of cars was now parked, glinting in the noon-hour sun. Limousines, buses, trucks, Smart cars, and bikes are all waiting to get around the flipped van.

He ran down into the ditch. After he'd gone twenty meters, he edged through a hole in the fence that lined the highway. It led to a large parking lot and what looked like a shopping center.

He still had his wallet and passport. He would go into the mall, buy new clothes, and use their bathroom to get fixed up. Then he'd rent a car or take a taxi and head back into Rome.

It was time to call Special Agent Greg Stinsen. He was the lead FBI investigator dealing with the Fuccini Family. Darwin had met him briefly back in the abandoned hangar.

Stinsen told him to call if Darwin ever needed anything.

He needed something now.

He needed the Fuccini Family boss on a spit, or he would be on the run forever.

3

Rosina couldn't help herself. The tears wouldn't stop. She felt like she was falling apart.

She ran from the airport to where the buses were ferrying passengers into Rome. She found one that took her to Roma Termini. After paying a few euros, she got on and took a seat.

Ten minutes later, they sat on the highway, not moving. The driver told them an accident on the road ahead had temporarily blocked all the lanes heading into Rome. He added that it wouldn't take long to clear.

She leaned out into the aisle and stared ahead at the top of a van that had flipped onto its side. At least twenty cars separated her bus from the accident scene.

Was that the same van she saw Darwin shoved into?

She leaned back in her seat and closed her eyes. It couldn't be.

Darwin, her man, her new husband. She couldn't let him face this alone. Not after all they'd been through together. Years of fighting with their parents and their stupid, old-world customs. Her mother said she should marry an Italian boy. His father said he needed a nice Greek woman. Her mother's reaction had disappointed her. Rosina expected better of family.

Darwin had proposed the idea to elope to Rome. Get married in Rome as a show of respect to her family and a honeymoon in Greece as a show of respect to his father. Deal with the repercussions later.

But now they were on the run, which had driven Darwin from her side. People were trying to kill them? Ridiculous. Everyone had died that fateful night back at the old airplane hangar. No one was alive to see Darwin hit that man.

What did her husband do? *Accident*, by definition, meant *not intentional*. Darwin didn't mean it. Darwin didn't *aim* his Ford at the guy.

Rosina looked out her window at the traffic easing by on the other side. She sighed deeply. Who were *they* anyway? The people Darwin mentioned in his letter. How could she find them? She just wanted her husband back. She'd waited too long to find the man of her dreams. When he came up with the idea to run to Rome, she lost control, running around like a crazy woman, laughing and screaming. His book sales had shot through the stratosphere in the last two months after the news had labeled him the *Hero of the Hangar*. His picture ran in every newspaper across North America, detailing how he *accidentally* killed a mafia killer with an American Ford Mustang.

The bus's engine revved, and the driver angled the bus closer to the railing at the median.

It took him several minutes, but then the driver was able to pass the accident. Rosina stretched upward to see out the window, trying to catch a look at the vehicle, but from her side, she couldn't see much.

She eased back down into her seat. Rosina would stand by her man whatever happened in the next few days. She would be there for him at all costs, whether he liked it or not. It was the Italian way. It was her way.

Then, maybe her parents would accept their relationship.

People couldn't kill with impunity. She was in a civilized country, *her ancestor's* country, and she would see any perpetrators of illegal activities put behind bars.

In the worst case, she'd walk into the Canadian embassy and demand her rights as a citizen of one of the best countries in the world. That would be better than calling local authorities.

Maybe that's what she should do in the first place. Just go to the embassy and explain to them what was happening. Show them Darwin's note. See what they could do.

She decided against it. First, she would return to the hotel and get a room again. She couldn't make a wrong move. If she contacted the wrong people, Darwin could be in worse trouble.

The bus entered the downtown area. She stared out the window at the buildings as they passed the windows and yearned for Darwin to sit beside her. She didn't think she could possibly miss him as much as she did at that moment.

The bus driver hit the horn, angled into his spot, and stopped.

The familiar Termini Station bustled around her. She exited the bus and started across the street. Her stomach growled, reminding her of how hungry she was. She hated flying on a full stomach, so she had eaten a small portion of the continental breakfast that morning, hours ago. After she checked back into the hotel, she would get something to eat.

The idea struck her that she wasn't being too cautious. What if Darwin's pursuers were following her at that moment?

She stopped walking and spun around. As far as she could tell, no one was paying special attention to her. She turned back around and stepped into the lobby of the hotel. After running up the front stairs, the clerk informed her they had a room available. After getting the key, she headed up to room twenty-seven. Inside, she parted the tall, white curtains, opened the long, slender doors, and stepped onto the balcony. To her surprise, it was the only room with a balcony. Rome bustled one floor below her. To the right sat the wall of Termini Station, to her left, open street.

She had to go to the police. Either that or the embassy. The image of Darwin getting put into that van left her with no question that he was in danger.

She breathed deeply and turned back into the room. Once the balcony doors were secured, Rosina grabbed her room key and fifty euros in cash and locked the room behind her.

A thought flitted through her mind. Could the men who had blocked traffic in the two Crown Victorias that morning when they went to the airport be connected to Darwin's trouble? Were they trying to get Darwin, even then, on the open, public highway? If they were, then these men, this organization, was fearless.

She descended the stairs to the lobby and then more stairs to the door that led outside. A long, sleek limousine sat parked across from the open door. As she approached it, the back door opened. A large man in a suit two sizes too small exited the limo. She eyed him suspiciously. Then, the man turned toward her.

Rosina looked away quickly. She didn't normally stare at people, but today was different. After several moments, she looked back. The man from the limousine stood behind her, arms crossed.

"Come with me," he said, barely above a grunt.

She looked him up and down. "I am not going anywhere with you—"

He grabbed her arm.

"Hey." She yanked backward, but his grip was too tight. "Let go of me."

He leaned closer. "Don't resist. You want to see Darwin again, yes?"

Her struggle stopped. She glared at him and let herself be guided toward the vehicle. She wanted to meet with them anyway. Give them a piece of her mind. A door opened as they approached. At the door, the man shoved her inside.

"Hey!" she yelled, trying to right herself in the back seat. "There's no need for that shit—"

The man jumped in behind her, and the vehicle got underway even before his door was shut.

Rosina righted herself and adjusted her blouse. The man who grabbed her sat to her right. Another man sat facing her in a backward-facing seat aimed at her. Both men grinned like they were in on some big secret.

"You two wanna tell me the joke?" she asked. "Or are you two going just to sit there smiling like a couple of faggots?"

They looked at each other and then turned their attention back on her. The man who threw her in the limo said, "It's all over now, sugar. That's why we're happy. We get to go home."

"What's over?"

"We have that rat bastard of a husband of yours, and now we have you."

"You have Darwin?"

"We're taking you to see him right now. Don't worry, it won't be long."

She looked out the window. They were in trouble. Big trouble. She decided on another question.

"Was it your people who shot at us the other night?"

The man sitting across from her raised a hand to his companion. "I'll handle her questions. I like toying with my prey."

"Prey?" She snickered. "I'm nobody's prey."

"Whatever you say, bitch. And yes, it was us shooting at you."

Her stomach twisted, and she thought she felt her bowels loosening as she realized how bad the situation was. "Why would you shoot at us? You could've killed one of us."

"We weren't trying to hit you. Believe me, if we were, we wouldn't have missed."

Confused, she asked, "Why were you trying to *miss* us? That doesn't make sense."

A grin slit his mouth upward at the corners. "We wouldn't want either one of you to die so easily. We don't believe in that. What kind of men would we be known as? Hitmen? Hired guns? Mercenaries? No, we like to do damage to our enemies."

Her stomach lurched. What little she had eaten that morning threatened to come up.

He continued. "All the time you two have been in Rome, we've been trying to find where you were staying. We hadn't gotten permission from the ruling families here to do our business, so we had to wait and collect information. We knew we were running out of time, so we thought we'd try to shoot at you, get you to call the police, file a report. But that didn't work. When we found out you were headed for the airport, we were granted permission to make our move, so we made our move, and here we are, nice and cozy."

He was lying. He had to be. "How would having us call the police help you?" she asked. "Doesn't make sense."

He guffawed for several seconds, then cut it off abruptly. He had bad teeth and a five-day-old beard. The guy looked unkempt, and yet he acted cocky and cool like it was part of the act.

"You really don't know who we are, do you, little girl? You live in your ivory towers and look down at us, not knowing that we're the ones who make the world go 'round. To us, you're just a fucking whore." His voice rose in volume. "You're a fucking slut. You have no idea the pain and anguish that awaits you."

Rosina didn't think of herself as stupid or naïve. She knew about mercenaries and hitmen. But why would they hurt innocent, regular folk like Darwin and her? She was barely twenty-five years old. She'd never even been in a fight except for a little hair-pulling in grade school. As far as dealing with extremely difficult people, Darwin had only ever dealt with his stepmother.

What was next? They kill Darwin and then kill her? No, she wouldn't believe it, *couldn't* believe it.

She watched Rome flash by the vehicle.

"My name is the Harvester of Sorrow," the man said. "I'm the distributor of pain."

Her disgust rose. They wouldn't intimidate her. She was determined not to show fear. She learned years ago in an after-school rape class that these kind of people relish the control they have over you. They yearn for the fear in your eyes. Don't fight to get away. Don't give them the pleasure. It may save your life.

"Seems like a stupid name."

"I'm the guy that gets to hurt you."

"Hey," the man in the suit beside her said. "We don't touch

her until the boss says we can."

The men looked at each other. "I know that. What the *fuck* do you think I'm doing here? You best watch yourself, Gabe. Your time will come, and I'll do you something special when it does."

"Fuck you. I'll be here long after you've rotted in an unmarked grave. Watch what the fuck you be saying to me. You're not bulletproof."

The Harvester grinned like he owned the world, and he knew it. Rosina sat on her hands to still the shaking. She could barely control the fear inside her, but as long as they had her husband and they were taking her to see him, there had to be a chance to work things out.

It took ten more minutes of negotiating Rome's traffic before they pulled into an underground garage. The limousine came to a stop beside several vans. Men approached the vehicle and opened all the doors in the back.

"Get out," one of the men ordered.

Rosina stayed silent as she followed a line of six men as they walked her to an elevator. She almost felt like she was in a Quentin Tarantino movie with six mafia men standing around in expensive suits in Rome, the home of the Italian mafia, escorting a helpless young woman to her final meeting. Then, she banished the thought as soon as it entered her head. Quentin's movies got bloody, and nothing about her meeting upstairs would be final. Nothing at all.

Ding.

The elevator doors opened. Three men filed in and turned around. Rosina was pushed from behind. She entered, and then the other three followed, with the Harvester standing closest to her.

The ride was quick, which was a relief as the thick air in the confined elevator was beginning to make her feel lightheaded.

The doors opened onto a gorgeous floor. The walls were marble, the carpets plush. Before they got too far, the Harvester twisted a key into the elevator panel, locking it out of service.

The men escorted her through glass double doors and into an office resembling any high-paid lawyer's domain back in Canada.

They continued down a hallway and walked, one by one, through a small door into a large room. It would easily seat fifteen men. Couches lined the walls, armchairs, and tables sat at random places. It looked like a luncheon room for the rich.

In the far corner sat a large banker's desk and, behind it, a man who appeared from a distance to be at least seventy-five years old.

"Come, sit," he said with a flourish of his hand.

Rosina was directed to a solitary chair positioned in front of the big desk. She approached it and stopped, remaining on her feet. All the men she entered the room with fell back. Some took positions near the door, and others sat on the plush couches.

"So good to finally meet you," the old man said. "Please, have a seat."

"I'll stand, thank you. But *I'm* the one who is happy to meet you finally."

He cocked his head to the side. Someone laughed under his breath behind her. The old man raised a hand, and the laughter ceased instantly.

"Why would that be?" he asked, his words clipped.

"So we can make some kind of arrangement to stop this petty bullying. Then we can all move on."

This time, it was the old man who chuckled.

"Where do you people come from?" he asked, almost to himself.

"I'm sorry?"

He reached for a cane beside the desk and started toward her, studying her face. He bent slightly to the left and right, gawking at her as if attempting to figure something out.

Rosina touched her cheek. "Do I have something on my face?"

"Not yet." He lifted his cane, put it in both hands, like he was about to bunt a ball with a baseball bat, and shoved forward with the strength of a boxer in the ring. The cane smacked into her chest so hard she had no time to recover. Her balance was lost, and she fell backward into the chair.

"I told you to sit down when you first entered *my* office. The next time you disobey me, the consequences will be more severe."

The old man walked away without a limp and the use of a cane.

"You and I have a unique problem," he said. "You, personally, have done me no harm." He reached his desk and sat down behind it. He picked up what looked like a gold-colored letter opener and began tapping it on the desktop. "But I have to do *you* harm."

"Why?" It was out before she could stop it. Her voice was weak, frightened, and limp.

"Because Darwin Athios Kostas does not have any children for me to kill."

What the fuck?

He continued. "I can see by the expression on your face you don't understand the gravity of the situation here." He stopped moving the letter opener. He looked down at it, and then, after a moment, he glanced back up at her. "The world is one big machine, living off the foundation of cause and effect. More specifically, I'm talking about consequences." He started tapping his letter opener again. "You do something—you have to answer for it. There are consequences, and there are debts to be paid."

"What has that got anything to do with my husband and me? We don't owe you any money."

"That's not the kind of currency that'll pay this debt. The currency I want is blood."

"What? Blood?"

The old man dropped the letter opener and stood, splaying his hands evenly on either side of his desk.

"Get me the water cure."

Men scurried away behind her. She had no idea what a *water cure* was.

"Look, what has my husband—"

"Silence!" he shouted.

Two men ran up beside her and grabbed her arms.

"Hey." She squirmed under their grip.

A man came from behind and wrapped a hand over her mouth. His hand was so large it covered her mouth and nose, cutting off her ability to breathe. She tried to struggle but felt paralyzed in their grip.

The man behind her inched closer and whispered, "The boss said to be quiet. I'd advise you to listen to him."

He eased up on her nose. Air rushed into her starved lungs. She gasped and breathed as fast and hard as she could. Lightheadedness set in, then eased off.

They placed her on the floor on her back. The man who had been behind her let go of her face. She breathed through her open mouth, trying not to make any noise. This would all be over soon. They'd let her go. The police would come. This didn't happen in her world. This couldn't happen.

One of the men stood over her with a funnel.

A squeaking noise behind her made her look back. The man from the limo, the Harvester of Sorrow, wheeled something that looked like a keg into the room.

The rest of the men surrounded her. She tried to get up but only made it a few inches before they shoved her back down. Hands grappled all over her body, holding her immobile.

A hand clamped over her mouth again. She couldn't scream. She couldn't move. She couldn't do anything but watch Harvester bend over her with the funnel and a plastic tube from the keg.

Fingers parted over her mouth. They were going to make her drink whatever was in the keg. She redoubled her efforts to get away but to no avail.

The tip of the funnel entered her mouth. Then water flowed through the funnel, and the hand on her mouth clamped her nose shut. To breathe, she had to use her mouth. To do that, she had to swallow.

Rosina tried to hold out, but lasted all of three seconds. She took swallow after swallow, as fast as she could, in a useless attempt to rid the water from her mouth to breathe. She also drank as fast as she could to avoid drowning. If one breath were forced into her lungs, it would be filled with water.

As fast as it started, it stopped. Both the hand on her face and the funnel were removed.

Rosina twisted sideways to rid her mouth of residual water and sucked in air. She blinked away tears, and then a hand returned to her face. The funnel jammed into her mouth harder this time. So hard she thought one of her teeth chipped.

Water coursed past her lips again. She couldn't take anymore. Her stomach was filling up. Her lungs were starving. She was going to pass out. Consciousness wavered, and yet she swallowed. They held her longer this time, and still, she swallowed.

Her eyes rolled back. At the last second, when she was about to breathe and drown on the floor of the expensive office, the funnel was removed, and she was bodily lifted into the air. Water sloshed out of her mouth and hit the carpet. Her stomach felt bloated to the point of bursting. Blackness hovered around her peripheral vision. She saw stars and coughed several times.

The men carried her to the side of the room where a large bucket had been placed. No one talked. She heard nothing but the rustling of their clothes.

They stood her up. She remained conscious but groggy.

Harvester stepped in front of her. Without warning, he drove his fist into her bloated stomach. She doubled over and coughed, on the edge of throwing up. Her eyes watered further, and she fought to keep everything down. Breathing became an even greater task.

The men on either side righted her, and Harvester rammed his fist into her gut even harder. She couldn't hold it back. Everything she just swallowed rushed out of her mouth and into the large bucket in a torrent. She gagged and vomited again. When she thought it was almost over, the men raised her one more time, and Harvester kicked her in the stomach.

She doubled over and threw up another time, wondering if someone could die from a kick to the stomach. She gagged so much she couldn't catch a breath. It felt like her stomach had closed up shop, and her diaphragm wouldn't cooperate.

Men jumped on her again, tossed her to the floor, and held down every movable part. Even if she wanted to struggle, she had lost any resolve to give a good fight. She could barely breathe, her vision going black.

Then, the funnel was jammed into her mouth. She tried to shout something, but the water flowed, and she couldn't swallow anymore. She couldn't breathe, and consciousness was coming to a close.

She felt the curtain dropping, the show over.

"Stop!" someone yelled off in the distance.

The funnel yanked away. She was manhandled to her feet but couldn't hold herself up. They let her fall to the carpeted floor, where she curled into a ball and tried to get her breathing back to a steady rhythm.

The wheels of the water keg squeaked away, much to her relief. Whatever the reason for the reprieve, she was thankful.

The chore of regular breathing took some effort, but once she felt better, Rosina opened her eyes and looked at the old man behind his desk.

"You come into my office and disrespect me by not sitting when I ask you to. You're Italian by descent, aren't you? Have you no manners?"

Fear, the kind you can taste, eat, and digest, consumed her. She wasn't in the company of men. She was listening to and being dictated to by a man Lucifer would consider a friend.

"Now, let's see if you have learned your lesson. Sit up in the chair that was provided for you. Do it now."

It's interesting how fear could also be a motivator. She had no strength to move or will to get up, but she somehow found the strength knowing what would happen if she didn't listen to him. Rosina crawled to the chair. She used its legs to pull herself onto the seat, and then she pushed off the carpet with her legs, dropping her butt onto the seat without falling back down once.

The effort further exhausted her. She panted like she'd been jogging. Her stomach felt foreign, and bile lined her mouth. She tried to swallow, but the desire had left her. Spittle slowly dripped from her lips, dangling in long beads, collecting on her lap.

"Someone, get her a Kleenex."

People shuffled behind her. A moment later, a handkerchief was shoved into her hand. She wiped at her mouth and brought her eyes up to meet the old man's.

"Good," he said. "Now I have your attention. I prefer you this way. No spunk. I believe a woman should be more docile than the demanding wench you were when you entered my office. Have I got your full attention? I really need to be clear on this. Tell me, are you listening?"

She tried to nod.

"I won't ask again." His face tightened, his eyes rigid.

"Yeah, yes, yes," she muttered. "You have my … attention."

"Good. Your husband killed my son, Vincenzo. Now, my son was no ordinary man." The old man began tapping his letter opener again. The tension in the room calmed, and breathing became easier with each intake of air.

"He was ruthless and sometimes stupid," the old man continued. "He walked into an ambush. All hell breaks loose, and yet, my boy, my son, was the only man who walked out alive, not a scratch on him. It's pretty incredible, really."

The old man stopped tapping the letter opener. He faced her full-on. His eyes rimmed red, face flush.

"My boy walks out of a bloodbath a hero, and your husband runs him down the road like he was a rodent. How does that happen, one might ask themselves? I know because I've asked it many times. How does that happen?"

The old man got up and walked to one of the large windows facing out to the lovely architecture of Rome. Beautiful Rome, where Darwin and she had walked around and enjoyed themselves twenty-four hours before.

"And I think I've got the answer," he added. "I think I've figured out how that was possible."

"Darwin was working for one of the other families. That has to be it. There can be no other reason. Tell me, was it the Gambino Family?"

The old man turned away from the window and looked at her. "I need you to tell me who hired him to be out there at that exact time. I need to know who set this up. If you make me believe you, I will collect my debt from them. You will be free to walk out of here and go on to live your life. So convince me, who sent your husband to execute my son?"

She tried to speak, but at first, nothing came. She tried again. "No one … did."

"That's not good for two reasons. One, you are left to pay the debt, and two, I don't believe you." He paused and sauntered over to her. "Do you really understand what you're in for? Do you realize how dire your circumstances are?"

She nodded.

"I asked you a question," he shouted.

"Yes," she said as fast as she could.

"Okay." He walked away from her and sat behind his desk again. Then he picked up that damned letter opener and started his insane tapping. She felt she was losing her mind.

"I will keep you alive as long as I can. Your husband was picked up at the airport. He's on his way here with two of my finest men. After he confesses, I will have to kill you first. I want him to watch as all of my men get a taste of you. How would you like that? I'm offering you the pleasure of having sex multiple times with every man here, as long as they like. Isn't that what women want, multiple partners and the sex lasting longer than a quicky?"

She didn't respond, couldn't respond. Her stomach rebelled at what he was saying, threatening to clench again.

"We will be aiming for as much blood as possible, as that is the debt. A blood debt. Darwin will watch everything. Then he will be killed even slower." He set the letter opener down. "Get her up, take her clothes off. Lock her in there naked for when Darwin gets here."

Her heart caught in her chest. She had nowhere to run—she was too weak to run anyway. Not a single human being knew where she was. She would die before she would let them touch her in that way.

She got up from the chair and bolted for the office window, intent on throwing herself into it. She didn't get three steps before they were on her.

A telephone rang. Hands pawed her stomach, her legs. Someone yelled something. Her shirt was torn off, buttons flying. Hands ran between her legs. She was going to vomit again. Hands pawed her breasts. Her bra stretched to its limit.

The phone rang again.

Then the hands released her. The man yelling was the boss.

"Leave her for a second. Let me get this." He glared at her.

"Make a peep, and I will personally cut out your eyes with this letter opener. Do not betray me." He emphasized his point by raising his index finger like a father disciplining a child.

He grabbed the phone. "Hello." A pause. "Yes, I understand. Okay. I'll handle it." The old man hung up. He scanned the room as if taking everything in for the first time. Then he picked up his letter opener, skirted around his desk, and ambled over to the men huddled around her.

"She is something, eh boys?"

The men nodded and mumbled their agreement.

With a violence that belied his age, the old man plunged the letter opener into the neck of the man he leaned on. Blood shot out in torrents. The man reached for his neck, eyes wide.

Acting on instinct, the other men reached in and restrained their colleague in the event he would try to attack the old man.

The old man gouged the letter opener back and forth and up and down as if digging in tough soil.

Rosina watched in horror. She had never seen a man killed before. She'd never seen *anyone* killed before. The man fell to his knees, color draining from his face.

In under a minute, it was over. A man lay dead five feet from her.

The old man wiped his letter opener on the dead man's shirt.

"It appears that your Darwin is more able than I previously thought. I will not underestimate him again. I assure you of that."

The old man walked behind his desk. "When I said stop, I meant it. Little Mickey didn't stop. He winked at her when I was on the phone. Defy me at your own peril. Now, we have other business to handle. Give her back her shirt. Get her looking reasonable again. No one touches her until we have Darwin. We may need her intact." The old man turned his attention to her. "I thought your husband would be here at any moment, but sadly, he won't join us quite yet. It seems he has killed two of my best men and escaped on foot."

"What happened, boss?" One of the men stepped forward.

"I don't know exactly. Two of our men are dead." He surveyed the men standing behind her. "Do not underestimate this man, Darwin. Apparently, he was seen running away handcuffed. Most of the driver's right ear is missing, and my informant said it wasn't because of the accident. They clearly saw teeth marks gouged into his head. Big John is dead, too. Nothing could kill Big John, but he is gone." He cleared his throat. "What kind of a man can be handcuffed, kill Big John, chew off the driver's ear, and then walk away from a van that apparently flipped numerous times? He must be caught. But until that time, no one touches her." He gestured with his hand dismissively. "Now, leave me. Find Darwin. But whatever you do, bring him to me with his heart still beating. I, and only I, will be the one who rips it out of his chest."

Rosina found the resolve to smile to herself. Hope was making a comeback.

4

DARWIN WALKED THROUGH THE shopping mall, feeling like a new man. He wore new jeans, a slim-fit collared shirt, and a black jacket. Rosina wouldn't recognize him. When he got to Greece, she would be so happy that he stayed behind and dealt with everything.

Stunned by what had just happened, in a daze as if that level of violence was so unreal as to be reserved for the world of fiction, he had washed up, gone on a shopping spree, bought everything he needed, and used the men's room to dress. Now, it was time to try to negotiate. He had to settle this.

He strode out the mall doors and looked toward the highway in the distance. A tow truck was trying to right the van. To his right, a police car entered the mall's parking lot.

He headed back into the mall. He had taken the cuffs off before entering the mall property, but there was a little bruising where they had chaffed his wrists. If the cops stopped him, looked at his wrists, and started asking questions, it could be a problem.

He hustled to the other end of the mall and saw a taxi idling through the double exit doors, the driver reading a novel.

He slipped out of the mall and hopped into the back seat.

"Termini Station, please," he said.

The cab driver closed his novel and looked at Darwin in the rearview mirror. "My time off."

Darwin pulled out a fifty euro bill.

"Roma Termini. Then have your time off."

The driver shook his head. "You want Termini, one hundred euros."

Darwin looked out the back window. No cops. It was only a matter of time. He grabbed another fifty, thought again, and yanked an additional twenty. He handed the driver the whole one hundred and twenty euros.

"Termini Station. And do it fast."

The driver set his novel aside, turned in his seat, and said, "You got it."

It took thirty-five minutes to get to Termini, making it almost three in the afternoon when he arrived. He jumped from the cab and walked into the station, unsure what he was looking for or how he would find it.

They would find him. He was sure of that, but he needed something to negotiate with before that happened. And he needed a weapon of some kind to defend himself with. He was prepared to deal, but what if they weren't?

People rushed past him, pulling luggage and yanking on their kids' hands. Beggars asked for money. Uniformed policemen stood at the entrance to the station in pairs. A normal day at Termini.

He entered the McDonald's, where he ordered two cheeseburgers for a euro each. After getting his food, he headed for the downstairs shopping area, which was quieter than the main floor where the train passengers gathered. He needed a private pay phone. The call he was about to make was the first move in solving the Fuccini Family problem.

Knowing Rosina was on her way to Greece was such a relief that he felt he could do this. Had she run off that plane, she would have been pissed, but after he told her what had happened and filled her in on what he was about to do, she'd understand, forgive him. When faced with the explanation or sending her to safety and explaining later, he chose the latter.

He reached a bank of phone booths, picked one at the end of the row, and slipped his credit card into the slot.

He dialed Special Agent Greg Stinsen's number and waited. On the third ring, he remembered the time zone. Three-thirty in the afternoon would be nine-thirty in the morning in Toronto. Would Stinsen even be at the office yet?

On the fifth ring, Stinsen picked up.

"Yeah?"

"Hi, Greg Stinsen?"

"You got him. Who's this?"

"Darwin."

"What? *The* Darwin? Our resident hero? How the hell are you? How's life treating you?"

"Not good. Speaking of my life, I'm lucky to still have it."

"What?" The phone moved like Stinsen was sitting down now. "Talk to me."

"You know the man I killed with my Mustang?"

"Of course, I know him."

"His *family* is hunting me. They've tried to kill me several times in the last four days. They kidnapped me hours ago, but there was a car accident, and I was the only one to walk away. Now, two more of their men are dead. I need help."

"How come this is the first I've heard of this? No one has told me about any renewed activity—"

"That's because it isn't happening in Canada. I'm in Rome."

"You mean Rome, as in Italy?"

"The very one."

Darwin looked around, but no one paid any special attention to him.

"What the fuck are you doing in Rome?"

"Rosina and I came here to get married—"

"You have Rosina with you? And they still tried to take you out? Are they going after her, too?" Greg sounded incredulous.

"I doubt they're worried about her. I need your help."

"Tell me everything. Wait, you're on a pay phone, right?"

"Yes."

"Good."

Darwin starts with the attempts on their life and finishes with sending Rosina off to Greece and the accident in the van in more detail, leaving nothing out.

"You bit the guy's ear off? You are one crazy bastard. But you are one *alive* crazy bastard. I always knew there was something about you that I loved, Darwin."

"I got lucky, Agent Stinsen."

"I know. Listen, call me Greg. No more Agent Stinsen, okay? Look, I'll catch the next plane out. Don't do anything without me. Stay low. Do not go anywhere more than once. Check into a ritzy hotel. They won't expect that. Stay away from the cops. They could be on the payroll. Stay low until I get there, okay? Don't do anything without me. I'll escort you home."

"Got it. How do we get in touch again?"

"You have my cell number, don't you?"

Darwin looked at Greg's business card.

"Yeah, it's here on your card."

"Good. Call me this time tomorrow. I should be on Italian soil. But be prepared for resistance."

"Resistance? What are you talking about?"

"I'm FBI, Darwin. I work for the American government. I had special clearance in Toronto to work on the Fuccini case. The FBI isn't a global police force. When I get to Rome, I will have to ask for clearance. It's a professional courtesy. If they deny it, I'll be just like you, a tourist. I'd have to have some serious shit on the Fuccini Family to be able to pursue them in Rome. Serious shit does not include your word that they're trying to kill you. Understand?"

"Got it."

Did the Fuccini Family have to kill him to get police help?

"Okay, stay low and stay alive. I can't have my resident hero dead because I couldn't get there fast enough."

"Will do."

Darwin hung up, discouraged. Sure, Greg was coming to Rome, and getting him there only took a phone call. But the idea that Greg had no authority over here, and Rosina was alone in Greece, made him feel like he was no further ahead. He had no idea the next step, yet his life hung in the balance.

He turned around and leaned back on the payphone as travelers shopped all around him, ignoring the despair on his face.

"Sorry, Rosina," he whispered. "Some man I turned out to be."

5

Rosina tossed and turned to the tune of a splitting headache. She lay on a small mattress on the floor of an adjoining office. Two men were posted outside her door. The room had no window. The only light came from a small lamp beside her mattress.

They'd left a couple of water bottles for her, but so far, she had difficulty even looking at them.

What kind of men were these people? They didn't see her as someone's daughter or friend. They'd seen her as a piece of meat. Was that really the way human beings were? Was she so idealistic that she was unaware of people like the men in the other room?

She dabbed the tears off her cheeks as she wept. How could she have been so stupid? She knowingly walked into their grasp. She could've been in Athens. She could've been far from these people. But she walked off the plane and right into their hands.

She did it for her husband. She had to remember that and stay as strong as possible because there was a real chance these men would capture Darwin and bring him there.

She rolled into a ball on the mattress, wrapped her arms

around her legs, and cried.

What a honeymoon this turned out to be.

A knock on the door startled her. It opened before she had a chance to say anything. Light spilled in from the hallway. The door shut behind the man who had entered, and the light cut off.

"Dinner," the man said.

He set a large plate of steaming lasagna down beside the lamp.

"I'm," she paused to clear her throat, "not hungry."

"Doesn't matter. Eat. You do not want to piss off the boss. If he says eat, then you fucking well eat."

The man walked over to the wall and leaned against it. As far as she could tell, he was staring at her.

"What?" she asked. "Are you supposed to stand there and watch me eat?"

The man pulled something out of his pocket and started twiddling it with his hands.

She waited.

After several moments, he pushed off the wall and returned to her mattress.

She edged away from him.

He squatted, clutching a rosary.

"Didn't anything that happened today give you insight?"

"Insight? The only reason they stopped torturing me was in case my husband proved difficult. So I'm still meat, just a different kind—bait."

The man shook his head and flipped his rosary in a circle around his palm.

"Just fucking eat when you're told to eat." He got to his feet. "I'm here to take you to the bathroom, too."

"I don't have to go."

"Oh yes, you do. Man, you're too defiant for your own good? I'm here to take you to the bathroom. That's it. I have a job to do. I do it. No questions asked. You're supposed to go to the bathroom, so you go. Whether you shit or piss makes no difference to me. But you're going."

There was enough light to witness his face change. His eyes seemed wider, his teeth closer together when he talked.

She was trying his patience.

She rolled off the mattress and got to her knees. Using the wall, she stood on wobbly legs.

"Follow me. Do not deviate."

She nodded, most of the fight beaten out of her.

The man led her out of the room, down the hall a few doors, and then opened the ladies' bathroom door. He stepped into the sink area and waited.

"I am not letting you out of my sight. I won't watch you piss or shit, but I'm staying right outside the stall door."

She stepped into the stall and tried to deal with the humiliation of having to go with a man just outside the door. When finished, she washed her hands and followed him to her room. The two men on either side of her door were new, spelling the others. They parted and let them inside.

The door shut behind them.

"Now what?" she asked.

"I can't leave until you eat."

Rosina knelt, eased her sore frame onto the mattress, and picked up the lasagna. It smelled amazing. She couldn't believe she was so hungry after all she'd been through.

The first bite woke up her stomach. Then, before she realized what was happening, the man hustled over and dropped beside her.

"Take this," he whispered, close to her ear.

He held out the rosary for her. She looked up into his eyes.

"I've only got a second, and then I must go. I won't let them kill you. I can't guarantee to stop them, but I'll do my best."

She took the rosary.

"The Fuccini Family showed up here four days ago, looking for you and your husband. They don't have the muscle in Italy like they have in Toronto. They had to reach out, ask for help from their family ties in Sicily, and ask permission to conduct business here in Rome. It was granted last night. I am one of a dozen men sent over to handle the Kostas situation. I've been undercover for three years, and my real bosses are about to pull me. I'll be taking you with me."

Salvation and hope coursed through her. It was like she was on a failing plane when, all of a sudden, everything righted, and the pilot came on and said he got the engine restarted. They were going to be okay. Speechless, she nodded at him.

"Just do what they say. Stop resisting so much. This'll be over soon."

He got up and stepped away. "Good," he said, his voice louder. "Eat all your fucking food, or I'll come back and force-feed you."

As he exited between the two men in the hall, he muttered, "Stupid bitch."

One of the guards slammed the door shut, casting Rosina back into the relative darkness.

But it wasn't as dark anymore.

6

DARWIN WONDERED WHAT HE would do for the next twenty-four hours. Greg told him to check in at a ritzy hotel, but which one?

He strode along the crowded train station in a daze, unfocused, rudderless. The first step would be a weapon. But what kind? Knives were out of the question, of course. After all those years of being tossed in the basement with no window. The things his stepmother would prick his skin with for hours made him despise anything sharp. He recalled how if he cried or even mumbled a single peep of protest, she would poke and prick him over and over.

He always said he would do it to her one day, and when he got the chance in that barn, he used a pitchfork. No one ever found out it was him, and he was okay with that. One less fucked up human for the rest of humanity to deal with.

One day, he would tell Rosina all about how he hid in a barn that didn't look used for anything other than hay storage. When his stepmother found him three hours later, she was furious. She saw a pitchfork against the barn wall and came at him. He recalled her saying something about pricking him *real* good this time. He dodged left, dodged right, and kept himself off the long tongs of the pitchfork, but he knew it wouldn't be long before she got lucky.

The sun was setting that afternoon, casting the barn into a shade of dusk. His ability to control his temper became too difficult. When she lunged again, he dropped to the hay-covered floor, reached up, and grabbed the pitchfork handle. After twisting it from her grasp, he moved at her with a quick jab. It entered her chest, and she died in minutes, her heart punctured.

Darwin ran from the area and never looked back. He knew no one saw him because it never came up later in the investigation. He wasn't a murderer. He wasn't a repeat offender. It was a one-time act of returning to the source of years of pain and anguish. Years of torment and torture at the hands of a psycho.

His father had been absent all those years, working late hours. When he finally broke down and told his dad what his stepmother had been doing, his father refused to believe it.

Darwin was left emotionally damaged and scarred. He developed a violent reaction, a wave of outright insane anger, to anything sharp being pointed at him. So, what kind of weapon would work? A taser? A stun gun? A pellet gun? But he had no idea where he would get those things in Rome.

Darwin took the escalator back up to the main floor and walked along the train tracks. He passed by a stationery store on the right and devised a great idea for a weapon. He bought exactly what he needed and exited the store with the weapon carefully hidden in his new jacket's pocket.

He spun on his heels, a full circle, looking in every direction. No one watched him longer than normal. No one appeared to be stalking him.

He moved to the wall and stayed close to it as he continued sauntering along, watching the faces of all the travelers. He looked for anyone without luggage. People from every culture ran by, heading in myriad directions, intent on returning to their loved ones or furthering their travel arrangements.

If only I could make it back to Rosina.

In thirty minutes, he had traversed the entire floor of Termini Station without seeing anyone who resembled a mobster.

Toward the front of the building, people stood in long lines buying train tickets. The roof was made of some kind of glass. Clouds rolled in, some gray, some darker.

Above him and to the left, people walked along a railing on the second floor near a restaurant and café. When he watched the people, he spotted one of the men from earlier, the slimmer of the two who had chased the bus Rosina and he had taken to the airport. The man sat on the second floor at a coffee shop, a beverage in his hand.

Darwin tightened his grip on his weapon and started for the side. He walked with purpose but without making his hurried step too obvious. Within twenty seconds, he made it under the railing of the second floor, and as far as he could tell, the guy hadn't seen him.

He skirted around and took the escalator to the second floor. Even though he was supposed to be staying out of sight, he wanted to send a message to the boss man that he wouldn't be intimidated.

He slowed as he neared the corner of the cafeteria-style café. The man still sat there, looking down over the railing, his attention on the lines at the ticket booths.

Darwin edged out and walked briskly toward the man's table, careful to stay out of his sightline. Once he was behind the man, Darwin stopped. He waited, watching the back of the man's head. The weapon grew slick in his sweaty palm.

This was the only way. Act insane and be insane. Insanity meant unpredictability. He eased forward, placed his weapon against the man's throat, and leaned down next to his ear.

"Move a *fucking* inch, and the next time you move any muscle will be convulsions from the lead poisoning in your neck."

He surprised himself. His own voice scared him. On the word *fucking*, spittle flew from his mouth. It felt good, liberating. That kind of madness and control at the same time gave him something of a rush.

To his credit, the man jerked at being surprised but didn't spin around.

"I'm going to sit down behind you, and we're going to talk. You will not turn around. You will not look at me, or I will kill you and shove your corpse over the railing. Then, I will calmly walk downstairs and catch a train to wherever. Are we clear?"

The man nodded slowly.

Darwin eased back, pulled his weapon away from the man's neck, and sat on the chair behind the mobster. The man just kept staring straight ahead.

Darwin glanced down at the weapon in his hand. A thick pencil, unsharpened. He couldn't carry a sharp one. Never could in school, couldn't now.

Lead poisoning.

He looked up. The man hadn't moved.

Darwin ground his teeth together and spoke through them. "Put your arms up on the railing. Your hands must always stay in my view, or I will cut them off."

The man lifted his arms up onto the railing.

"Good. Now tell your boss this has to stop."

"Can I speak?" the man asked.

"Yes, but first, tell me your name."

"Paul. My name's Paul."

"Okay, Paul—" He almost added *nice to meet you.*

Shit. Stupid Canadian kindness. I'm talking to a guy who wants me dead. It'd do me well to remember that.

"Go ahead. Fucking talk."

"I don't think the boss will walk away from this."

"Why is that?" Darwin asked, his teeth still clenched tight.

"Two of his best men are dead out on the highway."

They already know about that?

Darwin leaned forward and smacked the back of the guy's head. "That's for scaring my wife on the bus."

He snuck a glance left and right. No one walked toward them. Their little meeting hadn't gotten anyone's attention.

"Sorry about that, man. I was just doing my job. Anyway, after what you did, man, I just couldn't believe it."

"What are you talking about?"

"No one lays down, Big John. Never. But I was told you chewed the driver's ear off and snapped Big John's neck, flipped the van, and walked away. All that with handcuffs on? Man, you're one crazy dude. Everybody's fucked up about it. The word on the street is Big John is dead, and some crazy Canadian white boy has gone insane."

Suddenly, everything was clearer. They figured him to be a crazy rabid dog, so Paul took a position upstairs to watch the ticket line in case he saw Darwin. They were afraid of *him.* Paul wasn't challenging him at all. Not even trying to look around.

"That's right, I'm insane, and I'm pissed off. Killing Vincenzo was an accident." He leaned forward and made the rest of his words sound as intense as he could. "But then that asshole threw me down and put cuffs on me. The van pulled onto the highway, and Big John pulled a knife out of an ankle sheath. That was it. I went mad. Big John's neck was so severely broken that the skin was split right up the side."

Darwin sensed the fear coming off the guy in waves.

"Now I'm coming for Fuccini and anyone else who gets in my way because I've got nothing to lose."

"I'm sure if you go in and talk to him, he'll consider letting Rosina go," Paul said.

Rosina? They had his wife? He couldn't believe it. He left her on that plane. He waited and watched. She hadn't come out. It was impossible.

"Repeat what you just said, but don't use her name."

"They have your wife. Maybe you can set up some kind of exchange?"

"I don't believe you. I saw her get on that plane."

The guy shook his head. He stared out across the open expanse above the heads of ticket purchasers.

"They picked her up and took her to the boss's office tower after she checked back into your hotel."

"You know where they're holding my wife?"

Darwin thought he had this under control. Greg was coming tomorrow to help him sort it out. Rosina was supposed to be in Greece. He'd join her in a few days when everything was over. But tomorrow would be too late. Greg wouldn't make it in time for Rosina.

"Yes, I do, but I can't take you to see her. They'll kill me."

Darwin pulled the pencil out and leaned forward, placing the tip against the guy's neck.

"You'll die right now if you don't take me to her."

"Okay, okay, easy, easy. I'll take you to the building. I'll show it to you. You do the rest."

He eased the pencil away and placed it back in his pocket.

"Reach in slowly and remove your cell phone. Give it to me. Then, I want you to remove your weapon slowly. Any movement I don't like, you'll be dead before you hit the ground, one floor below."

With exaggerated slowness, Paul reached into his breast pocket and produced a small cell phone. He reached behind him, palm up, arm twisted, and handed the phone to Darwin.

"You really want me to give you my piece out here in the open?"

"Yes," Darwin said brusquely.

"Okay, take it easy."

Paul eased a hand inside his jacket.

Darwin moved closer. He touched Paul's shoulder and squeezed the jacket's material.

"Easy does it," Darwin whispered.

Paul brought the weapon out with two fingers on the butt of the gun. Darwin knew nothing about guns. He took it with his free hand and dropped it in the jacket pocket that didn't have the pencil.

"Now, get up."

"We're going to the office tower?" Paul asked.

"Not right away. I need to find out if you lied to me first. You better hope you didn't."

Darwin rose from his chair and stepped back. Paul got up, and half turned toward him. Darwin allowed one eye to twitch. Then he tilted his head slightly to the side. He wanted an insane look, someone who had gone over the edge and wasn't returning.

"Move," he instructed.

Paul started away from him.

"Don't do anything stupid. You know how this works."

Paul nodded.

Darwin followed him to the escalator and stayed two steps away on the way down. At the bottom, he told Paul to go to the right.

On the way out of Termini Station, a few people got close, but nothing happened. No one attacked or tried to stop them.

At the street, Darwin directed Paul down the side to where they would turn left.

In less than two minutes, they stood in front of Hotel Luigi.

"We are going to go up to the lobby. I need to see if my wife checked in as you said she did."

Paul nodded and entered into the building. He took the stairs with Darwin a few steps behind. Then, they entered the brightly lit lobby.

"May I help you?" the clerk asked.

Paul moved off to the side as Darwin stepped closer.

"Do you remember me? I stayed here for four nights with my wife, Rosina?"

"Ah, yes, of course. She already checked in. You're in room twenty-seven. I don't think she's in her room right now. Would you like your key?"

"No, it's okay. We'll come back later."

He turned away and motioned for Paul to join him, the entire time his hand in his jacket pocket, fingers wrapped around the butt of Paul's gun.

They got back outside without incident, and Darwin looked for a taxi. At first, he was surprised the guy hadn't tried anything yet. But then he thought of Big John and how he'd looked after the car accident. This kind of man understood what it took to take down someone like Big John. For him to do it in handcuffs would intimidate Paul to no end.

He hailed a cab with all the confidence of a man in complete control. He knew Paul wouldn't run. Bullets were faster, and, as far as Paul knew, Darwin had two guns on him.

Darwin stood on one side when the taxi pulled up and ordered Paul in first. Then he bent down to watch as Paul shut his door.

"Lock it," Darwin said.

Paul did.

Then Darwin slid in beside him.

"Where to?" the cab driver asked.

Out of the driver's line of sight, Darwin withdrew Paul's gun and rested it on his lap, keeping it pointed at Paul.

"Tell him where to go."

Paul looked down at the gun and then up at the driver.

"Take us to Via Roma in the Eur Zone."

The driver nodded, and they started off.

Rome's allure tempted Darwin to look out the window and take it all in, but he couldn't. The afternoon was waning, the sun was dropping, and his wife was a prisoner because of him.

Paul stared out the window. He kept his hands on his lap and waited until the cab ride ended. The driver eased up to a building at least five stories high. It was modern for Rome, with glass windows and an art deco front.

"That's thirty-eight euros," the driver said.

Darwin pulled out two twenties and handed them forward.

"Get out," he told Paul.

They exited in unison. Cars raced up and down Via Roma without any regard for safety. A horn blared, and then another. He almost turned to see what was happening but refrained, keeping his eyes on Paul.

"We made it this far. Where's this boss of yours?"

Paul turned to the glass building. "Up there. Top floor."

"What office or room number will I find my wife?"

"I have no idea where they have your wife. I've been at Termini all day, watching for you. And there is no room number. The Fuccini Family owns the building, and the boss's office takes up the whole top floor. But it won't be easy getting in."

Darwin cocked his head to the side. "Why's that?"

The sun had dropped behind the buildings in its final descent. Tension in Darwin's stomach caused him to consider abandoning this until tomorrow. He couldn't operate at night, in the dark.

"Because whenever the boss is up there, extra security detail is called in, and the elevators are put on service. That means no one can get up there without using the stairs, which are heavily guarded."

Darwin listened to Paul tell him that they'd come all this way for nothing. Paul had acted scared and compliant. Now, he looked smug, and he talked with attitude.

"What do you propose I do?"

Paul laughed. "You didn't think I was going up with you, did you?"

"Why not? You've come this far."

"Yeah, right. Fuccini would kill me if I went up there and let you walk right in."

"I'll kill you if you don't."

Darwin's stomach dropped as the sun did. It would be dark soon. He couldn't be out in the dark. He knew fear was irrational, but it wasn't a choice.

Back at Termini Station, Paul had been intimidated. Now, his tone had changed.

"So kill me," Paul said. He opened his jacket at the chest area. "Shoot me right here. Come on. It'll be a quicker death than Fuccini would offer me."

Darwin couldn't shoot him. He didn't even know how to use the gun.

In the blink of an eye, Paul launched forward. Darwin was hit with a sucker punch. Then another. He was falling, trying to keep his balance, his arms pinwheeling. If he fell, he wouldn't be getting back up.

Paul threw all his weight on top of him. Darwin landed on his back, the wind rushing from his lungs. Paul tossed punch after punch in the stomach and his side, and a couple connected with his arms.

Then, it was over as fast as it started. Paul got up, breathing fast and hard.

"You fucking idiot. You thought you had the jump on *me*?" he screamed.

Darwin wiped blood from the edge of his mouth. He reached for the gun in his jacket, but it was gone.

"That's right. Got my gun back." He turned the gun sideways. "See this here. That's called a safety. You can't fire the gun without the safety turned off." He looked down at Darwin, who lay there collecting his breath as the lights slowly dimmed on

Rome. "The whole time, you thought you had me. You couldn't even fire a gun. Actually, have you ever fired a weapon?"

Paul searched Darwin's face for an answer. Then he laughed and slapped a knee. "You haven't, have you? Holy shit, you're a fucking amateur. And the boss has everyone afraid of you. Damn, is he going to be happy when I deliver you?"

Paul grabbed Darwin's jacket pocket, where he'd stashed the pencil. He ripped it out and looked at it dumbfounded.

"A pencil. A *fucking pencil*. Lead poisoning? Are you kidding me? This is royal. This … I gotta tell the boys." He looked down at Darwin. "Get up. Get on your feet."

The sun continued its descent. His reality shifted for a moment. Maybe he was going crazy after all. If they had Rosina and they were going to kill him, then what was the point of living? What was it all for?

"I said, get up." Paul stepped closer and kicked Darwin in the stomach.

The blow knocked the wind out of him. He curled around and got on his hands and knees. He thought about his stepmother. He thought about all the times he sat in that dark room and got poked. He thought about blood. Big John's face came to him, neck split open, blood on his face, his shoulder, his arm.

Darwin got to his feet slowly. Paul talked about how he could never have taken Darwin prisoner and brought him to the Fuccini building so easily. It was much better to go as a willing captor. He thanked Darwin for the pleasure of delivering himself.

Then, a streetlight turned on overhead. The day had fallen victim to night and its ever-present darkness. Darwin shook as the darkness gripped him. He felt blind and lost, but most of all, he felt angry that he could be in this position. That he was the weak one again.

"Move," Paul ordered with a gesture of the gun.

Darwin wiped the rest of the blood from the edge of his mouth, used both hands to straighten out his jacket, took a deep breath, and said, "No. Fuck you." Then he spat out a red gob that landed on Paul's lapel.

"Ohhh, you are so dead for that."

"Uh, uh, uh," Darwin said, wagging his finger back and forth. "Temper, temper."

Paul lunged, but this time Darwin was ready. The two men connected at the chest, arms grappling for a hold. Darwin lifted his leg and kneed Paul between the legs.

Paul yelped and lost his footing. Darwin redoubled his efforts, pushing Paul, as he shouted out triumphantly, off the curb and into the street. A horn blared. A car swerved, and still, Darwin pushed.

Paul's resistance gave out, and he started to fall, grappling at Darwin. He shoved Paul one last time and turned around to jump out of the way.

Too many cars were coming. He made a choice and leap-frogged the trunk of a car. He cleared the road and landed hard on the sidewalk, rolling to a stop.

He looked for Paul, expecting to see a raised weapon.

Paul hadn't been so lucky. He sat on the road, his legs useless and broken. A car screeched to a halt after it had run over Paul's thighs. More cars were coming. They were going too fast. The streetlights were dim.

A BMW tried to slow down but waited too long. Paul screamed, and then the bumper connected with his face, almost knocking his head clean off.

What remained of Paul's face was driven into the concrete of the road. Blood squirted out like a stepped-on ketchup package.

For the first time since he'd started this, he wondered if he'd throw up.

Everyone's attention was on the accident. Darwin limped away, trying to act as normal as he could, considering the injuries Paul had just bestowed on him.

He chastised himself for not grabbing Paul's gun. Now, what was he going to do? He had no weapon. He walked around the edge of the Fuccini building and looked back to the road. The traffic had all but stopped. People milled around, and others ran out of the front of the building where they held Rosina.

The dark closed in. Another man was dead. The stakes had risen. There was no going back now. It was Fuccini or him.

That was the only way.

7

Rosina jumped as her door was smashed open.

"Get up. Now!"

She had been trying to relax. Darwin was probably on his way, and an undercover cop was in the building. No matter how much faith and hope she had, her heart rate spiked along with her breathing when that door banged open. It was all starting up again.

"Let's go," the man said.

She stepped into the hallway and followed him on legs that didn't wobble as much as before. She'd eaten the entire meal they'd offered her, buoying her system.

The man led her past the office where she had endured the water torture and into an adjoining room. As soon as she entered it, she gasped and brought her hands up to her mouth, stifling a scream. Everything in her being shouted at her to run.

The room was a torture chamber. A medieval stockade sat in one corner. A table with at least fifty metal tools and gadgets ran along one wall. Chains hung from the metal rafters above. To her right sat a square unit on wheels that appeared to be an electrical generator. She could feel tension in the air, thickened by the pain the instruments had caused.

She stepped backward, bumping into someone.

"Leaving so fast?"

She spun around to look into the empty eyes of the Harvester of Sorrow.

"Stay, join us, watch the show."

She tried to speak, swallowed once, and then tried to find her voice. "What show?"

"We haven't found your husband yet, so this isn't about you. Yours is coming. Of that, I'm sure."

Someone screamed. Like they were in massive pain, it came from down the corridor. She reached into her pocket and pulled out the rosary her new friend had given her. Rolling it through her fingers, Rosina eased away from the door and stepped toward the wall that was farthest from the torture equipment.

Noises in the hallway intensified.

Sorrow flipped a switch and turned on a machine. She had no idea what its purpose could be.

Then, the doorway to the room filled with men. For a brief second, she thought she'd seen Darwin among them. She almost yelled out.

Four men entered the room, escorting the undercover cop between them. His hands were behind his back. Blood smeared his face. When his eyes met hers, fear clouded his.

"Tie him to those chains," Sorrow ordered.

Rosina had watched horror movies before. *Hostel, Saw,* and other gore-fest flicks. But that was acting, scripted. This was real. She had no idea people could do this kind of thing to others.

They turned the cop around to tie him up to the chains, his hands cuffed behind his back.

She wanted to scream at the top of her lungs. She wanted every law official in Italy to watch so they would enact stronger laws against organized crime. She wanted so many things but would get none of them.

A nice man, a cop, was about to be tortured, or worse, and there was nothing anyone could do about it. In that moment, if she could have killed the men around her, she would have. Even though that would bring her to their level, it would be a pleasure.

She found it odd how the desire to murder came so easily to her.

The boss entered the room. He glanced at her. "So glad you could join us. I wanted you present. There's a reason, and I think you'll play a vital role in what will take place."

He stopped beside the cop. The men had hooked him up to the chains that hung suspended from the ceiling in a way that his arms were rigid and his mid-section couldn't move. It looked painful because his shoulders seemed to take most of the weight, and his feet could barely touch the ground.

"So, tell us your secret," the boss said.

The cop looked away as if he knew what was coming, and nothing would stop them.

The boss turned to Rosina. "I was talking to you, wench. Tell all of us your secret."

"What … what secret?" she stammered.

"That rosary. Where did you get it?"

"I, ahh." Rosina looked down at her hands. She looked back up at the boss. "I found it in my room."

He narrowed his eyes. "Did you now?"

The room was silent. The only sounds were the clinking and rattling of the chains as the cop tried to hold himself steady.

"Let me ask you again. I will give you a second chance. I don't believe in lying, but second chances are okay under certain circumstances, and this qualifies as a certain one." He inhaled deeply, closed his eyes, then asked, "Where did you get that rosary?"

Rosina looked at the cop's bruised face. Blood dripped from his right eye, his mouth, and a cut on his left eyebrow. His body language spoke of defeat. When he looked up at her, he nodded and tried to smile.

It's okay, he said. *Go ahead. Tell the truth.*

"I got the rosary from …" She couldn't condemn him. She couldn't say it. She thought of Darwin, dabbing at the tears falling off her cheeks, and selfishly said, "I got the rosary from him."

"From who?" the boss asked, his eyes open again.

Rosina pointed at the man in chains.

"And why would he give you such a thing?"

"Maybe," she paused, her voice caught, her body wracked with sobs. She couldn't hold it back. She just couldn't hold it back in a room full of men as mean as these men were. "Maybe because he wanted me to have a little faith before I died."

The old man raised his index finger. "Or maybe he's working against us. Tell me, what did he say to you when he handed you your little present?"

"I don't remember," Rosina answered defiantly.

"Maybe I could jog your memory."

The old man motioned for his men to move to her.

"No, no," she screamed through the tears.

"Oh, don't be such a crybaby. They aren't going to hurt you."

Two men stood on either side of her, their arms crossed. She knew what that meant. Don't move. No matter what you're about to see, don't move.

She was pretty sure whatever they were going to do, she couldn't watch anyway. She dropped her face into her hands and closed her eyes.

Someone grabbed her hair and yanked her head back. She screamed at the pain.

"You will watch everything," the old man said. "When I have finished here, you will get another chance to answer my question."

Men gripped her arms so tightly that even the slightest movement caused pain to flare.

"Sorrow, I want you to perform a hamstringing on our fine gentleman here."

The Harvester grabbed a long blade, a sword of some kind, and a roll of white cloth and made his way over to the cop.

The old man turned to Rosina. "We're just going to make a little cut and then bandage it up. Don't worry, there won't be too much blood. It'll be over in a second, and then we can get on with our little chat."

Harvester got set up quickly. He unrolled two long strips of the cloth and then fell on his knees. The other two men in the room walked over and got down on one knee in front of the cop, and each man grabbed a leg.

"If you close your eyes," the boss said to her, "I will rip off your eyelids with a pair of pliers and force you to watch the next session as your eyes dry themselves out of your head."

Rosina watched as the Harvester of Sorrow applied his blade to the jeans above the knee and walked around each leg. The bottom half of the cop's pants fell to the floor. The men who hunkered below him grabbed his legs again and held tight.

Harvester slid the long blade into the back of one of the cop's knees and sliced back and forth, almost severing his lower leg. Then, he began work on the back of the other knee. The cop screamed for all of ten seconds before his head dropped, and he passed out.

Rosina cried as she watched, the tears blurring her vision. The men holding her let go, and she fell to the floor.

The old man was talking again. "That's called hamstringing. My colleague here has cut the two large tendons at the back of the knees, thereby crippling this man for the rest of his life. We're bandaging him up because we wouldn't want him to bleed to death, now would we?"

She couldn't believe what was happening. Where was she? Who was she? This was her honeymoon. They were in Rome getting married because their parents wouldn't see eye to eye. And now she had witnessed this horrific act, an image she would never be able to put out of her mind.

She would never be the same. Whatever had hardened these men to make them who they are today, they passed along to her, but she didn't want it.

She opened her eyes. The room was still there. Everything remained real.

"I will start asking you questions again," the old man said as he approached her. He seemed to be enjoying this. Maybe, in the end, it was all an act for the men under his command. He needed to show this kind of absolute strength so no one would get out of line. She certainly hoped that was the reason because if any of them were enjoying this, there really was no hope for humanity.

"Do not waste my time, and don't lie to me," he said. "Why did that man give you the rosary? What did he say to you after delivering your dinner?"

Rosina made up her mind in under a second. She couldn't play here. The rules were too foreign. Life and death choices and answers seemed to be their only currency.

"He said he would help me escape."

The words carried a betrayal she'd never imagined could come from her. How could she do that after the man had bestowed hope on her? What kind of person was she?

"Anything else?"

"What do you mean?"

"Did he tell you anything else? Does he have a secret? Don't make me draw it out of you."

"He said he was working undercover. But you already know that."

The old man turned away from her.

"I want this cop to leave here with a Glasgow smile so all his other cop friends can know what happens when you attempt to betray me or my family."

She shuddered to think what a Glasgow smile was but felt relief at the words *leave here*. That meant he could leave. He would be free. Who knows, maybe they could fix his legs, and he would walk normally again.

The Harvester of Sorrow edged around to the front of the unconscious cop and surveyed his face. The thick bandages had staunched the blood flow. The Harvester nodded at his two helpers, and they stepped closer. Then Harvester pulled out a small utility knife and stuck it just inside the right corner of the cop's lips.

With a flourish of the wrist, he sliced the cop's cheek all the way to the ear on each side. The cop awoke from his blackout and screamed, his mouth opening in a grotesquery of horror.

Then the Harvester jabbed the utility knife in and out of the cop's abdomen, and his scream continued, louder, animal-like, unabated.

The horrid mask of open flesh was too much to bear. Rosina looked at the floor, afraid to close or avert her eyes entirely.

After a moment, the cop fell silent.

"What did you do?" the old man asked.

"Nothing, sir. We always stab them a few times to make them scream. It opens up the wound quite nicely."

"I realize that, but he looks dead."

The Harvester stepped forward and touched the cop's neck under the jaw. Then he turned back to the boss.

"I'm sorry." Harvester shrugged. "His heart must've stopped."

The boss's cell phone rang. He turned from the Harvester.

"Speak," the boss commanded into the phone. After a second, he said, "I understand. Thank you."

"It appears we're going to have company. Assemble all your men and head downstairs."

"What's happening, boss?" the man to Rosina's right asked.

He pointed at Rosina. "Her husband is here, and he brought Paul with him. But Paul is dead in the road out front, his head crushed." He glared at Rosina. "Paul still had his weapon on him. That means Darwin has his own weapon." The old man looked around the room. "Shoot Darwin on sight. We can play with this one later." He gestured to Rosina. "I want Darwin Athios Kostas dead within the hour."

8

Darwin stood at the back of the building, trying to find a way inside. There was no other option left. The sun had dropped past where he normally allowed himself to be exposed to the darkness. He knew, rationally, that there was nothing to fear just because it was dark. But that was the thing about a phobia—there was nothing rational about it.

His therapist called it *achluophobia*. He also diagnosed Darwin with *aichmophobia*—a *fear of sharp or pointed objects*, such as needles and knives. Darwin had looked them up and felt he really had *angrophobia*—a *fear of becoming angry*. He did horrible, unspeakable things when he got angry. It became a fury without limit. The only things that caused that fury were being in darkness or having something poking and prodding him like a needle or a knife.

The heavy darkness began to press down on Darwin, closing in tighter. He felt marked distress. His ability to function and think properly grew more difficult by the second. If he didn't find a door that opened to a lighted area within minutes, he would have no choice but to break the nearest window to gain entry.

Darwin ran toward two large green garbage bins at the back of the building, which sat directly under a bright streetlight shining onto them. He looked skyward, a dark black-blue color, the sun's presence all but gone.

Standing under the light, he scanned the building for a way in. There was one door with a *Keep Out* sign and a large hole in the wall about seven feet up, which looked like a garbage chute.

He ran to the *Keep Out* door and tried the knob. Locked.

A pile of broken skids were piled haphazardly, stacked about eight feet high. He leaned under the chute to look up. It reeked of garbage and looked very black up in there. Too dark for him.

Someone was talking close by. He placed his back against the wall and listened. The voices were on the other side of the *Keep Out* door.

Darwin ran around the skids to the other side of the garbage bin and dropped below sight. The door opened from the inside. He peeked around the edge of the bin. Bright light poured from the building. A man stepped out, a gun in his hand.

The man kicked something on the door near its bottom and then walked away. The door stayed propped open. Darwin got down on his hands and knees and looked under the bin to watch the man's feet.

He approached the other bin slowly. At the last second, he leaped forward and stared into the bin. "Shit."

Evidently, this guy talked to himself when he was nervous. Darwin watched the man's feet as he drew nearer to the bin Darwin was behind. The man repeated the previous performance, approaching slowly, using extra caution.

The man paused. Darwin braced himself. The man leaped up

and looked inside the bin. At that second, Darwin shoved the bin with his shoulder. It rolled forward faster than he thought, and he almost lost his balance. It was only six feet to the brick wall of the building, and, to the man's credit, he stayed on his feet all the way.

The bin stopped almost as fast as it had started, with a crunch and a short shout.

Darwin raised his fists and approached the man. The gun lay on the ground two feet from him. Darwin picked it up, checked the safety, and flicked it off. *Thanks for that, Paul.*

He pointed the weapon at the man.

But the man was already dead.

He eased the garbage bin off the wall. When the bin had pushed the man into the pile of wooden skids, at least six or seven rusty nails had made their home in the back of the man's head. But that didn't seem to be the killing blow. A large, sharp piece of wood had sliced the man's neck sideways as he fell across it, digging several inches deep. Blood covered the man's shoulder and the concrete around his feet. He had died quickly, the nails in his skull keeping him quiet.

Darwin couldn't believe his luck. Without wasting a moment, he entered the building, the gun in his hand, safety off. He kicked the stopper on the door and shut it quietly behind him.

Rosina was here somewhere, and he was determined to locate her as fast as he could.

He ran for the middle of the building where he supposed the elevators would be. He knew what Paul said about the elevators being locked out of service was probably true, but no one ever thought of the service elevator. The one contractors used for equipment and supplies was rarely locked out unless men were working on the building. But it was after nine in the evening. He doubted contractors were still working.

He cautiously rounded each corner, his new weapon at the ready, watching for overhead cameras. To his relief, the freight elevator was right where he thought it would be. He recognized the wider door right away.

He pushed the call button, and the cables and pulleys whirred into gear. He kept his back to it as it came down and watched the hallway.

The amateur in the building with hired hitmen was not the role he envisioned on his honeymoon, nor did he think his new bride would be kidnapped. There was no turning back. He only wished he had Greg with him. Someone trained in this kind of thing.

The elevator motors slowed. He prepared for anyone disembarking.

The doors slid open to reveal an empty lift. He jumped in, pushed the top button, and hit the *close door* button. Immediately, the door began closing. He watched the hallway until the last second, but no one appeared.

He knew a certain number of the Fuccini men would file out of the building to look into the accident out front. He felt that resistance would be minimized and that the ones inside the building would fear him more than Paul because of what happened to Big John.

What if a small army guarded the top floor? They would have heard the freight elevator, and now, as he rode toward them, they would be flipping off their safeties.

Two floors away from the top, he jammed his thumb into the button below the top. The freight elevator instantly slowed, then stopped.

Darwin sighed in relief and stood to the side to see if anyone was waiting for him.

His heart in his throat, stomach in knots, the door slid open slowly. The room was cavernous. Dark, too. That sealed his decision. He would have to go one more level and take his chances.

But he couldn't.

Going to the next floor could mean walking into an ambush. Getting off the elevator now only meant he needed to deal with the dark. As much as it terrified him, the dark wouldn't kill him like bullets could.

The door began to shut. He hit the *door open* button and waited. He knew the right thing would be to walk out now and find a way to get up one more floor, but he didn't know how. And it was *dark*.

He broke out in a clammy sweat. Adrenaline spread through his stomach. Fight or flight set in. He had to fight for Rosina. This was the only way.

The door started shutting again. He hit the proper button, and the doors stopped, then slowly opened.

Darwin stepped off the freight elevator and into the darkness of a floor under construction and almost fainted.

The door slowly closed behind him, taking most of the light with it. The door was closing on his salvation. All chance of survival was dying with that door.

It took everything in his soul to take one step. At every second, he waited for a knife to prick him, a needle to jab him. He wanted to scream, shout, and run, but all he could do was take one more step. Then another.

Paralysis threatened him. The only cure was chanting the

word, *Rosina,* under his breath. He whispered her name and took a step. He whispered it again and took another step. Only the dim red exit signs provided any light. He wanted to run to an exit and scream until his voice gave out, but he used every ounce of self-control to continue walking, one step at a time.

Three minutes later, he made it to the door that led into a corridor. An exit sign illuminated the stairwell in red.

He stepped out and touched the door handle, ready to twist it and leave the dark floor from hell.

He had no idea how he was still standing. A noise in the room startled him. Darwin spun around and saw the light from the freight elevator as its door opened. Three men exited, guns drawn, flashlights in their hands.

Darwin opened the door to the stairwell and closed it behind him as fast as he could. They were bound to have seen the light from the stairwell. They would be on their way toward him now. He couldn't just run aimlessly through a building he knew nothing about, chased by numerous men with guns. He would never have the time to find Rosina and get her out safely. Even if he ran right into her, the last thing he wanted was to be running from bullets with her at his side.

He had to take a stand.

He hustled up the stairwell to the half-level landing where the stairs turned. Eight more steps up was the door to the floor where they supposedly held his wife. He leaned into the corner so only his eyes could look down and see the top of the door to the dark floor.

He waited, breathing in and out in a controlled manner. He needed to focus and stay lucid.

The gun was heavy in his hand. He had no idea how many

bullets it contained or how to fire it exactly. But its weight and knowing to just point and shoot comforted Darwin.

He raised his weapon when his feet scuffled on the other side of the door. Someone spoke muffled words into a radio. He leaned forward until he could see the door handle. It slowly turned. Then, the door moved an inch inward.

He fell back against the wall to the point where he couldn't see the door at all, and if they looked up, they wouldn't see him.

He waited. He breathed softly, slowly. And waited.

At least two men moved into the stairwell. Possibly all three.

He waited.

He said numbers in his head for no other reason but to count. At four, he pushed off the wall, stuck the gun through the metal bars of the railing, and squeezed the trigger as hard and as fast as he could. The stairwell lit up with flashes and the sounds of cannon fire. He had never heard such ear-splitting sounds so close before. He tried to keep his weapon trained in the general direction of the three men standing at the open door, but the recoil thwarted him.

Something punched him in the left shoulder. Darwin twisted away from the railing and fell, landing on his back. He shut his eyes, breathing in rapidly.

The guns ceased firing.

Moans emanated from below. He must have hit some of them. The pain in his shoulder made him clench his teeth. Then one of the men spoke.

"We're in the south stairwell." The voice was strained, the speaker in pain. "I think we hit him. Two men dead. I'm hit but alive. And where the fuck did he get a gun?"

He listened for a reply. After a few seconds, one came,

muffled through static.

"Go now. Finish the job."

"On my way." The man grunted.

He was probably getting to his feet.

Darwin kept his eyes closed. The man was still at the level below him, so he took one large breath and held it. Then he waited. He stayed completely immobile, his weapon in his right hand, his left shoulder screaming in pain now, and focused on the sounds the man's shoes made as he neared.

As far as he could tell, the man was at or near the top of the stairs. He waited for one more sound. It came, but it almost made him jump and scream.

It was the clicking of metal. The guy had readied his gun.

One, two, three, four—

Darwin opened his eyes and lifted his gun in the same motion. He screamed and squeezed the trigger, aimed directly at the man's face.

But his gun didn't fire.

It was empty.

He looked at it, eyes wild. The man lowered his weapon until he aimed at Darwin's chest.

Darwin lifted off his back, supported by his elbows, and kicked upward. It made direct contact with the man's hand as the weapon fired. He felt, as much as heard, the bullet race by his right ear like an angry hornet. A solid thunk told him the bullet made a home in the wall behind his head.

The guy didn't lose his grip on the gun, though.

When Darwin lifted his leg to kick again, it wasn't aimed at the gun. He twisted his waist and kicked at the man's chest. He made solid contact as the guy's gun was coming around again.

The guy fell backward, rolling down the stairs at a weird, inverted angle.

Darwin used the railing to get to his feet, moaning at the pain in his shoulder. He had no time to inspect the injury. However bad it was, it was exactly that—bad, something to deal with after if he stayed alive.

He ran down the stairs, two at a time, and jumped, knees extended, toward the man struggling to reach his feet.

Darwin's knees connected high in the man's chest, part of his left knee jamming into the man's throat. Darwin continued forward, bumping the wall with his good shoulder like a solid body check in hockey. He stayed upright, all his weight on the man below.

The guy's eyes widened, and his hands came up to push Darwin off. It was obvious the man couldn't breathe. His hands flailed at Darwin, and his mouth sat agape like a fish flapping on a dock after being pulled from the water.

Darwin would have been appalled at this level of violence two weeks ago. But now, something felt good about the man under him succumbing to his injuries.

He ripped the radio off the guy's belt and grabbed his gun. He slipped it into the back of his pants and grabbed another gun off the floor.

He took a close look at his shoulder. The wound was exterior only. As far as he could tell, the bullet hadn't entered his body.

He moved his jacket up off the wound and saw a gouge in his skin about the thickness of his finger. It was already clotting, but blood still seeped from the center of the wound. It was big enough to hurt like a bitch, but not big enough to stop him or kill him.

He slipped his jacket gently over his shoulder and started up the stairs, the gun in his right hand aimed in front of him. At the top of the stairs, he put his ear to the door.

Nothing.

He clicked the radio several times to see if he'd get a response.

Nothing.

There was no other way in, and he'd lost any element of surprise. They knew he was here. All he had were two guns, one of their radios, and a love for Rosina that gave him more willpower than any man loyal to Fuccini.

They'd use deadly force, but so would he.

He twisted the knob, ripped open the door, and dropped back down two steps to avoid being hit by anything coming through. The door opened to its farthest point and slowly came back to shut.

He opened it a crack and peeked in at the corridor. Lights filled the hall. He opened the door the rest of the way. The hall was empty. He stepped into the corridor with no idea which way to go.

"In here," someone said.

He jumped and fired his weapon. The bullet shot through a ceiling tile, and bits of dust fell.

"Shit. My *fucking* nerves."

"There's no need for that. I'm unarmed," the voice said.

"Where, dammit?"

"In here."

He tracked the voice to the open door about five feet from him.

Cautiously, Darwin started for the door. An old man stood with his hands in front of him, clasped together. Darwin turned into the room slowly. Another unshaven and disheveled-looking man stood off to the side by some kind of electrical generator.

"Come on in," the disheveled man said. "Nothing in here to hurt you. We have no weapons."

Disheveled Man raised his empty hands in the air. The old man unclasped his and lifted them, too.

"No weapons," the old man said. "Please don't shoot us."

Darwin scanned the hallway behind him to make sure he wasn't about to be ambushed and then stepped into the room.

Then he saw Rosina. Darwin lifted his weapon and aimed it at the old man.

"Get her down."

He felt no pain at that moment. He felt steady, calm, and ready to murder ten men. His mind cleared.

Rosina hung suspended on chains. Her face was pale, eyes closed. Remnants of vomit stuck to her blouse.

"There's no need for further violence," the old man said.

He turned to the disheveled man and motioned with his finger. A moment later, Rosina was lowered until her feet rested on the ground.

The old man brought his attention back to Darwin. "She is merely unconscious. As you can see, she is unharmed. I can't say the same for my son."

Darwin felt the hate ooze off the old man in waves as his arm grew heavy. It wavered a little, and then he lowered the weapon.

"Let her go. This is over. There is nothing left between you and me."

The old man stared at him silently.

"What are you waiting for?" Darwin asked. "Let her down, or I'll kill that asshole with the sick grin over there."

The disheveled man laughed a violent, deep chuckle that spoke volumes of how disturbed he was.

"We are not finished yet," the old man said.

"How's that?"

"There is a certain debt that is owed to me. I always collect a debt. It has been my family's way since the beginning of time. I'm not about to make an exception for you."

"What debt? What are you talking about?"

Darwin stepped closer to Rosina. If and when she woke from her drugged sleep, or whatever it was these men had done to her, he wanted to be close to her.

"A blood debt."

"Blood debt? You're fucked?"

"Actually, no, I can't say I'm fucked. I'd say you are."

Darwin raised the gun again, aiming it at the old man in the center of the room. "And how's that?"

"If you shoot me, it won't end there. If you shoot my Harvester, it still won't end there."

Harvester? What the fuck?

"You're talking in circles, old man. Start making sense."

The old man nodded to the man he called the Harvester. "Show him."

The Harvester raised his right hand and displayed a little box with a button. "If I push this button, your wife will be jolted with enough electrical volts not just to kill her instantly but literally burn her on those chains. Her scorched skin will fall off in pieces, like the burned bark of a tree, seared forever." He smiled that sick grin again. "Are you aware how *horrible* that would feel?" He said *horrible* like a child would ask for cotton candy at the fair, with youthful glee.

"The both of you are fucking sick. But," Darwin raised his free hand to make a point, "if you did push that button, I will execute the both of you. So, who walks out of here? Huh? You have to ask yourself the right questions."

The old man shrugged. "I'm old. I'm already dying, and since you killed my only boy, I'm dead on the inside. You have killed me, Darwin Athios Kostas—"

"Don't," Darwin snapped. "Don't you ever say my name like that again. Do you hear me? Never, or this ends for all of us."

He breathed in and out between his teeth as every ounce of his body begged him to shoot the old man.

"I want something from you," the old man continued.

"What?" Darwin asked, his teeth grinding together. He had to think. He had to keep them talking.

"I want you to set all your weapons down and kick them over to me. I am an honorable man. Do this, and I will release your wife from that machine's chains. Do we have an agreement?"

"No."

"I'll ask one more time. Do we have a deal?"

Darwin tried to clear his head. Was there another way out of this?

They had him, and they knew it.

"You will unhook her? You'll keep your word?"

"Your word is all a man owns."

Darwin leaned down, set one gun on the floor, and then kicked it away.

"The other one, too."

"No. Two chains are holding Rosina. Unhook one for that gun."

The old man considered this and then turned and nodded to

Harvester.

Darwin watched as he pushed a switch on a small control panel. Rosina was lowered to the ground. The Harvester pulled one chain off her arm when she was spread out on her back. He left the other connected, the little button held up with his thumb on it.

"If we stop here, you'll have done worse damage to your wife," Harvester said. "With only one connection, she'll still die by electrocution, but it'll take longer." He offered Darwin a wicked half grin. "There'll be more agony, more screaming, and the smell of melting flesh will be ..." He stopped when he looked at the old man.

"Enough. Now, the other weapon."

The Harvester raised the button to give him a better view of it.

Against every voice in his head shouting at him not to do it, Darwin set the second gun on the floor and then kicked it toward the old man.

The Harvester took the mechanism out of his hand, set it down, and walked over to Rosina, where he knelt and unhooked her from the last chain.

"I keep my word, Darwin," the old man said. "Now, we can talk with less tension."

Darwin felt locked in. He needed to get out and run. He needed to gather Rosina and run away as far as he could. He was willing to run into the dark night outside for the first time since childhood.

"What could we possibly have to talk about?"

"The debt," the old man said.

"What debt?"

"The blood debt you owe me."

The old man nodded at Harvester, and then Harvester reached behind a small counter that was littered with metal tools of some kind and brought out a machete covered in what looked like blood.

The familiar stirrings of violence accompanied the sight of a blade built inside him.

Involuntarily, he backed up.

"You will bleed from as many places on your body as we can open. Then I will have you chained upside down, your legs spread wide. Two of my men will use a saw to cut you open from the groin down until the blade hits your heart. In that position, blood rushes to the brain, keeping you alive through most of the cutting. Quite the experience, really."

From the corner of his eye, he saw the old man picking up the guns. He was defenseless. They had disarmed him, and now they were the ones in power.

All he had was his wits, which effectively amounted to nothing.

Harvester stepped closer, swinging the blade in his hand.

"I enjoy sawing men in half. Only got to do it a couple of times."

To defend himself the best way he knew how, with no weapon of any sort, Darwin slipped out of his brand-new jacket and held it to the side. It wasn't too thick, but it was better than nothing.

"What's this?" Harvester asked.

"You wanna cut me? Here I am."

The old man stepped toward the door. "Cut him up, cut him bad. But Harvester, don't kill him." And then he stepped out of the room.

Darwin wrapped the jacket around his left forearm. Harvester was four feet away and moving closer.

"You really are a piece of work," Harvester said. "Rarely do I get to meet someone so interesting,"

Darwin had held himself together as long as he could. All the fury and anger from his childhood, everything he ever hated about his stepmother and all the people who had hurt his wife today, boiled to the surface and overflowed into madness so blinding and all-encompassing, a small part of him worried if he could ever regain normalcy again.

He dabbed at his bleeding shoulder, covered his hand in blood, then wiped it on each cheek as if it were war paint.

The Harvester hesitated a moment, eyebrows raised. Then he hollered and lunged. Darwin threw his jacket-covered left arm at the blade and ducked under it, his right hand going for Harvester's throat.

He clamped on, oblivious of where the blade was now, and squeezed with inhuman strength on Harvester's windpipe.

Raw strength pulsed through him, something akin to what mothers use to pick up cars that have trapped their babies. He tightened his grip so hard and fast that he dislodged Harvester's Adam's apple. He pushed forward and tightened his grip further, screaming in the moment's madness.

Harvester flailed his arms and lost his balance as he was thrust backward, dropping the blade while trying to dislodge Darwin's hand.

Their forward momentum tossed them to the floor. Darwin landed on top of the Harvester. As he rolled to the side, his hand dislodged from the man's throat. The Harvester was up on his knees in a flash, trying to learn how to breathe again.

Darwin rolled away and bumped into the tool tray. A metal

grip lay beside his head. On the other end of the grip was a bar, similar to a police baton, but with long metal spikes. He almost didn't touch it when he saw the spikes but knew he needed to be rash. He needed to use a sharp implement of some kind to end this.

Darwin grabbed the smooth handle and spun around, but he was too late.

Harvester brought his fist down onto Darwin's wounded shoulder. He screamed and gagged on the phlegm that had collected in his throat.

The Harvester raised his fist again when Darwin, in awe that he held something sharp in his hand, swung it in a swift arc.

The four-inch spikes embedded in the side of the Harvester's skull, one punching through his left eye, slicing deep inside his head.

Harvester moaned, mumbled something unintelligible, and sat down. With his good right eye, he found Darwin lying on his back in front of him. It was like he couldn't figure out who Darwin was.

Then he lost his balance and lay on the floor, his right eye staring at the ceiling.

Darwin got to his feet, his shoulder screaming, and glanced at Rosina. She was awake, watching in frightened silence.

Darwin stepped over to the Harvester. The man's one good eye met his. Blood dripped out of the four holes in his skull. The Harvester tried to smile, his lips twitching. "That hurts," he mumbled.

Darwin lifted his foot and brought it down on the weakened side of the Harvester's skull. Blood and bits of brain oozed out onto the floor.

Darwin unwrapped the jacket from his forearm and discovered the cut the machete had made. Harvester had gotten in one good hit. It would certainly need stitches. He used his right hand to rewrap his arm and stepped over to his bride.

"How about it?" he asked, trying to put on a cool face, his hand extended to help her up. "You ready to finish our honeymoon?"

She got to her feet and leaned into him, tears rolling down her cheeks.

"Did you hear that?" Darwin asked.

She shook her head.

"Sirens in the distance. Sounds like the police." He eased her back and looked into her eyes. "There was an accident downstairs. A man was killed in the street."

She nodded. "I know. A man named Paul. I heard them talking about it."

"I've done some bad things today. I didn't hurt anybody that didn't have it coming. And I'm sorry for trying to send you away. You have to know I was trying to protect you."

"I know," Rosina said.

"I could be in trouble. Once everything is ironed out, I'll come out looking okay, I'm sure, but understand, that may take time, and until then, unless that old man is out of the picture, our lives won't be worth much."

She nodded. "I understand. Let's find him before we leave."

With Darwin in the lead, they cautiously stepped into the room where the old man had gone before Darwin and Harvester fought.

The room was empty. Following Darwin's lead, they walked the hallway and looked in every room they could. Police sirens shut off outside the front of the building.

Down the corridor, the elevator kicked into gear.

Keeping an eye on the hallway, he asked, "Did they hurt you?"

"Not really. I was scared, but they were instructed to leave me alone until they had you. I watched them hurt someone else, though. They killed him." She looked into Darwin's eyes. "I'm so glad you killed the Harvester. That man shouldn't be allowed to live."

"How does someone get the name *Harvester*?"

The elevator door opened, and six Italian police officers stepped out, guns raised at them.

They were ordered to the ground and minutes later were handcuffed. The Italian officers led them downstairs to the main lobby, where they were told an officer in charge, who spoke fluent English, would come at any moment.

During their wait, Darwin saw a couple of the Fuccini Family men sitting in police cruisers at the front of the building.

A man in a suit and a tie approached them. The man's face changed to anger when he saw the handcuffs.

"Officers," he called out, then shouted something in rapid Italian.

Two cops ran over and undid their cuffs. Darwin checked his forearm cut. Still bleeding.

"I'm sorry they treated you like this. They don't know who you are. My name is Marco. I'll have an ambulance take you to the hospital, where we'll get you stitched up, and then I'll take your statement. How does that sound?"

Darwin nodded at him.

"I got a call from a colleague of mine, Special Agent Greg

Stinsen, with the FBI. He told me what was happening and that he'd be here in the morning. He said to offer you all the support I could. These men can piece together what happened here. We leave now. That work?"

Relieved it was over, Darwin, holding Rosina's hand tight, followed the officer to his car, even as the darkness surrounded him.

As the cop pulled away from the curb, Darwin said, "Can you turn on the interior light?"

"Yeah, sure," the cop said and flicked it on.

Darwin took a deep breath and stared down at his hands. He didn't want to look at the windows. All he'd see was blackness, and that didn't help anything.

It was over for now. A lot of men had died, but they were safe. They were in police custody, and the FBI would arrive soon. Together they'd launch an attack on the Fuccini Family to end the vendetta, that blood debt shit.

"You still need the light on?" the cop asked.

"Yes." Darwin looked up at the cop in the mirror. The cop smiled, nodded, and looked away to focus on the road.

***

He woke in the hospital the next morning, the sun streaming through the curtains.

"Rosina?" he called out, panicked as he rose from the bed.

"I'm right here," she said from the chair beside the bed. She stretched, arms above her head, moaning. "When I think about what happened yesterday, it feels like a dream. Then I see your shoulder and forearm, and I know we lived through it."

Darwin rested his head back on the pillow. "The cop, Marco, is he gone?"

"He left after he took our statements. I just heard from a nurse that Agent Stinsen called. He's five minutes away."

"What are we going to do?" Darwin stared at the ceiling tiles above his bed.

"We're going home," a man's voice said.

Darwin jerked upward, causing pain to flare in his arm.

"That's what we're going to do," Greg finished as he stepped into the room.

"Greg," Rosina gasped his name and ran to hug him.

"How's my favorite couple?" he asked.

"Great now," Rosina said. "It's so good to see a familiar face."

Rosina released him, and Greg walked up to Darwin. "What am I gonna do with you?" He smiled wide, his face beaming. "First, you kill Vincenzo by accident and then come to Rome to wipe out the rest of his family. Wow, if I hadda known you were like that, we could've used you on the force."

"Greg, it wasn't like that," Darwin said. "They kept coming after us. If they had accepted it was an accident in the first place, they wouldn't have hunted us in Rome. I flew my wife here to get married. I felt they were getting too close to us in Toronto. Death threats, people following me. They tried to kill us several times in four days."

"Marco told me everything."

"Doesn't that guy sleep?" Rosina asked.

"I'm sure he does at some point." He glanced over at Rosina, then back to Darwin. "I have you two booked on a flight from Rome to Toronto tonight. I can't protect you in Italy."

"Didn't you get clearance or something?" Darwin asked.

"Not really. Marco let me see the statements as a favor, but the diplomatic channels will take too long for me to do any good here. If you're in Toronto, I have backup and a sort of quasi-jurisdiction."

Darwin met Greg's eyes. "Thanks for coming so fast, and, yeah, let's go home."

"I'll talk to the doctor and get you checked out, but first, I must ask you a question."

"Go ahead."

"Did your father ever tell you why he called you Darwin?"

"Yeah, he said he wanted to always remind me to stay motivated and get out of life whatever I wanted. He put two words together to make Darwin. *Dare* and *win*. He claimed by saying my name was my dare to win."

"That's pretty good." Greg walked over to the hospital room door. "I thought there was another reason. Something to do with the survival of the fittest. You know, Charles Darwin and natural selection."

Darwin nodded his way in thanks. Greg was always high on the compliments.

Greg opened the door and made to step out, but his cell phone rang. He hopped back into Darwin's room and pulled out his phone.

"I gotta take this."

"Go ahead," Darwin said.

"Stinsen here."

Greg listened, his phone pressed to his ear. His face grew darker, and his eyebrows got closer until they connected in a look of consternation.

"Okay, I understand. Send units over to their house ASAP."

He flipped his phone shut and looked between the two of them.

"Sorry. Bad news."

"What? Tell us."

"It seems this shit isn't over yet."

"I didn't think it would be." Darwin sat up in bed. A dizzy spell hit him as he leaned back on his good arm. "What is it?"

"Your father," he said to Darwin. "Adrian has been kidnapped. He was taken from his home an hour ago, according to witnesses. That puts it around six in the morning, Toronto time." Greg looked over at Rosina. "Whoever's behind this may be headed to your parents' house in Brampton, too. Units are en route there now." He paused. "I'm sorry."

9

THEY LANDED UNDER CLEAR skies at Toronto's Lester B. Pearson International Airport.

Darwin had rested most of the flight, sleeping uncomfortably in the airplane seats with a bandaged left shoulder and left forearm.

Before leaving Rome, Greg had confirmed that Rosina's parents were safe. The police had secured their home before anyone from the Fuccini Family could get to them.

Rosina had been quiet on the way to the airport during their boarding procedure and the subsequent flight.

He turned to Greg. "What's next? Do they offer demands or something, or do they just kill my father?"

Greg looked up from the in-flight magazine he'd been reading and said, "So far, there have been no demands. These people don't call the police and ask for things."

"No, they kidnap people and kill them. It's a revenge thing, isn't it?"

Greg set the magazine in the pouch at the back of the seat in front of him. "Look, Darwin, this situation is as bad as it gets. There are many levels of problems with it."

The plane was taxiing in to a gate.

"What kind of problems?"

"A crime family as big as the Fuccinis runs deep. They have contacts all over the world. They have people on the take. I'm sure they even have police officers updating them on what's happening, but I'd never admit that publicly or to any other officer."

The plane stopped with a small jerk. People undid their belts and started to grab items from the overhead bins.

Greg continued. "Officers are working undercover. Deep cover. They report back at alternating times. In those reports, without breaking cover, I'll be told how your father is doing and what has happened to him. I won't find out from a phone call with a list of demands. The other thing you have to face is that this won't be a repeat of Rome. I mean, you did the right thing. But now—" He stopped as someone bumped him with their bag. He nodded when the passenger apologized and turned back to Darwin. "But now we're on Canadian soil. We have a lot of cops at our disposal, and they're all working overtime to find your father. They're also rounding up known Fuccini Family members and their employees to get answers. We'll work this out. All we'll need from you two is consulting. During this crisis, you two will stay where it's safe."

Darwin shook his head. "Nowhere is safe from them. When you have people that powerful after you, nothing will stop them. I'll always be looking over my shoulder until Vincenzo's father is dead. There is no other way."

The plane had emptied. Greg collected his things and grabbed their backpack. Their luggage was still in Athens, with arrangements to have it flown back to Toronto.

Because of Darwin's injuries, Greg handed the backpack to Rosina, and they started out of the plane. It was a long, quiet walk to customs. Once they were processed, Darwin said he needed a coffee. He couldn't leave the airport without a large double-double from Tim Horton's.

Outside, a cruiser waited for them. Six cars back, an unmarked vehicle with two men in suits and sunglasses watched them.

"They FBI, too?" Darwin nodded in their direction.

Greg nodded. "Good eye, Darwin."

They got in and were whisked away. Ten minutes later, the driver pulled into the Quality Suites Hotel.

"What's this?" Darwin asked. He looked at Rosina, who still hadn't said much. He was starting to get a little worried about her. She hadn't said anything since he woke up on the airplane.

"We've reserved six rooms at the end of the fifth floor. They're all adjoining rooms. You two will be in the middle. In each room surrounding yours, there will be two agents. No one will be able to get to you two unless they bring a small army."

The car pulled up to the front doors.

"You mean we can't go home?"

"Darwin, I told you in the airplane. Things are different. This won't be a repeat of Rome. You aren't free to drive a car, hang out with your friends, or go home and talk on your phone. You will have to remain in police protection at this hotel until we've located your father and found the people responsible for his abduction."

"That means my wife and I will live at the Quality Suites for years then."

"What does that mean?" Greg asked, his tone hurtful.

"Unless you're planning on killing the Fuccini Family boss, we will never be free," Darwin said and stepped from the car.

"Wait," Greg shouted.

The men from the car that had tailed them ran up.

"Don't get out of a vehicle without an escort," one of the men said.

Darwin ignored him and looked at Rosina. "Come on. Let's check in and go have a nice dinner."

They didn't have to check in as the rooms were ready. Darwin was surprised at how pleasant the rooms were. They were like small apartments with the bedroom separated by French doors. The room had a small fridge and a mini kitchen with a coffee maker.

"Looks like we'll be here for some time," Darwin said. He looked at Rosina. "You okay with that?"

She offered him a thin smile.

"Rosina, I need to hear it. What happened in Rome was tragic, but we survived. That part is over. We're alive and healthy. We're surrounded by the FBI now. I need to know you're still with me."

She walked over to the small couch and sat down. "I'm still with you, Darwin. I'm sorry. I just thought it was over. I saw what those men did to that cop who tried to comfort me. Thinking about your poor father and what he's going through … it just shakes me up. It'll never be over until we're dead or the Fuccini Family is dead."

Darwin sat beside her and wrapped his good arm around her. "I know, and I'm sorry, baby. I brought this on us. It's my fault."

She grabbed his lapels and yanked him around to face her.

"Don't you ever say that. Don't you ever. You did nothing wrong. Actually, you're the only one doing anything right. If you had waited until the police negotiated a release for me, I'd be dead. They weren't going to release me." She started to cry again. A shudder went through her shoulders. "I can't believe how close I came to being tortured, raped, and murdered, and you saved me."

"What were they going to do to you?" Darwin asked.

"Horrible, unspeakable things. What stopped them was the call that you had escaped from a guy named Big John. They said no one could touch me until you were caught. It was so scary. I saw these people for what they are, and I think Greg is wrong here. The police aren't prepared to execute them. So it'll never be over. I'm just really scared."

"I know, baby, I know," Darwin said as he pulled her closer.

***

Dinner was brought up to the room. They ate in silence, each lost in their own thoughts. While they ate, Darwin planned. He needed to have something to do, so he planned. He needed to end this. Staying in police protection wouldn't cut it.

He set his plate on the edge of the little sink and threw away the plastic utensils. They'd brought real cutlery, but he made them go back down for plastic. He used the bathroom, then walked over and opened the main door.

"Darwin, what're you doing?" Rosina asked.

"I don't know. Something, anything. We can't stay cooped up in a hotel room, brooding."

An FBI agent stepped up behind him. "Do you need anything?"

"Yes, I need to leave."

"I'm afraid that's not possible."

"So we're, like, prisoners now?"

"Not exactly. You are not a prisoner. We're here to protect you. This is for your own safety."

"No, we're prisoners by every definition."

The FBI man stared back without speaking.

Darwin shut the door. "What are we going to do, Rosina? We've been in Toronto for six hours, and we're already going stir-crazy."

The phone rang. They looked at each other.

"No one knows we're here, but the police," Darwin said before he answered. "Hello?"

"Darwin, it's Greg. I was hoping you picked it up. I couldn't tell Rosina what I have to say."

"Go ahead." His stomach dropped. *What now?*

"It's Rosina's parents. We had them protected. Six officers on the detail. Four of them are dead, and two are missing. There is no sign of her parents. I'm sorry, Darwin, we did everything we could. We lost good men today."

Darwin hung up and turned to face his wife.

10

No one had visited them since dinner, the phone hadn't rung again, and now it was midnight. Rosina had fallen asleep on the bed after crying for two solid hours. He'd waited until she'd fallen asleep. He was wide awake from his long rest on the plane and determined to do something about the threat that had befallen his family.

He put on his shoes and walked to the door. When he opened it, a new FBI man stood there.

"Do you need anything?"

Darwin stepped out into the hallway. "Actually, yes," he said, closing the door behind him.

"Sir, don't do that. You're not supposed to be in the hallway. Can I have your room key, please? Open the door."

"Oh, damn, I left it inside."

"Okay, stay here. Don't move. I'll radio down and have another one brought up. In the meantime, I'll keep you behind me while I watch the hall."

"That won't be necessary."

"Sir?"

"I'm leaving."

"I'm afraid I can't allow that."

"Well, you don't really have a choice, do you? I'm not a prisoner. I've broken no laws. Well, at least none that I've been charged with. Now, please, step aside."

The FBI man crossed his arms. "Sir, I have orders to keep you in your room with your wife."

"What's your name?"

"Special Agent Trent McMahon."

"Listen, Trent. How did they get to Rosina's parents? They were under police protection, too. Six officers, as far as I understand it. How many do we have here? Now, of course, I appreciate the thought, but there's been enough bloodshed. It's time I met with these people and ended this. I won't stay in the same room with my wife, endangering her further while these people are free, running around, conspiring to kill me and everyone I know."

"I understand what you're saying, and I sympathize. But I have orders, and I intend to follow them."

Darwin had been prepared for that but knew the FBI man wouldn't shoot him.

He looked past the cop's shoulder, widened his eyes, and said, "What about those guys?"

It was a stupid, juvenile trick, but Trent dropped and spun around, reaching for his weapon. By the time he turned back, Darwin was running down the hall, halfway between Trent and the door to the stairwell.

When he hit the door, he glanced back and saw Trent speaking into his wrist.

Darwin ran down the stairs two at a time. On the fourth, third, second, and finally, the ground floor, his shoulder wound ached at the raised heart rate and extra movement.

He headed into the lobby instead of running outside through the exit door. He walked past the front desk to a sliding door on the left, which opened as he neared it.

It seized him as soon as he walked outside and into the night. He hadn't put much thought into it. It was just after midnight, which meant darkness. What was he going to do? Run around Toronto in the dark? Impossible.

The familiar stirrings of anger surfaced. An image of his stepmother's face flashed in his mind.

A car raced up and squealed to a stop in front of him. Two men in suits ran toward him before he realized what was happening. They flipped open badges and grabbed his arms.

He winced and pulled his left arm away.

"Shit, that fucking hurts," he grunted, his teeth clamped together.

"Sorry," the agent on the left said.

They guided him to the car and put him in the center of the back seat. Both men got in on either side and shut the doors. A second later, the vehicle was underway.

"Turn on the interior light," Darwin said.

"What?" the driver asked.

"I said, turn on the interior light."

"Sir?" the driver said, looking in his mirror for approval.

The agent beside Darwin nodded, and the light flicked on.

No one said anything as the driver pulled out and exited the hotel parking area. He went through a green light and turned into a Park-N-Fly lot, grabbed a ticket, and then raced to the back, where it was relatively empty.

When the vehicle was parked, the agent next to Darwin said, "We need your help."

Darwin nodded. "Shoot."

"Rosina's parents' kidnapping was an inside job."

"I'm not surprised," Darwin said.

"You already know the man we're talking about."

Darwin frowned. "What? Who?"

The agents exchanged a glance. "We suspect it was Special Agent Greg Stinsen."

He felt cold, his forehead cool with sweat as he took in what the man had just said. "No way. You have to be joking."

"Wish I was. We followed him when he left your hotel before dinner was sent up to you. He drove to an adult store on Dundas and Dixie. He came out with a black bag. Normally, those kinds of stores have black bags for discretion. But the Fuccini Family owns and operates a lot of these adult stores. They do several payouts through them. Men can walk right out in public with large sums of cash, and no cop could ever see the drop-off taking place. The windows of these stores are covered, so unless I got a cop on the inside, for all we know, Greg rented a few movies."

"Let me guess," Darwin interrupted. "You think he told them where Rosina's parents were and collected a payout?"

"Exactly."

"Well, what about my wife? She's up there in her room alone. Greg knows where we are."

"She's being moved to a secure location at this moment."

"Where?"

"The less people know, the better."

"I'm not people. I'm her husband. You have to tell me where

my wife is."

"Calm down. If I do and Fuccini gets his hands on you, you can tell him."

The logic worked, but how could he trust this guy? How could he trust anybody?

"What we want you to do shouldn't be too dangerous. But we have to ask if you're willing first."

"What is it?"

Car headlights on the 427 Highway raced by behind them. The lights caught his eye as he tried to focus on what the agent was saying.

"We'll explain to Greg that we're moving you and your wife to a new location. We think there's been a leak. Your wife will be safe the whole time. She won't be anywhere near the area we tell him. We're going to ask Greg to deliver you to this location. He's the natural pick, as he was the one who brought you from Rome. We will stay close the whole time. If he veers from the route, we'll know. If someone tails you, we'll know. If he contacts a third party at any time, we'll intercept and take him out."

"We solve the Greg issue, but will this lead us to Fuccini?"

"When he makes contact with anybody, we can trace it. His cell phone is tapped now. Everything he does is being watched, but he won't do anything stupid. Without this, if he's already told them about your hotel, he won't make contact again. We have to force his hand. We need to get him to make contact again. He won't do anything to you personally. He will have to make contact."

Darwin watched the lights of the cars going by in the night. If he was going to stare out at darkness, he had to set his eyes on lights.

"Darwin, listen. I know how tough this is. I heard what went down in Rome, and believe me, not many agents could've pulled off what you did. The Harvester of Sorrow has an international reputation. Word on the street, and when I say *on the street*, I mean every street hoodlum from New York, Montreal, and Toronto all the way to Via Roma, has heard that a Canadian boy, under the nickname *Natural Selection*, crushed Harvester's skull. You are one serious fucker out there." The agents exchanged another glance. "I know what Rosina went through. You both should be home having a beer and watching a ball game. I get it." He patted Darwin on the shoulder. "But I need you here. Four of my men, guys I went to the academy with, were slaughtered tonight, and two of my men are missing. They took Rosina's parents. Someone blabbed the location to the Fuccini Family. We are pretty *fucking* sure it was Greg. We need you, man. Anything, at this late hour, that we do out of routine, Greg will suspect. The only thing he won't suspect is moving you and your wife, in separate cars, to a new, secret location as soon as possible. This he would consider normal, routine. So, that's why you're here. We're begging you to help. We need you. You're our only guy. What do you say?"

"I'm in. When do we do this?"

"Right now. Greg is meeting us here in." The agent looked at his watch. "Less than five minutes."

11

Darwin exited the FBI vehicle and got into the next one. He wasn't wired, and they hadn't given him a gun. He had no means of protection except for the agents following them.

While waiting, Darwin had posed a question. Since Greg was a seasoned agent, wouldn't he suspect a tail? They explained that they, too, were seasoned agents and that the tail would be a rotating one, where an agent followed for two to three blocks and turned off as another agent fell in behind the suspect vehicle, which was seriously hard to spot by even the best agents.

Now Darwin sat in the back seat of Greg's cruiser, the interior light already turned on for him.

"How're you feeling?" Greg asked.

"I'm worried about Rosina. When she heard her parents had been taken, it was seriously hard on her."

"I can imagine. I'm sorry, Darwin, I really am."

"How could they have found out where you guys had them?" Darwin asked.

The agents had warned him about asking questions. Greg was

a pro. He would catch on.

"We're still trying to piece it together. We have no idea." Greg glanced at him in the rearview mirror. "Don't read into this too much. If the kidnappers get boxed in, they wouldn't want to hurt the parents because they need them for whatever negotiation they're planning to get to you. They also took two of my agents. My agents will be disposed of when they get where they're going. That's the nature of this business."

"Why would anyone sign up for this?"

"I know. I keep asking myself that question every day. For the pay we get, it really is too dangerous."

"Where are we headed?" Darwin asked.

"Can't tell you."

"What? They didn't say anything about me not knowing."

Greg looked at him in the mirror again. "Sure. What if I told you the exact location right now? Then, in three minutes, I'm T-boned in this car and killed on the spot. They grab you, pull you out, and force you to tell them where Rosina is. It's a need-to-know basis now."

Darwin was done meeting Greg's eyes in the mirror.

"I think *they* think someone's on the take," Greg said. "They mention anything to you?"

Darwin looked up. "You think they'd tell me something like that?" Darwin asked. "Come on, they won't even tell me where I'm going or where my wife is."

"True. But I still feel they have a few suspects in their sights."

Greg looked in his mirror again.

"I'm sure they suspect someone." It was out before he could bottle it. He felt angry and betrayed. But he wasn't about to take it lying down.

"Did they say anything while you waited for me?"

"Who's following us?" Darwin asked, avoiding Greg's question.

"I have no idea, Darwin. I'm only checking my mirror out of habit. Why, is someone following us?"

Darwin stared straight ahead. It had been years since he'd spent this much time outside at night. Months ago, if he knew he'd be out in the dark this much, it would've caused him to go back into therapy. He would have asked to be committed for a few days to avoid the dark at all costs.

But something about it was getting easier. The sun had gone down on him in Rome, and he survived. It was the middle of the night in Toronto, and he was surviving. He could look out the window at the passing lights and know it was other cars out there and no *real* danger. He could look. A week ago, he wouldn't have been able to. But today, he could.

The therapist had used the term *flooding* a few times. Maybe that's what he had meant by it. Or maybe *flooding* referred to the anger he felt.

The man in the front seat no longer resembled a friend. He lowered his face but kept his eyes on the back of Greg's head, his pulse increasing. Triggers were set off, and he was powerless to stop them. The darkness closed in. His heart rate spiked, his breathing picked up.

"Darwin, you okay?" Greg asked.

Greg's cell phone rang. The moment he reached for it, a car rammed them from behind. Darwin's head snapped back, and then he was thrust forward. Greg screamed as he tried to regain control of the vehicle. Darwin spun around in his seat, his rage not yet dissipated. The act of looking directly into the dark, a pair of high beams aimed at him, only added to the rage he was dealing with.

"Get off the highway!" Darwin shouted.

"I'm trying, I'm trying."

Their car had swerved two times before Greg got it back under control. He hit the gas and launched them forward and to the right, his eyes trying to focus on their tail.

Red lights flashed in the front window. They were braking up ahead. A large eighteen-wheeler had slowed nearly to a stop in front of them.

"Watch it!" Darwin screamed.

His warning came too late. Greg hit the brakes hard and then cranked the wheel to the left, exposing the passenger side to the impact. They almost skirted past the back of the truck, but the undercover cruiser hit the rig, still doing thirty kilometers an hour. The passenger side doors crumpled like accordions, shoving the seat, glass, and metal toward the occupants.

Both men yelled as the contorted car buckled and bounced off the back of the rig, rolled off the highway, and down the grassy median.

Darwin jostled around, his head cushioned between the back seat and the headrest on the front passenger seat. Side airbags deployed, protecting him from anything sharp as the car tumbled.

When the vehicle came to rest, Darwin shook off the broken bits of glass from his hair. A light flared up just outside the car. He shook his head again.

Fire.

He reached for the door, but it was locked or jammed. The heat from the fire blasted against his face like he'd opened an oven door.

An explosion rocked the car from behind. Then another

explosion knocked out the back window, the glass flying over his shoulder.

The interior light had gone out.

He pushed on the passenger side door, but it wouldn't budge.

The flames were so high now that the inside of the car lit up. He was alone, the front seat empty.

Wasn't there a driver?

Heat covered him, flames licking closer. The door still wouldn't budge. The metal frame sat at an angle, twisted in the wreckage.

Rosina's voice called to him in his head. He saw the Harvester of Sorrow and his torture implements. Darwin had to save Rosina. He had to save his wife.

Her voice again. He rubbed his eyes. The window beside him was missing. He shoved his head through first and then crawled out, landing on the moist grass of the median.

He glanced back at the car as flames consumed the front.

Darwin pulled himself up and peered inside the front seat. It was empty. The car, or what looked like the car that had been following them, sat halfway under the back of the stopped rig, completely aflame, the driver's burned arm dangling out the crushed window.

That must have been the explosion moments ago.

Cars on either side of the 401 highway were slowing and stopping. There were no sirens yet, but he didn't want to be around when they arrived.

He tried to crawl away, but his left arm protested too much. The bandage over the machete wound was soaked through with blood again.

Favoring his arm, he struggled to his feet on wobbly legs and wandered off into the night.

*****

When Alfred's phone rang, Rosina had just ordered a burger and a large Coke. He stepped away to take the call. After paying the clerk, she gathered napkins and found a table in the corner.

Alfred watched her while on the phone. He snapped his phone shut but then didn't move.

She took a bite of her burger and, after a second, slowed her chewing. Finally, she swallowed and set her burger down.

"What?" she asked. "What is it? My parents?"

"Prepare yourself."

Rosina leaned forward. "After what happened in Rome, I'm ready. Just tell me."

"We have a safe house in Barrie. We're heading there in different vehicles."

Rosina rolled her hand around in a circle. "Go on. I already know this. And …"

"The vehicle your husband was in has had an accident."

"An accident?" she gasped, her voice too loud.

"Please, ma'am. Keep your voice down."

"Is. Darwin. Okay?" she asked, clipping each word with her voice back under control.

"We don't know."

"What can you tell me?"

"The vehicle he was traveling in hit the back of the rig."

"Why would there be no word on Darwin, then?"

The agent looked down at his shoes, then back up. "The car was fully engulfed in flames before the fire engines arrived."

"Oh. Oh, no … noooo," Rosina moaned, pushing the food away.

"There was another car that hit the rig. It, too, burst into flames. Multiple vehicles were involved."

She looked up at him, her food forgotten. "Where did this happen?"

"The accident took place on the 401."

She smacked the table. "What was his car doing on the 401?"

"I have no idea. I'm not given details about the other transport."

"You don't take the 401 to get to Barrie. When you knocked on my hotel room door, you said Darwin was already en route to Barrie and that I would come with you to relocate to the safe house. But you do not take the 401 to go to Barrie from where we were."

"I think it's time we leave. We're attracting attention."

"I want to know why Darwin was on the 401. You go north on the 427 and then across the 407 to the 400. The 400 goes north directly into Barrie. So tell me, a woman who has lived her whole life in Toronto, to the point where I could be a cab driver without the use of GPS, why was my husband on the *fucking* 401?" She was near screaming now.

Alfred stepped back a foot. "Ma'am, please, come with me—"

"Don't *ma'am* me. My Darwin did not fight the Fuccini Family in Rome to come home to die in a car accident. Don't you dare tell …" she choked, caught her breath. "Oh, my baby, my precious Darwin."

She tried to get up and slipped to the floor. She whispered his name over and over as Alfred lifted her up. He guided her toward the exit, passing the restaurant's night manager on the way. Alfred flipped out his ID, and the manager stepped back.

Alfred set her in the back seat, locked both doors and stepped away from the vehicle.

Thoughts of Darwin rolled through her mind as she tried to comprehend a life without him. She punched the seat beside her. Until they had a positive ID on a body, she wouldn't believe he was dead. No way. Not her Darwin. If he could walk away from Fuccini, he could walk away from scrap metal.

The driver's side door opened, and Alfred sat down in the driver's seat. He turned around before starting the car.

"They checked the car your husband was in. The driver and your husband weren't there. No one was in the car. They're still on the scene, but at this point, there are no bodies in the FBI vehicle."

"I knew it. Darwin's alive. I feel it. He can't die. You'll see. He'll come back around and kill everyone who has fucked with him. You watch. He's my husband."

12

HE WALKED FOR HOURS, keeping near street lamps as often as possible. The accident happened just before the exit to Keele Street, which he walked up and then went north on Keele until around five in the morning. He fell asleep for two hours behind a building on Ashwarren Road.

Once awake, he continued along Keele until he saw a drive-thru Tim Horton's. The line inside was short, but the place was busy as cars lined up over twenty deep at this early hour.

He got a large double-double and went looking for a pay phone. He found one, pulled out his wallet, and used his Visa for the charges.

He sipped his coffee while he dialed his father's home phone number. After three rings, he was about to hang up when someone answered.

"Hello?" Darwin said

"Hello?" a man said. "Can I help you?"

Darwin hung up. He leaned against the pay phone's Plexiglas shelter and wondered who to call for help. His friend Bill would already be gone to work, and he couldn't remember that number by heart. Bill would extend a hand, but did he really want to involve someone else he cared about? He decided to call Rosina's parents' number to see if the FBI would answer that one, too.

He dialed and drank more coffee while he waited.

The phone was answered after three rings.

"Hello?"

"Isabella?" Darwin said tentatively.

"Yes, who is this?"

"Isabella Capote? Is that you?"

"Who's calling, please?"

"Darwin."

"You. What have you got my daughter mixed up in? FBI agents came by. They wanted to set up stuff in my house. I told them to get out. Ohhh, Darwin, I'm so frustrated right now. Where's Rosina? Where's my daughter?"

It was so good to hear her voice, such a relief, that he wasn't formulating a proper response.

"It's so good to hear your voice."

"What? Darwin, are you on drugs?"

"I was told you were kidnapped—"

"Kidnapped? How absurd."

"Tell me about it."

The FBI had lied to him. Everyone was lying to him. The FBI had set him up, and Greg was involved at some level.

"Darwin, are you still there?"

"Yeah, sorry. I need your help."

"My help?"

"You're the only one I can turn to. I need to see you. Can we meet?"

"What's this all about? Rosina?"

"I will tell you everything. But you can't say anything to anyone about where you're going. Come alone, and I'll explain it all."

"Where do you want to meet?"

"How about the food court at Square One Shopping Center? I'll be sitting in front of the Tim Horton's."

"Darwin, I hate Tim Horton's."

"Well, you don't have to order anything," he said, completely offended.

"Meet me at the Starbucks in the bookstore across the street from Square One. Do you know where that is?"

"Yes," Darwin said. "When?"

"At ten, when they open."

"Good. But come alone. I need to talk to you and only you. Isabella, I'm sorry, but I'll have to leave if I see the FBI or anyone else. What I have to tell you is important, okay?"

"Why would I bring anyone?"

"Okay, see you soon." Darwin hung up.

He exited the pay phone booth and looked for a cab.

Why would the FBI lie to him? Was Greg on their side or working for Fuccini? Rosina would be so happy to find out her parents were fine.

He swung back to the pay phone. After inserting his card, he dialed information.

"Quality Suites Airport, please."

When the front desk answered, Darwin asked to speak to Rosina Kostas and told the desk clerk their room number on the fifth floor. After three rings, it was picked up.

At first, he heard nothing.

"Hello?" Darwin said.

"Darwin?"

"Yeah, who's this? Put Rosina on."

"Where are you?"

"Fuck you. Put Rosina on."

"Not until you come in."

"What's your name? Who are you?"

"Not important. Where are you?"

"Not important, eh? After what happened on the highway? How can I trust you, whoever the fuck you are? Now, put my wife on the phone."

There was a moment of silence. Darwin figured the guy was thinking about it.

"Rosina's not here."

"Yeah, right. Stop fucking around and put her on, or I'm hanging up."

"I'm serious. She's not here. She was moved to a safe house."

"A safe house? Where?"

"You know I can't tell you that, or it wouldn't be a *safe* house, would it?"

"I'm her husband. You can tell me where she is. In fact, you can tell me where she is right the fuck now, or I will assume you dickheads are the enemy."

"Darwin, tell us about your connection to the Gambino Family. Tell us everything, and we'll put you both in the program somewhere in the United States. Help us out here, and we can help you."

"The program? Gambino Family? What the fuck are you talking about?"

"The witness protection program. We can keep you safe.

Protect you and your wife. You can live a long life together. Safe. What do you say? Come on in."

"Are you mad? Have all of you gone crazy? I don't even know the name Gambino. And talking about safety, I sure was safe in a car with an FBI man last night. Sure, I was real safe. You guys have a knack for keeping folks safe."

"That was an accident. We can fix this. Just tell us about your connection—"

"Fuck you," Darwin shouted into the phone and slammed it down.

He ran from the pay phone before he tried to tear it off its mount. He had to get to the bookstore in Mississauga.

He'd left his credit card in the phone slot. He ran back, grabbed it, and then used the phone to call a cab. Ten minutes later, he was in the back seat of a taxi, heading to Mississauga to meet with Rosina's mother.

On the way there, he had the driver stop and wait at an Army surplus store. He needed a weapon. One that wasn't sharp or had pointy edges. One that wouldn't be lethal but would still be effective enough to repel attackers.

He found exactly what he needed and ran back to the waiting cab.

13

Rosina woke with a splitting headache. She rolled off the bed and got up slowly. The bed had been comfortable, but it was the first night since their marriage in Rome that she'd slept alone.

She spied the bathroom door. The house was gorgeous. She remembered being unable to appreciate it when they arrived earlier that morning. Alfred held her up as exhaustion finally won her over.

He'd explained how the house was on a normal city street, surrounded by normal neighbors. She remembered asking him to define normal. He'd ignored her and explained how there were hidden cameras everywhere. There was even one hidden in the clock on the wall.

"Where?" she had asked.

"There's a little black dot at the bottom of every number. On the six, that dot is a camera. We're surrounded by them outside, too. In the back, the house is on environmentally protected land. It's a ravine back there. If something happens and we need to leave, we go through the back, and there's always a car parked for us in a driveway two streets over. Everything's covered."

Alfred's phone had rung, and he moved away to answer it. She had wandered through the house and fell asleep in the room on the top floor.

Inside the bathroom, she couldn't find any headache medicine.

She used the toilet and went downstairs to find Alfred.

He sat in a lounge chair, staring out the front window. He eased out of the chair when he heard her coming.

"Ahh, you're up. How did you sleep?"

"Not good. I need something for my head and then coffee."

"On it," he said and slipped past her. "Some of my colleagues are coming by soon," he called over his shoulder. "They have news, and they want to talk to you."

"Talk to me?" she mumbled, afraid to raise her voice for fear of the throbbing in her head.

"What's that?" Alfred asked.

She waved him off.

A minute later, the coffee machine in the kitchen sputtered along. He brought her three Advils, and after taking all three, she told Alfred she'd shower and then be down for coffee.

Fifteen minutes later, she came back down, headache almost gone, ready for a couple of cups of coffee when she heard voices. Three men stood in a semi-circle around Alfred.

"Rosina, these are the men I was telling you about. Get a coffee and come join us."

She tried to determine if they were the kind of men who come to tell you personally that your spouse had been killed. She took her time preparing her coffee, dreading the news she feared was coming.

Finally, she dragged herself to the living room and took a seat. One man sported a stupid bushy mustache. The other didn't know how to tie a necktie. It hung too low with the knot askew. The third man seemed nervous, his leg bouncing up and down.

She decided she didn't want to know their names. She would call them Tie, Leg, and Stache.

"Rosina, the information we are about …"

Rosina held her hand up for him to stop. "First, is Darwin dead? That's all I want to know. Tell me about my husband."

Stache looked at Leg and Tie in turn. Then they all looked back at her. "Darwin is not dead. We have confirmation he's alive. He talked to one of our agents about an hour ago."

"Ohhh, what a relief," she said as she set her coffee down on the table by her knee. She bent over, holding her stomach.

They gave her a moment to digest the news.

Sitting up, she collected herself, adjusted her blouse, and sipped her coffee. Everyone in the room remained quiet, respecting the moment she needed.

"How did you receive confirmation?" Rosina asked.

"He called your hotel room at the Quality Suites," Leg answered.

She raised an eyebrow. "My room at the hotel? Why would he do that? He knew I wouldn't be there. We were supposed to be transported in separate vehicles to this safe house." She eyed them all and then asked. "What's *really* going on?"

"Well, Mrs. Kostas, we're here to talk to you about that."

She set her coffee down. "Go ahead. I'm listening."

Tie pulled a folder from a briefcase beside him and turned to her.

"Mrs. Kostas, do you and your husband ever watch adult

movies?"

"Excuse me? What the hell kinda question is that?"

"Ma'am, calm down, please. We have our reasons. We will explain. Bear with us. We have to get through our questions first."

She pulled her legs up under her and sat with her arms crossed.

"Have you ever heard of a man named Frankie Gambino?"

"No. Should I have?"

Tie ignored her question. "Have you ever shopped at the," he stopped to refer to his notes. "Adult Emporium and Toys on the corner of Dundas and Dixie in Mississauga?"

"What the hell is this? Why did you come all this way to ask if I use adult toys? My husband is in trouble, and you're asking how kinky we are as a couple? I hope this line of questioning is leading somewhere sane."

"Ma'am, look at this photo and tell me if you recognize anyone."

Stache handed her an eight by ten. She took it and gasped, a hand covering her mouth.

The photo showed the door to what looked like an adult store. It had a red stop sign on it and the number eighteen. The door was open, and a man stood there. That man was her husband, Darwin Kostas.

"What is this? My husband doesn't shop at these kinds of places."

She didn't know what to think. A thousand questions raced through her mind. She'd been with him for years and never seen any behavior that would make her think he would shop at a place like that. She would know. Darwin didn't even look at other women longer than anything cursory. He loved her and only her.

He'd asked her to marry him. He stole her away and her heart. Seeing him in that picture wasn't what made her cry. It was the embarrassment of not knowing what he was doing in an adult store with four FBI men looking for answers.

Leg stood up. "I'll get you a Kleenex." He stepped away.

When he came back, he handed it to her and sat down. "There are other pictures."

"Wait," Alfred said. He turned to her. "Are you okay? Do you want to continue?"

Rosina nodded and wiped the small amount of moisture from her eyes. "I'm ready."

Stache reached into a folder and produced another eight by ten. He handed it to her.

It was the same store, but this time, she recognized Vincenzo Fuccini from all the media coverage of his death and her husband's *heroic*, as they had put it, timing with his Ford Mustang.

She handed the photo back. "We all know who that man is."

Stache handed her another. Again, the same storefront, but a man she didn't recognize. This continued for six more photos, all men she didn't recognize.

Stache put all the photos back in his folder and gently placed them in his briefcase.

"Is anyone going to explain to me what this is all about? I think I've been patient."

The men looked at each other again, then back at her.

"We believe you've been telling us the truth."

"Good. I should hope so."

Tie nodded at her. "It's time we brought you in on this because we may need your help."

"I just want my husband back."

"That adult store has been under surveillance for some time now," Stache started. "We suspect the Fuccini Family use some of their stores as drop points."

"What's a drop point?"

"It's where payoffs are made. Drugs are distributed, too. There are never any kids in an adult store, and the windows are painted over. No one from the outside can see in. The person making the drop can browse the walls of merchandise and wait until the store is empty. Then he can walk to the counter, drop the message, money, or whatever his purpose is, get paid, and leave with a bag full of money. Their bags are always black. You can't see through them. It's a perfect setup. That's why they're so tied up in the adult business."

"How does this have anything to do with my husband? Does it answer why he was there? A drop-off?"

"It had been rumored for months that the four leading families in Eastern Canada were preparing a meet. Our job was to attempt to find out that location. We have men working undercover, but no one knows the exact location. During this meeting, the families agreed that an outside contractor would be brought in for security."

"I'll ask again," Rosina interrupted. "What does Darwin have to do with mobsters and adult stores?"

"That store was where the men attending the meet would get their final directions and destination. It happened hours before the meeting was to take place. All the men in those photos were representatives of each crime family getting the hangar's address. You know what happened at that hangar, as your husband was also there that night."

She placed her hands on her thighs and leaned forward. "Darwin wasn't *there*, as you put it. He was out driving around and saw the fire in the distance. He said it got dark too fast, and he took a wrong turn." Faced with the picture she'd seen moments before, it almost felt like she was defending him.

"That day, we took pictures of every person leaving that store. We ran all their faces through our system and came up with hits on the crime family pics. Darwin's face got no hits, so his picture was filed away. After what happened in Rome, the case of the Hangar Peace Accord, as we call it, was reopened, and we started going through everything. Darwin, being at that particular adult store on the exact day that directions were handed out, within an hour of the other crime family members, became suspect after knowing he turned up at the hangar."

"So what are you saying? Darwin, my husband, the man I've known for going on seven years now, the man I know better than his own father, is a mobster? Are you saying he's one of their hitmen or something?"

"Bear with us, please. Let us get through this, and we'll make conclusions together."

She nodded, afraid to say anything more.

"When you landed in Toronto with Greg, we received credible evidence that the Gambino Family paid off Darwin for the hit on Vincenzo Fuccini."

"That's preposterous," she shouted.

"This came to us from an inside source. Deep inside. It's sound."

"Are you saying you believe this source?" She shook her head. "I'm astounded. You have got to be kidding me. My husband is innocent in all this."

Alfred laid a hand on her arm. "Let them finish," he said. "Hear them out."

Tie waited, adjusted his stupid tie, and said, "We do not believe the evidence after all. We feel it was compromised. We only wanted you to see what we were seeing so you'd better understand what we did. You have to try to stay calm to understand everything."

"I am calm," she snapped. "Now, tell me, what did you do?"

"We acted on the information like we normally would. We separated you two last night and told Darwin we felt Greg was working for the Fuccinis. If your husband were, in fact, working for the Gambinos, he would have to make contact. Greg is one of the best agents we have. He has done this longer than any of us and had Darwin's confidence."

"Look, I'm sorry, but you must understand my side. I just got married five days ago. I'm supposed to be on my honeymoon. We were almost killed, more than once, by these guys, and now the FBI thinks my husband is one of them. The FBI sets us up, and then he almost dies in a car accident, and no one knows where he is. How do you think I'm supposed to feel?"

"We understand. We really do. But listening to us and getting through this is how we can return to work on bringing your husband home. Okay?"

She nodded.

"We thought it was credible given the evidence. If Darwin was sent to kill Vincenzo and then go after the Fuccini Family, it isn't odd that he would show up in Rome and start hunting them down. Again, if he was hired to do that, then he did a great job. Better than expected."

"We went to Rome to get married," she said, her voice low,

her tone non-threatening. "It was in respect to my parents as they are Italian. We were going on a honeymoon in Greece as Darwin's father is Greek. It was planned as respectful."

"Okay, but he shows up and takes out Big John. A hundred men have tried that and died. Then he walks a man into traffic and kills him. Greg tells him on the phone to stay calm and out of trouble. Don't do anything until Greg gets there. We thought Darwin was calling Greg to show that when he finished with the Fuccini Family, he could get his life back and still be an easygoing, calm, concerned citizen. Instead, Darwin heads to the Fuccini building on Via Roma, a known mafia haven. He succeeds in entering the building, getting to the top floor, after killing even more hired professionals, only to meet the Harvester of Sorrow unarmed."

She shuddered at the mention of the name. "I was there."

"You okay?" Alfred asked.

She nodded. "I saw firsthand what evil that man was. I'm happy he's dead."

"We are, too. The only men to compare him to were Nazi butchers. So, our question is, how did Darwin do all that with barely a scratch if he's just a writer from Toronto? We asked ourselves that question over and over."

"I'm his wife. I was their prisoner. You do not want to piss off Darwin. Turn out the lights, show him a knife, or ask about his stepmother, and you will have opened Pandora's box, and you won't be able to close it. Trust me."

They looked at each other. Stache turned to her, a frown twisting his mustache almost sideways. "What's that about? Lights, a knife?"

"Nothing." She waved them off. "Just go on."

Leg stopped bouncing his leg and said, "So, since Darwin didn't fit the profile, we looked at his past, reopened the Hangar Peace Accord file, and started looking at everything again. We saw his picture at the adult store and got a tip that he worked for the Gambino Family. See how it all came together."

"But you don't believe that anymore?" she asked.

They all shook their heads. "He never made contact that we could tell. Then, we contacted a known family member of the Gambinos, and they told us, on no uncertain terms, that they wanted to distance themselves from anyone like Darwin Kostas. He's too public, too dangerous, they said."

"My husband." She smiled. "How sweet."

"We found out the leak came from the Fuccini Family. They were trying to get us to move him. We did, and they attacked. That's how the accident happened. There was another car that hit the back of that rig. In it were two corpses of Fuccini Family members. Greg was located in the dark an hour after the accident. He'd crawled away from the burning car as he was worried other attackers could come. He's in the ICU over at St. Michael's Hospital. He woke up long enough to tell us about the car that rammed them."

"Oh, man." She felt tears coming again. The thought that the FBI sent her husband out into a trap after what happened in Rome, and now he's missing, really upset her.

"There's one more thing we must tell you about Darwin's father. We thought his kidnapping was directly related. Maybe he knew about Darwin's past or something, and Darwin had to remove him. What a great time to arrange it when he's still in Rome so he could never be blamed."

"Okay. Go on."

"This part is good news, but you may get angry."

"Go ahead."

"Your parents were never kidnapped. They're fine and still being watched. That was information control. We wanted to watch his reaction to things happening that weren't part of his orchestration. We needed to see who he would call. We also wanted to see if he would tell you or hide it from you. We're sorry. That was an error on our part. Your parents are at home, healthy and alive."

The fury Darwin always described to her when he saw a knife was what she felt rising as the FBI told her she'd been lied to about her parents. She didn't want to be a pawn in their game.

"I want you all to leave while I process this."

"Mrs. Kostas, we need to discuss—"

"Get out." She got to her feet and exited the room in three steps. Her headache was back in all its glory.

14

DARWIN USED HIS VISA to pay the cab driver. He got dropped off on the other side of Square One shopping mall. He had ten minutes until he was supposed to meet Rosina's mother, Isabella. That didn't leave him enough time to get a full disguise together, but he thought maybe a baseball hat would help.

The mall looked quite busy for a middle-of-the-week noon-hour crowd. On his way to the other side of the mall, he passed a store that sold hats, grabbed one, and bought it.

He also bought a new sports jacket. The weapon he picked up at the army surplus store earlier fit in his jacket pocket easily.

He used the doors of a large department store to exit the mall, as they were usually the less busy ones. As he crossed the parking lot on foot, he saw no one watching him or acting like they weren't supposed to be there.

At the main doors of the large bookstore, he took one last look around. Clouds were rolling in, the sun hidden behind them. The air was warm, a slight breeze cooling his damp forehead. As far as he could tell, no one observed him.

He entered through the double doors of the bookstore and headed for the Starbucks on the left.

Isabella was already there, drinking from a *tall* or a *grande* shit cup.

"Mrs. Capote. Thank you for coming."

"Darwin? Where's my daughter?"

"Rosina's safe."

"Where have you two been for the last week? Wait," she paused and tapped his wrist. "Get a coffee first. I can wait."

"No, thanks. I don't drink at this place."

"So why are we here? Tell me about this help you need."

She seemed off somehow. Like she was putting on an act. Could the FBI be watching?

Darwin cleared his throat. "Rosina and I went to Rome to get married."

"I knew you two would do that."

So unlike her. She was one of the most adamant against it.

"We had trouble in Rome."

"What kind of trouble?" she asked, holding up her coffee.

"People tried to hurt us, but we managed to leave Rome, and everything's okay now."

"Well, that's good. When do I get to see Rosina?"

He looked around conspiratorially, then whispered, "I need your car. I have to drive somewhere."

Mrs. Capote reached into her purse and produced her car keys with hesitation. A white piece of paper was attached to the key ring. She slid the keys across the table and tapped the paper.

Darwin waited for a breath and then looked down. Written in pencil, he read the words: *FBI listening.*

"Go, Darwin. The car is two rows up. Push the lock button.

The horn will honk to help you find it." She grabbed his hand and squeezed it. "Save my daughter again. Get the bastards who have done this to you two. I heard what you did in Rome for Rosina. I'm proud to call you my son-in-law, even if the men running to this table don't think so. You're a real man, Darwin. Now, get out of here."

Darwin squeezed her hand back and jumped from his chair so fast he knocked it over. He ran for the Starbucks door, spilling empty chairs behind him to block any pursuers' path.

He hit the door in full sprint and bolted for the second row of cars. He recognized the two-door BMW convertible right away.

He glanced over his shoulder and saw two men coming out of the Starbucks behind him. At the car, he dropped into the front seat, cranked the engine with the stick already in first, and popped the clutch. Spinning out of the parking spot, his door slammed shut with the forward motion.

He saw the two men coming to a stop in the rearview mirror.

There was only one place to go. He had no leads on any mafia family members. He knew nothing about them, where they hunkered down, or where they did business. But there was one place he knew where this had all started. One particular store was where he tried to do the right thing, and now he was paying for it.

The store where he had to shop—even though he hated going in there—for the mint tree lotion that Rosina had grown to love so much. He'd read about it online and looked everywhere for it until one day someone said you don't go to the Body Shop in the mall for that. You go to an adult store. The same adult store in Mississauga where he bought his wife her lotion. The same adult store where a man had carelessly dropped a piece of paper with the address to Buttonville's old airport location and the time for that night's meeting. The note had said *group therapy for phobia sufferers*.

When Darwin picked up the paper, he read the heading quickly to see if it was worthless and then tapped the man on the shoulder to hand it back to him. The two words *phobia sufferers* had caught his eye.

He'd gotten a cold stare, handed the man the note, looked away, and went to buy his wife her mint tree.

It was the same man he killed later that night when he'd ventured out in the dark, which he would never normally do, to see if he could join or sign up for the group therapy on phobias in his yearning to heal even more so Rosina didn't have to live with his darker moments. He wondered why it wasn't being held in a doctor's or counseling office. The fact that he had decided to go in the dark would be a step in the right direction, and maybe he would have triggers to deal with that could be discussed during the session.

It was all for his wife.

But that man, Vincenzo, had stumbled in front of his Ford. With the interior light on, Darwin hadn't seen him until it was too late.

It all started at the adult store.

It would all end there, too.

15

Alfred knocked on her door an hour later. She lay spread-eagle on the bed, staring at the ceiling.

"They're gone," he said through the door.

She didn't answer him.

"Rosina, can we talk?"

"What do you want?"

"Can I open the door?"

"No."

"I'm sorry. I agree. The FBI guys look like a bunch of bumbling fools. Remember, though, it's not me. I just came on duty. I, personally, didn't do any of that stupid stuff. So if you need someone to talk to, I'm here."

She waited a moment. "You can open the door."

The door opened a crack. "You doing okay?"

"Yeah."

"I have news. It's not good, but it's not bad either."

"What is it? Just tell me."

"We have visual confirmation that Darwin is alive and well."

She turned her head and looked at him sideways. "Where is he? Are you bringing him here?"

"Not exactly. He met with your mother at a Starbucks in Mississauga."

"Darwin went to a Starbucks? I don't believe it. He must be on the run for sure."

Alfred frowned.

"Never mind. Go on."

"He met with your mother, and she gave him the keys to her car. He left in her BMW when my colleagues tried to talk to him."

"I wonder if Darwin's figured out he's been screwed by the FBI and doesn't trust the very people we're supposed to trust?"

Alfred glanced at the carpet. "I guess we deserve that."

"They should go after the real bad guys and stop worrying about my husband."

Alfred eased backward and clicked her door shut.

Rosina rolled into a ball and prayed it would all end soon.

***

When Greg took his statement the night Vincenzo was run down, Darwin never revealed the adult store connection. He couldn't let Rosina know he would ever visit a place like that.

It wasn't a bad thing. Many good people shopped in stores like that. He was sure of it. He was a good person. He shopped there. It was more about her preconceived notions of what an adult store represented. Pornography, smut, lowlifes, and sexual deviants. Sure, there could be an element of that in some of the trashier places. But in the nicer ones, it was a nice store with real products for men and women and loving couples in healthy relationships.

Darwin believed it was something Rosina would accept better in years to come, but so far, in their relationship, anything too deviant had been taboo. He was fine with that. Their sex life was great. He just couldn't bring himself to tell her where he bought the mint tree bottle.

But after this mess was cleared up and behind them, he'd have to tell her. She was his wife now, and that meant honesty. Full disclosure. There was no other way to live.

He pulled into the store's parking area and found a spot in the middle where he sat idling, checking in all four directions to see if anyone was watching or following him.

After five minutes, Darwin turned off the car and got out. He locked the door and leaned against it, taking in the area. He was tired of running. He couldn't live like this all his life. He couldn't produce another novel if the stress level remained this high. These people and their sick, pathetic code of ethics weren't just fucking with his life and his wife—they were fucking with his livelihood, too.

He thought of Salman Rushdie and his book, *The Satanic Verses*.

"He did it, didn't he," Darwin whispered out loud. If Rushdie could run from the Ayatollah, with millions in bounty for his head, and live to publish again, then Darwin could run from a few mafia boys.

He pushed off from the car and crossed the parking lot. The clouds had moved in, blocking the early afternoon sun and casting a dim grayness on everything.

The store's door opened. A man walked out, a black bag in his hand. He looked at Darwin briefly, then looked away.

Darwin pushed the door and entered the adult store.

It was just as he remembered it. Movies on the walls by the door. Further in, the adult toys and the lubrications and massage oils. Near the counter sat the Kama Sutra section with bottles of mint tree and something called Honey Dust.

The clerk was on the phone, carrying on quietly like he was talking to his girlfriend. One customer stood in the far corner, surveying movie box covers. He nodded at the scruffy-looking clerk and tried to control his stomach. He hadn't eaten all day.

He headed for the toy section. Some of the items were so big that their use appeared humanly impossible.

"You need any help?"

Darwin jumped and pivoted around. The clerk stood beside him.

"No, just looking."

The clerk nodded and turned away.

"Wait. Do people actually use that thing there?"

"The Rambone?" The clerk nodded. "Oh, yeah. It's one of our better sellers."

"Wow. I'd assume after using it, the user would have to go in for surgery."

"They don't." The clerk smiled.

The door chimed as the other customer left the store. Darwin was alone with the clerk.

"There's one more thing."

"What's that?" the clerk asked.

The clerk wore beige khakis and a brown T-shirt. His hair was unkempt and smelled like he hadn't showered in a few days. He didn't look like a fighter. Darwin would ask his questions, get his needed answers, and leave.

"I want to speak to the Fuccini boss."

The clerk frowned. "Fuccini, who? I don't think anyone named Fuccini works here."

"No, not someone who works here. The Fuccini Family boss. I know this store is used as a contact point. Please get him on the phone or send out a note. Do whatever you guys do, but get me in touch with him."

The clerk put his hands in the air and stepped back. "Okay, weirdo, I don't take orders from you. I don't know anyone named Fuccini, and I have no idea what you're talking about."

Darwin grabbed him and tried to pull him back. The guy spun extremely fast, his hands wrapped around Darwin's forearm. He lifted up and turned again in a circle, throwing his hands above his head without letting go of Darwin. With his arm twisted like a windmill, Darwin was forced to bend and roll with it. Before he registered what was happening, Darwin was off his feet and flipping. He landed hard on his back, the clerk still holding his arm.

The clerk's foot came down onto Darwin's chest and applied pressure.

"Are you that fucking stupid?" the clerk shouted. "Holy shit. You really are just some silly kid who got mixed in over your head. Boy, do I feel sorry for you."

Darwin tried to twist away, but the clerk twisted his arm painfully.

"Don't try me. I'll break your *fucking* arm."

"What are you talking about?" Darwin asked.

"After what you did at the hangar and how crazy you were in Rome, everyone has heard of you. They hired me to sit here and see if you'd pop up. I had to serve all these asshole customers while I waited for you. I couldn't believe my luck when you walked in."

Darwin grunted. "You knew it was me?"

"I already called them. They're on their way. You actually got them scared. I looked at you and thought, *this dude. No way.* But they see you as some kind of killing machine."

"Listen, could you lighten up on the arm a bit?"

"What, like this?"

The clerk released his arm, and Darwin spun on the tiled floor. He kicked the clerk's feet out from under him in a foot-sweep move. The guy was a serious pro, though. Even on his way to the floor, he already had his arm coming out to attack Darwin when he landed.

As Darwin had thrown his foot out, he had reached into his pocket.

He aimed it just as the clerk hit the ground and attempted to elbow Darwin for his efforts. A stream of bear spray, quite potent in the space of one foot from the container, covered the clerk's face. The vile liquid entered the clerk's mouth, nostrils, and eyes as Darwin pressed the top button on the small canister.

Darwin held his breath while he sprayed and slit his eyes.

The clerk tried to ward off the attack but only swiped at his face and rolled away. Finally, Darwin stopped and rolled away, too.

He walked behind the counter, grabbed the phone, and hit redial while the clerk still writhed on the floor, screaming about how it hurt so bad.

"Get me some water!"

Darwin pressed the phone to his ear.

"Hello?" someone said.

"Fuccini?"

"Who's this?"

"Darwin."

He heard Fuccini's gasp over the clerk's wailing.

"I'm coming for you. However many men you've sent won't be enough. Double it. Unless you want to make a trade."

"I'm listening."

"Me for my father."

"I figured you'd understand my needs one day. My men will be there soon. Go with them, and we'll release your father."

"No. It'll be done on my terms." Darwin pulled the phone away from his ear and checked the number. It was local. He committed it to memory, recited it twice, and returned the phone to his ear. "I will call you at this number in two hours. Answer the phone, and I will tell you what to do. Then, I will surrender myself to you. Do we have a deal?"

The clerk wailed on. He'd made it to his feet, bloodshot eyes gushing water, his face a deep red. He used the wall to find his way to the back of the store, where Darwin figured there was a washroom.

"I don't have much choice if you won't go with my men. It's obvious that getting you to do anything will be a chore, so we have a deal. But if you don't call me, I will rip apart your father with my saw, and I will do it personally."

"I know what you'll do, big guy. Just answer the phone when I call. Don't disappoint me, Fuccini, or I might get *really* angry."

Darwin hung up and then quickly exited the store. He turned on the car and flicked on the satellite radio until he found Iron Maiden. Darwin waited as Bruce Dickinson sang about how many minutes they had until midnight. He saw Fuccini's men pull up and run into the adult store. Then he pulled away.

He had the perfect spot to do the exchange. Fuccini would be pissed.

He also had a surprise for him.

No one would see it coming.

16

DARWIN DROVE TO THE abandoned hangar, parked a kilometer away, and sat in the BMW as the sun began its drop behind the horizon. He had his bear spray, a new flashlight, and a new portable cell phone. As soon he had picked up the phone at the cell phone store, he programmed Fuccini's number in it and then Isabella's phone number.

Those would be the only two numbers he'd need.

He laid his head back on the seat while he waited. Ten minutes remained before he would call Fuccini.

Stone Sour's lead singer, Corey Taylor, screamed about being reborn on the heavy metal satellite radio station.

How appropriate.

Deep breathing, controlled thoughts, and a prayer were all he had. Rosina was out there somewhere with the FBI, men he couldn't trust. His father was in peril, and many people would probably die in the next few hours. All because of Vincenzo. All because of vendettas, revenge, and a mistakenly placed example of honor. How did doing the right thing get so fucked up? Why did humans have to kill each other to survive?

He steeled himself to get ready and make the call. Tonight, either Fuccini or Darwin would die.

He flipped off the radio and dialed Fuccini.

"Where?"

"The old, abandoned airplane hangar in Buttonville. Bring my father. Don't be too long, and *you*, personally, had better be here. I will not be giving myself up to a bunch of amateurs. I'm not a fan of the dark, and the sun is setting, so hurry."

Before Darwin hung up, he could tell how much coming to the hangar upset Fuccini by the barely audible gasp he'd heard. The death of his son took place on the hangar's soil. It would prove to be quite unsettling for the man.

Yet it was appropriate because of the Hangar Peace Accord. After tonight, there would be peace.

Darwin grabbed everything he needed, exited the car, shut the door quietly, and stepped away, but not before turning on the flashlight. He dropped the cell phone in his back pocket and the bear spray in the other pocket.

The walk to the hangar would take no time at all, but he wanted to walk the perimeter, head down the road on the other side a little way, and see what was around in case he needed to escape on foot.

Motorcycle thunder roared in the distance.

Right on time.

He smiled to himself as everything seemed to be coming together.

***

"How come it took me two hours of losing control, running through the neighborhood, and knocking on people's doors to get you to listen to me?"

"Rosina, you have done great harm here. That was a good, safe house. We'll have to sell it now. People will talk. You've cost the Bureau a great deal of money."

She looked out the car window as the exit for Newmarket raced by. They were on their way to Brampton so she could be with her parents.

Alfred had gotten a call with news but said he had to wait two hours before hearing more. Then, almost on the dot, his phone rang when they were already on the highway.

"Alfred, I don't care how much money I cost the Bureau. I've had my honeymoon ruined by the Fuccini Family, and now Darwin is out there, alone, while the sun is setting."

Alfred stared straight ahead, his eyes on the road.

When she looked up and saw the sign for the 407 West, which would take them to Brampton, she was surprised to see Alfred merge, heading for the 407 East.

"Alfred, you're going the wrong way."

He ignored her. He didn't say anything or even look at her in the mirror.

"Alfred, Brampton's the other way."

The car missed the exit. They were now turning along the ramp that would take them east toward Scarborough and Pickering.

"Alfred!"

A Plexiglas window rose between the front and back seats. She grabbed the top of it, but no amount of force would stop its ascent.

"Alfred!" she screamed.

Rosina pulled her fingers out in time as the dividing window hit the ceiling.

The back doors audibly snapped into the locked position. Alfred turned on the radio. Through the Plexiglas divider, she could barely hear Berlioz performing his "Symphonie Fantastique."

"Alfred!" she shouted, banging on the Plexiglas. "Where are you taking me?"

He didn't respond. She knew, wherever it was, it wouldn't be good.

17

Darwin reconnoitered the area as much as he could in the time he had. More Harleys had arrived, but Richard H had all of them park well off the property to keep the bikes out of sight. It had taken longer than expected, but the job was done.

"We're ready," H said. "My men know what to do. You better come through on your end."

"Richard. I assure you, I will write the book. I will promote it. I will make sure people know what I wrote about your motorcycle club in my previous novel was fictitious and that this novel is the real thing, the real deal. We have a deal. I won't back out."

Darwin held the flashlight near his face, aimed slightly away to avoid his eyes.

"Biker gangs aren't all about violence, extortion, and drugs as the media portray us," H said.

He swung a chain in his hand, wrapping it around his wristband and then unwrapping it. His aluminum baseball bat leaned against the hangar wall behind him.

Nothing violent about you lot.

"What you wrote in that other book caused some of our guys to leave the club. We got a reputation to keep."

"I know," Darwin said. "And I'm going to fix the damage I did. That's why I called you. I just need you to help me with my problem here first."

"The only reason I agreed to do this was so that you could see firsthand how we handle problems like that Fucconi idiot."

"Fuccini, not Fucconi."

"Whatever. Listen, is what happened in Rome true?"

Darwin arched one eyebrow. "You know about Rome?"

"It was in the Toronto papers. Is that how you got that bandage on your arm?"

Darwin turned the flashlight on his arm. "Yeah."

"Bastards. They actually took your woman and were going to torture her? You got a problem with a guy, you make him eat dirt. You don't fuck with the guy's woman. Well, unless she's hot. Then you *fuck* her, not fuck her up." He swung the chain around and wrapped it over his knuckles.

"You ready for tonight?" Darwin asked.

"Yeah, a couple guys in suits kidnapped your dad. We're gonna get you and your dad to safety and then hurt them real bad. That's it, right?"

"Sort of."

"What do you mean, '*sort of*'?"

Richard tilted his head back, his beard riding high on his thick chest.

"These guys in suits may have guns. They may choose to use them."

Richard nodded with confidence. "We got this. We've all been shot at before. But I gotta warn you, they start shooting; my boys won't tolerate that. Their side gonna lose a few men. You okay with that?"

"You have no idea. Kill 'em all for all I care."

"What I mean is, are you gonna publish that? 'Cause you can't really put murder in that book. It would fuck with our reputation again."

"I know, I know. I got it. Everything in the book will go past you first. I won't publish a thing without you approving it."

"And my picture still goes on the cover?"

"Yes, Richard, your picture."

"H. Call me H and consider your debt to my biker club paid when you write that book."

"Get me out of here alive tonight so I can write it, and I'm indebted to you for much more than a book, H."

"*In*debted? What's that?"

One of the bikers whistled from off in the woods to their left.

"This is it," Darwin said. "You know what to do."

"We got this," H said. "Get to safety." He grabbed the bat and hustled off, disappearing in the darkness behind a line of trees.

Darwin adjusted the flashlight and headed for the open hangar door. Once inside, he killed the flashlight and turned to watch a pair of headlights come up the road slowly. As it drew closer, he tried to see the make and model. It looked like an FBI-issued vehicle. The same kind of Crown Vics Greg drove.

It slowed and stopped on the road near the entrance.

The driver honked his horn.

Darwin stared at the vehicle. No one moved to get out. It was so dark already that he could barely tell if anyone sat in the back seat.

He leaned his head out the door, his stomach a ball of nerves.

The driver rolled down his window and shouted something.

"What's that?" Darwin yelled back.

"Get in the car."

He heard him perfectly this time.

"Are you alone?" the driver yelled. After a moment, he said, "Get in the car, or I'll drive away, and you'll never see her again."

Her?

Darwin stepped out. The driver turned on the interior light.

Rosina sat in the rear of the vehicle, shaking her head back and forth.

"You have mere seconds to decide if you ever want to see your wife again."

He couldn't think of a play here. This was an unexpected turn of events. The hangar was secure, surrounded by bikers. Getting in the car was too risky.

But Rosina?

He stepped closer.

"If you do not get in the vehicle, I will explain to Fuccini that you weren't interested in meeting him. Your father and your wife will be executed. Save us all a lot of trouble and get in the back seat beside your wife. I will drive you to where you're meeting Fuccini."

Everything he had planned was gone in a moment's decision. How could he think that he could deal with a man like Fuccini? Why did he ever feel that he could match the man with wits? Fuccini would always be more ruthless, more vile.

Against everything he had set out to do at the hangar, Darwin stepped forward, one foot in front of the other. He was in a daze. He was walking to his death. He had condemned his wife, and he was going to die for it. His father would be collateral.

It was over, and he was powerless to stop it.

As he reached for the back door's handle, it clicked to unlock. He opened the door and got into the car beside his wife. He barely had the door closed when Rosina fell into his arms, crying and asking him through her tears why he got in the car.

The driver locked the doors, skidded the tires in the dirt as he performed a U-turn, and raced away from the hangar.

"Rosina, I had to. I couldn't leave you. I started this. I have to pay for it."

She placed her head on his stomach and sobbed. He held her tight, rested his head back, and closed his eyes.

The driver got on the phone. Darwin listened. Maybe he could use his disposable phone to call the police before they got to wherever they were going.

"Yes, I know. No, no," the driver said. "I got him. Yes." A pause, then, "No, he came willingly. There was no one here but him. I know because I drove right up to the hangar. I flashed my headlights into the main door. He was alone. I would've been told if the FBI were supposed to be here. I got him. I'll be there soon."

The driver looked at Darwin in the rearview mirror and said, "I know. The guy's crazy. He was actually gonna trade himself in. Brave, if you ask me. Okay, okay." The driver closed his phone and tossed it on the seat beside him.

He looked back at Darwin and said, "You are one crazy dude. I gotta say, I've never met anyone like you. Wish you were on our side—"

Something hit the side of the car. It swerved so violently Darwin felt they were going to flip. The driver screamed like a teenager as he tried to correct the spin.

Another bang vibrated the car, which spun even faster. The

force of the spin caused Darwin to lean hard into the side door, Rosina up against him. He shielded her with his body as best he could.

After what felt like minutes, even though it all happened in seconds, the car came to a stop by the tree line. The driver's side window busted in, tiny diamond-sized pieces of glass cascading everywhere. Someone yanked the driver out while he grunted protests.

It all happened so fast. Darwin could only stare dumbfounded as their would-be kidnapper was lifted out of the car.

Something clicked beside him. The door he was leaning on opened, and Darwin fell out backward.

"I gotcha," H said, his hands wrapped in Darwin's underarms. He helped Darwin out, and Rosina followed.

"What happened?" Rosina asked. "What's going on? Who are these men?"

"This is H. H, this is my wife, Rosina."

"H?" she asked. "What's an H?"

"His name is Richard H, but we call him H."

"Yeah." H stepped in and extended his hand. Rosina took it.

"We heard about what happened in Rome, and it pissed us off. We're here to help, and Darwin said he'd write a documentary about us."

Rosina looked at Darwin. "You did?"

He nodded. "I'll be nice. I'll be fair." He turned his attention to H and looked him in the eye. "In fact, I'll write it any way you want me to."

Rosina let out a long breath and stepped up to H. Then, with both arms wide, she hugged him and whispered a *thank you* in his ear. She stepped back and said, "You saved our lives."

H didn't seem to handle compliments well.

"H, I'm going to walk back to the hangar. The meeting is still on. Can I trust you to take Rosina out of here?"

"I'm not going anywhere without you, Darwin," Rosina said.

"I understand, baby, but Fuccini is coming. H and his men and I need to deal with that. They have my father. If we don't end this tonight, it will never be over. Just go with H to where they've parked their bikes. It'll be far enough away that you can't get hurt, and we can deal with this guy."

Rosina hugged Darwin. "You had better walk away from this."

"You got it, baby. I will."

H gestured for Rosina to get moving. Before they were lost to sight in the darkness, H turned and said, "Hey, big D. You like how we stopped the car by shooting out the tires?"

"Yeah, H, brilliant."

H smiled, as far as Darwin could tell, and strode off with Rosina in tow. Darwin suddenly realized that the dark wasn't affecting him as much as it should've been.

He surveyed the wrecked Crown Vic. As far as Darwin could tell, the driver wasn't breathing.

"What happened?" Darwin asked the men gathered around.

"He wouldn't talk. We asked him where they had your father. We asked him where that Fucconi guy was. He wouldn't talk. We took it a little too far." The guy shrugged. "Sorry."

"Fuccini."

"What?"

"Never mind. Have an eye. The Fuccini people will be here as soon as their boy doesn't show. I will call them, so I'm sure they'll be along soon."

"Got it."

Darwin dialed the Fuccini number he'd committed to memory.

"Yeah?"

"You made a mistake."

"Darwin. How nice."

"You took my wife again. That was a mistake. You were supposed to trade me for my father. Because you didn't show, and you sent that man as your messenger, he's dead."

"I had to make sure it was safe. You could've had the place crawling with cops."

"Enough talking. I'm still at the hangar. I'm alone. I've got Rosina in a safe place. There's just you and me."

"I'll be there shortly."

Darwin hung up and dialed Rosina's mother. She answered on the third ring again.

"Isabella, I need to talk to the FBI guy in charge."

"Darwin, there's no …"

He knew she was told to deny that they were there. He waited. She waited. Finally, she said, "I'll put him on."

After a murmur, a man got on the phone.

"Darwin, where are you?"

"About to meet Fuccini. He's got my father. We're doing a trade."

"What kind of trade? You can't handle this alone. Tell us where you are."

"I'm at the abandoned hangar where it all started. Oh, and that guy you had taking care of my wife is dead."

"Alfred is dead? What are you talking about? Where's Rosina?"

"She's safe. Alfred brought her here. He was working for

Fuccini. I took Rosina back, and now Alfred is dead. Come and collect the asshole's body."

"Darwin, don't do anything stupid. Wait there for us."

"I'm not going anywhere."

The phone clicked in his ear.

Darwin tossed the phone into the bush.

18

DARWIN FLICKED A SWITCH for lights in the hangar, but the building remained dark. The only lights that worked were the red ones behind the exit signs. He needed to be inside, so he steeled himself and turned on his flashlight. He crossed the interior, headed for the back of the building, and stood behind a metal partition. No one could see his flashlight. If they came in shooting, he'd have some form of protection.

A car pulled up out front. Moments later, a man in a long trench coat stepped into the front door of the hangar and moved a flashlight around.

"You in here?" he shouted.

"Yeah," Darwin called out. The flashlight moved to find him, but he was too far back.

"I can't see you."

"Show me my father. And where's Fuccini?"

"No way. He ain't coming in here in the dark. You crazy? How do we know you don't have a gun?"

"Show me my father. Then I'll come out of the hangar."

The man stepped away. A car door opened and closed. Then another.

Darwin waited.

"You coming?" the same man shouted. "We aren't waiting all night."

Darwin stepped out from behind the metal partition. He walked along the inner wall of the hangar, ready to run at the first sign of a weapon coming through the door. He got to the open door of the hangar and peeked around. That's when he knew it was over. There was no way to come back from this.

Fuccini stood in front of his car, the headlights basking him in an eerie glow. He had his arms crossed, and he was grinning like an asshole. Four of his men stood with large weapons that looked like machine guns on steroids strapped over their shoulders.

At their feet were seven members of the biker gang. Four were dead, for sure. Darwin could see parts of their anatomy missing. One had half his face dangling from his jaw. The other three were bound and gagged on their knees. Darwin held his stomach, hoping he'd be able to hold its contents inside.

"We thought we'd wait to execute these other three until you joined the party. So glad you could make it, Darwin. Oh, and your father. He's over there." Fuccini pointed.

Adrian Kostas, Darwin's father, crawled on the ground, blood coming from his midsection.

"What did you do to him?" Darwin asked.

"I assumed you wanted him back alive. He's alive but with one stab wound to the stomach. If you staunch the bleeding, he could live out here in the bushes for a couple of days. The only way to save him from an injury like that is to go to the hospital. They could fix him up good. But that won't happen because no one knows we're out here, and all of your faggoty heroes in leather and chaps are dead or will be shortly."

Darwin seethed with anger. "You bastard."

"I know. I've been told. But it's only fair as you took out my Harvester and Big John, not to mention many other men. You've hurt my organization and cost me a lot of money. The only way to hurt someone like you is to take out your family. And I mean everyone." He turned to his men and pointed at two of them. "Go find that bitch wife of his and kill her. I don't even want to see her face again. Don't bring her back to me. Shoot on sight. I don't have time to play Darwin's games anymore."

Two men ran off, one behind the hangar and the other entered a door on the side.

"That wasn't the deal," Darwin said.

"Deal? There's no dealing with you." Fuccini raised a finger in the air. "A trade. You, for your father. There's your father. He's alive. I get you. I *already* had your wife in my possession, but you took her back. By the way, how did you handle that little feat? The driver told me personally that he had you with him."

Darwin's mind raced, but with each scenario he came up with, he couldn't figure a way out of this.

"Wait." Fuccini held up a hand. "Don't tell me. You had help from these goofs." Fuccini looked down at the three bikers on the dirt. "That's what they call you in prison, right? The name that's disrespectful? A goof? Well, if you aren't goofs, then you're fucking stupid to get mixed up with the likes of Darwin Kostas. Deal with him, and a lot of people die."

Fuccini turned to the man closest to the bikers and said something Darwin couldn't hear. The man lowered his weapon, chambered a round, and fired.

The head of the first biker exploded into a red spray of bone and blood. The biker's headless body stayed upright for a moment and then slowly teetered forward, finally falling on its chest.

The last two bikers screamed behind their gags. Darwin broke out in a sweat. His body shook all over. He'd seen a lot of shit in the past few days, but watching a man's head disappear in a vapor made him want to throw up.

A gunshot rang out in the distance. But this time, it came from the back of the building.

"There goes Rosina. Oh, I'm sorry, Darwin. Is the loss of someone you love hurting you? How about the loss of my only son? Do you know what I do to people who even raise their hands to me? Do you even know the kind of man I am?"

He walked over to Darwin and patted him on the back. "Darwin, my worthy opponent. Not many men *get* to me. You got to me. You hurt my organization. Actually, you're either really good or really lucky. You even gave me pause. I said to myself, maybe this is a trap. It couldn't be that easy. I'll force your hand. I'll get you to come with Rosina. But you didn't. You had bikers help you. How the hell you orchestrated that, I'll never know."

"A book."

Fuccini leaned closer and patted him down, feeling for a wire or a weapon.

"A book? Oh, that's fantastic. That's amazing. You know, I sent out the order to kill you on sight if I died. Do you know what that means? Even if I'm killed, you still die. I have hundreds of men who want a payoff. I have staff on fourteen different police forces, including the FBI. I have friends in Italy. Until you die, this will never end. That's how serious I am."

Darwin nodded. He suspected as much.

"You became, all on your own, Fuccini Family enemy number one."

"That sounds like an honor." Darwin looked out at the darkness, but it wasn't working like it used to. He couldn't trigger an angry response. "Pull a knife on me."

"Pull a knife? No, I don't think so. You're going to be shot in each foot with that gun, so there'll be no more running. Then I'll toss you in the trunk until we get back to my place, where I will treat you to days upon days of a certain kind of painful pleasure —"

The sound of another boom came from behind the hangar.

Fuccini looked at the corner where his two men had disappeared minutes ago.

"Why would there be two shots if there's only one girl? Johnny, go find out what's happening."

One of the men covering the bikers ran off.

"Now, where were we?" Fuccini asked.

He walked over to Darwin's dad, leaned down, and checked his pulse.

"Still breathing and bleeding. Not long now, though. Another day of this agony, and he'll be dead."

He whispered to Adrian, loud enough for Darwin to hear, "We'll be leaving in five minutes. So sorry you can't join us."

Darwin ducked as another crack from a weapon came from the back of the building. The remaining guard raised his and aimed it at the place where his colleague had just gone.

"Do you know something I should know, Darwin?" Fuccini asked and then turned to his guard. "Let's clear out. Kill these two fucking bikers, and then we're gone. Bring Darwin to the car. Put him in the trunk."

Fuccini stepped away and then ducked so hard he almost fell over when someone shuffled up close to him.

Darwin's dad had gotten to his feet and had hobbled to Fuccini with a large stone in his hand.

"Dad, no!"

The guard turned toward him. A shot rang out.

Darwin closed his eyes and fell to his knees. He thought he heard a siren in the distance but soon realized it wasn't a siren. His ears were ringing. When he opened his eyes, his father lay on the ground holding his wounded stomach.

To the right, the guard had a large hole in his abdomen. He looked down at his wound, then at Fuccini, and then dropped to his knees. He face-planted and didn't move again.

"Sorry I'm late for the party," Richard H said, his weapon trained on Fuccini. "Darwin. Snap out of it. Untie my men."

Darwin got to his feet and had both of them untied in seconds. They ran for Fuccini, but H held them back.

"Darwin, you have a beef with this man? If you do, speak now before we tear him apart."

"Rosina okay?" Darwin asked. "Those shots behind the building."

"I was taking them out as they came, one by one. Your wife is fine."

Darwin thought about the contract on his head when Fuccini was dead. It was over, and yet, it was just beginning.

"Fuccini and I are done. Do with him what you will."

Fuccini, for all his mutterings about torture, appeared frightened, with H holding the collar of his shirt, the large weapon's business end pushed up under his chin.

"Say goodbye," H said.

Fuccini looked at Darwin and said, "I'll see you in Hell."

H lowered the weapon and placed it against Fuccini's left arm at the elbow. He pulled the trigger, and the bottom half of Fuccini's arm flew off.

Darwin tried to look away, but his brain registered the flying arm. He ran for his father and knelt beside him.

"Dad, help's coming. We'll get you to a hospital."

The gun fired again behind him. Fuccini's other arm was missing now. Fuccini screamed so loud that they all missed the police sirens, but everyone turned at the red flashing lights.

H brought the weapon down to Fuccini's crotch and lowered the butt of the gun to the dirt.

"Sorry, I don't get more time dismembering you for what you did to my club members and our friend Darwin. You got lucky, asshole. When we're done here, we're going after anything named Fucconi."

H fired, and Fuccini was virtually split in half by the explosion.

The bikers wiped splattered blood from their faces.

H tossed the gun off to the side.

A line of cruisers pulled into the parking lot and quickly surrounded them.

Men in uniforms and suits, weapons out, screamed for everyone to get down.

Darwin whispered Rosina's name …

***

The statements read that Fuccini came to kill everyone and, in their defense, Richard H and his two surviving club members were lucky enough to get the upper hand in the end. Darwin's father was stabbed, and Richard grabbed a gun, shot the last guard, and then slid in like he was stealing home plate, shooting straight up into Fuccini himself. When asked why the man's arms were missing, H explained how his first shots had missed and gone wild. At least, that was what he thought happened. He said he had no idea he'd made contact with Fuccini's arms.

Darwin concurred with everything. That's how it happened.

Officers escorted Darwin and Rosina to the hospital to be with Darwin's father. Rosina's parents showed up to watch over him as well. They agreed it was long overdue for them to meet and start getting along.

Darwin kept a wary eye on everyone around them. He watched all the cops, the doctors, and the nurses every minute, looking for something suspicious.

He didn't take what Fuccini said lightly. He knew they were coming. He just couldn't tell when or how.

But they were coming, and he wanted to be ready.

19

Two Months Later …

Darwin opened the curtains in the kitchen and looked out at the morning sunshine.

It had been a long, hard road since the night at the hangar. He was writing again and loving it, even though he wrote under a pseudonym now.

Rosina really enjoyed her new home in sunny Florida.

The FBI had placed them into the witness protection program within two weeks of Fuccini's death.

The two bikers who had been tied up and gagged were gunned down within days of each other, and Darwin's name was scrawled across their chests in blood.

Richard H went into hiding, but they found him a week later. He fought hard and killed four men with his bare hands, even after they shot him three times. Darwin visited him in the hospital. H would live and walk again. The FBI was putting him into the program, too.

When Darwin went to visit H in the hospital, they tried to kill Darwin again. But they'd made a mistake. A man posing as a doctor turned on Darwin with a long needle and charged at him.

At the sight of the needle, all Darwin saw was rage. He lunged at the doctor. That lunge saved him as the needle had been thrust forward, and when Darwin dove, it passed his arm by an inch.

The fake doctor's neck had broken when he was thrown out the fourth-story hospital window. Darwin claimed he had no idea how he was already missing fingers and one eye. He couldn't remember much after seeing the needle.

The FBI, for the public's safety, and Darwin's had elected that he and his wife, Rosina, would have to go into hiding for good. They were handed over to the U.S. Marshals, and the witness protection program set them up in a house in Florida.

They allowed Darwin and H to email each other as H was detailing his life story so Darwin could write that promised book, which Darwin was writing with vigor.

"Another beautiful day," Rosina said as she entered the kitchen. "What's for breakfast?"

"I thought you said you were making breakfast this morning?" Darwin asked in his innocent voice.

"Of course I am." She giggled in her cute way.

He wrapped his arms around her waist and lifted her off the floor. "Let's have French toast and drown it in Canadian maple syrup. And coffee. How does that sound?"

"Perfect."

They kissed long and hard.

"Maybe we should go and have some fun first? Then have the pancakes?"

"You want sex now? Or *pancakes*?" he asked. "I said French

toast, woman."

She laughed and pulled away from him. "Okay, breakfast and then fun."

Rosina had taken the mint tree and adult store explanation well. She'd playfully slapped him when he told her. She understood how innocent it was and didn't care if he was in an adult store. Mint Tree was delivered with their groceries each week now.

"Rosina, honey. I will head down to the main gate and unlock it for Bruce to bring up our grocery order."

"I'll have breakfast ready when you return."

He put on his slippers and stepped outside into the already warm sun. He closed his eyes and took in a deep breath.

Amazing.

At the end of the path, he flicked the small button that allowed entry/exit and stepped out onto the driveway. He walked down it and swung his arms in a carefree way. Life was great. They were in hiding. He could relax. Let things go. He could write. He could love his wife.

They both missed their parents, but that was the way of things. Stay alive and miss them or visit them once or twice before being murdered.

They chose life.

A tall wrought iron gate at the end of the driveway stopped anyone from coming in unless they owned a tank.

The usual guard wasn't there. Darwin slowed his step and frowned.

"Hey, Mike, you around?" he called.

No one answered.

That's weird.

Rosina screamed from the house behind him.

He spun on his heels, ready to run back to the house, but a man stood behind him, a gun in his hand.

"Don't be stupid. A guard is patrolling the yard. When he's dead, we can leave. In the meantime, come with me."

Darwin nodded and walked in front of the man. They got to the house and entered through the front door. Darwin was led to the kitchen, the gun at the small of his back.

A man stood beside Rosina, a gun trained on her, eating Darwin's French toast.

"This is good," the man gestured at his partner, his mouth full. "You should try some."

"Not now, asshole. We have to get that last guard."

"I'm eating. You go and get him. I'll watch these two."

The guy closest to Darwin sucker punched him. Darwin didn't see it coming. The fist hit him in the face and knocked him off his feet. Rosina screamed.

"This one is feisty, so I've been told. Make sure he stays on the floor until I come back."

"No problem," the other guy said, his still mouth full. "Just go and get back here."

The guy who walked Darwin into the kitchen stepped back outside.

The guy at the table was still eating, not taking his eyes off the two of them. Rosina looked at Darwin, reached behind her, grabbed the knife holder set, and knocked it over. She raised her hands to show they were empty and yelled she was sorry.

The guy didn't shoot her. He didn't care that the knives had slid along the counter. One of them, a long bread knife, fell off and hit Darwin in the leg.

Nothing in a long time made him feel that angry. He launched off the floor and dove at the man so fast the guy didn't even get a chance to flip off the safety on his weapon.

He strangled the man in a fit of rage and then stomped on his throat until it had flattened on their kitchen floor.

Then Darwin stepped outside and went hunting for the enemy, a new gun in his hand.

It would never stop. He would be ready.

For Darwin and Rosina, a new life was unfolding. For them, killing was just the beginning. They could never go back to the way things were.

Marriage was just the beginning.

'Til death …

Part Two

The Blade

20

Without sunglasses, looking into his wife's eyes directly was difficult. "I'm sorry, honey. I didn't *want* to kill those men. But you know I had no choice. It was an us-or-them situation."

She nodded and looked at her feet. "I know, honey. I don't understand why it keeps happening. Why can't they just leave us alone? We don't want to hurt anyone. We just want to live our lives free of this shit."

Her tears always moved him to hug her, hold her. Darwin had an innate need to protect Rosina and keep her safe, and he would do anything to achieve that goal—even if it meant killing a dozen more men.

He stepped closer and held her in his arms as she cried. Cars raced by on the Florida highway, oblivious to the couple who wept for the dead men back at the *safe* house where Darwin and Rosina were supposed to be *safe*. Two of them, Darwin, had to kill himself.

The temperature was too hot not to be moving. The only breeze was when a car passed them. Darwin guessed it to be a little after the lunch hour. He was still dressed in his knee-length shorts and an oversized T-shirt that he slept in last night. Rosina did better in the heat with her red sundress, which allowed more ventilation.

He nudged her to get walking. She stepped forward and cleared her face of tears.

"I have to be strong," she said. "I'm sorry, Darwin. What happened back there wasn't your fault."

He knew why he married her in Rome months ago. She had a tough exterior and strong personality but remained soft and feminine on the inside. He'd seen her fight with the mafia and walk away. He loved her for her soul and only hoped that when everything was over, she'd retain some of that innocence and beauty.

He smiled in her direction. There was nothing more to say.

They walked on, feeling the weight of the heat, no one pulling over to offer them a ride. Maybe the blood on Darwin's T-shirt was distracting potential rides.

"We need to get inside somewhere," he said. "This heat is intense."

Darwin read a sign about a hundred meters ahead on the shoulder of the highway. "I guess we're leaving Folkston, Florida."

"Do you know where that is?" Rosina asked.

"Nope."

"So you don't know where we are?"

"Nope."

"Darwin." She stopped and put her back to the traffic. "What are we going to do?"

Darwin stopped two steps ahead. He moved back to her and

waited for a long truck to pass. The wind off it was refreshing.

"I don't know what we're going to do."

"Do we have any money?"

"None." Darwin shook his head.

"So we have no home because our safe house was invaded. We don't know where we are and have no money or ID. Where does that leave us?"

Darwin shrugged. "Wherever you go, there you are?" His attempt to lighten the tension with humor didn't work.

"Darwin, I'm serious. What're we going to do?"

"I have no idea. I wish I knew."

"What about my mother? We could call her. She'd wire money."

"She doesn't even know where we are. That was part of the deal. We had to take on new names when we entered witness protection and not contact old friends and family. Your mother understood. So you can't call her."

"Why not? We're out of protection now. We can go back to being us."

Darwin gestured up the road. "Come on. Let's keep walking. It's too hot to stand out in the sun and talk. We need to stay on the move."

"Okay, but agree to call her," Rosina said as she moved alongside Darwin.

"Not yet. Calling may lead our enemies to her."

"How?"

"They found our safe house, didn't they? Your mother would be an easier target."

"Who do you think they were?"

"I have no idea, but I can tell you who it isn't."

"Who?"

"No one from the Fuccini Family. I think they're done with us. Whoever wasn't killed in Toronto or Rome has been arrested. No one's left, last I heard."

Another truck rolled by, slowing to turn into the Burger joint coming up on the right.

"Then who?" Rosina asked. "If our enemies were the Fuccinis, then who would send professionals to infiltrate a safe house operated by the FBI to attack us? It doesn't make sense."

"I know. Come on." He grabbed her arm. "Let's go into that burger place and get a glass of water. Then we'll walk and talk more."

She agreed. Ten minutes later, after using the restaurant's bathroom to clean off as much blood from his T-shirt as he could and got refreshed from the complimentary water, they walked hand-in-hand along the side of the road again, their spirits buoyed.

"If you were to speculate," Rosina started, "who would you say was behind this morning's attack?"

"I've thought about that and come to two conclusions. Seeing as it was a safe house, only the U.S. Marshals would know where we were, and a select number of FBI agents would have access to that information. Therefore, I feel there's either a leak in the FBI, meaning we were sold out, or it was them."

"What? I'm confused. Why would the FBI attack us?"

"Maybe some of the *special* agents were screwed out of their mafia pensions when mob boss Fuccini was killed. Do you know how many of the authorities are on a mobster's payroll? Less has motivated people to kill."

"I hadn't thought of that."

"I know, me neither. Scary, huh?"

"Yeah."

They walked in silence until they saw a gas station coming up on the right.

Darwin grabbed her hands in his. "Look, Rosina, it's time to get serious. We have no money on us. We can't go back and get my wallet or your purse. I haven't eaten yet today. That asshole back at the house ate my French toast before I could kill him. My adrenaline rush is subsiding, and I'm starting to get the shakes. I have to eat."

"Okay, what're you saying?"

"I'm going into that gas station and stealing a sandwich or something for the two of us. They won't even miss it. We can discuss our next step once we have food in our stomachs. Is that okay with you?"

She cutely shuffled her shoulders and looked at the length of the highway. After a moment, she looked back at him.

"I don't like it. We have a fridge full of food at the house, just over an hour's walk from here. We have access to lots of money per our arrangement with the FBI. This sucks, but I won't say no because what else are we going to do? Somehow, some way, they did this, not us. So, okay, you can grab us something, but on one condition."

"What's that?"

"You don't get caught."

He clicked his tongue. "Don't be silly. It's just a sandwich. What could they do?"

Rosina followed a few steps behind as Darwin walked up the length of the entrance to the gas station convenience store part. Sweat beaded on his forehead. His hands shook from the ordeal an hour ago. His step wavered, and he reminded himself that his symptoms had nothing to do with nervousness. He had to take care of his wife, and if that meant stealing a five-dollar sandwich, he would do it.

As they neared the door, he turned and whispered to Rosina, "Run interference."

He grabbed the door and opened it but was stopped by a hand on his sleeve. Rosina gestured for him to come back out. He followed her a few feet from the door.

"What?" he asked.

"What does 'run interference' mean?"

"Avert the clerk's attention when I'm about to pocket our meal."

"How will I know when?"

"Look, Rosina, just keep an eye on me. You'll know, or I'll nod at you. Okay?"

"Okay. Just be careful. And no more killing."

"Of course not. I just hope the guy doesn't pull a knife on me."

She brushed his shoulder. "No jokes right now, either. Let's just do this and get walking again. I want to try to figure out what we will do next."

Darwin nodded and walked into the air-conditioned store and nearly gasped. It was such a contrast. They had humidity in Toronto, where he was from, but not the kind of heat Florida got in the summer.

He counted three customers and a bored-looking clerk. They split up. Rosina headed toward the drinks aisle, and Darwin walked toward the sandwich and hotdog section, where the wieners sat on steel rollers, constantly spinning.

After reading all the sandwich labels, he picked up two egg salad sandwiches and discovered he had nowhere to hide them.

"Shit."

He looked at the clerk leaning over the counter with a pen in his hand, an open notebook laid flat on the counter's surface.

The other customers paid him no attention.

What now?

He walked over to Rosina at the drinks fridge.

"You ready to go?" he asked.

"Yeah," she whispered. "What are you going to do with them? How are you going to, you know?"

"I have an idea. Follow my lead. Don't say anything. Let me handle it. Oh, and grab a couple of Cokes."

She frowned and gave him an angry stare. He gestured at the fridge with one of the egg salad sandwiches. "Come on."

Score points for the wife, he thought as she grabbed two Cokes. *I love it when she trusts me implicitly.*

Weird elevator music floated down from the speakers above their heads. Darwin walked toward the counter, blocking the music, his mind set on what he would do, having no idea if it would work.

He took one last look behind him. One customer read a magazine on the rack. The second stood in the small hardware section debating what antifreeze would best cool his car, and the third customer stood by the bathroom door, evidently waiting for it to become available.

He set the sandwiches on the counter and motioned for Rosina to do the same with the Cokes. She did, a smile on her face.

The clerk hadn't noticed them. Darwin cleared his throat. He couldn't waste time. He had to do what he'd planned as fast as he could for it to work.

The clerk turned slowly and looked at them. He stood up and set his pen down in a lazy, I-see-you-take-it-easy attitude.

Fuck you, too, asshole. I'm about to ruin your day.

The clerk grabbed each sandwich and scanned it. Then, the Cokes followed. The till rang up a total.

"You want a bag?" the clerk asked.

Even your voice is lazy. He made it sound like bagging their purchase would be so unnecessary that it would be a nuisance.

"Yes," was all Darwin could think to do. *Well, if you're going to ask that way, of course, I'm going to make you bag my shit.*

He didn't have the time to keep this up. He reached behind him and dropped a hand in each back pocket, exaggeratedly attempting to locate his wallet. He tried his front pockets and came up empty.

"Oh shit …" He turned to Rosina. "Honey, did you bring your purse?"

"No. Too hot for that thick strap. You don't have your wallet?"

Darwin heard the clerk chewing gum. He had opened his mouth and smacked his saliva to a rhythm like the bubbles in bubble wrap being snapped.

He turned back to the clerk, but not before making sure the other three customers hadn't moved.

"Look, I left my wallet in the car. That blue Impala over there." He pointed through the window at the vehicle parked at the pump. "I'll go and toss these in the back seat, finish pumping my gas, and come back and pay for it all at once."

He grabbed the bag and turned to leave. The bag jerked back, and Darwin lost his grip.

"Hold up," the clerk said. "You mean *that* blue Impala?"

"Yeah," Darwin said with all the confidence he could muster, sweat rolling down his face even though air-conditioning machines worked tirelessly to cool him.

"You didn't even start to pump gas yet."

"I'm going to do that now," Darwin said, pulling on the bag.

He felt resistance again.

"Next time, pump first," the clerk said. "Don't park at the pumps to come in and shop."

The clerk let go of the bag. Darwin pulled it in close.

"Right, okay, sorry about that." Darwin exited the store and headed toward the blue car, Rosina right beside him.

"What now?" she whispered.

"We get in and drive away if keys are in it."

"And if there aren't?"

"No idea."

"I was afraid of that."

She walked to the passenger side and got in the car. He tossed the bag inside the front seat, grabbed the pump, dislodged the latch, and went to open the hole, but the gas cap had a lock on it.

Shit!

He had to start pumping gas, or the ruse was over. He caught sight of the clerk watching him from the window of the store. No doubt he had to switch a button to start the gas flowing.

The guy waiting by the bathroom door at the back of the store emerged, shaking water off his hands. He slowed a step when he saw Darwin at his car. At any second, the guy would see Rosina in the passenger seat.

Darwin waved at him. "Over here," he shouted.

The man continued toward him, frowning.

"How much did you want me to put in?" Darwin asked,

knowing the clerk inside the shop was still watching.

"Twenty would do. I didn't know this was a full-serve station."

"It isn't really, but Andrew, the owner, he's trying it out for a month to monitor the response. He wants to see if he should change it over."

"Oh." The guy shrugged. "Okay."

"I'm going to need you to unlock the gas cap."

"Oh, right." The guy stepped forward, a key in his hand.

"Here," Darwin reached out his right hand. "I can do that for you."

The clerk still watched through the gas station's window. He used his free hand to wave and smile. The clerk didn't move, his face expressionless.

Darwin opened the cap, dropped the nozzle in, and started pumping gas.

"How about this heat?" he said, returning the keys.

The guy simply nodded.

He would be out of options as soon as the gas was pumped. Or before that, if the guy noticed Rosina in the front seat.

The pump hit twenty dollars.

Darwin stopped pumping, set the nozzle back in place, and extended his hand to be paid. He was so smooth that for a moment, he wondered if he had been a gas jockey in another life.

"That'll be twenty bucks."

He wondered if the clerk was still watching. Would he figure out that Darwin was taking the guy's money for gas?

The car's owner handed Darwin a twenty and made him step around him.

"You want a receipt?"

The guy shook his head. He opened his car door as Darwin opened his mouth to try to stop him, but nothing came out.

At the exact second, Rosina opened her door and slipped out, leaving the door open while she bent back into the car.

"Excuse me, sir," she said. "The guy who pumped your gas is in training. Sorry to bother you, but did he ask if you wanted your windows cleaned?"

"No, he didn't, but it's all right. I'm in a hurry. Thanks."

"Okay, sir, have a nice day."

Rosina shut the passenger door and walked around the car to join Darwin, the bag of sandwiches and Cokes wrapped around her wrist.

"Well done," Darwin muttered under his breath.

"It's not over yet. As soon as this guy—" she stopped talking when the blue Impala turned on, "leaves, the clerk will not only want the money for the food but also the gas."

"I know. I'm thinking."

The blue Impala pulled away. Darwin waved at the mirrors.

"We're out of time. The clerk just disappeared from the window."

The door of the gas station opened, and the clerk ran out.

"Hey!" he shouted. "What're you doing?"

The noise of the pump behind them ceased churning. Darwin turned to see a man in his fifties standing by the gas pump. The old man put a hand to his chest and mouthed the word, "Me?"

"No, those two," the clerk shouted.

"I think he means you," Darwin said to the old man who stood at least five feet behind him.

"What do we do?" Rosina asked near Darwin's ear, a sense of desperation in her voice.

Darwin's stomach growled as he contemplated their options. He was tired of being beaten up, pushed around, and having to defend himself. Stealing a sandwich had to be easier than this.

"Come with me," he whispered to Rosina as he approached the man in his fifties.

"I just filled that guy's tank," Darwin said.

The man shrugged. "So."

"Well, now we're in trouble with the boss because I'm not filling your tank. That's why he was yelling. Help us out, move aside, and let me fill your tank?"

"No."

Darwin looked at Rosina and then back at the old man. "No? That's it, just no."

"This ain't no full serve. *I* fill my truck," he said as he tapped his chest. "Fuck off."

The clerk yelled behind them. "I'm calling the cops."

Darwin snuck a glance at the clerk. He had a phone at his ear.

Darwin made a decision. He grabbed the handle of the gas pump, drove his right foot down into the back of the old guy's knee, and yanked the hose at the same time. The old guy shouted profanities as he fell to the side, letting go of the pump.

"Sorry, didn't see you there," Darwin said as he held down the lever on the handle, shooting gas out onto the hot concrete.

"What are you doing?" The clerk sounded insane as he yelled from twenty feet away. "You can't do that. Stop!"

With the lever pushed all the way up, the nozzle sprayed gas where the blue Impala had been moments before. Then he turned and sprayed the lower legs of the old guy.

"Be careful you don't get burned when I light this gas station on fire," Darwin said to the old guy.

Rosina leaned in close. "You're not really going to burn anything, are you?"

Darwin shook his head.

A car entered the gas station. Darwin looked quick to make sure it wasn't the authorities.

He tossed the hose onto the concrete, grabbed Rosina's hand, and ran to the front of the pickup as the old guy tried to get up.

The keys were in the ignition.

After helping Rosina up, he jumped in, gunned the engine, and slammed it into drive.

"Hey," the old man shouted behind them.

They hit the highway and accelerated to ten miles over the speed limit.

"Holy shit," Rosina said. "What just happened? Did we just steal a car?"

"Yeah, I think we did. It kinda got out of hand."

Rosina opened the bag and handed Darwin a sandwich. "Well, at least we got the sandwiches and Cokes. There's that."

He looked over at her. "You're right, baby. There's that."

They drove in silence; both lost in their thoughts while they ate. Rosina opened a Coke, and they shared the first one. Then she flipped the air conditioning dial to full.

"You know, cops will be looking for this pickup soon."

"I know," Darwin said, wiping egg salad off his lip. "We'll find some old road to pull into and wait until dark. Maybe change the plates or something."

"What are we now? Criminals on the run? Bandits? Bonnie and Clyde? That's not us. We were attacked at the safe house. Why can't we just dump this thing and call the U.S. Marshals or the FBI?"

"Because," he looked sideways at her. "I have a feeling the feds hit us or leaked our position."

"You said earlier that that was one of two possibilities. Now you think it was them?"

"They were experienced in ways feds would be."

"And you don't think the mafia has guys like that?"

"I'm sure they do, but I still feel the feds hit us. Call it a hunch. Feds go on hunches all the time. I'm gonna go with mine."

"There's another problem," Rosina said.

"What's that?"

"We can't hide out until dark. You know what happens to you in the dark. That won't work."

Darwin thought about it for a minute. "You're right."

"I vote we find a cheap motel to let us stay for cash. Use that twenty you got off the Impala guy. We do that within the next ten to fifteen minutes and ditch this truck along another road to send them looking the wrong way. We walk back to the motel and are safe for the night. No one would know where we are. Sound good?"

Darwin snorted. "Sounds like you've done this kind of thing before."

"What does that mean?" She sounded wounded.

"It means I love your intelligence. What you just came up with, my love, is a brilliant idea."

They drove on until both sandwiches and both Cokes were gone. Less than a half-hour north on 301, Darwin saw the sign for a small town called Nahunta. Five minutes later, they were through it to the other side, where they saw a small motel called Sleep On Inn on the right.

"Perfect," Darwin said. "If it's over twenty, I'll tell the clerk a story and offer to do the dishes." He smiled. "Let's check in first, and I'll leave you behind in the room. I'll go and dump the truck, okay?"

"No way. I'm not being left alone. We go everywhere together."

"Normally, I'd agree. But we can't walk back to the motel once I dump this pickup. The cops are looking for a young couple. They'll have our descriptions. If it's just me, they may not take a second look. Also, it's fucking hot. I can take my shirt off, and all they'll see is a white-skinned boy walking along the road in a pair of fucked-up shorts. They won't look at me and say, 'There's the guy that just robbed a gas station and stole a pickup truck.'"

As he pulled into the front of the motel, Rosina nodded her agreement.

"Okay, but you have to come back. You can't get caught by anybody because I don't know what I'd do without you."

"Don't worry, baby. Nothing's going to happen to me."

At least, I hope not.

21

Carson Dodge pulled up to the front gate of the safe house and laid on his horn. A throng of reporters and media vans looked like they'd been spread out and layered on thick as one would spread butter on toast.

He cracked his window, the heat hitting his face like he'd opened an oven door. "Out of the way. FBI coming through."

Men and women picked up tripods and camera cases and slowly drifted to one side or the other, taking their time.

Carson smacked his horn repeatedly for them to be quicker, then called Rudy on his cell phone. "Who's in charge of keeping the media back and out of the way at the gate?"

Special Agent Rudy Earlton responded. "We have a guy down there. A rookie from the local police force. Don't remember his name."

"He just lost his job. Fire him." Carson ended the call.

He drove through the small opening the reporters offered and stopped on the other side of the gate. The rookie cop stood off to the side, examining his fingernails.

Carson got out, left his car door open, and strode toward the rookie.

"Hey," he called.

"Yeah?" the rookie asked, biting his thumbnail. "What's up?"

Carson had been a Bureau man since his twenties. When he lost his left thumb in an accident at a firing range, the FBI stood by him. When he returned after spending four months in India and lost most of his left eye's eyesight, the Bureau looked the other way. No new eye exams, no tests. If it didn't affect his job, no one cared. That's how much respect they had for him and his successful career. He had already tagged and singlehandedly bagged four of America's Most Wanted in his late forties.

Carson removed his trademark sunglasses and held up his left hand. "You see my thumb here?"

The rookie shook his head.

"Do you know how I lost it?"

"I'm sorry. Who are you?"

Carson retrieved his badge with his right hand, keeping his left in the air.

"Oh, shit, sorry." The rookie stood to his full height.

Carson put the badge away and asked, "Do you know how I lost it?"

"Uhm, sorry sir, lost what?"

"My thumb, asshole."

"I have no idea, sir."

The rookie's posture had changed when he saw the FBI badge, but Carson was too pissed to stop there.

"Do you ever want a promotion?"

"Yes, sir."

"Do you like being a cop?"

"Yes, sir."

"Then listen to what I have to say."

The rookie nodded, his eyes wider.

"When I started at the Bureau, about your age, I was minding a gate like this one. Not paying attention, like you. My boss came over, pulled his weapon out to scare me into doing my job better, and it fired by accident. I lost my thumb. I felt I deserved it, so neither one of us said shit about the accident. I got promoted soon enough, and now look at me—I'm the lead guy on this Darwin and Rosina Kostas case. So, I will ask you again. Do you want a promotion?"

"Uhm, yes, but I …"

Carson pulled out his sidearm and held it by his thigh so the reporter's cameras wouldn't see it.

"Hold out your thumb."

"Sir, I'm sorry."

"I know you are. I can hear it in your voice." Carson leaned in until his nose was an inch from the rookie's. "Did you know the men who died here today?"

"No."

"They were good men. All of them. I knew each man by their God-given names, and I knew their wives. I'm the guy who gets to drive to each of their homes and tell their wives that their husbands are dead. Two of these men have kids."

"Yes, sir."

Carson could see the rookie was on the verge of tears.

"Mind that *fucking* gate. Keep the reporters back. Allow official traffic only. Do not fuck this up. I am way too pissed off to tolerate any kind of shit. Either set your gun and badge on the pavement, walk away, or do your job. If I come back here and things aren't how they're supposed to be, you will lose both thumbs. Are we clear?"

He slipped his weapon back into its holster as the rookie nodded faster than a bobblehead figure on a race car's dashboard.

"Good," Carson said.

He backed away, glanced at the line of reporters, smiled for whichever camera might be rolling, and got back into his car.

In his mirror, on the drive up to the house, he saw the rookie cop standing in the middle of the lane, shooing reporters back to keep an opening clear.

Two ambulances were parked in front of the safe house, along with six police cars and a police van. The only other unmarked car was Rudy's. Carson parked behind it and got out. He removed his suit jacket, not caring how big the sweat stains were under his arms. It was a hot day, and his men were dead. Men he'd worked with over the years. Comrades. No one would have the nerve to say anything to him or even to give his wet shirt a second glance. Not today. They wouldn't dare.

He walked by one of the ambulances and lifted the blanket off the face of the man on the stretcher.

"John Simmons. You guys know how he died?"

"We can't confirm what caused his death until the autopsy, but it looks like he was strangled with a belt or something like a belt," the guy to his right said.

"A belt?" Carson let go of the blanket.

"Yeah, same with those two guys. But not until they fought with someone. All three were beaten up badly. They look like they were tortured first."

"What about the other two?"

"We found one guy in the kitchen. He had just eaten breakfast, by the look of things. Stab wound to the neck and cheek."

"The cheek? Who the fuck does that?"

The ambulance attendant shrugged. "It's not as bad as the last guy."

"Tell me."

"We found the fifth victim in the woods a little way from the gate. He also fought, but not a lot of bruising, which indicates the fight didn't go on long. The thing about the last guy was he had a pen jammed into the side of his neck just below the ear. It even looks like it was his own pen because of the ink stains on his shirt."

"Darwin," Carson whispered under his breath.

"Excuse me?"

"Nothing. Finish up here." Carson walked away.

How the hell could a little pudgy boy from Canada take out five decorated federal officers? To beat the three on duty the way he did and strangle them with a belt was unconscionable. To stab one in the kitchen and use a pen to kill another was insane.

Everyone had heard about Darwin Kostas and his fight with the Fuccini Family. Everyone at the Bureau bugged Greg Stinsen about it constantly. How should they hire Darwin to go after more bad guys. He could clean up the city. Greg always insisted that Darwin was harmless and that he just got lucky.

No way what Darwin did in Rome and Toronto was luck. He was a killing machine, plain and simple. The evidence lay on stretchers on the property where Darwin and his wife had been living in secrecy. Only four agents knew where the safe house was, excluding the rotation of agents who acted as guards for the Kostas, and two of them were dead now. Nick Johnson and Lee Michaels worked with Greg and Carson, and they were pivotal in making the safe house safe.

Carson entered the front door of the house and walked the length of the front hall until he reached the kitchen, where he met with Rudy and a crime scene team.

Cameras flashed, and men sifted through items on the floor while Rudy talked on his cell phone. Carson caught Rudy's eye.

"Okay … yeah … I have to go. Get back to me soon." Rudy slapped his phone shut and dropped it into his jacket pocket. "This is a clusterfuck, isn't it?"

"Fill me in. What've you got?"

Rudy picked up a notebook that had been on the kitchen counter and flipped back four pages. "Looks like the three men on duty, Simmons, Ouellette, and Baron, were similarly attacked by the same aggressor. We can tell by how all three men were beaten systematically without putting up much of a fight. I have a theory." Rudy raised his right finger.

Rudy's theories drove Carson nuts, but he was all ears today. He needed to listen and digest everything. He waited for Rudy to continue.

"I think the three men on duty were held at gunpoint as they were beaten. Or at least something was preventing them from fighting back. These weren't men who would go down that easily. It also looks like they were beaten so badly that whatever they were strangled with only sped up their deaths. None of them has a bruised knuckle or a shred of skin under their nails. They didn't fight back when being strangled."

"What about the other two?" Carson asked as he moved a few feet into the living room to make way for a CSI photographer.

Rudy stepped ahead of him and sat down on one of the dining room chairs. Carson followed suit. To his credit, Rudy didn't look at Carson's shirt with the stained underarms.

"The other two were murdered with a different MO. Nick Johnson had eaten breakfast and was stabbed in the kitchen. His gun was in his hand, but the safety was still on. He still had French toast in his mouth when he died. Whoever attacked him was seriously fast and good at what they did. Either that or extremely angry. The kind of rage that sets men apart."

"What do you mean?"

"The stabber hit so fast that he had no real aim. He used a kitchen knife from the set on the counter. His first jab went in Nick's cheek and the second one in the side of his throat. That was the killing blow. A look at the blood splatter pattern indicates Nick was sitting at the kitchen table minding his own business when he was hit."

"What about Lee? What've you got on him?"

Rudy flipped another page. "Lee Michaels was found on the property out by the woods. He got a bunch of blows in, which makes him the only one to have scuffled with his attacker. His hands were bruised and covered in blood. But somehow, whoever he fought got a hold of his pen and jammed it into his neck like he was trying to do an amateur tracheotomy and missed the whole point about it helping someone breathe."

"Not funny," Carson said.

"Sorry."

"Where's the couple they were protecting?"

Rudy frowned. "Darwin and Rosina Kostas?"

"Yes. Who else was in this safe house? Just tell me where they are."

"We haven't found them yet. Whoever attacked the safe house and killed our guys must've taken them."

"We don't know that. What we have is five men down and the couple on the run. We all know what that boy can do. Nobody has gone up against Fuccini in decades. Yet, this kid did it on his own and walked away. That makes him dangerous—very dangerous. Just look around the house where he lived, and what do we see? Five dead Bureau men."

"We don't know *that*. They could've been kidnapped."

Carson shook his head. "I guess we'll see when we find them."

"We're pulling the camera feeds from the property and surrounding area. I'll be watching them myself."

"What part of the house did the cameras cover?" Carson wondered how he'd forgotten that particular detail about the house.

"There's a camera on the front gate and two covering the perimeter, but they don't cover everything. Then we have three on the inside of the house. The kitchen camera covers the back door."

"Show me."

Carson followed Rudy back into the kitchen, stepping around Nick's body, crossing himself, and saying a quick prayer under his breath. The CSI team was cleaning up their tools, but blood remained on the floor and cupboards below the sink.

Rudy pointed to the clock on the wall.

"It's in the clock?" Carson asked.

"Yup. At the little dot where the six is. See here." Rudy pointed.

Carson nodded. "Where're the discs?"

"Come on, I'll show you."

Rudy led him outside to the police van. He opened the back door and stepped in, gesturing for Carson to follow. The van had a raised roof, but at six foot two, Carson still had to duck.

"I had my guys going over the discs here to give me a preview of whatever they found." He smacked the back of one technician's chair. "That's your cue. What have you found?"

The tech pushed a couple of buttons, and security camera footage from that morning began to play.

"Cameras three and five had nothing for us," the tech said. "But the gate camera shows Nick and Lee coming inside the property. After that, we don't see them again until the kitchen. The three men on duty were executed off camera, as was Lee out by the perimeter fence."

Rudy slapped the back of the tech's chair again. "Show us what you do have, then."

"This here is the kitchen."

The screen changed. On the small monitor, everyone saw Nick Johnson eating French toast and smiling as he talked to someone off-camera.

"Wait, here it comes. Three seconds."

Carson eased closer. He recognized Rosina Kostas as she appeared on the screen. The camera caught her knocking over the knife set on the counter. Then Carson watched as Darwin rose from the floor with a knife in his hand so fast that he was at the bottom of the screen one second and attacking Nick the next.

The camera picked up two fast knife jabs, although Darwin's back obscured most of the detail. Then Darwin stepped away, and Carson watched as Nick clutched at his face, his mouth jammed with food before he toppled off the chair, where he bled out and died on the kitchen floor.

"Holy shit," Rudy said. "That's the first time I've seen that."

"Yeah," the tech said. "I just watched it myself a minute

before you came in."

"Seal everything up tight," Carson said. "No mistakes. Rudy, come outside."

Both men stepped down the two stairs to the driveway.

"Make sure no one else sees that. I want everyone looking for this Darwin kid, but I'm bringing him in. He's my collar. Got it?"

He waited until the stunned Rudy nodded.

"Good. Make sure when one of your men spots Darwin or his wife, they call me. Understood?"

"Yeah …"

"You okay?" Carson asked. "Are you hesitant?"

Rudy ran a hand through his hair. "Nick and I played a round of golf last week. He took me to Vegas to play Shadow Creek. You know how Nick loved to gamble. He got these two passes for free rounds at Shadow Creek through the New York New York Hotel. They drove us to the course in limousines." Rudy paused to exhale a deep sigh. "I just watched my friend murdered by the guy he was protecting. Stabbed in the face. I refused to believe it when I got here. I kept telling myself that Darwin and his wife needed our help, that they had been kidnapped or something. I'd never have guessed that Darwin did all this."

"Well, now you know. He'll pay for it. I assure you." Carson grabbed Rudy's shoulders and gripped them tight. "Hold it together. Do this right, and we'll get him, okay? Now, I have to go and issue a statement to the press. When I'm done, I'll return to the office to learn everything I can about Darwin. I'll find out where his and Rosina's parents are and talk to Greg Stinsen. We'll nail him. He'll make a mistake. We'll get him. But I need you to keep it together."

"It's okay, I'm good."

Carson let him go and started for his car.

"Wait, Carson," Rudy called after him.

"What is it?" Carson asked over his shoulder without turning around. He reached his car, opened the door, and waited.

"Why were Nick and Lee here in the first place?"

"What?" Carson shook his head. "What are you talking about? They're FBI. They know about the safe house. It's their job."

"Yeah, but why were they here? They weren't relieving the guys on duty. They know about the safe house, but they don't work it. Too much official traffic coming and going could raise questions with the neighbors. They know that, so I find it confusing that they would just show up for breakfast."

"Look, Rudy, just do your job. Don't worry about that. We can't ask them now, can we? They were here, and now they're dead. You saw for yourself how Darwin stabbed Nick. It doesn't matter why they were here. They're dead, and we have a murderer to catch."

Carson got in his car and drove away.

"Why were they here?" he asked out loud. "It doesn't fucking matter."

***

The rookie guarding the gate had done a fine job. Carson pulled up to the inside of the gate and was relieved that he didn't have to shoot the guy's thumb off.

He exited the car, put on his jacket, and turned to the rookie.

"Good job. I'll put a word in for you."

The rookie's face blanched as he forced a smile.

Carson turned to the media assembled near the gate and said

loud enough for the rookie to hear, "Fucking maggots."

Cameras flashed in multiple succession as at least a hundred reporters surged forward for a statement.

Carson understood what it was all about. He hated it, but he understood it. They were itching to get the details of his friends' deaths for the evening news. They all wanted to be the first to air the dirty laundry. This would be the story of the year. Five agents of the Federal Bureau of Investigation had been killed in the line of duty at the same location.

Questions were volleyed at him. Reporters talked over one another, hoping for him to answer them personally. He waved both arms in the air to signal quiet.

"We'll answer all of your questions in time," he said.

"How many dead are there?" a pretty brunette from CNN shouted from four feet away.

"We have five dead, all federal agents."

"Can you give us names?"

"Not at this time. Not until the next of kin are notified."

"Was this a crack house?" a man with three letters on his microphone Carson didn't recognize asked.

"I'll tell you what I can, but there's still a lot of investigation to take place."

The throng jostled closer. Over twenty black microphones crowded Carson's face. At that moment, all he felt like doing was smacking the microphones away. He didn't want to talk to the media. It was Darwin he wanted to talk to. But public information had to be managed. The five men lying dead behind him deserved respect. He would do it his way and find Darwin and his wife.

"We have five FBI agents dead. The murderer was caught on camera." He wondered why that spilled out so easily when he asked Rudy to keep it to himself. Maybe he was past caring. Maybe he wanted the world to know what Darwin had done. "The person of interest is known to us." Carson's face tightened. "We are actively looking for Darwin Kostas and his—"

The reporters exploded in a fury of new questions.

"Hold it!" Carson yelled to be heard over them. "Take it easy. Your questions will be answered in good time."

The CNN brunette asked, "Do you mean the Darwin Kostas who fought the Fuccini Family in Toronto a few months back?"

"Yes, that's who I'm talking about."

"Isn't he one of the good guys?" she asked. "I thought the FBI protected him."

"That's what we thought." Carson turned to look directly into the lens of the CNN camera. "Darwin Kostas, I know what you did to the Fuccinis." He knew he'd hear about this later. His superiors would be pissed. He cleared his throat and tightened his jaw. "Darwin, I will find you. There's nowhere you can hide. These were men I worked with. They have families. They didn't deserve this. Turn yourself in, Darwin. That would be the safest bet for you and your wife."

Carson rolled thick saliva on his tongue, spat onto the pavement at his feet, and turned for his car.

A barrage of questions assailed his back, but he'd said all he was prepared to say to the reporters.

He was done. He wanted Darwin now, and he knew he'd catch him.

It was just a matter of time.

22

Three hours after leaving Rosina at the motel, Darwin had dumped the pickup behind an abandoned barn two side roads off the main highway and trudged back to the motel. The clerk had asked for thirty bucks but said they could have a double room for a single price as most rooms were vacant. As far as Darwin could see, no other room key had been missing from the board behind the desk.

He approached their room as the sun descended and used his key to enter it. Rosina sat in the room's chair, rubbing cream onto her legs, a towel on her head, and one wrapped around her body. "I had a shower while I waited. It was so hot today. It helped me to cool down and think."

Darwin looked outside to ensure he wasn't being watched and closed the door. After securing the deadbolt, he sprawled out on the bed with a deep sigh.

Rosina moved off the chair, crawled onto the bed, and lay beside him. Her towel loosened and fell open.

"Oops," she said, a hand in front of her mouth in a gesture of innocence.

After Darwin didn't respond to her invitation, she wrapped an arm across him, and they lay there, holding each other.

After a few minutes, Rosina said, "Do you think we'll ever be out from under this?"

Darwin arched his head back and looked downward to see her. He moved a lock of hair that had fallen from the towel and stared into her eyes. "I swear to you, this will all be over one day. When that day comes, it'll be just you and me together. We'll live our lives any way we want. Maybe we'll even get a dog." He inhaled, then continued. "Sometimes I feel like I can't face the day. I don't know where the courage comes from. But then I see you smile, hear your voice, and remember where the strength comes from." He brushed at her hair again and rested his hand over her shoulder. "I love you, Rosina. I don't say it enough, but I'm so very happy you're my wife." He kissed her and held it a moment. "I promise that I will figure this out. The people responsible will be held accountable. We'll leave everything behind and move on. You'll have your dream house. We'll go shopping in a grocery store, and maybe one day we'll even play Bingo at some flea market."

She shoved him playfully. "No, I don't wanna play Bingo."

"Okay, baby, whatever you want."

A tear escaped his eye. He let it fall to the pillow. Rosina dabbed her thumb at his cheek, tracing the line of his tear. "I love you, too, Darwin. I'm the lucky one. Not many men would have come for me like you did in Rome. I'd be dead without you. I'll support you and do whatever's necessary to end this. But when it's all over, no more violence, no more fighting, and no more killing people. We have to stop murdering everyone." She giggled. "Doesn't that sound ridiculous? When we decided to get married, if anyone had walked up to us and said that we'd be fighting the mafia, killing *people*," she used air quotes with her fingers to illustrate the last two words, "and on the run, I would've never believed it."

"Me neither."

They snuggled closer and held each other until they almost fell asleep.

Darwin jerked awake, then angled off the bed. "We should check the news. See if there's anything on the car theft at the gas station or safe house."

He could tell she didn't want to know, but moving forward without knowing anything would be more dangerous. He sat on the end of the bed and flipped through channels while Rosina adjusted the pillows to lean against the headboard.

"Here," Darwin said.

A news anchor sat behind his desk, waiting for the TV station's intro music to finish.

"Breaking news this evening coming out of Florida near Jacksonville. Five FBI agents tasked to a safe house in that area have been brutally murdered. Our own Kate Frankson has the story."

As the camera panned onto the street in front of the house they'd occupied peacefully for the past two months, Darwin turned to Rosina. "This is it. Shit, my stomach just dropped."

"Hi, Michael? Yes." The woman on the screen tapped her earpiece. "There, I have you now." Her head lifted, and she stared into the camera. "It has been confirmed that we have five dead FBI agents on site. They aren't releasing many details yet as there's an investigation still underway, but it does look like the people they were supposed to be protecting are being looked at as suspects in the murders."

Darwin leaped to his feet. "I didn't kill the three other guys. The two rogue agents broke in and killed the other three." He looked back at Rosina. She had started to cry. "Fuck!"

"We received a statement from Special Agent Carson Dodge with the FBI."

The camera changed, and Darwin watched as a man with veins sticking out on either side of his neck, his face red, talked directly to the camera.

"Darwin Kostas, I know what you did to the Fuccinis." The guy cleared his throat, clenched his jaw, and paused briefly. "Darwin, I will find you. There's nowhere you can hide. These were men I worked with. They have families. They didn't deserve to die. Turn yourself in, Darwin. That would be the safest bet for you and your wife."

The guy on camera spat onto the pavement and walked away.

"There you have it, Michael." The newswoman tapped her earpiece again. "That was Special Agent Dodge reporting at the crime scene. Other media outlets are calling Darwin Kostas "The Blade." The police here are looking for a quick closure to this mess. They've put out a BOLO on Darwin and his wife, Rosina. If you see them, do not approach them. They are considered armed and dangerous. Call the number on the bottom of the screen." A telephone number flashed on the screen. "Tell them where you saw these people and let the police handle it."

Two pictures filled the screen on the small twenty-inch TV in the hotel room. Both were shots of Darwin and Rosina from a year and a half ago when they had their passport photos done.

"How did they get those?" Darwin asked.

"Does that really matter?" Rosina said, her voice breaking.

Darwin closed the distance between them and leaned into her. "I'm sorry, honey. We'll sort this out."

"They think we killed everybody. There were no witnesses. They'd never believe our side of things. We're finished. This is bigger than killing mobsters."

"We'll find a way. I didn't touch those other three. We killed the guy eating my breakfast because they were going to kill us. Then I went outside and fought with the other one who had punched me to the kitchen floor. It was self-defense. We're innocent. There's nothing to worry about."

"I wish that were true." Rosina dabbed a Kleenex on her closed eyes. "Promise me one thing."

"Of course, honey. Whatever you want."

"No more killing the feds."

"Well, I don't know—"

"Darwin." Her face grew serious. "It's one thing to tell the judge you're sorry you killed the junkie when he broke into our house and pulled a knife, as an example. But it's completely different to say you killed federal officers who were hired to protect you in your own home. This is going to be really hard to get out of."

"I know, I know. I understand."

She was on the verge of more tears. The TV had moved on to another news story. The mention of a gas station caught Darwin's ear. He focused on the screen.

"A couple of hours ago, a pickup truck was stolen from this gas station. Police are combing the area to locate it. All active members of the local and state police are involved as it has come to our attention that Darwin Kostas, known as The Blade, and his wife, Rosina Kostas, were caught on the gas station's security cameras stealing sandwiches and beverages before pouring gas at the clerk from one of the pumps when he tried to approach them. We have the clerk here."

The camera panned to the face of the gas station clerk.

"They both came in and were so rude. I asked if he wanted a bag with his purchase, and he nearly bit my head off …"

"That's not true," Darwin shouted.

"Then he just grabbed everything and walked outside like it was free. He pumped gas in one guy's car like he owned the joint and took the customer's money. Then, he stole the pickup from another customer. I'm just happy he didn't want to kill me, too. I've never met such a brazen criminal before. It was like the world owed him everything, and we little people were in his way. I can't believe I made it out alive."

The camera panned back to the newswoman. "There you have it. Darwin and Rosina Kostas are suspects in the murder of five FBI agents just over four miles from here, and now they're on the run in a stolen Ford F-150. If you see this vehicle, license plate number …"

"I can't believe this. We were just hungry. All I wanted to do was get us something to eat. Now it looks like we're on a crime spree across America."

Rosina got off the bed and dropped her towel. She slipped on her panties and proceeded to get dressed.

Darwin muted the TV. "What're you doing?"

"Getting dressed."

"Rosina, I can see that. Are you going somewhere?"

"Yes."

Darwin waited, but she didn't offer a destination. "Where're you going?"

"To the nearest police station."

"Why?" Darwin asked as he got up off the bed.

"Because we can't stay here."

"I'm not following. Why can't we stay here?"

"The clerk who rented this room has seen our faces. If he watched the news, the police would bust that door down in ten minutes. I'd rather go in willingly than have that FBI guy Dodge chasing us. If they come through that door, there's no telling how dead we will be with no witnesses." She paused to lower a purple shirt over her head. "Tomorrow's news will have our names in it again, but this time, they'll be reporting our deaths. I can see it now. 'Darwin Kostas, known as The Blade, was killed last night in a motel on the outskirts of wherever-the-fuck-we-are, Florida or Georgia, or who knows, as he resisted arrest.'"

"Rosina, I don't think your leaving is a good idea."

She undid the towel on her head and shook her hair out. "All cops can't be bad. We'll be safe there. Wait, why did you say, 'You leaving'? We're not going together?"

Darwin moved closer to her. "Look, just think about this for a second—"

An explosion outside cut him off.

"What the hell was that?" Rosina asked.

"No idea, but it doesn't sound good."

Darwin peeked out the curtain. Long shadows lay across the barren parking area of the vacant motel as the sun continued its descent. Not a single car sat parked in the lot. Vehicles traveled along the highway a hundred yards away.

"I don't see anything," he said.

Rosina came up behind him and put her hand on the

doorknob. "You're coming with me, I hope?"

"Rosina, I want to talk about this a while longer. As much as you believe this is the right thing to do, I don't. Can you at least wait ten minutes so we can discuss it? Give me that much time."

"Okay, ten minutes."

Another explosion made him jump. This one felt closer than the first.

"Whatever it is, it's closer."

"It could be highway workers blasting a new road."

"Did you see construction signs anywhere when we came in?"

"No, but maybe they're blasting behind us."

Darwin shook his head. "That was too close. Like in the next room or the one after that."

"How so? The place is empty."

"I know, but something's not right. Get away from the door."

Rosina walked the length of the motel room and stood by the door to the bathroom at the back. "You're scaring me, Darwin."

"Until we know what that is, we must be careful."

Someone knocked on their door. Darwin turned and placed his index finger across his lips to indicate silence. Rosina nodded.

"Come out, come out, wherever you are. Or you can talk to my little friend."

It came to Darwin in a rush. The explosions were from a powerful gun. Whoever was outside their motel room was shooting doors in, searching for them.

He looked to the back of the motel and into the bathroom.

"Last chance," the voice on the other side of the door yelled.

Darwin ran for the back. He grabbed Rosina's arm and pulled her into the bathroom. He hopped inside the bathtub and made room for her. Once she was laid flat out, except for her knees, which were tented, he wrapped his body around hers and waited.

The sound of the speaker's muffled voice traveled to them.

"Who do you think it is?" she whispered. "The owner of the pickup?"

"Doubt it. Sounds like a cop."

"A cop? Shooting motel room doors in like that?"

"Sure. If they know we're the only people here, what does it hurt to shoot a couple of FBI murderers accidentally?"

She grabbed his hand and held it to her chest. "Promise me we'll get through this, and I'll do anything you need to help make that happen. Just promise me."

He maneuvered into a position where he could look down on her. "I promise with all my heart that I will solve this and do my best to get us out of this mess alive and well."

"Good, because I couldn't live without you."

The door to their motel room blew inward. Darwin ducked his head and wrapped his right arm over his wife. No debris entered the bathroom.

"Ho, ho, ho, Santa's come to pay a visit bearing gifts. I see someone lives here, but I don't see any stocking by the fireplace." The man's voice changed to a deeper, gravelly moan. "Where are my little children?" he asked in an accent.

They stayed down. Footsteps approached.

"There you are, my little munchkins. Come on, out of the tub. Bath time is over."

Darwin moved first. The man was dressed conservatively in khaki slacks, a sports jacket, and black dress shoes. What struck Darwin was the police badge dangling from his neck on a chain.

"Come on, let's go," the guy said, gesturing with the business end of a double-barreled weapon.

"We're coming."

"Shut up. No talking. I do the talking."

Darwin nodded and made sure the guy saw the nod. He stepped out of the tub slowly and helped Rosina out. They stood beside the bathtub a moment later, hands raised shoulder height, waiting for instructions.

"Empty your pockets. Remove everything, but easy does it."

The guy's nose showed signs of alcohol abuse. His teeth were stained from years of smoking, and his eyes were watered as if he were on the verge of tears.

Darwin lowered his right hand, reached into the pocket of his shorts, and pulled the inside of his empty pocket outward. Then he did the same on the left.

Rosina didn't have pockets in her black pants.

"Don't fuck with me. Pull out your weapons. Place them in the bathtub behind you. Stop fuckin' around."

The guy's gun hand shook from strain.

Darwin pointed at his mouth.

"The weapons are in your mouth?"

He shook his head. He pointed at his mouth again and used his hand to illustrate talking.

"Oh, you want permission to talk?"

Darwin nodded.

"Talk then."

"A moment ago, you said no talking."

"I did? What do you wanna say?"

"I have no weapons."

He snuck a peek at Rosina. Her face was pale, but behind her eyes, he could tell she was thinking.

"Bullshit, you have no weapons. And stop looking at her. I

know how married couples talk with their eyes. Now, one more time, pull out your fucking knives."

The cop's breath smelled of cigarettes in the confined bathroom. A waft of tobacco and whiskey hit Darwin's nose. That alone made Darwin want to throw up.

"I'm serious. I. Do. Not. Have. Any. Weapons."

"Fuck you. There's no way I'm believin' that shit. They don't call you The Blade for nothing. I heard what you can do. Breaking people's necks with your bare hands, knifing people in the face. Jamming pens in people's necks. You're a legend, Darwin. You singlehandedly killed the Harvester. There are not many men who could do that. Now, dump the weapons, or I shoot you. It's that simple."

"I got lucky with Sorrow."

"Tell that to Fuccini. Oh wait, you can't. You killed him, too." He cleared his throat. "Stop wasting my time and dump the weapons."

Darwin patted his waist and did a half circle to show he concealed nothing.

"The look on your face says you're not bluffing." The cop grinned. "I can't believe this. The Blade doesn't have a knife on him. Must be my lucky day." He backed up and grabbed the chair Rosina had sat on ten minutes before. "Come out of the bathroom."

The cop walked the chair to the broken front door and sat on it backward, resting his gun and arm on the back.

"Sit on the bed closest to the bathroom."

They did as they were told.

"Now, Darwin, since you're the one I'm most worried about, take off your clothes."

"What—"

"You fucking heard me," he shouted, his voice booming like he had a bullhorn attached to it. "Do it now." Something on the weapon in his hand clicked.

Darwin lifted his large T-shirt over his head and let it fall behind him. He undid his shorts and stood to let them fall at his ankles. With both hands out at his sides, he did a half-turn to reveal no hidden weapons.

"Those, too. I'm not gay, but I gotta look."

Darwin glanced at Rosina and then dropped his boxers.

"Okay. Get dressed."

Darwin lifted the boxers and shorts, setting them back in place. He grabbed his T-shirt and dropped it over his head.

"Your turn," the cop said, gesturing with the end of the gun at Rosina.

"Now, wait a minute," Darwin said.

The cop jumped from the chair and rushed Darwin. He jammed the shotgun up under Darwin's chin and shoved him onto the bed, physically restraining him.

"Little honey," the cop said to Rosina. "Undress right now and show me all your pretty parts or your husband will lose his *fucking* head. Just so we're clear, I'd prefer you leave your clothes on. That way, I can kill your husband, and then I get to be the one to take your clothes off." He looked down at Darwin. "Sorry, no offense, but I don't like anyone watching me with a woman."

"It's okay, Darwin," Rosina said. "I'll do it."

The barrel made it hard for Darwin to swallow. Breathing was almost impossible with the extra weight of the asshole on him. He worried that any move would make the guy fire the weapon and splatter his brains against the headboard.

His anger boiled up. He nudged an arm for position. The shotgun pressed against him harder, jamming his tongue to the top of his mouth. Everything in his being screamed to roll the guy off and break every bone in his body. But the drunk on top of him had the gun in a position that made it almost impossible for him to move without being shot.

Rosina had removed the purple top and unclasped her bra. She slid her black pants down and, without pause, lowered her white panties.

With his wife humiliated and standing absolutely naked in front of the cop, it made him want to tear the guy in half. But Rosina had asked him not to kill any more cops.

The guy's breath stank like a dead raccoon had curled up in his mouth. If he didn't get off soon, Darwin would have to shove him off or die from the fumes.

The cop kept his attention riveted on Rosina's body. "A very nice, cute little body. Nice tits." He looked back at Darwin, his face three inches away. "You are one lucky sonofabitch."

Then he pushed hard and got back to his feet. Darwin took in a long, deep breath and waited to see if the guy would touch his naked wife.

"Okay, fun's over. Get dressed. I'll play with you later. We have to move." He shook his head and laughed. "I cannot get over the luck. I picked up The Blade, and he isn't armed." The cop looked at Darwin on the bed. "I actually thought I was going to have to shoot you in this fleabag, fuck motel. Look at you. You're nothing. How the hell did you take out the Fuccini Family?"

Darwin didn't answer him as he helped Rosina get dressed. What surprised him was her strength. Not a single tear escaped her during the entire ordeal.

"Now, let's move. There's someone I want you to meet before you die. The man you're going to meet happens to live thirty minutes from here. He's got a seriously great idea the both of you might like."

23

Carson was getting nowhere. Most of the files on the Kostases had been sealed. Other than rumors, only a few people knew what actually happened to them and the Fuccinis all those months ago. One of them was a biker named Richard H. He now spent his days in a safe house, but no one was letting Carson in on where that was located.

The only other person with any knowledge of Darwin was Greg Stinsen, who had worked with the men that were murdered at the safe house. Since the files were empty and no one was talking to Carson, he'd decided to wait for Greg to show up in Jacksonville. Greg was due on a private jet from Washington that evening.

Carson would be waiting for him, and Greg would tell him everything he knew whether he wanted to or not. Greg would help in the investigation no matter how much he liked the Kostas kid because they were on the same team and they were hunting a killer. Once a man kills a federal agent, as Darwin had done, no one is safe.

Carson checked his watch. He still had two hours until Greg touched down in Jacksonville.

He rustled up the files on his desk, placed them neatly off to one corner, and stood, pushing his chair away with the backs of his knees. As the afternoon turned to evening, the Jacksonville Bureau office was still quite busy and would be until they apprehended Darwin. That many agents killed in a single event kept the office jumping.

He stepped away from his desk, walked out the main doors, and headed for his car. When he got in and turned it on, he realized just how angry he was. Five federal agents were beaten and killed by one man. And no one will talk about Darwin because his file is sealed.

"What the fuck is wrong with this world?"

His cell phone startled him.

"Hello," he snapped.

"Just thought you should know," Rudy said.

"What?"

"A motel north of that gas station that Darwin hit has been shot up pretty bad. The clerk said he was asleep. He woke up when the shotgun went off."

"Shotgun?"

"Yeah, apparently he had one room rented to a couple who paid cash—a couple he just saw on the news. Three rooms got hit. The motel clerk called in and said it was like the shooter had randomly shot into motel rooms. This guy sounds really fucked."

"How come this is the first I'm hearing about this?"

"Local authorities took the call and are responding. I have all our guys out looking for that pickup truck. We thought Darwin was long gone. Who would have guessed he grabbed a room a few miles from the gas station?"

"What's the name of the place?"

"The Sleep On Inn."

"I know the one."

Carson tossed his phone onto the passenger seat and squealed his tires as he drove away from the federal building.

"I got you, Darwin, you sick fuck."

He leaned across the seats and opened the glove box. After another glance out the windshield, he retrieved his unregistered gun. A Taurus PT145. Made in Brazil, his came with a blued finish, a ten-round magazine, and a double-action trigger. A wonderful killing machine, it weighed just over twenty-two ounces. The serial number had been shaved off. The gun had disappeared from the evidence room two years ago.

Carson smiled to himself as he eased the Taurus into its holster.

"I have a surprise for you, Darwin," he said out loud. "There will not be a courtroom, no jail cell where you would serve your time. That's for the crooks, the rapists, and all the rest of the bad guys. No, for you, Darwin, there's only one way." He slammed his hand against the steering wheel. "You will die by my hand, you worthless piece of *fuck*. You will bleed, and I will be your judge and jury, and when I'm done, I will shoot your fucking wife in the face. How do you like that?"

Carson turned on his siren and added weight to his foot.

24

THE COP HAD ORDERED them into the back of an unmarked cruiser. The doors were locked on the outside, with Plexiglas separating them from the driver.

Along with his spirits, the sun had dropped far enough to be lost behind low-level clouds. After getting underway, Darwin held Rosina's hand as she stared out the window at the passing scenery.

Rosina turned to him. "I saw his badge, but I don't think he's taking us to a police station."

"You may be right."

"What are you talking about back there?" the cop asked. "No talking."

"Stop the car," Darwin said.

"Fuck you."

"You don't want us to talk, so pull over and make us stop talking. Otherwise, mind your own fucking business."

They had nothing to lose. If the driver wanted to get him to stop talking to his wife, he would have to get out of his seat and do something about it. If the cop were sent to kill them, then he would've already done it.

"Just keep quiet. I don't want to hear your bullshit."

"Rosina, I don't want to worry you, but this looks bad. We'll have to make a break for it when we get a chance."

"We need to piece together who's behind everything. We both know it isn't Fuccini. He's dead. And it's not the feds themselves."

"Why do you say that?"

"I've been thinking. They wouldn't send two FBI agents over to the safe house to kill three other FBI agents. If it were the feds, those guys would've staged our deaths, and it'd be all over."

The driver applied the brakes. Darwin scanned the area outside his window and saw a sign for the Markville Family Funeral Home on the left side of the two-lane highway.

"I know all those answers," the driver said as he turned right and started up what looked like a driveway away from the funeral home.

"Then tell us. Who's behind all this?"

"In time, in time."

Trees lined each side of the lane as it wound left and right. Darwin watched it unfold as best he could with the limited light left from the sun. He had broken out in a sweat, thinking about how dark it would be in the car's back seat if the guy didn't get them where they were going soon.

Darwin hated that he'd come out of his childhood with two phobias. One was *aichmophobia*, a fear of sharp or pointy objects like needles or knives. Rosina knew this about him. That's why she'd knocked the knife set off the kitchen counter back at the safe house—so Darwin would go crazy and attack the guy at their breakfast table.

The other phobia was *achluophobia,* a fear of darkness. He hated the dark. He had to drive with the interior light on if he was out after the sun went down. When eating out at restaurants, he ate with spoons or plastic cutlery.

The car came to a halt in front of a huge water fountain. Whoever owned the house they were visiting had to be seriously rich. The sprawling grounds were manicured and perfect, with bushes and flowers lining each walkway. Everywhere he could see, tiny lights under the foliage made him think of a landing strip.

The five-car garage was larger than any house Darwin had ever lived in. Even though the sun had dropped far enough to leave only a purple hue in the sky, bright lights illuminated the front of the house, designed to enhance its beauty.

The water fountain filled the windshield. A mermaid sat, leaning on a rock, water spouting from her mouth in torrents. It reminded Darwin of the one in Copenhagen, Denmark.

The driver exited the car and disappeared around the edge of the fountain.

"What're we going to do?" Rosina asked.

"Don't know yet."

"Just make sure, whatever it is, you don't get shot."

"I won't, honey. It'll work out."

"You should find a way to call Richard H. I'm sure he'd help. Maybe he could send a few guys over."

"He's still recovering from the bullets he received the last time he helped us. I'm supposed to be sending back a piece of his manuscript later today. I hope he doesn't think I bailed on him."

"Darwin, seriously, he'll see what's happening on the news.

He'll know we're on the run."

"True," Darwin said and then thought of something else. "Maybe I could call Greg."

"Do that. As soon as we get to a phone."

The driver came back around the corner with men behind him. Big men, all carrying large weapons, hung on straps over their shoulders. Darwin did a quick count. Eight men, plus the driver.

"What the hell is this?" Darwin grabbed Rosina's hand. "Listen, honey, think on your feet and follow my lead."

Rosina pulled him in and kissed him on the lips, hard and fast. "You're everything I could've asked for."

The doors ripped open in unison, and the tips of long guns jammed in each side.

"Out," someone ordered.

Slowly, Darwin and Rosina got out of the back seat of the police cruiser and stood on opposite sides.

"Why is it called 'cold-blooded' murder when humans are warm-blooded?" Darwin asked.

The guy holding a weapon at Darwin's forehead frowned. "What?"

"Nothing," Darwin said. He lowered his voice and talked through his nose to sound like Darth Vader. "Take us to your leader."

The guy glanced at the driver. "Is this the guy that Frankie told you to go get?"

"That's him. Darwin and his wife, Rosina."

The gunman looked back at Darwin. "You gotta be fucking kidding me. This is the guy that took out the Fuccinis? No way. I don't believe it."

Darwin looked at his shoes. "You know, I'm getting sick and

tired of everyone underestimating me." He looked back at the gunman and stared into his eyes. "I killed the Harvester of Sorrow. I killed Vincenzo Fuccini and his father and many of the men he had working for him. They're all gone. You should have a little more respect for what I've done. This body is a disguise." Darwin waved his arms up and down the length of his sides.

The guy with the gun stepped back. "Careful."

"Darwin," Rosina said from the other side of the car. "Don't hurt them. They're just doing their jobs. Let's at least meet who they've brought us to meet."

The cop stepped closer and nodded at Darwin. "What are you talking about, disguise?"

"Under this lovely pair of shorts and this large T-shirt is a midget ninja always selling myself short."

The cop closed his eyes for a brief moment. An unlit cigarette dangled from his lips. "What?"

The gunman laughed. "I get it. He's a comedian. Canada has lots of them. John Candy, Jim Carrey, Michael J. Fox."

The cop looked at the gunman. "You're fucked, too. Michael J. Fox isn't a comedian. He was that guy in *Back to the Future*."

"Don't say I'm *fucked* ever again."

The gunman moved his aim slightly.

"Threaten me with that weapon, and I will shove it up your ass so far you'll be putting a straw in the barrel to drink."

"Okay, okay," a man shouted from behind them. "Enough of this. Bring them inside."

The gunman sneered at the cop but stepped back, giving Darwin room to walk.

"Let's go."

Darwin headed around the front of the cruiser and met up with

Rosina. Together, surrounded by eight gunmen and a cop, they approached the front of the huge manor.

He counted sixteen windows in the front of the house, with two of them an entire floor high. As they approached the stairs that led to the two massive wooden front doors, he saw the man who had spoken moments before.

The man standing on the front steps had a barrel chest, a slim goatee, and a physique that shouted muscle.

"Good evening," he said.

His greeting reminded Darwin of Dracula welcoming guests to his castle.

"Come," the man said as he opened the front doors.

The foyer was massive, with two sets of stairs winding up in a half circle on either side. Darwin saw money in everything he set his eyes on, from the Afghan carpets to the crown molding.

He took it all in with a sense of hope. Whoever had the money to own a home like this couldn't only profit from illegal activities. Eventually, they would have gotten caught. Living outside the law and enjoying the comforts of a house like this would be too risky.

Crime doesn't pay this well, does it?

He glanced at Rosina, winked, and smiled to reassure her.

They entered a hallway and started for the back of the house. At the end of the long hallway, it opened to the rear, where Darwin was shocked again. An Olympic-sized pool had two bikini-clad girls frolicking around with a beach ball. To the left, about twenty meters from the pool, at the gates of a tennis court. On the right was a large square that resembled a chess or checkers game board but was life-sized. Exterior lights illuminated the entire area in amber.

Lounge chairs were spread around the circumference of the

pool. The man leading them moved toward the checkerboard and sat in a large, leather, padded office chair. He motioned to his right, where Darwin saw another such chair.

"Darwin, come, sit beside me." The man turned to his guards. "Take Rosina to one of the lounges."

Darwin gave Rosina a nod, and they separated, sitting in their designated spots over a dozen meters apart. He scanned the back of the property. A fence, at least twenty feet tall, lined the perimeter.

More armed men appeared guns slung over their shoulders. It didn't look like there were too many escape routes. The large man beside him leaned back and looked Darwin up and down. He had a half smile on his face like the other half of his lips were immobile.

"So, we finally meet," the man said.

"Yes, we do," Darwin said. "But I didn't get your name."

"Frankie Gambino," he said and leaned forward, his hand extended. "Pleased to meet you."

Darwin took the man's hand. Gambino's grip was like getting his hand caught in a car door. He made an impassive face, his own grip intense.

"Can you tell me why we're here?" Darwin asked.

"Sure. I sent for you because I had to meet the man who finished the job for me."

"I'm not sure I understand."

The cop who brought them here shuffled his feet and cleared his throat. Gambino looked over at him, and the cop averted his gaze.

"Don't move," Gambino said to their driver. "You're staying for the game. Got it?"

The cop nodded and sat down in a nearby chair.

Gambino turned back to Darwin. "I'm sure you're aware of a certain meeting that took place many months ago in an airplane hangar on the outskirts of Toronto between different powerful families in that area."

Darwin nodded.

"Of course, you were there in your Ford Mustang. You *accidentally* killed Vincenzo. Then, in Rome, you took out more of Fuccini's men and, finally, back to the hangar where you and your biker friends killed the Fuccini Family boss."

"Most of that was luck."

Gambino laughed and held his stomach, acting as if it hurt. On cue, all the gunmen laughed with him. Gambino slowed and then stopped laughing. The men surrounding him became silent.

"I'm serious," Darwin pleaded. "They kept coming after me. I was just defending myself."

Gambino held up his meaty hand. "You're not on trial here. You don't have to defend yourself. For whatever reason, they're all gone now, and you're the man who aided them in their hasty retreat from this shitty world. Am I right so far?"

"Yeah, but—"

He moved his hand up again, cutting Darwin off. "Simple yes or no would do. Are you Darwin Kostas, the man who has been put into an FBI safe house for your protection because of the high-level killings that took place a few months ago?"

Darwin nodded. "Yes."

"Okay, that's why I sent those two assholes to get you."

"What two assholes?"

"Nick and Lee, the two agents who fucked it up. They were sent to kill the three men watching you and bring you to me. But instead, as I understand it, you killed them. I'm fascinated by that. Tell me, how'd you do it? How do you kill so easily?"

"I don't kill easily."

Gambino leaned back in his chair and clasped his hands together, resting them in his lap. "You know, I'm not really into laughing right now. Answer my questions. Converse with me. Man to man, I don't mind a little ribbing from someone I know, but I don't know you, and we are talking in front of all my men. Don't try to embarrass me because I'll win. I always do."

Darwin nodded, his stomach dropping another foot. His mind raced, but there was nothing he could do. He had to play along.

"I sent for you for two reasons. One, I wanted to thank you for finishing the job I had started when I tried to execute everyone at that meeting in the hangar. Two, I wanted to find out who hired you. Why did you go after the Fuccinis?"

"I am a Canadian boy, born and bred. I watch hockey and drink beer." He grabbed his small belly. Just recently, it had started to slip over his waistline. "And I want to live a peaceful and quiet life. No one hired me. I didn't know the Fuccinis before that night. I don't do well in the dark, so I was driving with the interior light on when I hit Vincenzo. It was purely an accident. Nothing else."

Gambino started clapping. "Nice speech." He lowered his hands to his lap. "Now for the truth. I warned you a moment ago. No fucking around. What you just said is impossible, absolutely and utterly. If that were true, why did you fly to Rome, willingly walk into their hands, and then attack the Fuccini building? Why did you then fly back to Toronto and drag Fuccini to that hangar and kill him where you killed his son? It looks like execution to me, and I know a lot about that. Appears well-planned, too. Also, a touch of revenge, which I also know something about. I heard you had help. A biker gang? The FBI? Come on, Darwin Kostas, if that's your real name, tell me who you are and who your employers are." Gambino waved his arm out toward his guards. "I don't have to threaten you. I won't go into what will happen if you continue to lie. We're bigger than that. Just tell me what I want to know."

Darwin swiveled his chair until he was face to face with Gambino. Armed men stepped closer. "I *am* telling you the truth," he said in his most serious voice. "What you've heard has been filtered and made to sound wild and crazy. I don't work for anybody unless you consider my publisher an employer, and last time I checked, Amazon has killer books. Still, they aren't employing their authors to execute members of the mafia."

Gambino nodded. "I checked you out. I saw your books online. Nice job. Who does your covers?"

"My wife is a graphic designer."

Gambino turned and gestured at Rosina. "Great covers."

She waved a hand in thanks.

Gambino leaned his elbows on his thighs and stretched closer to Darwin. "You have to understand something. When one man goes up against the Fuccinis and has the kind of success you had, it causes concern. What if that man decided that the Gambinos needed to go? What if that man started a war between me and rival families? Do you see where I'm going with this? I needed to meet you to see for myself. After everything I heard, you don't look anything like I pictured. And where did you get those shorts?"

Darwin looked down at his lap. "You know, I have to tell you, I'm really getting tired of people thinking I'm some professional hitman. My wife and I were in trouble. I handled the situation. That's all. It's what any husband would do."

"Like what Hernandez did."

"Hernandez? Who's that?"

Gambino motioned to a guard out by the pool who was watching the two girls as they swam—a lot quieter now, the beach ball all but forgotten as the tension between Gambino and Darwin increased.

"Take those two out of the pool and keep them out of sight. Bring in the entire Hernandez family and get them in position."

The guard barked an order, and the two girls, who couldn't be more than eighteen, exited the water and followed him out of sight.

Gambino continued. "I ordered an execution in Las Vegas six months ago. The man I had ordered killed had been gambling with my money, borrowing more, and getting so far in debt that I knew he'd never pay it back. I worked out a deal and secured most of my money through his business assets in the event of his death. He agreed. But I still didn't have my money, so I had him killed to get back what was due to me. In the rear access area of his hotel, my four men showed up and executed him. Mr. Hernandez saw the whole thing. He knew the faces of my men. A half-hour before, they'd been playing high-stakes blackjack at his table. Hernandez *was* a great card dealer, but now he's dead."

Sweat gathered on Darwin's forehead, and his hands wouldn't stop shaking. He glanced at Rosina. She looked somewhat composed, but he could tell she was terrified of what was about to happen.

"Why would Mr. Hernandez be dead?" Darwin asked.

"The police arrived and asked if anyone saw anything.

Hernandez was the only witness. He told the cops everything. He gave them the identity of my men from the casino cards the casinos give out to add points to your account as you gamble. That's what cops have to get warrants for, but Mr. Hernandez was really helpful. Signed a statement and was prepared to tell his story in court. But I couldn't let that happen. My men are too valuable. Two weeks later, Mr. Hernandez was found missing his hands, his feet, and his head. That was three weeks ago. They're still trying to figure out whose torso they found in the Grand Canyon. They're also trying to figure out what happened to his entire family. Extended family, too." Gambino gestured toward the pool. "The whole lot of them have been our guests here for the past three weeks. Funny, huh? The investigators think the Hernandez family skipped town. No one suspects where they actually are."

A woman followed the guard around the pool. Behind her were three girls, differing in age, two boys in their teens, an old man walking with a cane, and three women in their fifties. After a brief pause, four more adults walked out, two Asians and two with darker skin, making Darwin think of India. In total, he counted fourteen people standing by the pool.

"Set them up on the board. Split them evenly, seven on each side."

A group of guards stepped away to help make sure everyone was where they were supposed to be. Darwin had no idea what he was about to witness, but he was pretty sure he wouldn't enjoy it.

"Take the shirts off the white team."

Guards stepped in and ripped the shirts off the people standing on the right. The two older women didn't protest. They appeared resigned to their fate. But the teenage girl protested. Two guards jumped on her, tore her shirt off, and lifted her back to her feet. One of the guards held her while the other whispered something in her ear.

Whatever he said made her blanch. She stood stock still in her pants and bra as the men eased away. Seven men and women stood fully clothed on the left, and seven men and women, some as young as fifteen from what he could tell, stood on the right with no shirts on.

"We're going to have us a game of human checkers. We don't have the full twenty-four pieces, but this'll do. We'll assume the other five pieces have already been taken off the board. Are you ready?"

"Ready for what?" Darwin asked.

"To play."

"Uhm, I haven't played checkers in years. I'll pass."

Gambino nodded.

A guard rushed in close and drove a fist into Darwin's stomach, knocking the wind out of him. Darwin gasped and bent over until his face hung over his knees, trying to gather any air back into his lungs. For a brief moment, he thought he would vomit.

"Darwin, you don't get the option not to play. Do you understand?"

Darwin barely heard him. He was still trying to breathe.

"I asked you a question. Do *not* make me ask it again."

Darwin pushed himself up with a hand on each knee, breathing better with every inhale. He nodded. "What happens if I win?"

"Here are the rules. Play me human checkers, and I guarantee, if you win, you will be blindfolded, driven out of my home, and delivered to a destination of your choice. Deal?"

"You serious?" he asked, finally returning his breathing to normal.

"Of course I am." He looked over at the fidgeting cop. "Bob, tell him I'm serious. You know me after all the years I've employed you. Can you honestly say that when I guarantee something that I come through?"

"It's true," the cop said. "He comes through."

"Good enough for you?" Gambino asked.

Darwin nodded.

"I need to hear it. Since we won't have a written contract, a verbal one will have to suffice. So say something."

"I agree."

"There will be consequences if you decide to stop playing. Are we clear?"

Darwin nodded again, breathing much easier, even though his stomach ached.

Gambino waited. Over thirty people, some standing with weapons, others standing on the large checkerboard, stood silent.

"Oh, shit, sorry. We're clear."

"Good." Gambino turned to the people on the board. "Marcus, move the old man up one and to the right."

Darwin watched from his elevated position as the old man with the cane was maneuvered into place.

"Your turn, Darwin."

"Okay, the Asian man. I want him to move onto the right square against the side."

What the hell am I doing? This is ludicrous. He snuck a glance at Rosina. She didn't look well.

A guard stepped in and moved the Asian man.

"Place the man with the cane to the right, in front of the Asian man on Darwin's team."

After that move was completed, Gambino looked at Darwin, expectation on his face. "Well? You know what to do."

"What?"

"In checkers, at least the version we play in my home, the rules state that when presented with a jump, you *have* to make the jump."

Darwin looked back at the board. "Okay, jump the old man with my Asian player."

Two guards stepped in, removed the old man with the cane to the side of the board where he stood by himself, and got Darwin's Asian player into place.

Then, half the old man's head disappeared. His cane flipped in the air when his body got hit, and for what felt like a minute, the old man's body stood, defying gravity while his legs shook. In an animated version of a mime falling down the side of an imaginary wall, the old man slumped and then dropped sideways, his head leaking out brain matter mixed with chucks of skull and blood.

"What the fuck!" Darwin shouted as he stood from his comfortable chair. All the responsibility fell on his shoulders. He had moved the Asian. He had made the jump. Therefore, by his actions, he had killed the old man.

Two of the remaining players moved off the board to throw up. Guards surrounded them instantly. Guns were raised and aimed at the remaining thirteen players, who seemed to all be crying, their faces displaying their fear and panic, paralyzed by the weapons trained on them.

Darwin looked at Rosina. Her face was white as she stared at the people on the board. He felt an overwhelming need to be with her. To hold her. To protect her. He'd let her down. She watched him participate in a game that had resulted in an innocent man's death.

Life was not a game, and a man like Frankie Gambino should not be that powerful.

Gambino sat just a few feet away, smiling like someone had told him a good joke.

"Do it," Gambino said. "Attack me. Try to kill me. I know you want to. I know you hate me. Go ahead, see how far you get."

Darwin wasn't having trouble breathing anymore. Torrents of air rushed through his nose as he contemplated death. He knew he wouldn't live if he attacked Gambino, but what pleasure he would have with Gambino's eyes crushed under his thumbs.

"Tell me," Gambino continued. "Tell me who sent you to take out Fuccini, and we'll stop this nonsense."

"No one did."

Gambino turned to his men. "Set it up like it was. It's my move, and I'm already down a man." He looked back at Darwin. "Sit down. Now."

Darwin eased back into his chair, his gaze moving from Rosina to the checkerboard. The old man had stopped twitching, and the blood from his open head wound had slowed.

"Take that young girl and move her up one and to the right."

Guards stepped in and did so. One guard stayed with the girl as she had difficulty standing. Her knees shook so badly that Darwin wondered if she would faint.

"Your turn," Gambino said.

"I'm not playing anymore."

"Oh, yes, you are."

"No, I'm not. I will not actively partake in the murder of these people."

Gambino lifted a finger to his mouth and started biting a nail with the indifference of a man at a coffee shop discussing baseball. Darwin understood he was dealing with a man who defined the word insane.

"I explained there would be consequences if you stopped playing."

"What do you expect me to do?" Darwin asked, his anger coming through in this voice.

"I expect you to play my game, and now that you've refused, I have one consequence that must be dealt with first. Then, I'm sure you'll be delighted to continue our little game of checkers." He motioned toward Rosina and the men watching her. "Bring her over here."

"No!" Darwin shouted, standing back up. "Don't touch her."

Several guards moved in on Darwin.

"Can't you see the odds are stacked against you? Are you that stupid? There's nothing you can do. You sealed your fate, Mr. Kostas, and your wife's fate. Just sit back down and enjoy the last game of checkers and the last show of your life because it is truly over for you, Darwin."

25

Carson Dodge stopped in front of the motel office at the Sleep On Inn. He had an hour before Stinsen's plane landed. That gave him enough time to talk to the motel clerk and then head to the airport.

Darkness had settled on the area. The middle word in the motel's sign had burnt out. All it said was 'Sleep Inn' with a long space in the middle.

Two police cruisers were parked in front of the rooms at the end with the damaged doors. Carson saw Rudy talking to someone on a cell phone by the check-in counter. Carson entered the office and spoke to Rudy as if he wasn't on the phone. "What do we have here? Tell me what you got and do it fast because I haven't much time."

"I'll call you back," Rudy said into the phone and snapped it shut. "All we have is the clerk who checked them in. He said he recognized them from the news on the TV after they were settled into their room. A shotgun blast has hit three doors, but that's it. Nothing else so far."

"No bodies?"

"None."

"No other damage?"

"Nope."

"Something's not right. Think about it, Rudy." Carson watched Rudy for a prolonged moment, then said, "Did you think about it?"

"Yeah."

"Anything?"

"Nope."

Carson shook his head. "Where's the clerk?"

"Over there." Rudy pointed.

What looked like a bedraggled junkie sat in the corner, bouncing his legs up and down, eyes darting left and right.

"Hey," Carson shouted.

"Hey, back," the clerk said.

Carson started over to him. "Why do you look so nervous? Need a fix?"

"No, I don't do that stuff."

Carson stood over the clerk and leaned into the wall. "You don't take drugs of any sort?" he asked in a suspicious tone.

"Only prescription drugs, man. I wouldn't touch that other stuff."

"Let's say I believe you. Assuming you have no withdrawal symptoms, tell me why you look like a junkie waiting for the next fix? Because if that isn't it, you're really nervous about something."

"Look, mister, I don't do drugs."

"Then what are you nervous about?"

"Other than the fact that someone just shot up my motel? You mean other than that? You know, random acts of gun violence? Maybe you see it all the time with your job, but up here, this far from Jacksonville, we don't get that kind of noise."

"You'd be surprised at how little gun violence we actually see. Ain't that right, Rudy?"

"Yup, that's right."

The clerk adjusted himself, twiddled with his hands, and bounced his legs again.

"I'm going to ask you a few questions, and I would like honest answers. I get those honest answers, and I'm out of your hair. Deal?"

"Those other cops already asked me a bunch of questions. Go talk to them. They'll tell you what you want to know. And move all the police cruisers off my parking lot. No wonder the motel is empty tonight. Nobody gonna rent a room at cop headquarters."

"Number one, I'm not a cop. I'm Special Agent Carson Dodge with the FBI. Number two, the motel is empty because it's a dirty motel, probably rife with cockroaches and termites, and three, you will answer my questions, or you'll piss me off, and I'll be forced to shoot you."

The clerk stopped bouncing his leg and looked up at Carson. "You threatening me, Cop?"

"Yes." Carson leaned in close and whispered, "Five fellow FBI agents were slaughtered like fucking pigs in an abattoir this morning. The man who did it was in your motel just hours ago. It is my life's duty, no, my *American* duty, to locate this maniac, and you had him here hours ago as a *fucking* guest. If you have answers that I need but refuse to give them to me, you're no better than the fucking puke who killed my men. In fact, you're colluding with him by helping him to hide. That tells me that you're on his side, and anyone helping that asshole gets arrested for obstruction of justice. So, questions and answers, or the night in jail?"

The clerk nodded, sweat beading up on his forehead.

Carson stepped back and cleared his throat. "Who kidnapped your guests?"

"I don't know—"

Carson slapped the clerk's face in mid-sentence. "I said," he shouted, "don't lie."

Rudy came up behind him. "Hey, Carson, take it easy. The kid already told us everything."

"No, he didn't. Not everything. Go back and watch the door. If anyone comes to the door, tell them the clerk went to the hospital."

Rudy hesitated.

Carson looked over his shoulder. "Do. It. Now," he said through his teeth.

The clerk held his cheek, which was already turning red.

"Let's start again." Carson lifted his hand, closed it into a fist, and paused. "Who came and took the man you gave the room to?"

The clerk looked at Carson's face and then his fist. "It was a cop."

"Now we're getting somewhere," Carson said, lowering his fist. "Do you have a name?"

"No, but I can tell you he looked pretty bad. I can smell drunks from a mile away. This guy smokes like a chimney, and his nose looks pretty bad from all the alcohol—Rudolph-like. I should know. My dad was a drunk."

Carson turned to Rudy. "Sound like Bob Freska?"

Rudy nodded.

Carson turned back to the clerk. "What was his deal?"

"He gave me five hundred bucks. He said he wouldn't kill anybody and that I wasn't to worry. All I had to do was tell him the room number and then wait twenty minutes until after he left to call the police."

"What else?"

The clerk lowered his hand from his reddening cheek. Carson saw the length of his own fingers in red imprints on the guy's skin.

"He said he would make it look like I didn't inform him. That's why he shot two other doors first to make it look like he was trying to find them."

"Anything else?"

The clerk shook his head. "Nothing. I got the money, gave him the room number, heard the shots, and waited until after his car pulled out before I started the twenty-minute countdown."

Carson moved closer to Rudy. "Now, do you see what I mean when I said think about it? It didn't add up. If the gunman was just shooting randomly into motel rooms, he could've hit and wounded or killed Darwin. Or he could've killed innocents. But he intended to take them alive. Otherwise, we'd have two murders on our hands right now and not two missing persons. You would've found bodies when you got here and not empty rooms."

"But who would want to kidnap Darwin and his wife? And if Freska wanted to kill them, why not just kill them here and leave?"

"I don't know, but I'll find out. Call it in. I want a BOLO for Bob Freska, and they will report directly to me when they find him. Detain him if you have to, but find him. We have a two-hour window. Find him, Rudy. I'm more serious than terminal cancer."

Before Carson heard a reply, he walked out of the motel office, got in his car, and raced away en route to the airport.

26

GAMBINO BROUGHT ROSINA CLOSER. He had her sit ten feet in front of Darwin. Five guards surrounded Darwin, with one pointing his weapon at Darwin's temple.

"Now, Darwin," Gambino said. "This is how it's going to work. If you move more than one foot, I will have my guard use his weapon to behead you."

Darwin glared at him.

"Good. The first consequence will be a simple one. All I'm asking is that Rosina swallow one spoonful of cinnamon. That can't be that bad, now can it?"

Rosina nodded. "I'll do it."

"Will it just be cinnamon?" Darwin asked. "You're not going to add anything?"

"What, you don't trust me?"

"No."

"Fair enough. I'll have a spoon and a spice-rack-sized bottle of cinnamon delivered to us with its seal still on. Will that work?"

Darwin nodded.

Gambino motioned with his hand. "Get it for me," he said to one of the guards.

The people on the checkerboard were offered water. Two guards walked among them with a jug. Everyone averted their eyes from the old man's dead body not five feet from them.

The cop who brought them to Gambino's home sat off to the side, a cigarette between his lips. Gambino stared at the back of the cop's head. Then he looked at a nearby guard and tilted his head toward the cop.

The guard moved soundlessly behind the cop, lowered his weapon, and pulled the trigger. The sound was deafening.

The cigarette shot out of the cop's mouth and landed in the pool. The cop's head bounced back and forth on his shoulders a couple of times, and then he bent over, his head between his knees, as if he was in a safe position on a plane. The man had sustained a mortal wound.

Gambino turned his attention back to Darwin. "He was careless. The FBI has been investigating him for a few years, as I understand it. They were very close to apprehending him, meaning he would talk because he was a spineless snake. I can't have that." He glanced at the man who had just murdered the cop. "Take his body and tie it to the front of his car. Leave it a mile from the motel where he picked these two up and scrawled on the windshield, 'Death to all cops.' Got it?"

The guard nodded. "Consider it done." Other men came in to help. After a moment, the cop's body was gone, and a woman in an apron showed up with a bucket of water to start wiping up the blood.

The five men watching Darwin took turns holding their weapons at his temple as fatigue slowly set in.

Gambino clapped his hands twice. "Having fun yet?"

"No, not yet. That comes later."

"Whoa," Gambino said, turning in his seat. "I like you. Big words for a man in this sort of trouble. Maybe there is something to the rumors we heard about you."

Gambino's cell phone rang. He picked it up and hit a button. "Speak." He waited and then said, "It's done. He'll be a mile away from the motel soon … okay, got it … I did my part. You do yours."

He snapped the phone shut. "While we wait for the cinnamon, we should talk a little. I checked out what your name means. Kostas is Greek, and it means constant and steadfast. Usually, the Greeks use it as a first name, but who cares, right? I'd say that about describes you, doesn't it? Constant and steadfast."

Darwin didn't move or reply. He just stared at the psychopathic mobster sitting on his fancy chair.

"If it's the bodies you're worried about, don't be. I own the funeral home across the street. Not sure if you would've seen the sign on the way in."

"Markville Family Funeral Home. Yeah, I saw it."

"Good observation skills. I use that to eliminate all the bodies I seem to be disposing of lately. Our private cemetery has so many burials it's getting out of hand."

"I'm not surprised."

"You know, I'm not all bad. I'm a businessman. What we're doing here is just business."

Darwin nodded.

"I also have a collection of some of the most sought-after World War II memorabilia. Did you know that?"

"No, I didn't," Darwin said.

"In a warehouse, just over there." He pointed in the distance. "You can barely see the lights from here. I collect war machines and have them rebuilt as close to the original as I can. You wouldn't believe it. I have a Japanese Zero, fully intact and able to fly. I have an American Hellcat and a P-51D Mustang that can also fly. I take them out to air shows once or twice a year. One of my favorites is the German Stuka I snagged off a dealer a decade ago. The wings on the Stuka are quite amazing. Too bad we don't have the time to offer you a tour."

One of the older women in her fifties standing on the checkerboard with no shirt on had edged off the board as Gambino talked. When there was a pause in the conversation, she bolted for the perimeter fence. Even though it was too high, she ran anyway, no doubt in search of a gate or some other way out.

Four guns roared at the same time. The woman's back exploded in red, and she was temporarily lifted off her feet, flying forward in a grotesque ballet routine. She hit the grass hard and bounced once before stopping, arms and legs askew.

"Wow, that was exciting," Gambino said. "We get a runner every so often during one of our games." He turned to the group of men on his left. "Grab another pine box for her and bury her tonight across the street."

Darwin felt his bowels loosen and his insides adjust. He wasn't sure how much more he could take. Sure, he'd killed before, but that was life or death and in the moment of extreme anger. This was different. This was a slaughter.

Gambino turned to him. "Now, what was I saying? Oh yeah, my collection. The highlight is an authentic German Panther World War II tank. Still works great. I had it rebuilt, had new treads made, and even armed it. Did you know that four and sometimes five men operated inside those things? Sometimes, I see myself under attack by a rival family. I run for my tank and use it to repel the attack just as the Nazis did in World War II. I mean, I'd lose the house, but it's insured." He beamed, obviously proud of himself. Gambino was putting on a show.

Darwin saw their future at that moment. He saw they weren't just cornered; they were finished. If Gambino hadn't had a change of heart, they wouldn't see the outside of this mansion's walls again. The only thing the mobster couldn't take from him was hope, and he had that in abundance.

There has to be a way.

"I have a buyer for the tank," Gambino continued. "They're coming by this week to pick it up." Gambino looked down at his fingers and picked something from under a nail. "I'm going to miss my panther. Maybe one day I'll get another one."

The players still stood on their required squares. The armed men stood around where needed, weapons at the ready. Rosina sat, hands shaking, and waited for her spoonful of cinnamon.

A door opened behind them. Darwin wanted to turn to see who approached them, but the gun on his temple forbade it.

"Ahh, here we are," Gambino said. "The cinnamon."

A man came into Darwin's view carrying a small bottle of cinnamon and a tablespoon. He moved to Rosina and sat beside her.

"Rosina." Gambino leaned on the front of his chair. "All that's got to happen is you take one spoonful of the cinnamon and swallow it. When you've done that, we'll be able to move on. There will be no water. Are we clear?"

Rosina nodded.

"Okay, but I should warn you. When taken like this, cinnamon can feel a little spicy—even hot, so prepare yourself. Are you ready?"

"Yes," Rosina said.

Gambino nodded, and the man beside Rosina cracked open the safety seal on the bottle and poured cinnamon out onto the spoon. He handed the spoon to her, recapped the bottle, and stepped away.

"Wait," Darwin shouted. "Stop. Is there something you're not telling us?"

Gambino looked at him sideways. "You're too late to ask for a reprieve. You should have taken your turn. There are consequences. The only other option is a pine box for Rosina. Take your pick."

"Darwin, I'll do it. Everything's fine. It's only a little cinnamon. Even if things go bad, I'll swallow it, and it'll be over."

Darwin could see her strength and loved her for it. But he could also see her nerves as the hand holding the spoon shook.

He nodded, fear enveloping his entire nervous system.

Rosina lifted the spoon. Her eyes locked with Darwin's. In his eyes, he tried to convey his love for her.

She put the spoon in her mouth, cleared the cinnamon off it, and handed the empty spoon to the man who had brought it out.

The entire back terrace and pool area fell silent. Everyone watched.

Rosina's cheeks were puffed out like she was blowing up a balloon. Her eyes widened as Darwin watched her throat work to take on the cinnamon. Early signs of distress showed.

"This is great," Gambino said. "I've always wanted to see what happens to someone who tries this."

Rosina's eyes widened. She seemed about to panic.

"Water," Darwin said. "She needs water."

"I *said* no water. Swallow it dry."

Rosina coughed inside her mouth and couldn't hold it in. She opened her mouth to cough. A cloud of airborne cinnamon spewed out as she coughed again and again.

"That's called dragon breath," Gambino said. "I expected that."

Rosina hacked and tried to catch her breath. Nothing seemed to be working. Dark clumps of wet cinnamon hung from the inside of her lips. Her face turned a deeper red as she leaned over, holding her stomach.

"I can't watch this," Darwin said as he moved to get up.

Someone wrapped their arms around his shoulders and yanked him backward into a full-nelson hold, greatly limiting his ability to move.

"Come on," he shouted, his anger rising. "Give her water."

"That wasn't the deal. One spoonful of cinnamon, unaided."

Rosina was coughing so badly now that Darwin wondered if she'd start to bleed internally soon. She fell to one knee and then started to crawl along the concrete-tiled deck, coughing and gagging, droplets of brown cinnamon falling out of her mouth.

As she leaned up to get some air, her stomach let go. She vomited down her chin, onto her shirt, and down the front of her pants.

As horrible and humiliating as that was Darwin only hoped it dislodged whatever blockage was causing her to gag.

Gambino clapped his hands when she vomited, and he started shouting 'olè' like a matador.

Darwin shed a tear as his wife crawled. He wept because he

was powerless to save her and because it was his fault she was here in the first place. He struggled against the hands that held him, his vision clouding as tears flowed.

Gambino laughed louder as Rosina crawled on the concrete floor, searching for an elusive breath. Many of his men laughed along with him.

A desire to embrace hatred and live up to the moniker, *The Blade*, swept over him. He struggled again, loosening the hands behind his neck. Another man stepped in and drove a fist into Darwin's stomach, punching the air out of his lungs. He gasped and struggled to breathe, stars forming in his vision. After a few breaths, he saw what Rosina was crawling toward.

The pool.

When the guards realized it, they were too late. Rosina hopped and landed in the pool head first. For a brief moment, Darwin worried about her as breathing had proven difficult moments before entering the water. How was she expected to have enough air to be underwater? Was she going to drown?

After what felt like too long, Rosina surfaced and gasped. She coughed even harder and gasped again. Most of the cinnamon had washed away from her mouth area. Her shirt was cleaner but still stained from the stomach acids. Her face had gotten some color back. To his relief, she was coming around. She just needed water, and since no one offered a glass, she chose to put a little chlorine in her water—a life-saving move.

"Get her out of there and take her to one of the rooms in the house," Gambino said. "Have the maid clean her up and clean up the vomit." He clapped his hands.

The man holding him in a full nelson released his grip and stepped back. Darwin spun toward Gambino and glared at him.

Gambino slowed his clapping, then stopped, his hands suspended in the air.

"You have an expression of hatred on your face, Darwin. Would you like to kill me?"

Darwin's gaze didn't waver.

Gambino continued. "There are a lot of people in your position. I make enemies easy. Friends prove more difficult to make." He opened his arms wide. "But that's what these men are for. To control the desires of my enemies."

Darwin measured the distance and knew he could have his hands around Gambino's throat before bullets stopped his heart.

"Wasn't that a show?" Gambino asked. "Didn't you know that cinnamon doesn't dissolve in water? It sounds easy to swallow a spoonful, but it isn't. As soon as it's in your throat, it causes gagging—you want to regurgitate. It sucks all the moisture out of your mouth and clumps up. The risks are choking and an uncontrollable cough. I've even heard of people being hospitalized. One girl had a collapsed lung doing this same thing at home. It's all over YouTube. I've just never seen it live before. Very cool," he said, shaking his head. "Very cool."

Armed men standing around him nodded and smiled. Two of them echoed his words about how cool it was.

Darwin waited. There would be a moment. Soon.

"Now," Gambino said. "Shall we continue our game?"

"No."

"No? I'm afraid that's not an option."

"I will not play God. I will not indulge you with your twisted game of checkers."

"Okay. Fair enough. Johnson, Mackering," he pointed at two beefy guards. "Line everyone up to go back to their prison cells."

The guards stepped in and started putting everyone in a line near the back of the checkerboard, where it met the grass.

"If that's how you want it, you and I will move on to the next phase of our evening."

"Which is?"

"You'll see. Everyone, back to your posts. The game is over."

The men surrounding Darwin stepped away from him. He sat by himself, the closest guard a few feet away and moving farther.

Gambino got up and started toward his house.

The Hernandez family and the Asians were being lined up.

Armed men formed a row opposite them.

Darwin understood what they were doing, but it was too late for him to do anything. He felt a horror like nothing he'd ever felt before.

The six armed men brought their weapons down, aimed, and released a torrent of bullets. Darwin fell out of his chair as the Hernandez family was murdered. Every single human being in the line got hit. Only two stayed on their feet, bullet holes in their abdomens, gasping at the reality of what had become their end.

Darwin saw faces chewed up by the stream of weapons fire. The remaining two men fell to their knees in unison, a twisted performance straight out of a Rob Zombie outtake, their faces adorned with the reality of death, their bodies the evidence.

Finally, they fell to the grass, one after the other, as dead as the rest of the fourteen people.

Darwin lost his fight with his stomach, vomiting in a spray that almost hit the shiny black shoes of the guard eight feet away.

"You wanted the game to end," Gambino barked from the door of his home. "You ruined the fun tonight, Darwin Kostas. You also lost the game by forfeiting. Which means you don't get your freedom." He turned to face the guards. "Kill Darwin. Shoot him down like the fucking swine that he is."

Darwin lunged from the chair, almost toppling it over. With each step he got toward Gambino, he felt it a minor victory. He felt absolute insanity. Yet there was a power to it, a liberating rush that propelled his feet.

He was still seven feet from Gambino when a hired thug stepped between the two of them, aimed his weapon, and fired.

Darwin saw the recoil of the weapon before he shut his eyes. He felt the impact. It hit him in the center of the forehead, less than an inch above his eyes, snapping his head back.

He didn't get a chance to feel the second bullet as it hit him in the chest, a little left of center.

27

THE AIRPORT WAS TOO busy for the early evening. The hustle and bustle of travelers irritated Carson as he tried to get around people on his way to the arrivals screen.

He probably shouldn't be carrying his unregistered gun in the airport, and he forgot the flight number Greg Stinsen was supposed to be on. All he remembered was the time.

He looked at the little digital clock on the arrivals screen and saw that whatever plane Greg was coming in on would've landed ten minutes ago.

"Shit." He pounded a fist into his open palm.

A woman holding a child in her arms watched him, irritation on her face.

"What's your fucking problem?" he asked.

Her face changed to disgust, and she moved away.

On the board, he noticed that international flights all deplaned and entered the airport at certain gates, and domestic flights did the same. The three domestics were all coming in through gates D and E.

He ran off in search of gates D and E.

He found a small kiosk by the gates offering everything from books, newspapers, and gum to toothbrushes, tiny reading lights, and travel pillows. He bought a Red Bull and stood back by the gates to watch for Stinsen.

He'd seen Greg several times at the office over the past few months as Darwin and Rosina were processed and set up in their new home. Greg always reminded him of a goody-two-shoes. Either that or he had an unusual love for the Kostases because everything had to be just right. He oversaw their setup to the last detail.

Carson had even asked him once if he'd known Darwin before the Fuccini incident. Stinsen said that Darwin had saved the FBI a lot of undercover work, a lot of paperwork, and tons of money in the courts by offing the Fuccinis. The amount of money the government would spend housing Darwin and his wife would never come close to what he'd saved them. Stinsen just wanted the best for a couple who had been through hell and back.

The doors opened, and travelers piled into the terminal, hugging relatives as they went. Some blocked the doors. A security guard asked people to keep moving.

Finally, after a fifteen-minute wait, the doors opened, and Agent Stinsen emerged, looking haggard, his hair a mess, his face showing the years. He had a small carry-on bag in one hand as he walked right past Carson.

"Hold up," Carson said.

Stinsen stopped and turned around. "Oh, hey."

"I'm your ride."

"No, it's okay. I called ahead. I have a car waiting outside."

"Yeah, you do. My car."

Stinsen ignored Dodge and started away, dragging his carry-on.

"Special Agent Stinsen," Carson said as he hustled to keep up, "you're coming with me whether you like it or not."

"Oh yeah. News to me."

"We have five men down. Good men. And you're the only person who knows Darwin. This is my case, and I intend to find the prick and fix it. I need you, and you need me."

Stinsen stopped walking and turned to face Carson. "'Prick'? So you've decided he's guilty? Without any evidence or the aid of the system?"

"Are you saying there's another conclusion? I mean, if you are, tell me now."

Stinsen shook his head and turned away again. Carson grabbed Stinsen's shoulder and spun him back.

"Don't you fucking walk away from me," Carson said too loud. People slowed to watch. "Five good men were shot and killed like they were in someone's way. Families have lost brothers, fathers, sons, and husbands. These were men I worked with. The evidence we have so far leads to Darwin. You know him better than anybody at the Bureau. If you don't come willingly, I will have you assigned to me, and I'll make you wipe my *fucking* ass every chance I get."

Stinsen leaned in close and said, "Two things. One, *fuck*. And two, *you*. Are we clear?"

Carson felt an urge to raise his fist and slam it into the asshole's face. As his hand twitched, his cell phone rang. He grabbed it too fast, making Stinsen step back in defense.

"What?" he said into the phone.

"Bob Freska's dead."

"What?" he said, louder this time.

Stinsen remained beside him.

"We found him ten minutes ago about a mile from the Sleep On Inn Motel. He was shot in the back of the head and strapped to the hood of his car. Someone scrawled, 'Death to all cops' on the windshield. This Darwin kid is on a rampage."

"Okay, call me back when you have more." Carson hung up.

He glared at Stinsen. "Do you know what that was all about?"

"No idea, but I'm sure you will tell me."

"Rudy Earlton—you know the name—just called to tell me they found another one of Darwin's victims."

"How do you know this is Darwin's doing?"

"Bob Freska, a local degenerate cop we all know at the Bureau office, went to the motel where Darwin and his wife were holed up after stealing a pickup from a gas station a few miles down the road from their safe house. We have witnesses to corroborate what I just said. The motel clerk even talked to Bob when he came to fetch the Kostases. We couldn't reach him for the last hour and wondered why. Now we know. Freska was just found strapped to the hood of his car. He's been shot in the head, and there was a message on the windshield of his car. It said, 'Death to all cops.'" He paused to let it sink into Stinsen's thick skull. "We will get Darwin with or without your help. I suspect it'll be easier with you, and there's a chance he will make it out of this alive if you're around. Otherwise, I can't make any guarantees."

Special Agent Greg Stinsen looked along the corridor and then fixed his eyes back on Carson.

"Where's your car?"

28

ROSINA ROLLED OFF THE mattress and got to her feet. She paced the little room they'd put her in. She had heard the gunfire and the commotion and guessed what had happened. She didn't know if her husband had been hit but refused to believe Darwin could be dead. Not after all they'd been through.

There was nothing she could use to defend herself in the simple square room they put her in. It had four walls and a mattress, which was stained and beyond repair but softer than the floor.

Her hair sat heavily on her shoulders, wet from the pool. Even though she'd taken in half a dozen gulps of chlorinated pool water, she could still taste cinnamon on her breath. It would be a long time before she ever bought anything with cinnamon in it again.

The door to her room clicked open and almost banged into her. One of the guards entered the room, his eyes roving her body.

"A sweet young thing," he said. "Man, you're going to be fun."

"Just try. We'll see how much fun we have."

"Oh, don't you worry. We have whips and chains. Once you're tied up, all you can do is take what we give you."

"There's only enough room in my pants for one asshole. Sorry."

"Cute."

The guard eased aside to make room for the other men behind him. She counted seven in total. The seventh guard held two pairs of cuffs.

She wondered if she would be better off dead.

"You need this many men for widdle ol' me?"

The guards closest to her moved quickly. In seconds, her wrists and ankles were bound. In their eagerness to secure her, one of the men elbowed her in the mouth. They pushed her onto the mattress and stood back to survey their work.

She tasted blood. "You bastard. You cut my lip."

"Next time, I'll cut your face. Now, shut the fuck up. The boss wants to talk to you."

"What if I don't want to talk to him?"

One of the guards handed a black bag to the man talking to her. He looked in the bag, smiled, and pulled something out.

"This is a douche," he said, holding it up. "You're expected to shower in the morning and change those filthy clothes. No one will touch you with vomit on your shirt. Then you will use this douche to clean and prepare for your day. New douches will be provided throughout the day as needed." He reached inside the bag and pulled something else out. "This is an enema kit. You'll use one of these first thing in the morning as well. New enema kits will be provided daily. Do you understand what is required of you?"

There was no way she would do what they were asking. "I'd rather be dead."

"That can be arranged. It will be forced upon you if you refuse to do this willingly. We have enough chains to hook you up and have a maid douche you. Do it willingly, and there'll be no restraints." He placed the items back in the bag on the floor.

"Fuck you. Kill me first."

The door moved as someone new entered the room.

Frankie Gambino. He held a laptop in his hands, the screen shining on his face.

"I see you're learning our rules. That's good. You'll fit in nicely for the last few weeks of your use. You will be killed if you are a troublesome nuisance by the end of your first month here. If you're a loving, willing partner during your stay here, you may remain on as a maid. Your future is in your hands."

Revulsion coursed through her. She would never let them touch her.

"Now, for the reason I brought this with me." Gambino gestured at the computer. He motioned with his head, and six men stepped closer, three on each side of her. "Hold her if she becomes hostile."

"I have terrible news for you."

Her mouth dried out, and her stomach twisted into a knot.

"I offered your husband a deal. Play checkers with me and win, and I will let you two go free. You're aware he decided not to play with me. You probably heard the gunshots?"

She nodded, dreading what he was about to say.

"Because Darwin decided not to play, he forfeited the game. I executed the Hernandez family, as the players weren't needed anymore. You two have lost your freedom. But there was another problem."

He looked around the tiny room. She detected a subtle message being told to each guard. Her wrists tested the bond of the cuffs.

"Your husband didn't agree with my method. He ran at me. My men had no option but to protect me. Darwin was shot twice. Once in the forehead and once in the chest."

Numbness overwhelmed her. She didn't hear him right. The world tilted in her vision.

"This house has cameras and listening devices everywhere. I brought this laptop to prove what I'm saying."

Gambino turned the computer around and aimed the screen toward her. He hit the spacebar, and the video started. Two men on either side gripped her shoulders to keep her down. She barely noticed them as Darwin appeared on the screen, the camera a little to his left.

"I chose this camera," Gambino said. "Because it shows him coming at me from the best angle."

Gunfire erupted as the Hernandez family was executed. She saw Darwin's face in profile from the shock of what he'd just witnessed. Projectile vomit shot out of his mouth. It almost hit the guard standing several feet in front of him. She didn't want to watch anymore, but they forced her to.

Darwin jumped from the chair so fast that he almost toppled it. He ran at Gambino, who stood near a door at the top of the camera lens. She watched as a man next to Gambino stepped between him and Darwin. She saw and heard the gun's report. What happened next made her so sick she thought her heart would stop.

Darwin's head snapped back at an enormous speed. He lifted

off his feet and tilted like a seesaw to the concrete-tiled deck floor. He slid a few feet until his forward motion ceased.

On the screen of the small laptop, she saw blood seep from the forehead wound. He didn't move.

Her husband had just been murdered.

"One last thing to see, and we'll leave you for the night. In the morning, you have your cleaning instructions. Follow them to a tee, or there will be consequences."

Gambino fumbled with the computer's buttons and then angled the screen toward her.

"Watch this on your own, or I will have my men force your eyelids open, and I guarantee you don't want that."

The screen showed what looked like a morgue. Pine boxes lay side by side on a table or raised platform.

"This video was taken fifteen minutes ago. These are the bodies of the Hernandez family. They are being buried as we speak across the street at the Markville Family Funeral Home. Notice the last coffin in the row."

Even though every inch of her body screamed for her to look away, she stared at the screen, mesmerized.

Whoever held the camera slowed and then aimed it into the last pine box. Darwin lay there, his face at peace, a small trickle of blood still sitting on his forehead.

He's being buried in the T-shirt he wore to bed last night ...

Her body went limp as consciousness, in a merciful gesture, left her.

29

CARSON DODGE PASSED TWO media vans and front gate security to enter the safe house grounds and drove up to the front of the building.

"I told you to take me to the hotel," Stinsen said.

Greg was angry with him, but Carson didn't care. Nothing mattered more than catching and stopping Darwin Kostas.

"I need you to walk through the crime scene first. Help me understand Darwin. It may save his life. If you care anything for the fellow agents who lost their lives here today, and if you care anything for Darwin, you will do this first. Then I'll take you to your hotel."

Carson turned off the car and waited in the driver's seat for an answer. After a moment, Greg got out and slammed the door behind him.

"Fucking child," Carson whispered to himself.

He walked Greg through the crime scene, detailing what they figured had happened. Once he got to the kitchen, Greg stopped and held up a hand.

"Wait," he said, examining the layout under the dim lights. "Where did Darwin get the knife from again?" Greg asked.

"That knife set over there." Carson pointed.

"Where did you find the set?"

"Toppled on the counter," Carson said. "Right here."

Greg measured the distance. "Explain the injuries on all five victims. As many details as you can."

Carson went through the preliminary findings and explained the autopsies would be performed within the next few days.

"Interesting that only one agent had bruised knuckles. Tell me, who was on duty at that specific time?"

"John Simmons, Don Ouellette, and David Baron were the three on duty. Nick Johnson and Lee Michaels were showing up to relieve them."

Greg walked over to sit on the chair where Nick Johnson had sat and ate French toast that morning before being knifed to death. "Do you know these two well?"

"What two?" Carson asked, a feeling of agitation brewing under his skin. "We're supposed to be talking about Darwin Kostas."

"Humor me."

Carson glared at him, looking for an angle, but failed to see one. Then he nodded. "I knew all five men," Carson said.

"How well did you know Nick and Lee, the two relievers?"

"Like I know most of the other agents. They're there. I see them once in a while."

"Get on the phone and call whoever's performing the autopsy or whoever's at the morgue where Nick and Lee are right now."

"What? Why? It's almost midnight."

"I want to find out if we can reenact the fight from the

external features of the bodies." When Carson didn't move to call anyone, Stinsen added, "I'm onto something here. I've figured it out."

Carson pulled out his phone. "I'm lost. I don't know where you're going with this."

Greg clasped his hands together on the table and stared down at them, lost in thought. "Listen to everything I have to say before interrupting."

Carson nodded and took a seat opposite Greg at the table.

"My guess is the three on duty were here all night, and they had an uneventful evening."

Carson nodded.

"The two relievers show, and breakfast is being made. Lee is out at the gate and holds his weapon on the agent posted there while Nick beats him and strangles him. They come into the house without pause and do the same to the agent on the inside. Two dead. That leaves one out securing the perimeter. Nick stays in the kitchen to guard the Kostases while Lee goes outside to kill the last guy. That's why you have only Lee's knuckles bruised up, and the three night-shift guys are beaten and then strangled."

"How do you know Darwin didn't do all the beatings?"

"Because you're a good detective. One of the best. Am I right?"

"Stop playing with me. Tell it straight."

"I figured you're so good that when you interviewed that motel clerk, you would've found out that when the clerk met the Kostases only hours before, the clerk would've seen how badly bruised Darwin's knuckles were. Or someone would've mentioned it at the gas station where the other incident occurred. Since I've heard nothing of Darwin being in a fight, and it didn't look like the three night-shift guys put up a fight, I deduced that he didn't beat and kill the three on duty."

Carson sat back in his chair. He didn't want to believe it, but it could be possible. "So then, what happened here in the kitchen? How did Darwin get the jump on Nick? He was a trained federal agent."

"First, let me tell you a little about Darwin. He has a few phobias. These phobias cause an odd reaction in him. Because he has a highly developed sense of fear due to the phobias, he has learned over the years to despise that fear."

"You're talking in circles."

"I'll give you an example. Say he's threatened. That threat causes fear. Because he hates fear and has lived under it for more than half his life, he does whatever he can to eradicate that threat as fast as possible because he will not live with a threat over his head."

"We all do that."

"Not quite like Darwin," Greg said, waving his index finger back and forth. "One of his phobias is knives and sharp things. If you pull a knife on Darwin, he doesn't just see red, he doesn't just get angry or feel a natural sense of self-preservation. He feels a rage akin to splitting an atom and acts on it without thinking. He removes that threat with extreme prejudice."

"Are you saying Nick pulled a knife on Darwin, and Darwin wrestled it from him and stabbed Nick? Because that didn't happen. We have a recording of the kitchen stabbing."

"No. I'm saying that they were being held against their will, and Rosina knocked the knife set over so a knife would fall and land on Darwin, turning him into the killing machine she knows he is when presented with one of his phobias."

Carson raised his eyebrows. "And you believe this?"

"Absolutely. I was in Rome. I saw what he did in the Fuccini building by himself with no backup. The Harvester of Sorrow had a long blade. He's dead now. The two guys that picked him up at the Rome airport were almost torn in half. I saw what he did in Toronto, too."

"That is all the more reason we need to get this maniac off the streets."

"You're misunderstanding. He's a soft, happy, polite Canadian boy. There's nothing dangerous about him unless you pull a knife and threaten him or his wife. It's really what you'd expect of any citizen, except Darwin is faster, stronger, and more out of control when in a rage."

Carson leaned forward, rested his elbows on his knees, and stared at the floor where Nick bled out. Something about what Stinsen said made sense, but he couldn't believe Nick and Lee were rogue agents.

"That would mean someone was paying off my two agents," Carson said. "Two good men were on the take. And if that was the case, then who? And what about Bob Freska, shot in the head and tied to the front of his car?"

"Whoever paid to have Darwin taken care of grabbed Darwin from Bob and made his death appear to be Darwin's handiwork."

"What about the gas station?" Carson asked. "We have him on security cameras stealing food and a truck."

"I would be hungry too if my potential kidnapper entered my home and sat down to eat the French toast that my wife had just prepared for me. They're scared. They're hungry. They stole the truck to get away fast. Look where they checked in—a couple of miles away and then ditched the truck. They aren't on the run. I'm sure Darwin wants to find out who is behind all this as much as you do."

"Correction," Carson said, raising his hand. "I just want Darwin. He'll be able to answer all my questions."

"Make that call. Find somebody to check Lee Michaels's body for signs of a struggle. If he was the only one beating people and Darwin's hands are clean, then he's the one who beat his fellow agents."

Carson grunted before dialing. It took him ten minutes to get through to the medical examiner.

"Working late?" Carson asked.

"Yeah. Too many dead people. Do something about that, will you, Carson?"

"I'm trying, I'm trying. Listen, I need you to do me a favor."

"What?"

"Pull the bodies of John Simmons, Don Ouellette, and David Baron. I need you to look at something for me."

"Their autopsies haven't been completed yet."

"I just need you to confirm something topical for me."

"Give me a minute."

Carson held the phone away from his ear. "He's going in now."

Greg nodded and looked back at his folded hands.

"Okay," the medical examiner said. "I'm here. I've got all three rolled out of their holes. What do you want me to look at?"

"Their hands. Tell me if you see any sign of a struggle. Is there any skin under their nails? Did they put up a fight?"

"Give me a sec."

Carson waited patiently, hoping Greg's theory didn't pan out. The last thing Carson wanted was to believe two agents went rogue.

"There's nothing on John Simmons's hands. Moving to Don Ouellette's."

Carson could hear the slab being rolled back into place. He waited.

"Nothing at all on Don's hands but a little dirt. Normal, though."

"Okay, last one," Carson said. "David Baron."

Carson looked at Greg, who sat staring at him across the table.

"Nothing on the first two men," he whispered.

Greg nodded. "It'll be this guy. My guess is Nick was alone in the kitchen and killed here. Lee went out alone to take care of David and left Nick to guard the Kostases. If there's anything to find, it'll be on the agent who didn't have Nick holding a weapon on him."

"Carson?" the medical examiner asked.

"Yeah, I'm here."

"Strange. There's no blood or skin under his nails."

"But there's a few flecks of plastic. Like you find on those fake leather jackets. And two of his nails have recently been broken. By recently, I mean within twelve hours of the time of death. Without a full autopsy report, I can't confirm anything. But it does look like he struggled with someone before he died."

"Okay, thanks. I'll swing by in a few days to see what you find in the autopsy."

Carson hung up and turned to Greg. "He found flecks of plastic under David's fingernails and evidence of a struggle based on the condition of the fingers."

"What was Lee wearing when he was found?"

"An imitation leather jacket. We'd have to confirm the state of the jacket."

Greg sat back in his chair.

"Doesn't prove anything," Carson said.

"No, but it offers doubt, the kind that's beyond reasonable."

30

THE JOLT WOKE HIM. Something banged around him. He heard it again and felt the pain. It rushed him like a strong wind. He moaned and rolled to his side, but his movement was restricted. He opened his eyes and saw nothing.

Using his hands, he felt around his immediate area. A wall, only inches from his face. But he still couldn't see it. Frantically, he roamed his hands along the wall and felt where it started and stopped. The sides were small, the top and bottom wider.

The pine boxes Gambino had his men prepare for the Hernandez family. He tried to calm his breathing. He touched his forehead. There was a large bump between his eyes where the top of his nose met his eyebrows. He felt a slight pain in his chest where the other bullet had hit him.

Rubber bullets.

He'd seen them used on protestors in the past. But why use rubber bullets? Why not just kill him outright?

Maybe shooting him was too easy a death.

"Help," he shouted. With his fists, he banged both sides of the makeshift coffin and called again. "Someone! Help!"

The thickness of the earth dulled the echo.

Am I already underground?

He grabbed the top of the box and searched for holes. In the middle of the lid, above his stomach, he felt a small slit where the wood had warped. His little finger slid through the opening. If he were in a building or outside, somewhere with even a small amount of light, he would see that light through the hole. But there was no light.

He was already buried.

Darwin screamed. His bladder released, and warm urine filled his shorts. He broke out in a sweat and pounded his fists against the top of the coffin. He was worn out and fatigued within a minute, panting when he should have been conserving oxygen.

"Oh, Rosina, I'm so sorry."

He thought about oxygen. A quick calculation figured the area of the box to be quite small, with maybe enough oxygen for a couple of hours. He kicked the back of the box. Dirt dribbled down along his ankle.

He wiped away the sweat from his face and the collected tears that had started.

"Why?" he asked out loud. "Oh, God, please help me here. Tell me what to do, and I'll do it."

He recalled something from his Sunday school days when he was a kid.

God helps those who help themselves.

He rummaged in his pockets. No wallet, no keys, no flashlight, and no cell phone. Even if he had a lighter or a match, he wouldn't want to use it due to the oxygen it would consume.

The darkness felt heavy, like it crept closer, tightening its grip on his breathing tubes. He casually thought about his fear of the dark and how he wasn't absolutely certifiable yet.

"Get control of yourself, Darwin. Think, dammit, think. The dark can't hurt you anymore."

He laid his hands down beside him and focused on his breathing.

Slow the breathing. Take it easy. I can get out of this.

"But how?"

The dirt above the coffin would have recently been replaced. He knew the depth was likely six feet. He may not be that deep, but in the worst case, he'd go with six feet.

Since he was five foot, eleven inches tall, he could reach above the grass if he could stand and raise his hands above his head.

But how do I stand with all this dirt above me?

Displacement.

Science class, grade nine, discussed displacement. He had to displace as much dirt as he could.

Just like when they built that tunnel in The Great Escape.

The pine box was six feet long and two feet high. If every inch inside the box took the dirt above it, he could have a chance of standing and digging himself out.

It could work. But how do I breathe when my head is above the box and in the dirt?

A hockey fight filtered through his mind. He could raise his extra-large T-shirt over his head where he would tie the sleeves together as tight as he could to form a seal.

He kicked the top again. More dirt cascaded down. He kicked again, harder this time.

The weight of all the earth above him could be quite heavy. If he broke a large piece of wood off, in seconds, he would be smothered and unable to move. He had to work slowly and displace bits of dirt at a time, but yet work fast enough to get it done before the oxygen ran out.

He grabbed the warped piece of wood by his stomach and applied pressure. Then he waited and listened. He heard nothing above him. The only thing he could hear in the absolute darkness was the beating of his heart.

Lucky claustrophobia isn't an issue.

His fear crept up again. The fear of being locked in a dark room when he was a child. His stepmother came in and poked him with the tips of steak knives and large syringes. For a moment, his vision filled with the image of the pitchfork. He saw lights where there were none. He heard a voice.

"Rosina?"

The voice of his stepmother intruded. She told him how horrible he'd been and that dinner wasn't a place for jokey jokes. Now that his father had gone to work, it was her job to teach him what was right and wrong. He felt the sharp edge of a blade and screamed.

Was he losing his mind? Could someone be so consumed by fear that they die of insanity?

He shuffled left and right and felt dirt under him, then grabbed the warped edge of the wood and pulled downward. A piece broke off, and dirt poured in. He touched the hole and figured it to be the size of a baseball.

He used his right knee to plug the hole and lifted his shirt. Once he got the bottom up to his neck, he heaved it over his head and pulled his arms out. Next, he reached above his head and brought the ends of the sleeves together, tying them in the tightest knot he could. Then, he secured the bottom of the T-shirt to seal it over his head.

The fabric laid across his face, causing an even more claustrophobic feeling. He eased the shirt away from his nose and breathed in deeply. Air traveled through the fabric with ease. He grabbed a hand full of dirt and dropped it onto the shirt in front of his mouth, testing its integrity. Not a single drop came through.

He released his knee from the plugged hole. As dirt dropped into the pine box, he used his hands to shovel it to the back and used his feet to push it into the far corners. He did this for what felt like an exhausting thirty minutes until he plugged the hole with his knee again to catch his breath.

When he'd researched phobias to get answers on why he couldn't look at a knife and why he needed to drive with the interior light on at night, he remembered seeing there was a phobia for being buried alive called *taphophobia*.

"Fuck, am I glad I don't have that one either."

He collected his breath, counted to three, and began displacing dirt again, thinking of the day he married Rosina in Rome. She was so beautiful. The church had been magnificent, and the people who witnessed the wedding were awesome. Everyone involved made them feel welcomed and cherished. He remembered thinking how happy he'd been to elope—to take Rosina to Rome and marry the woman of his dreams.

He dug upward and moved the dirt as far from himself as possible. Soon, the bottom of the coffin was getting so full that his legs were becoming stiff from the exertion.

It was almost time to attempt to stand. He began the arduous task of bringing the dirt up and above his head. The work grew harder as his arms stiffened. He wondered how much dirt he'd moved. Would it be enough? Was the earth loose enough to push through and try to stand?

He would have to work fast when he broke the piece of wood in the lid out of the way. Dirt would fill the coffin quickly. He would need to be ready and stand with determination, using his hands to pull the dirt down below himself, constantly making a path for the top. Air would be an issue, but if he stayed where he was, air would be an issue soon enough.

Dirt now filled the box almost up to his waist. It sat packed to his triceps and up around his T-shirt-covered face to the top of the coffin above his head, leaving him enough room for his face to remain exposed to the little air left.

He grabbed the board where the hole was and pulled downward.

Nothing happened.

He pulled again, harder, but it didn't budge.

"What the fuck?"

He yanked on the piece of wood, but nothing moved or broke off.

The air seemed thinner. He gasped and tried to breathe in deeper. Small amounts of dirt trickled around his right knee. He rested his weary hands at his sides and waited for the nausea to go away. Throwing up in his T-shirt-covered face would be the end.

He felt his anger, allowed its freedom, and drew power from it. The darkness closed in a notch more.

He raised his right knee and slammed it into the opening it had plugged only moments before.

Wood cracked and split.

Hope filled his sluggish brain. He did it repeatedly, feeling the dirt coming in around his leg.

He grabbed the broken wood and pulled a piece toward him. With the aid of the weight of the earth, the wood gave and broke inward.

At the last second, Darwin inhaled and struggled upward, digging with his hands at a mad rate. He pushed with his feet and scrambled like a mole, making a path where one hadn't been moments before.

Seconds later, he was kneeling and sitting outside the pine box, which came up to his waist. Dirt rested on his shoulders like the weight Atlas once carried.

He pulled his shirt away from his mouth and nose as far as it would go and breathed out. He breathed in again and coughed. Minute amounts of dust filled the small space. He figured the air inside his shirt limited him to mere minutes at best.

Tiny items scattered throughout the dirt scratched his skin. He reached above his head and dug deep, pulling the dirt down and around him to fill the now half-empty coffin. He pushed hard with his legs and forced his body to stand, the dirt filling the rest of the open space inside the coffin below him. Darwin pushed up and dug using his thighs, breathing as little as he could.

Finally, his arms above his head, still buried in dirt, his right hand broke the surface first. He felt emptiness and wondered for a crazy second if he'd hit some kind of air pocket, but realized his hand had dug up past the surface.

Pain wracked his body. He paused and breathed inside the shirt mask as he did a mental inventory of the pain. His forehead wound ached the most. Second were his hands. He was sure he'd broken at least two fingernails as he had dug frantically. Scrapes and cuts littered his body. His shirt still sat above his head, the sleeves still tied, but below his neck, he was exposed. The nerdy shorts he wore only came to just above his knees. Below that, his shins were also cut and scraped.

Dizziness set in. Lightheadedness overcame him.

Air. I need air.

He dug but soon realized he had nowhere to displace the dirt below him. Both hands broke the surface and tossed dirt left and right, but it wasn't quick enough.

His head remained buried approximately a foot below the earth's surface, which might as well be quicksand. The dirt was so heavy around him that none of his body parts could move too well. His shoulders ached from the strain to the point where they felt like they'd been pulled out of their sockets.

He hadn't lost his will now that he'd gotten so close. It was his strength he was losing. When he stopped to catch his breath, no air was left.

He tried again. He struggled, his eyes closed, focused on the ground above him, but it was useless. It wasn't going to happen. They would know he'd tried when they came in the morning and saw his hands sticking out.

In his oxygen-deprived brain, one last conscious thought came to him. The sides of the coffin were wood. They were strong and now supported by dirt on either side.

He opened his eyes in the absolute darkness. He allowed it in. All the years of hating the dark. All the rage he felt when confronted with a phobia. He called upon that dark place inside him and used every ounce of strength he had left to lift his right leg onto the right side of the coffin wall. Dirt shuffled and moved as most of it was relatively looser down there.

Once his right foot was centered on the edge of the coffin wall, he placed his left foot on the opposite wall. He brought his hands back under the earth's surface, putting them right above his head. Then he counted to three and pushed with his legs, his hands digging.

With the added height of the coffin's walls, Darwin's head burst through the topsoil and into the open air.

The dirt came to his chin. He quickly grabbed the T-shirt and ripped it off his head, breathing in the sweet air. He breathed so fast that he became dizzy as the glorious oxygen filled his lungs.

He didn't move for at least ten minutes until his breathing was under control and the dizziness had abated. He stood under the ground, buried to his neck in dirt, surrounded by headstones, and breathed.

His thoughts cleared. His muscles felt less tired. Piece by piece, he picked dirt up and tossed it away. Then, more dirt. He chanted his wife's name under his breath. He figured it had taken an hour to get halfway out of the hole. He kept digging. He wanted to go after Gambino before sunrise because he had a plan. One that he knew would work. Gambino would never expect it.

"I'm coming, Gambino. I'm back from the dead, and I'm fucking pissed."

31

CARSON AND GREG STOOD in the headlights of Carson's car. They sipped two large coffees as they watched Bob Freska's body be removed from the hood of his car.

"I want this kid, Darwin," Carson said. "He'll have to answer for what he's done."

Greg sat on the hood of Carson's car. He took another sip of his coffee. "What makes you certain this is Darwin's handiwork?"

Carson glared at him. "I read the kid's file. I know him."

Greg shook his head. "No. You don't. You only think you know him."

Carson set his coffee down on the hood and dropped his arms to his side. "You've got some nerve."

"*I* know Darwin better than any agent at the Bureau. I helped him with the Vincenzo fiasco. I was in Rome with him at the end and was there for the Toronto attacks. That's where I got these scars." He pointed at his arms. "We were in a car accident on Toronto's main highway. So, *I* know Darwin better than anybody and especially better than someone who *read* his file."

"Is this a competition?"

"Clearly, it is for you."

Carson studied the man's face in the light of the headlights. "What about that cop who got killed in Rome? The report said the time of death was estimated within an hour of the Harvester of Sorrow's time of death. This nonviolent little boy can waltz into the Fuccini building and kill all the Fuccini hitmen *and* the Harvester, but he can't save a cop. Something's fishy."

"Maybe he got there too late."

"What about the security cameras showing him leaving the airport in Rome and walking into one of Fuccini's vans?"

"What about it?"

Carson stepped back and took a longer look at Greg. "Are you fooled by all this, too?"

"I have no idea what you're referring to. The Fuccinis hunted him. They followed Darwin to Rome because he accidentally killed Vincenzo, and the Fuccinis wanted revenge."

"I don't buy that the Vincenzo thing was purely accidental. Fuccini wouldn't travel the globe looking to kill one man. Too stupid and too risky."

"He did, though. Maybe that's why he's dead."

"I still think Darwin is connected somehow, and it's above my pay grade to get all the answers. But that doesn't matter anymore. When you kill feds in my jurisdiction, you go down for it."

"We still don't know if he was acting in self-defense. As far as Bob Freska here goes, anyone could've done this. I'm trying to figure out who would target Darwin now that Fuccini is dead?"

"None of that matters to me," Carson said as he picked up his coffee cup. "I'm not the jury or the judge. My job is to arrest people and let the courts figure it out. I hope he gets a good lawyer, and if he's innocent, he'll go free, but I don't think that'll happen. Too much dirt on this guy's hands for him to be clean. Sorry, I'm just not buying it."

Freska's body had been removed from the car. Men stood around the vehicle with small brushes, examining the car under floodlights. Carson watched as Rudy finished talking to the coroner and then waved him over.

"Found something?" Carson asked.

"Nothing. His wallet and badge are missing. The car looks clean. This was a professional hit. If Darwin did this, he's getting tips from Gambino."

"Everything points to Darwin. He was the last person seen with Bob at the motel."

Greg pushed off the car and walked around Carson. "What was that about Gambino?"

"Gambino has a vacation home in the area," Rudy said. "Lately, he's been spending a lot of time down here as his family does their business in Toronto. It keeps him isolated to be this far south."

Stinsen kicked at the gravel underfoot. A plume of dust rose around their feet. He stepped away and slammed a fist into the palm of his other hand.

"What got into him?" Rudy asked.

"Who knows? He's been a dick ever since I picked him up at the airport."

Greg turned back to face them from five feet away. "Are you two clowns saying that Gambino, as in Frankie Gambino, reputed Canadian mob boss, has a residence in this area?"

Carson put up a hand. "Watch how you're talking, Stinsen. I'm not a fucking clown."

"Just answer the *fucking* question. Does Gambino have a local residence?"

Rudy stepped forward. "Yeah. It's about a ten-minute drive from here."

Greg tossed his coffee cup into the brush and headed for the car. "Let's go."

"Where're we going?" Carson asked.

Greg got to the passenger side door and opened it. He stood holding the door. "You serious?"

"Yeah. We can't just barge into Gambino's residence. Too much security. We can't assume that he has anything to do with what's happening today just because he has a vacation home in the area."

"You do know the famous shootout at the abandoned hangar in Toronto was reportedly orchestrated by the Gambino Family?"

Carson nodded. "I've heard that."

"They missed Vincenzo that night. Darwin killed him by accident. Fuccini went after Darwin, and he paid the ultimate price for that. Wouldn't you think Gambino wants to know who Darwin is and who he works for? That's how these assholes think. Fuck, *you* even think Darwin isn't on the up and up."

Stinsen dropped into the car.

Carson turned to Rudy. "Did he just call us assholes?"

Rudy shrugged. "I'm not entirely sure. Probably not."

"Hey," Stinsen shouted from inside the car. "Whose bright idea was it to set up a safe house for a mafia killer like Darwin only a short drive from Gambino's vacation home? There are hundreds of places the Kostases could've gone. Wait, don't tell me. Nick Johnson and Lee Michaels, right?"

Carson nodded.

Greg waved at Bob Freska's car. "Gambino did this. It's a message. Darwin doesn't do this kind of shit. The mob does. Gambino's too stupid to know we'll see through it. Bob picked up the Kostases at the Sleep On Inn and delivered them to Gambino. Then Frankie did this to make it look like Darwin's work." Greg slapped the roof of the car. "Come on. Let's go pick up Darwin and his wife before they're killed. If Gambino has them, they're either dead already or will be shortly."

32

DARWIN LAY ON HIS back and stared at the stars, thanking them for being lucky and thanking God. He waited until his breathing was under control and his body had a short rest.

After ten minutes, he got to his feet, slipped his dirty T-shirt back on, and stumbled away from the unmarked grave toward the road.

What he had done in the past haunted him. Nightmares were a regular visitor in the night. He had killed people. He'd done it out of anger, but it was always in self-defense. Today, he would kill again. Once Gambino was gone, Darwin couldn't think of another mafia boss who even knew his name. Maybe the nightmare would be over after that.

He made it to the darkened road and leaned against a tree to catch his breath. Thoughts of Rosina kept him upright. Without her, he was dead anyway.

Nothing moved on the other side of the road. He couldn't see security detail anywhere. Keeping to the darkened shadows of the trees on the side, Darwin walked parallel to the road, guessing how far to the warehouse where Gambino kept his prized World War II collection of airplanes and artillery. It was at least two or three in the morning, and the darkness didn't bother him as much as it normally would. There was certainly more light now than in that pine box. As far as he was concerned, the old Darwin, the idealistic one who assumed that there was goodness in everyone, passed away in that grave.

The road turned to the right. He stayed ten feet back, deep in the trees' dark shadows, searching for a route to the warehouse. At the side of the road, he closed his eyes and listened. Nothing moved. The only sounds were the crickets. He opened his eyes and stepped out of the trees.

He made it to the other side of the road and dropped down to the cover of trees and darkness again, where he waited a heartbeat and listened.

His guesstimate of just over a hundred yards had worked. Ten yards in front of him, light glistened off a chain-link fence. Staying in the shadows, he walked around the fence and climbed over a small stone barrier until he landed on Gambino's warehouse property.

At this point, he expected to see security guards or even dogs, but no one approached him.

The wall of a building came up quickly. In the dark, he hadn't been able to see it. All he needed now was a door.

He hopped over a fallen tree, landed hard, and slipped to the side, falling onto dead leaves. He clamped his lips down hard to quell the grunt that escaped him. He waited on the ground to see if anyone heard him fall.

From inside the warehouse, the rhythmic sound of boots thumped as someone walked close by. He lay flat out on the damp ground and waited until silence returned. Then, he slowly got up and searched for an access point along the wall.

A twig scraped across his cheek, but he held the groan in. The trees thickened at the corner of the building. At the edge of the tree line, he saw an opening. A guard held the backdoor to the warehouse open while he puffed on a cigarette. The lights inside the warehouse shone brightly, illuminating the trees Darwin stood behind. The density of the trees blocked the light from getting more than four feet past them.

He waited with shallow breath until the man butted his cigarette and stepped back inside. When the door clicked shut, Darwin ran from his hiding place. He gripped the handle and turned it, expecting resistance. But the door was unlocked.

He peeked through the crack in the door. The man who had just finished his smoke break retreated toward the main offices in the rear of the warehouse.

The door's hinges were well-oiled as Darwin eased it open far enough to squeeze through. He stepped onto the warehouse floor and stopped as a piece of cold steel pressed against his neck.

"Oh, man, won't the boss be so happy with me when I show him what I caught trying to break in here? Are you so fucking stupid that it didn't surprise you that the door was unlocked? We saw your approach on camera and motion sensors, you fucking dumbass."

Darwin turned enough to see the crazy look on the man's face. He held an assault rifle strapped over his shoulder, the tip pressed into Darwin's skin.

"You know, I'm wondering something," Darwin said.

"What you wondering, asshole?"

"Where do you guys come from? Like, do you all have the

same mother or something?"

The gun pulled away from his neck. A flash of movement, and Darwin felt the sucker punch as it connected with his left temple. His shoulder smacked the doorframe, and he fell backward out the door and onto the grass. The fall hurt more than the punch.

"Shit, that sucks," he muttered.

The pain where the rubber bullet had hit him in the forehead had recently subsided but now pulsed again.

"Wha's that you be saying about us? You wanna talk shit again before I kills ya?"

"Wait," Darwin said, his hand raised to ward off an attack. The assault rifle was aimed at his forehead. "I need to know if you all have the same mother because if you don't, then how does Gambino hire you guys? I mean, it boggles the mind. Does he put out a classified ad in the newspaper saying something about asshole thugs needing to piss and shit all day while looking scary and holding a big gun?"

The guy smiled. "You got some balls, kid. I like that."

"Are you gay? All this talk about my balls makes me think so. I'd never have noticed. You look too tough to take it in the ass. Are you the wife in the relationship or the husband?"

The guy shook his head to clear it of Darwin's words. "What the fuck are you talking about?"

"You just complimented my balls, so I was wondering if you take it in the ass or give it? Which way does your boyfriend like it?"

Darwin braced himself. He waited.

The thug lifted the assault rifle over his head and removed the strap. He tossed it back inside the building and rolled up his sleeves.

"I think you need to learn how to talk to strangers. You break into *our* facility and then insult *me*. I will kill you, but first, I want you to feel an enormous amount of pain."

"I meant no harm," Darwin said. "You were the one who admitted to being gay. I was just curious, is all, and I wanted to know how a guy like Gambino could have so many assholes on the payroll—"

The thug lunged down, grabbed Darwin by the front of the T-shirt, and brought him to a standing position.

"Please, mister, don't hurt me," Darwin cried.

Then he pushed off the ground, jumped up, and wrapped both legs around the man's midsection. The guard stumbled backward, let go of Darwin's shirt to use his arms to break his fall, and dropped back toward the step. Darwin opened his legs at the last second so his feet wouldn't fall under the man's back.

The moment they landed, Darwin formed fists with both hands and pummeled the thug's face over a dozen times before he stopped to catch his breath.

Blood oozed from numerous cracks in the guard's skin. His nose was broken, and the man's eyes would swell shut in a matter of hours.

Darwin pulled the guard's unconscious body away from the open door and behind a copse of trees. He ran back to the door, stepped inside the complex, and grabbed the assault rifle. After a quick inspection, he found the safety and clicked it off. Then he wrapped the rifle strap over his head, held it in front of him, and started along the wall toward the front.

He passed two planes with World War II insignia on them. An old jeep with a broken windshield sat parked in the back corner.

A light turned off in the offices at the back of the facility where the smoker had gone earlier.

Then he saw what he came for.

The authentic, restored German Panther tank sat facing Gambino's house. The gun stuck out proudly from the turret. The tracks were wide and slightly different from other tanks he'd seen with the wheels interweaved. They were placed almost side-by-side so that certain areas weren't visible. The front of the tank had a slope that probably repelled enemy artillery.

Gambino had said that the tank was fully restored and operational and that a buyer was coming to pick it up.

Darwin swung the rifle around to his back and climbed up the side of the tank. He stood on top and looked around to ensure he wasn't being observed. Then he grabbed the circular opening at the top of the turret and pulled. Nothing happened. He pulled again.

A lever in the middle twisted under the pressure of his hand. He pulled upward, and the top opened.

The crack of a weapon made him swing his head around as a bullet ricocheted off a wall. The smoker stood at the back of the building, sighting him down with his weapon.

"Get off the tank, or I will shoot you," the guy shouted from fifty yards.

"You're not that good," Darwin shouted back as he got into position and dropped down inside the confining space of the turret. He bumped his right knee and left elbow on the way in, numbing his left hand.

"Shit, that fucking hurts."

He grabbed the top and pulled it shut over his head as bullets careened off the tank. A quick twist and the hatch locked from the inside. Small lights flickered on, illuminating a tiny interior.

He took off the rifle and scrunched down to move into another compartment. The guy outside shouted frantically into a phone about how some guy had just jumped in the tank. Reinforcements didn't bother Darwin. Short of another tank or a massive amount of explosives, nothing could stop him now.

He found where the driver would sit in the lower forward compartment and eased into the small black chair.

How the hell did four or five men operate in something so small?

He quickly ascertained that the tank had seven gears. On either side of the turret, he saw ammunition for the gun but had no idea how to load it or fire it.

All he needed to do was get the thing turned on. He touched the black steering wheel and placed his other hand on the gear shifter. Two lights hung near a black panel on his right. He saw the ignition button and pushed it. The tank fired up like the day it was built. It was so loud the voice of the guy on the phone standing just outside the tank was drowned out.

He maneuvered the gears on his right and tried to find the first one. Once he had it where he thought it should be, he put his left hand on the steering wheel and looked straight ahead at a metal wall.

"How the fuck did the driver see where to go?"

There was a small rectangular slit about eye level. He unclipped it and flipped it open. The first thing he saw was the guy on the phone.

Their eyes met. Then the guy dropped the phone, yanked up his rifle, and aimed at the slot Darwin stared out of. Darwin slammed the slot closed and clicked it back into place. Bullets ricocheted off the exterior.

He decided he didn't need to see out the rectangular slot. The tank was already aimed at Gambino's house, which was his target. He would just drive forward until he hit the building.

He couldn't detect a gas pedal at his feet.

"Hey, you in the tank. Listen carefully. We have orders to blow the tank up with you in it. Get out of the tank, and we will let you live. We have a large quantity of C-4 sitting under the tank right now. I give you ten seconds to exit the tank, or I will blow the C-4."

He couldn't see the clutch pedal because the lights were slightly above his head. He felt around until his foot bumped into it, then pushed his foot on top and pushed. He slipped the gears into what he assumed was the first gear and slowly let the clutch out.

The tank chugged forward, knocking him back in his seat, his foot coming clean off the clutch. The tank stalled and stopped, the engine dead.

"Fuck."

"Last chance." The man's voice was loud and clear now that the engine was off.

"Fuck you," Darwin whispered.

He pressed down on the ignition switch, fired up the engine, dropped the clutch, and let it ease out slowly.

The tank moved forward. It teetered as the front came off its concrete platform. It met the grass, dug in, and started across the lawn toward Gambino's house.

As soon as the back touched the grass, the tank shuddered as an explosion behind the tank sent out a shock wave.

Darwin pushed in the clutch, dropped the Panther into second gear, opened the view slot, and headed for the back patio of

Gambino's house, intent on murdering anyone in his way.

"I'm coming, baby. I'm coming."

33

Carson had the sudden urge to shove his passenger out the door. He hated everything about Agent Greg Stinsen at that moment. He had predetermined ideas and attitudes about Darwin, and the facts spoke for themselves. Darwin had killed federal agents. Darwin had stolen a pickup truck, and, as far as anyone was concerned, Bob Freska was dead because of Darwin Kostas.

But Stinsen thought mobsters were involved. He'd proclaim that Darwin was innocent despite the evidence if he had his way.

"Hey, Rudy," Carson said as he looked in the rearview mirror at him in the back seat, "what's your take on all this? You think the mafia orchestrated everything? Or is this carnage Darwin's handiwork?"

"Carson, seriously, I have no idea. We'll gather what proof we can and charge the people responsible like we always do."

"Waffling much?"

"That's not waffling. It's what we do. We don't assign blame. The evidence and facts lead us to suspects and arrests."

Carson slapped the steering wheel. "I was asking for your

opinion. So let me ask you a different way. Who, or what is behind all the killings of federal agents?"

"I'm gathering that Darwin and his wife have a lot to do with it, but I can't say they are the only guilty party. I think the Freska thing had more to do with the Gambino Family than it had to do with the Kostases."

"Why's that?" Carson asked.

"Because everyone knows Bob's been on the take for a long time, and no one could prove it. Gambino has at least half a dozen local cops around here in his pocket. Good men, too. Men who wouldn't normally consort with guys like Gambino, but he had something on them. Do I think some kid from Canada took Bob out like that? No way."

Carson stared forward at the road. As much as he wanted to pin everything on Darwin, Rudy had a point. But why did Gambino take care of Bob Freska the day Darwin was on the run? Just to make it look like Darwin did it when Darwin's profile would suggest otherwise?

Somehow, someway, he was going to figure out who killed his men, and whoever was responsible would pay.

He turned onto the side road that led to Gambino's vacation home.

"What will we say when we get to the door at three in the morning?" Carson asked. "Oh, hey guys, just wanted to check in and see if you're keeping anyone hostage here?"

"We're going to knock on the front door," Stinsen said. "We're the FBI. A man and his wife known to the Gambino Family are missing in the area, and federal officers have been killed. We're canvassing the area to see if anyone heard or saw anything. We will do everything to get inside."

Carson looked at him. "And you think they're just going to say, 'Oh, those two. Yeah, we got them tied up in the basement'?"

"You know, Carson, you're more an asshole than your reputation lets on."

"What the *fuck* does that mean?"

"It means your reputation is better."

"What?"

"We'll study their response. Watch to see if they're edgy. Did we wake a sleeping guard, or are all the lights on and—"

The sound of automatic gunfire from somewhere on the right stopped him mid-sentence.

"What the fuck was that?" Carson asked.

"Sounded like a gun," Rudy said from the back.

"What we just heard was probable cause," Stinsen said. "We're going in now. Rudy, get on your phone and call for backup. Bring everybody available."

They passed a small gravel road and came to the main entrance. On the left, Carson looked at the funeral home sign and wondered how many more bodies would be buried before the night was over.

A huge explosion rocked the car as they turned onto Gambino's driveway. A fireball rose in the air over the treetops.

Carson aimed for the house. "That looks like it's coming from Gambino's warehouse."

"A warehouse?" Stinsen asked.

"Yeah, he stores old war relics in there. Harmless shit."

"Doesn't sound too harmless to me."

Stinsen pulled out his gun and placed it on his lap. "We're going in hot. My hunch is Darwin and his wife are here, and if I have any wits about me, that explosion was because they pissed

Darwin off, and he's fighting back. He'll need our help, and I intend to give it to him."

34

THE WORLD WAR II tank started down an embankment and headed toward the pool and hills behind it. He had to turn left to continue toward the main house, but the steering didn't respond like a car.

He pulled on the steering wheel, forcing it as far left as possible, but the large machine continued to lumber straight forward. When he released the wheel, the panther turned to the right and headed toward the trees beyond the property.

"Fuck, shit."

An external pinging sound alerted Darwin that he was being fired upon. Regular bullets would do nothing to a German Panther. Then, a thought occurred to him. Would the tank's steering respond like when steering a boat?

The brake pedals were lost to darkness at his feet. Feeling around, he detected numerous pedals at once. He chose the pedal on the left, pushed down softly, and saw through the rectangular slot that the tank turned slightly to the left.

He quickly learned to hit the brakes on one side to turn easily and fast. Using the brakes on the treads on one side, the tank turned as if he were in a canoe and had placed one oar in the water. He kept the tank moving at ten miles an hour so he wouldn't have to anticipate a turn too early.

Through the slot, the house came into view. A line of men carrying assault weapons stood between him and the house. The last thing he needed was one of the guards getting a lucky shot that slipped through the view hole and into his eye. He set the tank on a course to barrel into the patio furniture at the back and enter the house through the back windows, where it would drive through the living room and out the front. Once in the main driveway, he planned on turning it around and driving back through the house. He would do this over and over until the house fell around him or they released his wife.

Once the tank was positioned, he calculated two minutes to impact. Then he shut and locked the rectangular view slot.

Bullets continued to smack into the body of the tank like rain hitting the roof of a car. He checked the gears, the gas, and the steering wheel to ensure nothing had moved and he wasn't destined for the pool.

Something bumped the tank, causing it to lift at the front.

The edge of the patio.

Someone shouted with a bullhorn for him to stop the tank and get out. The table and chairs fell victim to the treads and weight of the tank.

Someone pounded on the top of the turret, attempting to gain entry.

Darwin pushed the clutch inward, shifted into third gear, and released the clutch. The tank shot forward. Glass shattered as he entered the house. The man's voice with the bullhorn resembled

Gambino. He was asking who the fuck was in the tank and what they thought they were doing.

Darwin felt the tank tilt to the right and then drop. He braced himself. Maybe the tank was too heavy for the floor. Did the house have a basement? But then the tank leveled out and continued forward. More gunfire smacked the body of the monster machine. Glass shattered as he drove out through the front of the house. The tank dropped to a forty-five-degree angle as it descended through the front flower bed and hit the driveway.

He waited to the count of three and hit the left brake while dropping the clutch and pulling the tank out of gear. It performed what he assumed to be an almost perfect 180-degree turn. He wanted to risk a peek to see where he was aimed but chose not to. They had to have men holding a bead on the view slot. He put it into first gear and started forward. Within five feet, the tank hit something hard that slowed it almost to a stop.

What the fuck?

If something was in his way, it may be more difficult to shoot at the view slot. He risked a quick glance.

The tank had hit a four-door sedan and driven it into a line of thick trees.

"Shit."

After all, the tank hadn't turned enough to aim back at the house.

"Where's reverse?"

He slammed the view slot closed and held down the brake on one side. Once he pulled the clutch, the engine revved. The screech of metal being torn and shredded accompanied the maneuver. There was some resistance at the start of the turn, but after a ten-second fight, the strong tank ripped through the sedan and pulled back in line with the house.

He grabbed the view slot and held the edge. He needed one look to make sure he didn't make another mistake. He waited. No bullets hit the tank. He couldn't hear anyone on the bullhorn. The only sound was the engine of the tank.

Ready to slam the view slot shut if he saw something he didn't like, he flipped it open, looked outside, and gasped.

Gambino stood by the huge hole in his house with Rosina, a gun to her temple. Darwin shut the view slot and locked it.

"Shit."

"Darwin?" Gambino shouted with the bullhorn. "I know you're in there. Come on out so we can talk."

Darwin kept the brake on but revved the engine in response.

"I'd like to know how you did it," Gambino continued. "How the hell did you get out of that coffin? I saw the backhoe drop the dirt onto its lid myself. Which one of my men helped you? Come on, talk to me, or I will have to kill your lovely wife here."

"Darwin," Gambino shouted. "Special Agent Greg Stinsen is here, too. You remember him, don't you?"

Darwin sat up straight in the seat.

"There are three federal officers here who are pretty pissed that you destroyed their car. You literally wrapped it around those trees. What will it take for you to come out of that tank?"

He was beat. There was nothing left. He could ram the tank back and forth through the house and then drive down the street until the gas ran out, but he wouldn't have Rosina. They would kill her, and Gambino would use insurance money to rebuild his house. Darwin's meddling would only be a setback.

For guys like Gambino, setbacks were all he ever had to deal with.

"Okay," Darwin shouted. "I'll come out. What assurances do I have?"

"Not many," he heard. "But with three feds here, you can be assured that the odds are in your favor. For now."

Darwin turned off the tank's engine and exited the driver's seat. He crouched low and hobbled to the door at the top of the turret. A quick twist and the door unlocked. He pushed open the top and lifted himself up, waiting for the bullets to rain down.

No one moved. No guns were fired.

He estimated over two dozen men stood around the front of the house staring at him. He knew he looked bad. His forehead had a large bump from the rubber bullet. His T-shirt and shorts were covered in dirt, and his hair was tussled up into a mess of filth. He must be like a ghost to them because they thought he was dead and buried.

"This is some pretty sick shit, eh?" Darwin pointed at the house. "That's fucked up."

Gambino looked over his shoulder at the damage. "It's going to be a month or two to repair that." He turned back to Darwin. "Say hello to our guests."

Three men were on their knees. Greg Stinsen kneeled in the middle.

"Hey, Greg. How's it going?"

"Not good. You think you could kill everyone so we can go have a drink? I'll buy."

"Enough," Gambino shouted. "Darwin, come down off that tank. You have caused me a lot of trouble. I can fix a house, but the people coming to buy my German Panther are going to be pissed with what you've done to it."

"I didn't shoot it up. Your goons did."

"I said, get down."

Darwin slid off the turret and climbed down the side. Five feet to his left was the man who had shot him in the forehead with the rubber bullets. "I have a score to settle with you, asshole." Darwin pointed at his head. "This is one fuck of a headache."

"Gambino," Greg shouted. "You can't kill anyone."

"Oh yeah, and why's that?"

"Because we're federal officers. We would be witnesses to murder. I don't see you getting off on that charge."

Gambino laughed. A few of his men laughed along with him. Goosebumps formed on Darwin's arms in the cool breeze. He looked at Rosina. She'd been crying, her eyes red, makeup running. She offered him a smile and mouthed, *I love you.*

Darwin mouthed it back.

"I can kill whomever I want. You're on my property. Darwin here has broken, get it, *broken*, into my house. He's an intruder. I can shoot him and his wife and have twenty-five witnesses say that's how it went down. Then, I can decide whether or not to kill all three of you. Doesn't matter to me. Don't you see?" Gambino let go of Rosina and walked onto the driveway, moving closer to the three officers. "I'm above the law. I won't hire a lawyer. I'll hire a *team* of lawyers, and they'll parade every one of these men standing around you before the jury. Each man will tell the same story. Then I will give them all a hundred-thousand-dollar bonus just because I can. That's what your life means to me." He stood over the three men on their knees. "Except, of course, I wouldn't hurt Rudy here, would I?"

The man on Greg's right stood up. "No, you wouldn't dare."

"Rudy, what the fuck is this?" the man on Greg's left asked.

"Carson, you asshole, the Russians recruited me before I

entered the Bureau."

While the men talked, Darwin moved closer to the man who shot him before he was put in the pine box.

"Gambino will be working with the Russians," Rudy said. "He has successfully passed his initiation rite."

"Which was?" Carson asked.

"He needed to take out the three rival families in central Ontario and then retire to his home here to meet my people. We thought he'd done that, but then *Darwin* showed up." Rudy pointed at Darwin. "He fucked everything up. No one knew who he was or where he came from. Gambino's final task was to grab Darwin, find out who he was, and then execute him. But that hasn't worked out so well, either."

Darwin lowered his center of gravity, twisted toward his mark, and drove his right fist into the man's Adam's apple. The guy fell backward, clutching at his throat. As he fell, Darwin ripped his weapon up and over his head, then spun and leveled it at Gambino.

Before he could find the safety switch on the weapon, half a dozen guns pressed into his temples and cheeks.

"Don't," someone whispered beside him.

Gambino clapped his hands. "Bravo, bravo. What a performance." He stopped clapping and crossed his arms over his sizable chest. "You really are a fucker, aren't you?"

"Can I speak?" Darwin whispered.

"Step back a foot," Gambino motioned to his men. "All guns remain aimed at Darwin. Kill him if he flips off that safety." Gambino fixed his gaze on Darwin. "You were saying?"

The only sound was the choking and hacking behind him on the ground. Rudy stepped away from his old colleagues, who remained on their knees and grabbed a handgun from one of Gambino's men.

"If I'm going to die, I want to do it with dignity," Darwin said.

"And how do you intend to do that?" Gambino asked.

"It appears as though my wife and I are going to die tonight." He glanced around at the firepower surrounding them.

"I agree, but you're like a fucking cat that keeps coming back. How many lives do you have? If I don't see you die, feel your pulse cease, I won't believe you're dead."

A few men snickered. A man on his right eased the tip of his weapon onto Darwin's cheek.

"My offer is this," Darwin said.

"You have an offer? Interesting." Gambino looked over at Rudy. "Should we hear him out or just have him turned into pig food?"

"Hear him out," Rudy said and stepped farther into the shadows behind more of Gambino's men.

Darwin's heart beat so hard that his chest hurt, yet his hands remained steady.

"Let me kill Agent Greg Stinsen for setting me up."

He hoped Greg would understand the reference to what happened in Toronto only a few months ago. The expression on Greg's face told him otherwise.

"Are you serious?" Gambino asked.

Gambino's face scrunched in concentration as he tried to figure out what Darwin was up to.

"Yes," Darwin said. "I'm serious."

Gambino and Rudy exchanged a glance. Rudy nodded.

"Okay, be my guest. Everyone, step back. I want every weapon you have aimed at Darwin. When he flips off the safety, if he turns his weapon away from Stinsen, execute him."

The men surrounding Darwin backed away. Only the gun pressed into his cheek remained. Gambino stepped away from the two remaining feds on the ground. The last of his soldiers stood in Darwin's periphery.

"You gonna get this animal off my cheek?" Darwin asked.

The report of a weapon made him jump. The guy beside him slipped to his knees, half his head missing. The man's body convulsed in the throes of death as it shook for several seconds before coming still, his blood staining the ground a dark red.

"There, he's off your cheek," Gambino said. "I have no use for men who don't follow orders. I told him to ease back."

Darwin lifted the weapon. He clicked off the safety and brought the gun up to aim at Greg.

"Sorry, Greg, but it ends here."

A look of acceptance washed over Greg's face. He had to know the chances of leaving Gambino's alive were slim to none. This was better for everyone, and it was the only way.

Darwin fired. The bullet hit Greg an inch above the eyes in the center of his forehead, right about where Darwin had gotten shot earlier.

Greg's head whipped back, followed by his body. Blood squirted out where the bullet had broken the skin.

Rosina screamed behind him, "Darwin, how could you?" She was crying. "Greg was our friend."

Still on his knees beside Greg, the federal agent edged away, his face showing confusion and fear. Darwin couldn't see Rudy anymore. He'd fallen in behind the men.

Gambino clapped loudly. "Well then, there's one down. Who's next?" he asked.

Darwin stepped forward. Guns tracked his movement. "I'd like to finish the job."

"What are you proposing?" Gambino said as he stepped in front of Darwin, daring him to aim. "You want to shoot yourself?"

"Not exactly. I'd like to shoot my wife now."

Rosina gasped. Gambino looked at her and then back at Darwin. "No way. We have special plans for such a cute young thing. Don't worry, we'll be gentle at first. Wouldn't want to damage her too early. But you were kidding, right? You'd never shoot your own wife. This is some kind of joke, isn't it?"

Darwin shook his head. "No joke. This was always about my initiation into the Russian mafia. I knew your men were coming. How else do you think I could take out five agents? Why am I still alive after you buried me? Ask yourself how I made it to Fuccini and the Harvester of Sorrow all by myself. You have to ask yourself, who has been helping me behind the scenes?"

Gambino faltered, then stepped back. His eyes searched the men around him. His gaze fell to the house, a look of confusion on his face. "Where's Rudy?"

No one answered.

"He's not needed now that I'm here," Darwin said, hoping desperately that Gambino would believe even a little of what he was saying. "That's why I stole the tank. I wanted a test drive before I took it to my people."

"But you're nothing." Gambino fidgeted under his collar at an itch. "I had you checked out. You couldn't even play checkers with me. That was sincere."

"Wrong."

"Then explain why you were so believable."

"Training. Ever heard of Keyser Söze?"

Gambino shook his head. Darwin gripped the weapon tighter.

"Darwin, honey, what're you saying?" Rosina asked behind him.

"Rosina, shut up. This doesn't concern you anymore." He looked at Gambino with all the hatred he could muster. Because of the man in front of him, he was forced to talk like that to his wife. "With the proper training, even polygraphs are useless. I'm one of their forward soldiers. I was sent to finish the job you fucked up in Toronto. Vincenzo was to be killed, too. The Fuccini head was supposed to be at that meeting. He wasn't. So, as I said, I finished your job for you. You should be thanking me and not burying me in six feet of dirt." Darwin spat the last word out. "If I'm lying, then how is it I'm standing before you, alive, and so many men lay dead by my hand? If I'm really a little boy looking to live out his years married and raising kids, then why am I shooting feds and discussing business with you? That leads me to one more thing for you to think about."

Gambino appeared confused. He scanned the faces of his men in search of Rudy. "What do I have to think about?"

"Whether you will willingly let me shoot Rosina and the five men who helped me escape the grave."

"There were five men who helped you?"

Murmurs erupted among the men standing around. They were buying his bullshit with all their stupidity.

"I will point them out as soon as Rosina is dead."

"Fine. Shoot her."

Darwin aimed his weapon at Rosina from ten feet away.

"Fuck you," Rosina spit. "I loved you, and I don't believe a single word—"

Darwin fired, cutting her off. The bullet hit high in her

forehead near the hairline. Her eyes rolled back, and she crumpled to the floor, blood seeping from the wound. The men who had been standing on either side of her stepped away.

"Now, tell me who helped you," Gambino said.

Darwin examined everyone's faces and met the eyes of each man. He caught a glimpse of Rudy in the living room window, talking on a cell phone. Darwin chose five men at random. They all protested and had to be brought to the ground by the butts of their friends' weapons. One of the five got quite vocal, protesting the charge and declaring his innocence.

"Quiet them," Gambino ordered. "No one speaks. I want silence." Then he turned to look at Darwin. "Wait. Johnny was with me after you were taken away to the cemetery. He couldn't have helped you escape. You're lying."

Darwin lowered the weapon to his side and raised his right hand. "Stop," he barked at Gambino. "Watch what you say. The mistakes you've made are plenty. Rudy," he pointed up at the living room window without looking, "is on the phone right now, detailing your mistakes to our bosses. Questioning me again will cost you. Look at your house. That's just the start. Ask Fuccini how I deal with mistakes."

Gambino nodded. "I can't. He was torn in half."

"I had a local biker gang do that for me. So, question me again. Please, because I'm pretty pissed at being buried alive."

Gambino's forehead glistened in the floodlights coming from the house. He moved off to the side and leaned against the tank.

"Line those five men up and kill them."

All five were put in a line. Before they could fight or run, half a dozen other men emptied weapons into their bodies, making them dance on the ground like puppets with broken strings.

Darwin turned to Gambino. He pointed at the dead men on the ground. "May I?"

Gambino nodded. Darwin walked over and emptied his weapon into them, making sure he aimed high so any ricochets would fly into the trees and disappear in the darkness beyond. Then he tossed the assault rifle into the bush and grabbed one from the dead man at his feet.

"Now, let's talk business."

"Not so fast," Gambino said. He waved at Rudy in the window. Rudy nodded and headed toward them.

"Can you verify anything Darwin is saying?" Gambino asked Rudy.

The Russian contact stared at Darwin. "No, I can't. But I will say this. His story fits."

Gambino looked back at Rudy. "Fits what?"

"How many people do you know who could do what Darwin has done?"

Gambino gestured with his hand. "Go on."

"There are others working for my people. They don't tell me everything. I only know what I'm supposed to do."

"Who were you talking to on the phone?"

"That's none of your business. We have a deal. You've passed your initiation. If Darwin says he's one of them, I wouldn't believe him. But if he says he's one of them and shoots a fed and his wife, then I would be careful before I say otherwise."

Darwin held the new weapon tight, waiting for his moment. He counted eight men in total, including Rudy and Gambino. The fed named Carson was still on his knees, another guard holding a weapon behind him.

"Gambino, you know how this works," Rudy continued. "I

haven't met Darwin because his people and my people didn't feel it necessary. If they did, we would've met. There's never a face-to-face without a recommendation by a third party. But after what he has done here tonight, I would take him at his word. For now."

When Gambino faced Darwin, Rudy aimed his weapon and fired at the back of Gambino's head. The back of Gambino's skull exploded, his head taking on a grotesque shape. Gambino's facial muscles twitched as he fell to his knees before dropping face-first to the ground.

No one turned to shoot Rudy. They were all afraid of who he was and who he represented.

"The Red Mafia is moving into new territories. All of you men are now standing employees of my people. Your wages just increased. Now, secure the property. You and you," he pointed at two men nearest him, "come with me."

Rudy turned around and walked into the house, followed by the two men. The rest of them lowered their weapons and stared at Gambino's body.

That gave Darwin the edge he needed. He fired at the guard by Carson, cutting him nearly in half. He swung back, cutting the other three men down before they could respond. In a matter of four seconds, only Carson and Darwin were still alive.

Darwin kicked a rifle toward Carson. "Help me get those other three. Let's end this."

Carson grabbed the gun and aimed it at Darwin. "You die first."

"Aim that somewhere else. I'm with you."

"You just killed a federal agent and your wife."

"No, I didn't. That gun was loaded with rubber bullets. They're only unconscious."

Darwin watched the front of the house. Carson dropped to check Greg's pulse and stood back up. "How'd you know?"

"That was the same gun they shot me with before they buried me alive. The handle has a piece of blue duct tape on it. I covered it with my hand so no one else could tell what gun I was using."

Carson saw the blue tape, then blinked twice, and looked stunned momentarily.

The two men who had followed Rudy inside came running out of the front door. Carson and Darwin fired in unison, killing both men before they got past the threshold.

"One left," Darwin said.

"I got him," Carson said. He stepped by Darwin and then stopped. He put a hand on Darwin's shoulder. "You're a smart fucker. You even had me believing you. How did you come up with that shit?"

"No idea. We'll talk later. Get Rudy."

Carson disappeared inside the house. Darwin knelt by Rosina and lifted her head to rest it on his legs.

"I'm so sorry, baby. I had to. You'll wake to a splitting headache and be mad at me, but we're married. You'll have to forgive me. I'm your husband. To save your life, I can do no wrong, right?"

"Right," Rosina mumbled. Her eyes fluttered. "You are an … asshole sometimes. But I love you, Darwin."

They held each other as sirens approached in the distance.

35

DARWIN RECLINED IN THE office chair of Carson Dodge's plush office. It had been a week since Gambino's death. Darwin had spent the first few days of that week giving long, drawn-out statements to the FBI.

Rudy Earlton had escaped. Carson had gone into Gambino's house after him, but Rudy was already gone. A SWAT team had been dispatched. For the next twelve hours, they searched every square foot of the Gambino property and surrounding area without turning up anything. On the second day, work crews began digging up graves at the funeral home across from the Gambino residence with the arduous task of identifying the bodies. The expected count of over one hundred unmarked graves was a low estimate.

Two days ago, Rosina had been taken to stay with Greg Stinsen in a secret location that only Greg and Carson knew about.

It had been seven full days, and Darwin was eager to finish at the federal building and return to his wife. His wounds healed fast, the bump on his forehead only a small, purple bruise now.

Carson entered the office, followed by two other men holding file folders.

"Darwin, I want you to meet Special Agent Mike Keans and Special Agent Victor Ivanovich."

Darwin stood and shook their hands. He nodded at each man in turn and then took his seat. Both men were dressed in suits and clean-shaven. They looked so good. They could easily have passed as two guys on their way to a wedding. Mike and Victor sat on the small sofa beside Carson's desk.

"I asked these men to join us before you leave today. They have information you should hear."

"Do I want to hear it?"

"You *need* to hear it. It's about you and your wife." Carson turned to his colleagues, laced his hands together behind his head, and leaned back in his office chair, placing his feet on the corner of the desk.

"Darwin," Victor started, "I'm the local Russian mafia expert. Much of the information coming and going that deals with the Red Mafia channels through me."

"And how has that got anything to do with me and my wife?" Darwin asked.

"New information has come to light." The agents exchanged a wary glance. "Your name has come up."

His stomach dropped, and a cold sweat broke out on his forehead and upper lip. *Not again.*

"I'm listening."

"Recently, we discovered that Gambino was moving his interests into arms dealing. The tank and his private planes were converted to war machines with specific modifications. He stored munitions in the back of that warehouse where you found the tank. The kind of stockpiles he had would shame a small country."

"But he's dead. That's all over." He turned to Carson. "It's all over, right?"

"Bear with me." Victor opened the file folder he'd brought with him. "Do you recognize this man?" He handed Darwin a black and white five-by-seven photo.

The picture was taken in the street of a busy downtown area like New York. The man had stepped from a limousine and turned to the camera. Darwin stared at the face and drew a blank.

"Should I recognize him?" Darwin asked.

"No, but he knows you."

"And why does that matter? I'm sure my name has traveled the circles of mobsters after what happened in Toronto. Who is this guy?" Darwin asked, handing the photo back.

"This is Arkady Andropov, also known as AA. Arkady has been seen in Jacksonville as recently as three days ago."

"For fear of sounding retarded and repeating myself several times, what does this have to do with me?"

"Arkady Andropov is reputed to be the boss of the Russian Bratva in Toronto."

"Bratva?" Darwin asked.

"It's Russian, meaning brotherhood. As far as we can tell, Arkady runs the most dangerous mafia in the world this side of Russia, and he does it in Toronto."

Darwin crossed his legs to keep them from bouncing. "Who gets to determine which one is the most dangerous mafia in the world?"

"The U.S. State Department does, and they've given that

distinction to the Red Mafia. They aren't like La Cosa Nostra."

Darwin uncrossed his legs and leaned forward, elbows on his thighs. "You have my attention. What does the Bratva want with me?"

"La Cosa Nostra is just another word for the Italian mafia," Carson said. "Gambino and Fuccini were both bosses in La Cosa Nostra."

"Okay … Rosina and I are going to where no one will ever find us. How does this affect us?"

"I'm afraid that won't be possible," Mike said. "You can't leave."

Darwin looked at the man who had remained quiet so far.

"I'm afraid to ask, but why is that? Why can't we leave?"

"There's a contract on your head. They want you dead within forty-eight hours."

"Bullshit." Darwin looked at Carson, who didn't offer any support. "You're saying if I walk out that door," he pointed at Carson's office door, "and go to my wife, someone will kill me within two days?"

Mike nodded. "It has been ordered if you don't do what Arkady is asking of you."

Darwin grew suspicious. "And you know what Arkady wants with me? Wait, can't the FBI protect us?"

Mike nodded. "We know what he wants."

Darwin walked to the door and placed his hand on the knob. He turned the knob and opened the door. No one waited on the other side to stop him.

"Darwin," Carson said, "Mike Keans has been with the Bureau for twenty-six years. After working deep cover for eight of those twenty-six years, he's our resident expert on the Russian mafia. He has seen things that would make an average man kill himself to rid the images. Mike is one of the most dedicated soldiers the FBI has. There's not many men like him." Carson dropped his feet from the corner of his desk and pulled his chair in. "He has informants all over the country. When he says your name is floating around and there's been a contract put out on your head, I'd listen to him."

What he thought was the end of the nightmare was just the beginning. As upset as he was to learn about the hit on his head, it also pissed him off.

"What the fuck am I supposed to do to get these maggots off my shit?"

Carson gestured at the chair Darwin had vacated. "Please, shut the door and come sit. We have an opportunity to help you end this once and for all. Hear us out."

Darwin pondered his options but knew he had no choice. He closed the door and walked back to the chair, defeated. "I hope what you have to say cheers me up because my life just got gloomier again."

Victor opened another file and pulled out a newspaper folded in half. He flopped it down on the table in front of Darwin.

"Read the headlines. Don't lose control. Only the people in this room and Greg Stinsen knows what it says. The paper will be released later today."

Darwin picked up the paper, flipped it open to the front page, and almost vomited. His stomach clenched, and he bent over like he'd gotten kicked in the abdomen.

The paper had a picture of Rosina from her high school graduation on the front page. Beside the picture was the article on the Gambino house shootings from seven days ago. The report said the shootings claimed another victim. Rosina Kostas (nee Capote) died in the hospital due to the fatal bullet wound caused when her husband, Darwin Kostas, shot her.

Below that, Greg Stinsen was featured as a valued officer with the FBI, also dead by Darwin's hand. When the article was written, Darwin Kostas was still at large in the Jacksonville area. He may be armed and dangerous. Do not approach if you see him. There was a 1-800 number for people to call, and his high school graduation photo featured by the number.

"What's this?" he asked, placing the newspaper on the table. "Why would you guys do that?"

"To save your life."

"What're you talking about?"

Mike motioned with his hands for Victor and Carson to stay quiet. He looked at Darwin and said, "We are on the cusp of the biggest mafia war we've ever seen on our soil. Scratch that, *the* biggest mafia war the world has ever seen, and you're at the center of the storm."

Darwin sat back, eyes wide, and stared at the ceiling. He was sure his face was white. Pins and needles tickled his hands as the blood rushed to his major organs. Adrenaline pumped into his stomach, and the first signs of shock settled in on his system.

"The Russian mafia are muscling in on Toronto. There are seven known crime families in Toronto, three of which have been disbanded or killed off. You know of the Fuccinis, who were the strongest family. The other four left are scrambling for territory." He got to his feet. "Darwin, can we get you some water? You don't look so good."

Darwin nodded. "Yeah."

Carson got up and left the room. They waited. Mike looked

out the office window while Victor rummaged through the folders he had with him.

Carson returned with two bottles of Evian and handed one to Darwin and the other to Mike. After Darwin had a few sips, Mike raised his eyebrows. "We good?"

"Yeah, go on."

"Okay, the Russian mafia are into everything. They're active throughout Russia and have connections with the Chinese Triads, Italy's Cosa Nostra, and biker gangs. The Reds have spread to Israel, Hungary, Spain, the United Kingdom, Canada, and the U.S. They started in Brighton Beach, but none of the history matters for the here and now. They're actually on friendly terms with numerous biker gangs, and our undercover agent says there's confusion in the ranks. They can't figure out how a guy like you had the help of a biker gang to deal with Fuccini. I don't think you realize just how powerful you look to them right now."

Mike drank half the water in his bottle and set it on a corner of Carson's desk. He paced the floor in front of the window.

"The gang you're talking about," Darwin said, "helped me in exchange for a book deal."

"A book deal?" Carson asked. "What the fuck?"

"They were just supposed to be muscle, and things got out of hand. I asked for their help, and in exchange, I would write a nonfiction book, like a biography, on the leader, Richard H, and his biker gang. We've been sending emails back and forth recently, working on the first draft. He's in a safe house somewhere."

Carson laughed. "Where the hell did you come from? Biker gangs killing made men and all to write books? Unbelievable."

"The Reds don't see it that way," Mike cut in. "You've shown that you've got clout, and not even the FBI can keep you down."

Darwin grunted. "I was afraid of that. I just wish it would all go away."

"The Reds are involved in human trafficking, drug trafficking, smuggling of weapons, which include nuclear weapons or dirty bombs, and money laundering, not to mention prostitution. The big money," he raised his right hand to emphasize a point, "is in weapons. Russia fell apart at the end of the Cold War, and free enterprise sprung up. Many soldiers in the Russian army stopped getting paychecks. People still needed to eat to survive. For the right price, and if you had the right contacts, anything could be bought. The DEA busted a couple of guys attempting to sell a Russian submarine to a Columbian drug lord who wanted to bring his cocaine into America underwater. The Reds are so dangerous, they've been known to shoot someone just to see if their gun works."

Darwin felt sick. That he could be so involved in the underworld after a simple accident months ago boggled his mind. He just wanted it all to go away. Life almost wasn't worth living if he had to live it like this.

"Darwin, are you listening?"

He looked up and met Mike's eyes. "I don't know where you're going with this, but when you're done, I will meet up with my wife and leave the States for good. No one will ever hear from us again."

Mike looked at Victor and then Carson. He drank the rest of his water, tossed the empty bottle onto the sofa, and addressed Darwin.

"They want to know how you're still alive. You were ordered to be killed by Gambino for meddling with the Fuccini affairs.

This doesn't mean they weren't happy with what you did—they were. But they're asking, who is this Darwin Kostas? Is that even his real name? Survival of the fittest. Natural selection—"

"Stop. I'm so sick of that connection. All my life, same shit."

"I understand, but you need to listen. We have men on the inside of the Red Mafia. Yesterday, we heard that Arkady wants to meet you."

"Why me?"

"Because Gambino was supposed to find out who you work for and then kill you. They want to know how a man as powerful as Gambino could grab you and your wife, and after shooting you and burying you in the ground, Gambino is dead, and you're still breathing. They are starting to think you're seriously connected somehow."

"I won't be breathing for long from the sounds of it," Darwin said.

"To them, you're either a hero or the biggest enemy the mafia has ever encountered. Arkady has requested a sit down with you. How that plays out depends on how well you play chess."

"What? Chess? I don't know the game."

"The Italians play ball in their downtime. The Russians play chess. What I'm saying is the Red Mafia is smart. These men are very serious and very dangerous. Darwin, they want you dead or working for them. That's it. According to the inner circle of Russian power, you've become too powerful. They want their German tank. They want their arms shipments to come in on time. They want their territory to cover all of Toronto. But most of all, they want you."

"Well, I don't want them. So it's settled."

"You're not getting it. Dead and buried for good or alive and working for them are your only two options. While working with them, you can help us make arrests. We know Rudy Earlton was involved with the Bratva. He saw you handle Gambino at Gambino's estate. He reported back that you shot your own wife and Greg Stinsen. He said you claimed to be a part of the Red Mafia, but you didn't offer to show your tattoos."

"Tattoos? I don't have any tattoos, and I never will."

Mike loosened his tie and pulled it off. He undid the top half of his shirt and opened it to reveal several tattoos across his chest.

"This rose here," Mike pointed to the center of his chest, "was given to me after my initiation. The barbed wire counts for how many years I spent in jail. The rest of these tattoos represent a person's rank, their sins, the number of murders, and prison sentences. As you advance through the ranks, new tattoos are added. They've got over half a million members worldwide, and they're all looking for you. You pose the largest threat to their organization, and they want to know why. You've killed more Cosa Nostra in three months than anyone in history. The Reds aren't stupid. They know you're not a simple vigilante. That would be impossible. It's rumored that you work for us, and since the American justice system is soft, we've let loose a crazy fucker in their midst to off as many as we can."

"So they already think I work for you? That's great. I'll just go have this sit-down while *still* working for you. That'll get me killed real fast."

Mike buttoned his shirt. "Darwin, you can't escape this. You can't just walk away. You will be dead inside two days if you leave this office unguarded. There's nowhere in the world you can go without a new face, a new name, and a lot of praying. Even then, they have informants in the FBI like Rudy. Somehow, some way, they'll find you. The only way to deal with this is to go to them. Tell them what you did with Fuccini and Gambino was to serve as a resume for entry into the Russian mafia. Convince them to take you on, and once you have something concrete on them, we pull you out, arrest the lot of them, and send you to South America for the rest of your life with a new name like Bob or Ralph."

"No way. Can't do it. I'm no mafia guy. I like bacon and eggs for breakfast. I write thrillers for Amazon. I snuggle with my wife in bed and cry while watching sappy movies. The last few months have been hell, but it was all to stay alive. I've been lucky. When the bad guys came, I got away each time. That's it. I will not walk into their den willingly. I've been running from the swarm of bees after accidentally knocking the beehive off the tree. I won't lie down on the beehive and not expect to get stung. That's just fucking crazy."

"That's what they're expecting, though," Carson said. "Your actions have been labeled as crazy. They think you're fucking gone in the head." He pointed at his temple. "They're afraid of you. If they can have you on their team, it removes their fear."

"I don't care about their fear. I care about mine."

The room fell silent for a moment. No one spoke as Mike retook his seat beside Victor.

"You understand why we had Greg and Rosina reported as killed, right?"

Darwin didn't say anything. He just wanted to leave.

"So that the hits on them would expire. We can't fake your death, too. They would want to see the body."

Darwin got up and walked to the door. "We done here?"

"Is there nothing we can say to help you understand how dire your situation is right now?" Victor asked.

"You have done that. I know shit's gone bad. But when I leave, no one will find me or my wife. I've had a lot of people try to kill me over the last three months. I've been lucky, I know, but if they come, I will do whatever's necessary to remove the threat, and if that means more bodies, then so be it. Maybe they'll all learn just to leave me alone next time."

Darwin opened the door, stepped into the hallway, and slammed the door behind him.

36

The FBI was right. He couldn't live the rest of his life wondering who was around the next corner, the constant threat over their heads. Yet the alternative was worse. How could he go into deep cover and work with the Bratva?

The choice had been made for him—he had to deal with the Reds whether he liked it or not. But he had to do it his way, not the FBI's, which meant running from Carson's office. He needed to leave the federal building without being seen by anyone. If the Reds ever thought he'd struck a deal in Carson's office, his life was forfeit.

He had to consider the possibility that the FBI would make him wear a wire, and that would be too risky. If he had no choice but to deal with this new problem, he would deal with it on his terms and no one else's. There had to be a greater purpose to his life. Otherwise, he'd be dead by now. Someone had looked out for him, and he needed help one more time.

He waited for the elevator. When it arrived, he got on, pressed Lobby, and then changed his mind. He couldn't be seen leaving a federal building through the front door. The light for Parking Level Two lit up when he pushed it. The doors shut, and the elevator began to descend.

All he could think about were Mike's mafia tattoos. What if Arkady did decide to work with Darwin and made him go under the needle? He'd lose his mind and end up killing the tattoo artist. A needle? A *fucking* needle? On his skin? No way.

The elevator slowed and stopped. The doors opened in the lobby. Darwin leaned into the wall in the back left corner of the elevator to avoid being seen. The doors sat open for mere seconds and then started to close.

A hand shot through and stopped the doors at the last second. They opened, and two well-dressed men got on. Both nodded at Darwin, and one of the men turned to the buttons, pressing Eighteen. The doors shut, and the elevator descended again. At parking level two, the doors opened, and Darwin walked out between the men, turned to the right, and disappeared around the concrete corner.

Light from the elevator spilled out onto the floor. He watched it from behind the corner. Then the doors closed, and Darwin heard the mechanism lifting the elevator to the floors above.

He couldn't live as a paranoid maniac. Just because two men got on an elevator didn't mean they were assassins.

He slid down the wall and sat, bringing his knees to his chest. He wrapped his arms around his knees and bowed his head.

He could grab Rosina, run to the train station, and head to the Mexican border. Once across the border, they could continue south. Panama, Costa Rica, and maybe even Brazil. How could anyone find them in South America? If they shacked up on a beach somewhere, no one would know who or where they were.

But what kind of life was that? How could he provide for Rosina? He needed his MacBook Pro to write. He needed an American address and bank account to get paid. That meant he would have a bank card and leave an electronic trail to wherever he was. Just to get food, clothing, and shelter, he would expose them to the constant threat of being murdered in their sleep. He refused to sleep with one eye open for the rest of his life, however long that would be.

The decision had to be made. Run with Rosina or locate the Reds and offer to work with them. But for how long? When could he get out? One day, one week, or one month? When was enough enough?

He slapped his knee. Then he answered his own question.

It's over when I say it's over.

And the only way to do that was to go to the Russians, find out their interest in him, and then go to the next stage. He'd make new decisions at that point. At least he would have given it a try. Just running meant they'd always be running. Joining the Bratva had the potential to remove the threat.

Rosina was safe with Greg. The world thought they were dead. He had to do what any good husband would do and leave her where she was safe. He had to deal with this last issue.

He got up and stepped out of the shadows. No one was visible. He walked down the rows of cars on his way to the clearly marked exit. Something moved to his right. He jumped back and looked, but nothing was there.

He shook out his arms and started walking again. It was warm in the parking garage. Sweat broke out on his forehead and back. He wiped at it and bumped the string around his neck. The FBI Visitor Pass. He lifted it over his head and tossed it between two cars.

The exit ramp was narrow and meant for one car only. He didn't want to take the stairs as that was an obvious exit. Walking out of the building on the ramp wouldn't be expected.

He stopped at the sound of a noise reverberating throughout the parking level behind him. He stepped back and peeked around the edge of the wall. A woman had exited her car and was walking toward the elevator bank.

A moment later, a man exited the same car and shut his door quietly, scanning the area around him. His gaze stopped when he saw Darwin watching him.

Darwin yanked his head back behind the wall, then jogged up the ramp until he reached parking level one. At the far end, the sun shone through large concrete holes ventilating the parking area.

Dress shoes clomped hard behind him.

Darwin hustled down four cars over and two back, dropped to his knees, and lay on his belly. From under the car beside him, he could see the spot where his pursuer would exit the ramp.

Just as he expected, the man came around the corner and stopped. The bottom of his legs turned and twisted as the guy looked everywhere, evidently confused about where Darwin had gone.

After a full minute, he turned back to the ramp and disappeared from view.

Darwin stayed on the ground for another five minutes. Two cars came and went in search of parking. Then he walked down the aisle of cars, staying close to the concrete abutment at their front bumpers, which kept him relatively out of sight from the ramp the man had disappeared down.

Halfway to the concrete holes where the sun shone through, the man popped back out.

"Hey!" he shouted.

Darwin ran. He had no way to explain his presence because he'd discarded the visitor pass. Talking to the man and verifying who he was would take time and mean another hour or two in the FBI building, which Darwin didn't want.

He reached the end of the lot, ran between two parked cars, and hopped onto the three-foot concrete wall. The drop down to the grass was easy eight feet. Beside the grass was a sidewalk, and beyond that was the access road to the parking garage. The street twenty yards away bustled with activity. Getting to the street was all he needed to do. He could easily lose the guy in the crowd out there.

He looked back and saw the man six cars behind him and advancing fast. There was a certain rush from being chased and having to think his way out of the situation that he enjoyed.

Darwin swung his legs over the edge. A green electrical box sat in the center of the grass. He pushed off the wall and aimed for the box. When he hit it, he bent at the knees and let the forward momentum roll him off the top of the green box and onto the grass, where he tucked and rolled. He got to his feet and looked up. The man leaned over the edge and stared down at Darwin.

"Don't move. I'm coming down there. Stay where you are."

Darwin lifted his middle finger and backed away. "Fuck you." Then he turned and ran for the street. He looked back once more, but his pursuer had disappeared.

He had to stop on the street to let a crowd of people go by on the sidewalk. It was a busy downtown street. He wouldn't be able to tell if someone was watching him or not. He had no idea how to contact Arkady to get the sit-down over with. When they finally met, he would tell him he'd had a score to settle with Fuccini. Gambino brought on his own fate by coming after Darwin. If he would've left well enough alone, he'd still be alive today.

If the Red Mafia were as smart as the FBI said they were, Darwin didn't feel he'd have a problem getting through to Arkady without playing chess.

He decided to catch a cab and head back to his hotel. He would pack and then meet with Rosina, and together, they would leave Florida and head to Mexico.

Perhaps it would be better just to disappear. They would never see Darwin again if he hid them well enough. Maybe after a while, my interest in Darwin would wane.

He raised his hand to hail a cab. A checkered cab pulled out of traffic and approached him, the passenger window down.

"Where do you need to go?" the cab driver asked.

"The Howard Johnson's out by the airport."

"Hop in."

He opened the door and slipped into the back seat just as the door on the other side opened.

"Cab's taken," Darwin shouted at the new passenger.

A man on the sidewalk broke from the crowd and stepped up to the door on Darwin's side, preventing him from opening it as the stranger sat in the back seat beside him. The stranger was small and thin and wore a hoodie covering his face.

The cab driver looked in the mirror. "Everything okay back there?"

The stranger produced a handgun from his pocket and tapped the driver's shoulder with it. "Drive the fucking car."

Darwin tried the door, but it remained blocked. He leaned away in his seat as if moving deeper into the corner could get him farther from the stranger. He had caught the hard accent when the man spoke English.

The cab driver pulled away from the curb and joined the traffic heading south.

"Where to?" the driver asked, his voice changing to reveal his nerves.

"Just drive. I'll tell you when to stop."

The man pulled the hoodie back. His head was clean-shaven, with tattoos on his scalp. He had a deep scar on his neck and two silver front teeth.

"We finally meet," the man said.

All Darwin could think about was the weapon. "I'm so glad you brought a gun and not a knife."

The stranger frowned.

"I wondered how long it would take for you to show yourself," Darwin continued. "Now that I've got your attention, how can I be of service to you?"

37

"Looks like we fucked up," Carson said.

"Not really." Mike shook his head.

"And how do you figure that? The guy has no surveillance, he has no wire, no formal training, nothing. And we let him go. He'll get killed out there."

"He's made it this far."

"Mike, our job was to scare him. We were supposed to bring him up to speed on the people looking for him. Tell him how dangerous these people are and then offer him a sweet deal."

"That wouldn't have worked with Darwin," Victor interjected. "He does things his way. He reminds me of Charles Bronson in *Death Wish*."

Mike and Victor exchanged a smile.

"We just killed him," Carson said. "If the Reds pick him up, he's done, and you guys are giggling like schoolgirls." Carson walked over to the office window. "Just over a week ago, I would've put a bullet in his head myself, but I saw what he did at Gambino's place that night. I saw the dirt all over him from being buried alive. I saw what he did with a *fucking* German tank. What that man did to get to his wife—I don't know many men in the Bureau who could do better. I was wrong about him. My gut is rarely wrong. At least not *that* wrong." Carson turned to the men still seated on his couch. "Darwin deserves better. And yet we allowed a citizen in serious danger to leave this office. Sure, we had a deal—get us inside information so we can make busts, and then we'll protect you—I can see why he wouldn't take that. We couldn't protect him before." He pulled out his chair and sat hard. "How could he expect us to protect him now?"

Mike got up and walked to the door. "If it's any consolation, Darwin has done the right thing here."

"How's that? Tell me."

"Walking out of this office and refusing to work with us may save his life. If the Reds ever found out he struck a deal, we wouldn't find him in the river with concrete weights on his feet. We'd find body parts in several states. And it wouldn't end there. They would do the same to Rosina and her parents, too. The best thing he could do was leave here naked. They can break anyone. They'd break our Canadian boy, and that would be his death."

"Do we have any leads on Arkady's location?"

"None."

"Do we have anything on where the Russians frequent? Anything at all?"

"They don't come around Jacksonville. If you want to find the people in the Russian mafia interested in Darwin, you have to go to Toronto. Or better yet …"

"What? Or better yet, what?"

"Go sit with Rosina and Greg. The Reds will show up there soon enough."

"This is fucked," Carson said. "Do you know how fucked this is?"

Mike stepped out and closed the door without responding. Victor collected his file folders and the newspaper off the floor and stood.

"Do you know where Greg is keeping Rosina?" Victor asked.

"Yeah, why?"

"You want my opinion?"

Carson nodded.

"Find Darwin and get him and his wife out of the States. The situation's too hot. It'll cool. The feuding families will duke it out. The territory will be established, and Darwin's fight with the Cosa Nostra will become a legend. Darwin gets older, grows a beard, and assumes a new name. Everything's back to normal. We go after the bad guys and protect the good guys, like it should be."

"I like that. I really do, but this isn't a perfect world. We had to tell Darwin about the Russians' interest in him. The director wanted to offer Darwin a deal. Wouldn't you, after Darwin's track record? On the outside, the guy sounds like a regular *fucking* John Rambo. But that is where we failed him."

Victor nodded, walked to the door, and left without saying a word.

Carson punched his desktop.

"Fuck!"

38

"WHY WERE YOU HAPPY I brought a gun and not a knife?"

Darwin had settled back in his seat as the taxi continued through the city, speaking slowly and sure to not make a mistake.

"I hate knives. Anything sharp or pointy angers me. I use plastic utensils when eating at a restaurant. But guns, I don't mind."

"You've meddled where you shouldn't have," Arkady said. "But I like that. Tell me, why'd you do it?"

Darwin looked out the window. They were driving over a bridge. An airplane flew overhead. They were near the airport. The cab driver looked back a few times but did what he was told and continued to drive without a word.

"I did it to survive." He looked at Arkady but couldn't meet his eyes for over a second. They were dark pits, black orbs. He wondered what the man had seen and done in his life to be where he was. "I did it because they pissed me off. But most of all, I did it for you."

"How do you know what I want?"

"After I killed Fuccini, there was a certain rush to it. I waited. I knew someone else would come. Then Gambino sent his men, and now Gambino's dead, and here we are. If a man makes himself a worm, he must not complain when he is trodden on."

"Immanuel Kant."

Darwin nodded. "No great genius has ever existed without some touch of madness."

"Aristotle. I'm impressed."

"I don't play chess," Darwin said. Arkady's eyebrows raised. Darwin detected the edge of a smile. "I play checkers. When someone gets in my way, I jump them—piece removed. Game over. Checkers is about *becoming* the king, not acquiring the other's king. Use the walls to keep your men safe. Never back into a corner unless there are two spots and an exit. It's all black and white. There's something to think about in that."

Arkady leaned away and tapped the driver's shoulder. "Pull in to terminal two."

The driver nodded.

"I want to talk further," Arkady said. "I'm assuming you will come willingly."

Darwin nodded.

Arkady slipped the gun away. "We have much to talk about. If everything works out, maybe we can do business. I saw how you escaped the feds. What did they want?"

Darwin hoped the feeling in his stomach wouldn't show on his face.

"They wanted me to work with them to help track you. I was told that I would work undercover."

"What did you tell them?"

"To go fuck themselves. They have no idea who I am or what

I want. They don't know my motivations."

"And they are?"

"To work with men of honor, which is only found in the brotherhood."

"But you're not Russian."

"Is every hitman you use Russian? What counts is not the size of the man in the fight—it's the size of the fight in the man. I can help you claim your territory rights in Toronto. That's my city. I set meetings up and take care of whatever you need. Your transition into Toronto would be seamless. The families of the Cosa Nostra are in disarray because their bosses are dead. They're naming new captains and trying to maintain control. This is the best time in Toronto's history to make a play. In a matter of months, Toronto could be yours."

The cab pulled over near the terminal. Arkady motioned for the door. Darwin opened it and got out, followed by the Russian. The cab squealed away without getting paid.

"Come with me," Arkady said, taking Darwin's arm and leading him into the airport.

***

When they entered the private plane, two skinheads met them. Both men spent considerable time frisking Darwin in a manner he thought too rough. He would definitely bruise from the pat-down. Once the plane was airborne, both men joined Arkady in another section of the aircraft. For the entire flight, Darwin remained alone.

They taxied to a waiting limousine at the Toronto airport under a sky darkened by rain clouds. As they stepped from the plane, six men stood on the tarmac, surrounding a stretch limo. The air cooled with the imminent threat of rain.

Arkady pointed to the car. Darwin got in the back. Inside, one of the toughest-looking men he'd ever seen sat on the opposing seat. The man could've been Dolph Lundgren's brother. His head was shaved, as well as his bony face. He wore a white tank top that showed off his tattoos and muscles. The scowl on his face made him look permanently angry. If they ever met in an alley, Darwin knew any ordinary handgun wouldn't stop a man like this unless the bullet entered an eye, and even then, he couldn't be sure.

The other door opened, and Arkady got in.

"Go."

The limo pulled away.

Landing in Toronto was bittersweet. He would normally be happy to be home, but he was being chauffeured in a limo with high-ranking members of the Russian mafia under false pretenses. Anything he learned from Arkady, Darwin would definitely be taken back to the authorities because people like Arkady needed to be stopped at all costs.

He just hoped to stay alive long enough to relay that information to the feds and see his wife again.

39

THE LIMOUSINE ENTERED A warehouse in Etobicoke, a section of the Greater Toronto Area. They drove in silence, Dolph clenching and unclenching his fists as he stared at Darwin. Arkady turned toward him more than once, but Darwin kept his attention aimed out the window.

A sickening thought made him feel faint. What if they were delivering him to the other families of the Cosa Nostra as a peace offering? With Darwin Kostas out of the way, they could make a deal.

He had to stop thinking about worst-case scenarios. He had gotten lucky with Fuccini and luckier with Gambino. Could three times be the charm?

The garage door descended, closing off the falling sun and dark clouds from view. Armed men approached the limo from all sides.

"Get out," Arkady ordered.

Darwin grabbed the door handle and stopped when Arkady's hand landed on his shoulder.

"No sudden movements out there. These men don't know you. You're not Russian. They've only heard of you. Your reputation scares them, which makes them testy. There are a few who don't believe in what I'm doing. Do you understand this?"

"Yeah, I get it."

Darwin got out and stood by the open door. The men closest to him didn't retreat. Two of them tilted their heads back and watched him down the length of their noses, jaws tight.

"Give him some room," Arkady said as he came around from the other side. "This is the man we've all been hearing about. Darwin's here for a sit-down. We will have our talk, and then we'll decide what to do next." Arkady turned to Dolph. "Take him to the second floor. We'll meet in five minutes."

Dolph grabbed Darwin's arm and almost broke it. The guy's grip was worse than a vise. It felt like he had a Hummer parked on his arm as he was dragged to a metal staircase and pulled to the second floor.

In the room, he was pushed to a chair in the middle. Dolph stepped out and shut the door behind him, leaving Darwin alone. A table with folding legs sat in front of a chair near the far wall. A rectangular light fixture suspended from the ceiling reminded him of the kind they had in grade school. He felt exposed in the center of the room. He fumbled with his hands, checked for dirt under his nails, and waited for Arkady.

There was something surreal about what was happening. It was like he was living someone else's life. He wrote thrillers—he didn't live them. The men outside the room were murderers. They ran drugs and weapons to make money. He was not of their ilk. He felt a greater fear and tension from waiting, like sitting in reception at the dentist's office to have teeth pulled or a root canal.

Eventually, Arkady entered the room, a gun in his hand. He closed and locked the door, then sat facing Darwin. He placed the weapon on the table, the barrel aimed at Darwin.

"We need to talk."

Darwin nodded.

"Tell me what happened with the Fuccini Family."

Darwin considered what to say. He talked about how he learned of the meeting in north Toronto and drove there to observe. When he saw Vincenzo leaving the premises alone, he killed him with his car to make sure Gambino's job was complete.

He continued, telling Arkady that after taking out the rest of the Fuccinis, Gambino would come calling, so he waited. He explained that Arkady should already know the rest because Rudy Earlton had escaped the Gambino mansion thanks to Darwin.

"Where's Rosina?" Arkady asked.

Darwin dropped his head and stared at his hands. "She's no longer with us."

"You mean she's dead?"

Darwin met his eyes. "Read the morning papers."

"I don't understand something," Arkady said as he stood. "Why would you bring your wife into this? Wasn't that dangerous?"

"It was a checkers move."

"What?" Arkady asked. He lifted his weapon and walked around the table to sit in the front corner. "What kind of move?"

"She was my partner. The Fuccini Family had killed her brother. She wanted revenge. We met and decided to fly to Rome, where the Fuccinis had an office. We married in Rome to make it look like we were eloping. No real threat to anyone. As the Cosa

Nostra attacked, one by one, we executed them and flew back to Canada, where we contacted Richard H and his biker gang to back us up in a meeting with Fuccini. You know the rest."

"So you're actually married?"

It was the first time Arkady cracked a full smile.

"Yes."

"I kill liars. You know that, Darwin. I kill them in this room. It's easy. I ask questions, and when I catch the first lie, I shoot them in the knee. Shortly after, the next knee. Three strikes, you're out. Bullet in the forehead." He raised the gun and tapped his temple. "The fish rots from the head first."

The thought that Arkady knew something and caught him in a lie freaked him out. He wanted to shift in his seat but didn't. He wanted to run at Arkady and strangle the life out of him but didn't. He sat and waited for a bullet.

"But so far, everything you've said makes sense. I checked you out and saw a real marriage license. I'm impressed with the lengths you will go to create a cover. Not many people could take down two Cosa Nostra bosses and live. The families around here want your head. Other families in the old country want you dead."

"That's why I want to work for you. The fear that my name instills adds to your strength." A cool sweat broke out across Darwin's body.

Arkady stood and started pacing. "We'll get to that. But first, I want to ask you a series of questions, and I want the most honest answers you can give me." Arkady walked around behind Darwin. "I want you to picture a cube in the desert."

"What do you mean, a cube?"

"Any cube. It can be made of anything. You picture it. Later, I will want as many details as you can offer about the cube. Do it now."

Darwin assumed this was some kind of test. Passing the test would mean life or death.

"Next, I want you to picture a ladder," Arkady said. "I want to know what it's made of and where the ladder is in relation to the cube."

Darwin's knee bounced, and he stopped it for fear of looking nervous. He wanted to wipe the sweat from his brow but chose not to.

"Are you ready?" Arkady asked, still standing behind him.

Darwin nodded.

"Okay, two more things. Picture a horse. I want to know the kind it is, where it is, and what it's doing now."

Darwin did and waited for the last item.

The Russian gangster stepped to Darwin's right and looked down at him. "Are you ready for one more?"

"Yes. Go ahead."

"Picture a storm. Tell me everything you can about this storm. Where is it? How far are you from it? What kind of storm is it? Got it?"

Darwin nodded.

"Okay, I will let a few people in to hear your answers."

Arkady opened the door, and half a dozen Russians entered the room.

He remained stone-faced as the men formed a semi-circle around the desk. The only man who stayed slightly behind him was Dolph. He leaned against the closed doors and folded his meaty arms.

Darwin studied their faces, wondering if one could be undercover FBI like Carson had told him. Maybe more than one of the men in the room worked for the feds. Would that matter if Arkady lifted his weapon and shot him in the face?

"Tell us about the cube first."

Darwin nodded. "I pictured a large cube. One made of hardened steel and impenetrable. Nothing can hurt it, mark it, or destroy it. Like a cockroach after a nuclear war, the cube would keep sitting in the desert, the sun reflecting off its surface."

Heads turned, eyebrows raised. A couple of the men nodded to one another.

"Very good," Arkady said. "The cube represents you."

"Me? How so?"

"The cube is a look into your self-esteem, how you feel about yourself. What you just told us is that you're unbeatable, unbreakable. You're as strong as steel, and even after the war, you will be the last man standing, untouched. I like that."

Darwin was shocked. He had no idea how they linked the cube to him, but he was happy his description was good.

"The ladder," Arkady said. "Tell us about your ladder."

"It's strong, too, but not as strong as the cube. Its metal frame can be bent with enough pressure."

"Where do you see the ladder in relation to the cube?"

He thought fast and decided on what to say. "The ladder is lying down under the cube. It's stuck, and unless the cube is moved or decides to move, the ladder isn't going anywhere."

More nods. He knew this answer worked also. Two for two.

"The ladder represents law enforcement and how you feel about them. You just told us that they are not a threat to you—at least, you don't see it that way. You're on top of them, like the cube on the ladder. The rungs are made of metal, but they can be bent, which leads to how you can get them to do what you want when you want, like in the help you've received using the FBI. Brilliant, actually."

"How do you know all this?"

"It's an examination of sorts prepared by a German psychologist for us to begin the initiation process. If you pass this successfully, you go to the next level. That is something we'll discuss another time. First, we must finish with the horse and the storm. Tell us about your horse."

Arkady pulled back the action on his weapon to chamber a round. He checked to see if the selector was off safe and lowered the weapon to his side.

Tension filled Darwin's body, and his heart rate increased. There was no way he could get past the amount of men in the room. Weapons bulged under shirts and in the pockets of every man in the semi-circle. Arkady had just readied his gun, and Dolph guarded the door. Everything seemed to weigh on the horse answer.

He made a decision and went for it. "The horse I pictured is dead. Completely dead and rotting. It was an ugly thing. I had to kill it because of how ugly it was. Fucking horse. Who would want one?"

Arkady lifted his weapon, looked at Darwin over the top of it, and flipped the safety back on. He set the gun on the table by his side and clapped three times.

"Bravo. That is amazing." He turned to the men around him and addressed them. "See how accurate this shit is?" He met Darwin's eyes. "The horse represents love in a couple of forms. Mostly, it is supposed to deal with the one love in your life, but it can also deal with how you feel about love if you're single. Since your horse is dead, that confirms to us Rosina is dead. You said you had to kill your horse, and we know you shot Rosina. But did you know," Arkady waved his finger at Darwin, "you're the first person ever to say their horse is dead? Of all the men we've done this on, the horse always described the woman they were in love with and how much they loved her. Amazing," he said, shaking his head. "Now, tell us about the storm. Where is it in relation to the cube, and what kind of storm is it?"

"The storm is so far from the cube that I can barely see it. Four winds from different areas have joined together to form a wicked tornado. I can see it in the distance, but it doesn't pose a threat to me. Even if it came my way, nothing fucks with the cube. There's no tornado big enough to even move the cube. I don't fear it."

"The storm tells us how you feel about problems in your life, such as law enforcement. It also tells us how close they are to you. We've caught two guys working undercover with the storm as they said that it was over their heads, raining down on them. According to what you just said, the law is so far away, you can barely see them, and even if they came at you, it'd mean nothing because you're the motherfucking cube."

Arkady turned and pointed at each man in the room. After a moment, each man nodded at Arkady. Darwin had no idea what that meant, only that it was probably a good thing.

Dolph opened the door and stepped out, followed by the rest of the men. Arkady stopped at the door and waved at Darwin.

"Come on. I'll give you a tour of our warehouse while the men set up the initiation rites. You're going to like what we have in store for you."

Darwin got up from the chair, happy that Arkady had already turned away, and didn't notice his knees almost give out. How he managed to pass their test eluded him. He wondered when his heart would calm down. Before leaving the room, he looked back and saw the telltale sweaty moisture on the seat he'd been sitting on.

He followed Arkady along the raised metal walkway and then down the stairs. They turned a corner and started along another hall with doors on either side. Music blared from two rooms on the left, their doors shut. On the right, the rooms had no doors.

Arkady stopped in front of the first room and stepped just inside.

"Take a look at what we have here," he said, his face showing no emotion.

Darwin entered the room and saw a pointy apparatus of some kind. It was covered in a red and black liquid. It looked like someone had haphazardly painted the whole unit, dripping the darkened paint on the floor around the unit's base. Small white cubes were scattered on the floor at the base, as well as what looked like hair.

"What is that thing?" Darwin asked.

"That's a Judas Cradle."

It looked like a regular wooden stool from any bar, but there wasn't a seat. Instead, there was a cone-like pyramid with a sharp-looking tip. From where Darwin stood—and he swore to himself he wouldn't step closer—the top appeared to be metal with four sharpened edges coming to the pinnacle that formed the tip of a large dart. It wasn't paint that covered the surface. It was blood. Chains were suspended above the unit with weights and different pulleys that, at first glance, Darwin couldn't make sense of.

"It looks pretty dirty …" Darwin broke off before his voice caught in his throat. The sharp tip of the cone caused a disturbance in him. He suddenly felt like he had to vomit again.

"We never clean it," Arkady said.

Darwin frowned but didn't say a word.

"Four days ago, we found an informant amongst our ranks. He was stripped of his clothes and placed in those chains above the Judas Cradle. Then, with the support of gravity and his own body weight, he was eased down onto the top of the cone, strategically, until the steel tip entered his ass." Arkady chuckled, his shoulders hitching. "Man, did that guy scream."

Darwin had heard enough. If he continued, he was sure stomach acids would cover Arkady's head in seconds.

"The blades on the top of the cone are so sharp that as the man is lowered, he gets opened from the anus and spread as wide as the base. When it's over, you could place a large watermelon or pumpkin in the corpse without touching the edges of the hole in his ass. The informant was literally torn apart from his rectum up to his neck. Amazing, isn't it?"

Darwin felt seriously ill. He worried that if Arkady caught on, he would be the next Judas Cradle victim. He stepped back to the shadow of the door, made a trip, and stubbed his toe hard against the door to have something else to focus on. The pain was sharp and did its job. Anger fueled him as the pain coursed up his leg.

He turned to Arkady, his face placid, and asked, "What are the white cubes on the floor at the base?"

"The guy screamed and begged to be taken off. We told him we would stop. At that point, the damage from the first foot of the blades inserted in his ass was enough that after surgery, he'd be able to shit again the normal way within a month. But he had to do something for us."

Arkady turned away from the door and started walking down

the hall again. Darwin followed.

"He agreed. We handed him pliers and told him to take out as many teeth as possible because that's how we feel about informants—they shouldn't talk right after what they've done." Arkady stopped in the hall and slapped Darwin's arm. "Can you believe this guy? He took the pliers and started pulling his own teeth out. Blood was pouring from his mouth. We were taking vodka shots and having a real party at that point. After he was done, he tossed the pliers away, screamed as loud as he could, and showed us his broken and bleeding gums. The guy's fucking mouth was shattered." Arkady banged the wall beside him with his hand. "I'll tell you, that's a will to live."

"Did he make it to the hospital?"

"You serious? Fuck no. After that little demonstration, we added the weights to the chains and dropped him hard onto the cone's top, slicing it right through him to the top of his fucking head. He almost got cut in half." Arkady didn't laugh. His face had grown serious. "That's what happens to informants. Nobody rats out the brotherhood."

"You want to know something?" Darwin asked. He waited until Arkady nodded. "We got in that taxi, drove to the airport, flew to Toronto, and came here. In all that time, I have not taken a fucking piss. Where can I take a piss?"

Arkady smiled and patted him on the shoulder. "Down the hall. It's the last door on your right. When you're done, meet me right here."

"Got it."

Darwin stepped away and almost vomited. He hit the bathroom door, ran for the toilet, and threw up nothing but liquid, his stomach heaving as it clenched. He hadn't eaten since the morning before his talk in Carson's office. He flushed immediately, urinated, and washed his face and hands. To add color to his face, he got in the pushup position on the floor, lifted his feet up on the counter, and did five inverted push-ups at a forty-five-degree angle.

He left the bathroom and joined Arkady, who hadn't moved a foot. The tour resumed as if it hadn't stopped. Arkady opened the door to the room on the left. What Darwin saw was a different kind of shock to his system.

A woman, who appeared to be high on drugs, was chained to a bed, naked. Four different men straddled her, with two of them forcing their genitals into her at the same time, the other two men stroking themselves, no doubt waiting their turn.

"That's Lisa. She gets all the drugs she wants for free, and my men take turns relieving their stress. She services about twenty men a day here. I'm sure she'd be happy to take care of you later. Just let me know, and I'll introduce you to her."

Arkady shut the door and headed to the room with music next door. Inside, two women, both on their knees, were performing oral sex on two men covered in tattoos. One of the men looked up and nodded at Arkady, who shut the door.

"If you're looking for something quieter, more intimate, you can always take one of the women who work for us and find an empty room. Lisa and Mona are two of the best. We have dozens of women coming through here all day. Some are getting off work, and others are heading out. They come here to pay their protection dues and get high. Our hottest girl holds the record of fifty-five customers in twelve hours. After that, she came back here to do fifteen more men in our warehouse. Not bad for a day's work. She bled at the end, but isn't that what Alice Cooper said,

'Only women bleed'?"

Darwin followed Arkady to the last door on the left. Arkady turned to him before they entered the room.

"You're not queasy, are you?"

Darwin shook his head, afraid to speak. He was horrified that humans even existed like the man he stood beside. What those women were going through was atrocious. He had to do something soon. Killing Arkady was out of the question. Did he have enough to tell the FBI? Could the tour alone have all the Russians in the building rounded up, arrested, and taken to jail for dozens of years?

Arkady stepped aside, and Darwin moved into the room. He willed his eyes to close, but they remained open.

Strung up on chains with hooks embedded in his skin, an Asian man was bleeding in dozens of places.

"Ivan here is slowly killing this member of the Triads. He attacked our men and disrespected one of our women. She's still in the hospital, having surgery to correct the smashed orbital bone around her eye. He broke her face in half. No one does that to our girls. This is called 'death by a thousand cuts.' Ivan spends the day cutting the Asian's flesh, piece by piece. He bleeds, it clots, and Ivan cuts again somewhere else. The process is slow, and the cuts are painful and agonizing. Imagine the last week of your life being slowly cut apart—hell would seem appealing."

"What ahh …" Darwin paused. "What's next? Can we go get something to eat?"

Arkady smiled at him. "You just saw the Judas Cradle, and this man here bleeding all over the floor, and you're asking about food. I like that. You'll fit in well here."

Arkady led him back to the stairs and up to the room where

he'd been asked all the questions about the cube and horse. Before they entered the room, Arkady turned to him.

"The Bratva have decided to let you in. While we were downstairs, they set up the initiation ritual. After that, you will be given our commandments and sent out on your first job. Your time has come. Only enter the room if you're prepared to go all the way."

Darwin moved past him, grabbed the doorknob, and entered the room. Over thirty men lingered along the perimeter, leaning against the walls. No one sat at the table. There was one chair that he guessed was for him. The light in the room was off. A candle had been lit and burned strong on the table. Also on the table by the candle was a human skull, a gun, and a dagger.

The dagger made him falter. He stopped and stared at it, a renewed fury growing inside. He hated knives. The threat of a knife made him lose his mind. He knew the initiation would involve the dagger. Otherwise, it wouldn't be on the table. He was already trying to find a way to get rid of it. He couldn't possibly run now. He'd seen too much. He was stuck in the Russian lair as rage boiled in him. He could not fight the number of men in the room and make it out alive.

But he had to do something.

40

CARSON DODGE DROVE HIS car hard, leaving Jacksonville as fast as he could. The last thing he wanted to do was tell Rosina that Darwin had left his office and disappeared.

As he drove, he cursed the Bureau, the system, and the men he worked with. How could they let Darwin walk away? The Bureau was so intimidated by the Russian mafia that sometimes they would charge members with lesser crimes to get them off the streets for a few years instead of taking bigger risks to go for the bigger fish.

He recalled a case where two men had offered weapons to two undercover agents. A meeting had been set up. Once a deal was made, a delivery date established, and the proper amount of vodka drunk, the two suspects offered a bigger item for sale: a dirty bomb. The threat to the agents had grown exponentially. The order came down to arrest both men on the weapons charges. Getting a dirty bomb into the States could have consequences no one wanted to face for the sake of an arrest. Both Russian brotherhood members spent three years in jail, got released, and flew home.

Three years. Carson shook his head. *That's nothing but another tattoo of honor.*

Greg had insisted they use the same safe house where Rosina and Darwin had been before Gambino came after them. No one would expect them to stay there. Carson was the only contact they had with the Bureau office in Jacksonville, and Carson was the only one who knew where they were, other than Darwin.

He made the last turn and started up to the gate. Two men stepped out of the shadows. It was nearly midnight. Shift change had already taken place. Carson wondered who he'd have to deal with to get inside.

He pulled up to the gate and lowered his window.

"Carson Dodge, here to see Greg Stinsen."

"ID, please," the guard said as he stepped close to the vehicle, his hand on the butt of his weapon.

Carson detected movement in his mirror. Another guard had exited the woods and stepped up to his trunk, with the third one staring in at him from the passenger side.

He reached inside his suit jacket slowly and produced his Bureau ID. He handed it to the guard, who walked away and entered a little booth.

Crickets sang in the bushes, and a light breeze rolled over his forearm as he rested it on the door. After several moments, the guard stepped out of the booth and nodded at his men. The gate began to open.

"Special Agent Dodge, Agent Stinsen is waiting for you. Go on up."

Carson took his badge back and drove through the gate. When he looked in his mirror, the guards at the gate had disappeared.

"Bit late for a meeting," Greg said. "Everything cool?"

Carson stepped through the door, past Greg. "We need to talk. Alone."

"She's in the other room watching a movie, trying to keep her mind off everything. She's worried sick about Darwin. Where is he?"

"Gone."

Greg took a step back. "Gone? What're you talking about?"

"Take me somewhere private."

"Outside. We'll go out the back door."

Greg shut and locked the front door. He led Carson through the house and onto the back deck.

"You want a beverage of some kind?" Greg asked.

"No, thanks."

They sat opposite each other at the patio table.

"What happened?" Greg asked. "I thought you were going to tell Darwin about the Russians."

"We did. Darwin wanted no part of it."

"He's not trained to do undercover work. Frankly, I'd be scared for him if he met the Russians, especially if they thought he was working for us."

"I know, but we discussed this. If he ignores the problem, it won't go away. The Russians ordered him to be brought to Arkady or executed. He became too big a problem for them. Have you heard from him?"

"Nothing. When did you last see him?"

"I brought Special Agent Mike Keans and Victor Ivanovich in to talk to him. I think we pushed too hard and scared him. He walked out of my office midafternoon. No one has heard from him since."

Greg looked up at the stars.

"What are you thinking about?"

"You," Greg said and turned to face him. "A week ago, you were trying to find Darwin to kill him, and now you're trying to find him to save him, and both situations are eating away at you."

"Cut me a break. I didn't have all the facts last week. Let me ask you something. Do ants sleep? Can a horse vomit? What color is a hippo's sweat when they're upset?"

"What?"

"Answer any one of those questions."

"As far as I know, ants don't sleep."

"What about the horse or the hippo?"

"I have no idea."

"Because you don't know the facts, does that make you an idiot? Are you to be laughed at?"

Greg looked skyward again. "Tell me?"

"Horses cannot vomit, and a hippo's sweat turns red when they're upset."

"Wow, that's something. Didn't know that." Greg turned his chair to face Carson. "What's next? What do we do?"

"Nothing, really. We have no leads on Darwin. Arkady's disappeared. No one knows where either one is. Our two undercover agents in Toronto have nothing for us and won't report back for a day or so. We have nothing."

"Darwin's a survivor. Don't sweat it. I'm worried about him, but if there's nothing we can do, then have a drink with me."

"I didn't come here to drink."

"Don't move," Greg said and got up to enter the house. He came back with two glasses half-filled with an amber liquid.

"Islay Scotch whiskey. Nothing like it. A good quantity of

peat gives it a smoky feel going down. Try it."

Carson sipped his drink and savored the smoky aroma as it traveled up through his nose. "Good shit."

"Tell me some other trivial facts."

"A rat can last longer without water than a camel."

"Wow, didn't know that either."

"The total weight of skin in the average adult human is six pounds. Hugo Boss designed some of the Nazi SS uniforms, and the original name for a butterfly was flutterby because that's what they did."

"Wow, where do you get all this stuff—"

The lights in the house blinked and went out, cutting him off. Carson set his glass of whiskey on the patio table and yanked out his sidearm.

"Is there ever an end to this shit?" Carson whispered. "Where's the power box?"

"In the basement or the garage. I normally know this stuff, but I just got here," Greg whispered. "You take the garage. I'll check on Rosina and do the basement."

Greg entered the house with Carson close behind. He followed until Greg turned down a corridor.

Rosina stepped out of a room on the left. "What happened to the lights?"

"We don't know yet," Greg said as Carson moved past them toward the garage.

"Who's that?" she asked. "It's too dark."

"Carson Dodge came over for a drink," Greg said. "Everything's fine. Come with me to the basement to check the fuse box."

Carson moved toward the front and looked out the living

room window. He detected nothing moving outside. The door to the garage was positioned beside the front door. He walked across the window, grabbed a flashlight from the front closet, and stepped into the garage.

Automatic weapons fire broke the silence of the night outside and brought goosebumps to his arms and adrenaline to his stomach.

He found the fuse box and checked the master power switch. It was in the On position. He yanked it up and down to no avail.

"Shit."

He reached for his cell phone but realized he'd left it in his car. A vehicle revved its engine outside. Tires squealed somewhere.

The Taurus PT145 in his hand was loaded with its ten-round magazine. The rest of the ammunition was in his glove box.

He ran out of the garage and almost bumped into Greg.

"You find it?" Greg asked.

"Yeah. No good. Power's been cut from the outside. Maybe they knocked down a transformer."

"I thought the lines to the safe house were buried."

"Guess not," Carson said as he leaned to look out the front door's window. "Whoever it is, how did they find us?"

"Followed you here, maybe."

"Impossible." He turned to look at Greg in the dark and could barely make out his head but could tell Rosina stood behind him. "I would've noticed a tail."

"What now?" Rosina asked.

"We wait," Greg said. "I tried the phones. All dead. If that gunfire from a moment ago meant our guards are down, how much ammo you got on you?"

Carson waved his gun. "Just this. The rest is in the car."

"We have to get to the car."

"We could wait and, as they approach, pick them off one by one. The dark is as advantageous to them as it is to us."

"I don't like this," Rosina said, a slight whimper in her voice.

"We don't either," Greg said.

Carson felt his weapon slip in the moisture on his palm. "I'm going outside. I'll try to get my extra ammo and stay hidden behind the car. You take Rosina out the back door and get ready to run for the back fence. Find something in the garage to cut through the fence."

Carson slipped out the front door. He ran bent over and dropped to the ground by the right front wheel of his car. An engine idled somewhere down the driveway. Whoever had arrived was taking their time advancing on the house.

A branch snapped to his left, about twenty yards away, close to the edge of the house. A red light moved up the pavement and stopped on his chest. Carson understood what it was and moved away as quickly as he could.

The bullet came faster. It hit his left hand, the one with the missing thumb passed through, and ripped open the skin at the edge of his left eye, the bullet falling useless in the trees behind him.

Carson dropped to the pavement. He hadn't been able to see out of his left eye since his time in India. He'd lost his vision in that eye after meditating and drinking a batch of homemade liquor for three days straight. He ended up in the hospital and almost lost a kidney, too.

His hand was numb, but he knew the pain would come soon. The ache in his face near his left eye grew in intensity, the blood running. He remained as still as he could, letting his blood flow onto the driveway for whoever watched.

Getting shot in the face was devastating to most. If the shooter wanted to finish off the job, there wasn't much Carson could do to stop him. But if the shooter was after Rosina and Greg and had felt his shot at Carson was good enough, it could give Carson the edge he needed.

Scuffling noises surrounded him. He tried to count the number of feet running by, but he stopped at eight as the pain took over. Nausea threatened him. He wanted to curl into the fetal position and wait for an ambulance stocked with painkillers.

Rosina screamed from behind the house. A gun fired. Then another.

Carson lifted himself off the pavement and raised his weapon. The tall silhouettes of the trees surrounding the property and the house were all he could see in the dark. He started around to the back of the house, wobbly on knees that were losing strength as shock set in. Blood flowed freely down the side of his face. He held his wounded left hand near the base of his neck, above his racing heart.

Another gun fired in the dark ahead of him. He heard two words in Russian that sounded like, "Get her."

Russian?

He stepped around the corner and balanced himself against the edge of the house, leaning on the wall. Six men stood with automatic rifles slung over their shoulders. One of the men held a large white box in his hands.

A drinks cooler?

The reflected light from the moon glinted off the edge of a long blade.

A sword? What the fuck?

He felt like falling to the ground and lying out flat. Sleep would be good. Rest for a while, and think about everything later.

A man kneeled in front of the six men. The man with the sword raised it. Carson understood what they intended to do.

He aimed with his one good eye. The gun erupted in his hand, and the six men jumped and spun to look at him. Carson slipped behind the wall and fell to the pavement, but not before two more bullets entered his right shoulder.

Run Rosina ...

He fell asleep on that thought.

41

"Darwin, this is how we welcome our new soldiers," Arkady said. "You passed the test in the other room. Now, you must pledge your life to us and acknowledge our commandments. Take a seat at the table."

The men around him looked permanently angry. A team of psychiatrists could spend years studying their childhoods and discover that it wasn't bad parenting that created men like this. It was raw anger. Their parents were angry, and their parents before them.

He stepped forward and stopped. He couldn't do it with the dagger on the table. Whatever plan they had for the blade had to be substituted.

"The knife has to go," he said.

The room erupted in a soft murmur as the men whispered to each other.

"What did you say?" Arkady asked.

Dolph stepped away from the door, moving closer to Darwin. He didn't care. All he could feel was the power the knife had over his ability to remain calm.

"The knife. Get it out of the room. Then we carry on."

"It's part of the initiation. You need to bleed. Aren't you 'The Blade'?"

There was no way in hell he could hold a knife, let alone prick himself with it. Through gritted teeth, he said, "You want me to bleed?"

Arkady nodded.

Darwin stepped past him, walked up to Dolph, and kicked him in the stomach. It happened so fast that Dolph didn't respond in time to defend himself. As he bent forward, Darwin dropped his foot to the floor and elbowed Dolph in the left cheek. Dolph's head snapped sideways, and then he crumpled to his knees.

Arkady wouldn't like what he'd just done.

"You want blood?" he asked. "Draw mine."

Arkady held up a hand as his men converged. "Impressive. I've heard that you were insane." He turned to a skinny, tattooed man who looked to be in his mid-thirties. "Draw blood." Then he waved his arm.

The Russian ran at Darwin, his fists flailing. Darwin took several punches to the face before he raised his arms to fend off the blows.

"You're not defending yourself, Darwin," Arkady shouted. "Miklos, back off."

The blows stopped. Darwin dropped his arms, got to his feet, and opened his eyes. The pain didn't come right away, but the numbness did. His face felt twice the size. He could taste blood on his tongue.

"You bleed—"

"That's right," Darwin cut him off. "Now, we don't need the

dagger. Let's remove it and carry on."

Arkady nodded to the men behind Darwin. The dagger was lifted off the table and taken to the door.

"Wait," Arkady shouted. The men stopped. "Take this lump of muscle with you. He can wake up in one of the rooms."

It took four men to carry Dolph out. While they waited, Darwin walked over to the table and sat in the chair before he fell. The aftereffects of the adrenaline weakened him.

The others returned and closed the door.

"Lean over the skull and bleed on it," Arkady ordered. "Get as much blood on the skull as you can. If enough blood covers the top of the skull, then it was meant to be that you are a member of the Bratva. This proves your loyalty as a man ready to die for the Bratva."

Darwin hovered over the skull, dripping blood from his facial wounds.

"A Toronto police officer once owned the skull," Arkady explained. "We don't remember where the rest of his body is. That's not important. Every LEO we have to fight is beheaded and brought here."

"What's a LEO?" Darwin asked.

"Law enforcement officers. We have a collection in the back of over a dozen, and it grows each year."

Arkady produced a piece of paper from his back pocket. "I'm going to read the commandments to you as you bleed on the pig's skull. At the end of each commandment, you will verbally acknowledge whether you agree or not. Understood?"

"Yes," Darwin said.

"Number one. No one can present himself directly to another member of the Bratva without a third person arranging the meeting. For each member, this third person vouches for the brotherhood that is to meet."

"Agreed."

"Number two. Never look or act mischievously or inappropriately toward the wife or girlfriend of a Bratva member. If that member has selected them, they are off-limits."

"Agreed."

"Never be seen with authorities such as cops, FBI, or any other legal representative."

"Agreed."

"Earn and honor rank."

"Agreed."

"Always being available for the Bratva is a duty, even if your wife is giving birth or on her deathbed."

"Agreed."

"Appointments must absolutely be respected. Commitment before ego."

"Understood."

"Not understood. Agreed."

"Agreed."

"Honor the truth. When asked for anything from a member of the Bratva, it must always be the truth."

"Agreed."

"When ordered, kill whoever, whenever, without question."

"Agreed." Blood continued to drip onto the skull of a cop long dead.

"Swear to secrecy. Never talk about the Bratva to outsiders. Respect confidentiality."

"Agreed."

Arkady laid the paper over the top of the skull and produced a lighter.

"Stand up," he ordered.

Darwin stood.

"The last commandment has to be completed while standing. Take the skull in your hands."

Darwin picked it up and almost dropped it as the blood collected near the base made it slick.

"I'm going to burn the paper with the commandments. While it burns, you will not let go of the skull. I will read the last one to you. When the fire goes out, you will have joined the brotherhood."

Darwin nodded.

Arkady lit the edge of the paper. The small flame grew, heat coming off it.

"If you betray the Bratva, your flesh will burn like this paper, as will the rest of your immediate and distant family."

The paper burned slowly across the top of the skull. He wanted to ram the skull into Arkady's teeth. The whole ritual was fucked. How could groups of people act like this? Mothers with children were shopping at the mall a few kilometers away. People were running errands and going to birthday parties while the men around him were performing rituals and killing cops.

Rehabilitation didn't stop men like this. Courts didn't stop men like this. Psychologists couldn't break down the hatred that built up in these men after years of anger and fighting.

What stopped men like the Bratva was death. A pedophile has to be castrated to cease his urges, and men like the ones standing around him needed to have not just their balls ripped off but also their heads.

As the flame burned down, he wondered if that made him the

same as them and realized it didn't. He was a better man because he could walk away and have a good life, never hurting anything bigger than a housefly. The fire went out, and one of the men turned on the lights.

"Congratulations," Arkady said. "You are now a member of the Bratva."

He patted him on the back. Darwin set the skull down on the table and wiped at the blood dripping off his chin. The men circled him, hugging him and slapping his back. A couple of them smiled.

"We will get you some food and drink, and then you leave to handle your first assignment."

"What's my first assignment?"

"We have been wasting our time for the last eight months meeting two men in the food court of Sherway Gardens. They had expressed interest in buying weapons. They have been professional, and everything is checked out. We have proven unsuccessful in following them until our last meeting."

"You want me to follow them?"

Arkady shook his head. "We've done that and found out they are cops. We have a meeting scheduled for an hour before the mall closes. You are to meet them, offer to show them a sample of the weapons they're supposed to be buying, and once they're outside by the mall's loading docks, you are to execute them both with two bullets to the forehead. Are we clear?"

Darwin nodded without hesitation. "Clear."

"Good, but you won't be going alone."

The door opened, and Dolph stepped back into the room. He smiled at Darwin and walked up to him, examining the fresh marks and blood on his face. Darwin expected to be broken in half. He waited for the blows to come, but Dolph only extended his hand.

"Brother," he said.

Darwin gripped the proffered hand as tight as he could but still felt his bones grind in Dolph's grip.

"He will join you to watch the kills and report back to us. If anything goes wrong, I will have two other men in a car near the van you take the pigs to. Now go. Clean yourself up first, and then kill those filthy pigs. Bring back their heads."

42

DARWIN SAT IN THE van's passenger seat and wondered what the point was. Since he ran from the federal building in Jacksonville, he had been with Arkady. He had toured their warehouse and went through their blood ceremony, with bruises on his face to prove it.

But for what? He couldn't kill a cop. He couldn't kill anybody just because. Kill or be killed was the only way he could take another life. Unless, of course, they were hurting Rosina. She seemed a world away from him now.

He pledged to make it up to her. He would contact the authorities and tell them where Arkady's warehouse was. They were bound to have enough evidence to put them all away for a long time. The Asian being killed by a thousand cuts would still be there. Blood on the Judas Cradle would leave a DNA trail to its victims. The rape and sodomy performed daily would have numerous charges brought up on the rest of the men present, not to mention all the drugs that were probably on-site.

All he had to do was get past Dolph at the mall.

They wanted him to shoot cops. They would give him a gun to do that. He would make his play then.

"You doing okay?" Dolph asked. "You look white, pale."

Darwin turned to face him. "I'm fine. It's a big job, wasting cops on my first day."

"You scared?"

"Not scared. Smart."

"Smart?"

Dolph pulled into the huge parking lot of the mall as rain began to fall. He hung a right and headed for the loading dock at the back.

"This is a chess move. Arkady is being strategic with me, and I think I see where he's going with it."

"Where's that?"

"When we're done tonight, I'll tell you."

"If he's playing chess," Dolph said, "what piece are you right now?"

"A pawn. But if everything goes right tonight, I'll be either a rook or a knight."

Dolph nodded, backed the van to the docks, and cut the engine. He grabbed a duffel bag from behind his seat and pulled out a small handgun.

"This is what you will use to kill both men." He clicked it open and nodded. "Four bullets are loaded. Two in each man's forehead."

Darwin nodded.

"Good. Here's the safety." Dolph held the weapon up on its side and pointed. Darwin nodded and took the weapon.

"Our backup is right there." Dolph glanced out the windshield and nodded to the right.

Two skinheads sat in an older model Pontiac 6000, seven cars away.

"Let's go," Dolph said.

They got out of the van and entered the mall by way of the back door as Darwin slipped the gun into his waistband at the back. He searched Dolph's body with his eyes but couldn't see a weapon anywhere.

Shoppers bustled by them as they entered the corridors of the main mall.

"Food court's this way," Dolph said. "Don't forget. I'll do the talking. We're to show them the product. We escort them to the van. I open the doors slowly. Stay back. When the doors open and the van is empty—shoot both men in the forehead. Do not shoot me." Dolph looked sideways at him. "That'll piss me off."

"The chance they come alone is low," Darwin offered. "Others may be watching."

"We know. That's what our backup is for. We hop in the van and leave with our backup guys running interference. The highway is one exit away, and the warehouse is five minutes away. Once there, the van is stripped and repainted by the morning. We've done this before."

Several stores were already closing their doors as it was nearly nine-thirty. The food court was almost empty. Dolph headed to the middle, where two men sat at a table with four seats near a white railing. Both men were dressed casually in jeans and T-shirts. One had a mustache and two-day growth on his face. The other was clean-shaven and could easily pass as a cop.

They sat opposite the men, who were drinking coffee. The smell of Taco Bell and other fast food restaurants in the food court made Darwin's stomach growl. He hadn't eaten since breakfast before seeing Carson, and he'd thrown up what little he had in his stomach in Arkady's warehouse bathroom.

After the introductions, Dolph got right to the point. Once it was agreed that the buyers would view their purchase, all four men got to their feet and started the long walk back to the empty van.

The foursome made it to the hallway door leading to the van. Darwin entered last, taking up the rear, Dolph in the lead.

He idly wondered what Dolph's real name was. He'd been calling him Dolph since they first saw each other in the limo at the airport.

Dolph stepped onto the loading dock and pulled the keys out of his pocket. He fumbled with them and wasted a few precious seconds for Darwin to ready himself.

Darwin gripped the butt of the weapon. Both officers caught Darwin's move and slowly turned their attention to him. He waited, holding the gun in his waistband. The second seemed to drag on.

"Got it," Dolph said.

With Dolph's back to them, Darwin motioned the two cops to step back and get out of the way. As they did, Dolph opened the back door of the empty van and turned to stare at the gun in Darwin's hand.

"Empty your pockets," Darwin ordered. "It's okay, guys. I'm working with the FBI. You can verify me by calling Carson Dodge at the Jacksonville Bureau office in Florida."

No one moved.

Dolph grinned so wide he showed teeth. "This is chess. You *were* the king on the opposing side."

"What?" Darwin said as he edged to the right to be closer to the van. "I told you to empty your pockets."

"Checkmate," Dolph said.

Darwin lowered the weapon and fired at Dolph's right thigh.

Nothing happened. He fired again.

"Did you actually think I would give you a loaded weapon?"

Darwin grabbed the back door of the van and slammed it into Dolph. It caught the man off guard. He stumbled backward.

Darwin ran for the front of the van and the mall doors beyond it, the other two men reaching for him. The backup car with the two skinheads squealed out of their parking spot. Darwin caught a glimpse of metal in the passenger's hand as the car came around to bear down on him.

With three men on foot and two in a car, all bent on killing him, he had no choice but to take cover back in the mall.

He ran through a door on the left and bolted into the mall, racing past the bookstore and turning down the corridor toward a large department store. He looked back once and saw the two fake cops closer than Dolph, who ran slower because of his size. The two skinheads in the Pontiac probably stayed outside in the car to head Darwin off wherever he exited.

With the empty gun in his hand, he ran through the men's clothing racks in a department store, grabbed a hoodie, rolled it into a ball, and headed for the exit. A lone clerk closing his till out for the night glanced up as Darwin passed.

"Hey, you gotta pay for that."

Darwin held up the empty gun as he raced by. "Call the cops if you don't like it."

Then he was out the door. A city bus pulled in through the heavy rain to pick up passengers.

Darwin slipped the hoodie over his head as he ran for the bus.

He glanced behind him, hoping his new hoodie would make it look like he was just another mall employee running for the bus. Dolph and the two cops exited the mall at the same door Darwin just came through and saw him immediately.

He raised the gun and shouted for everyone to step away from the bus. Then he bounded up the steps and grabbed the driver by the lapel, thrusting the gun under his neck.

"Everyone off the bus, now, or the driver dies. Go!"

It took all of five seconds for the four people already seated to dive out the side door of the bus.

"You, up and out."

The driver began to protest, but the windshield cracked in front of him as a bullet penetrated it.

Darwin ducked and shoved the driver out the open door. He dropped into the driver's seat, set the gun between his legs, and hit the gas pedal. The bus lurched forward as another bullet entered the glass, passing one foot from Darwin's head.

Dolph stepped out from behind a row of cars and lifted his arms. Darwin yanked the wheel to the right to make less of a target of himself and then ducked as he yanked the wheel back left, aiming the large bus at Dolph.

What sounded like a firecracker went off four times before the bus rammed into the line of parked cars, knocking Darwin off the seat and onto the pedals on the floor. He bumped his head on the driver's metal lunchbox beside the stick shift's base. He shook his head to avoid losing consciousness and crawled back into the driver's seat. Blood ran freely over his right ear.

Dolph was squished between the bus and a black pickup truck. His face was pressed into the bottom of the bus's front windshield, eyes not moving, blood covering his shirt.

Others were coming. He dropped the bus into reverse and pulled away from the wrecked cars. Dolph's body slipped to the ground and disappeared. When he put the bus in drive, the Pontiac 6000 with the two skinheads turned the corner up ahead.

He hit the gas, and the bus shot toward them. Lights flashed from his right. Mall security raced across the parking lot. A siren blared from somewhere behind the bus.

Darwin shoved the accelerator as he drove at the Pontiac. To his surprise, the Pontiac reversed and spun its tires on the wet pavement toward the exit.

Mall security and the police would box them all in soon enough.

Darwin followed the Pontiac, heading toward the exit. He turned too wide, hoping the long bus wouldn't clip a streetlight. After straightening out, he pushed the bus as hard as it would go along the Queensway in the heavy rain. He needed to get to Arkady's warehouse and bring whatever authorities were following him there, too.

It took under five minutes to get to the warehouse parking lot. By that time, three Toronto Police cruisers had taken up pursuit along with the mall security Ford SUV.

He rammed the fence that secured the parking lot, the bus easily breaking it. Darwin aimed the city bus at the large warehouse door the limo had entered through only hours before.

The door buckled and tore from its mounts as the bus broke through it. Halfway down the warehouse, a line of four naked women stood five feet apart.

Darwin jammed on the brakes and yanked the steering wheel to miss the women. The bus skidded sideways as it slid toward the four women, its wheels slick with rain.

"Get out of the way," Darwin shouted from the driver's side window.

He tried to brace himself as he lost control of the bus.

Then the unthinkable happened. Something caught on the back wheels ceased its slide and made the bus tilt dangerously. The sound of twisted metal screamed as the bus fell onto its side and crashed down with a heavy thud, knocking Darwin into the window he'd just been sitting next to.

The blow to the ground knocked the wind out of him. He tried to breathe and, for the first few seconds, wondered if he would. He pulled himself upright, got air moving into his lungs again, and started to climb to the top of the bus, which was now the right-side seat.

He lifted his head through the bus's open door and looked around quickly before dropping back inside. No one took a shot at him.

A cell phone rang somewhere in the building. Darwin looked over the edge of the door again and saw nothing. No movement, no one attacking the bus. Nothing.

He took a chance and crawled out the window at the top of the bus.

The cell phone rang incessantly.

He hopped onto the warehouse floor and ran to the back of the bus so as not to be seen through the warehouse's open door. Multiple sirens blared outside, and vehicles pulled in front. He may get arrested, but he'd finally get back to his wife once his story checked out.

From his position, he couldn't see any of the four naked women. Either they were under the bus, or they'd gotten away.

He stayed low and ran for the hall in front of him.

A cop identified himself and called out on a bullhorn for everyone in the building to come out with their hands visible.

A quick look in each room convinced Darwin that Arkady and his crew had left the building. How could they leave so fast?

The cell phone began ringing again. He looked up and saw the phone on the metal walkway on the second floor. He wiped blood from the side of his face and ran for the stairs.

The man on the bullhorn outside announced they were entering in one minute if the occupants didn't start exiting.

Darwin climbed the stairs two at a time, turned the corner, and ran along the walkway until he hovered over the cell phone.

It rang again. He picked it up and hit the talk button.

"Darwin?"

Arkady.

"Where are you?" Darwin shouted into the phone as he started back toward the stairs.

"I thought I told you. I play chess. Everything we did was a strategic move."

"What're you talking about?"

The bullhorn sounded outside, giving him thirty seconds.

"I know you're friendly with the FBI. I also know that I couldn't hand you over to La Cosa Nostra. I wanted to kill *The Blade* myself."

"Come and get me then, asshole. Come kill me." He was halfway down the steps to the main floor.

"I already have."

Darwin heard air rushing past an open car window. Arkady was mobile.

"I'm still breathing."

"Let me check my watch," Arkady said. "In half a minute, that building will be destroyed, and I'm assuming you're still standing where the phone was placed."

Darwin hit the warehouse floor running.

"That means you will die along with any evidence you thought you could lead the authorities to. Except, of course, for the Triad member in the back who has been killed by hundreds of cuts to his body by a man known as 'The Blade.' Everything leads back to you. Also, I left you four hookers. In addition to the murder charge and the anger the Triads will direct at you, you'll have human trafficking charges as well."

Darwin headed toward the bus. "Why not just shoot me? Why go to all the trouble of that initiation and setting up meetings in the mall?"

"I needed time to get to your wife. This is personal, Darwin. I knew she wasn't dead, and I aim to be the one to kill her."

The man using the bullhorn outside said they were coming in.

"You don't have my wife. If anything happens to her, I will put you on the Judas Cradle and cut your fucking body in half and then piss on the remains."

Arkady laughed. "I'm sending a picture to the phone in your hand."

Darwin made it to the bus. He didn't have enough time to go out the front of the warehouse and persuade the police to fall back. If he ran outside, they would probably just shoot him. The back of the building was probably covered, too. The bus was his only chance.

He pulled the phone down and clicked on the picture. He could barely tell what he was looking at, and then it became clear. It was a white box that resembled a cooler of some sort. Inside the box was a human head.

Greg Stinsen's head.

He brought the phone back to his ear, gasping for air. "This madness has got to stop. Greg Stinsen was a good man. A friend."

"Somehow, your wife escaped my men, but we'll find her. She can't be far. My men in Jacksonville are only minutes behind her. Die peacefully. At least it'll be fast. You betrayed the Bratva, so now your flesh will burn. Goodbye. Checkmate."

"I'm not playing chess, asshole," Darwin whispered into the phone as men with assault rifles started filing in the front of the warehouse. "I'm playing checkers and just kinged up on your side of the board. I'm more powerful than you bargained for. I'm coming for you and every single family member associated with you and all of your men. The Russian mafia has a new enemy. Remember my name. It's *The Blade*."

Darwin tossed the phone away, climbed up the side of the bus, and rolled his legs around and inside the open door.

"Everyone get down," he shouted. "There's a bomb. The place is going to blow."

He dropped into the bus as something exploded behind him. The bus jerked a few feet, and then another explosion roared throughout the warehouse. The bus jerked again.

He tried to position himself between two seats at their base, but a larger explosion tore through the building. The shock wave hit the bus and knocked it so hard that Darwin smacked his head in the same spot the metal lunchbox hit earlier.

The last thing he saw were bright orange flames licking across the warehouse's roof.

One more huge explosion turned his lights out.

Part Three

The Scythe

43

YURI PAVEL SAT IN his palatial home in Toronto, sipped his vodka neat, and stared at the TV as it broadcasted the hell falling down upon his territory.

"I'll kill them all," he shouted at the TV.

He picked up his plate of *pirogue*—Russian pastry shells filled with spicy pork and topped with a dollop of sour cream—and took a large bite.

"We are live at the scene of yet another raid on the Russian mafia's strip club called The Mistress," newswoman Juliet Lawrence said into the camera, a microphone in her hand. "Inspector Carl Michaels, what can you tell us about the current raids?"

A strong man with a jutting jaw, standing in full Royal Canadian Mounted Police regalia, with his hands clasped in front, moved closer to the microphone.

"After the explosion at the factory in Mississauga the other day, we have ramped up our attack on the Russian mafia. Just as we did in Ontario and Quebec years ago against the biker clubs, we're raiding all their known establishments and hideouts."

"And what're you hoping to find?"

"As it stands now, Ontario is the money-laundering capital of organized crime worldwide. We have dealt with the Italian mafia, the Triads, and the bikers for many years, but the Red Mafia is smarter and stronger. They don't seem to care who gets hurt. We lost a few good men in that explosion in Mississauga. Our goal is to shut them down, and in doing so, we're also looking for Arkady."

"Just Arkady, Inspector? A man with one name?"

He shook his head. "We only have the name he's known to go by."

The newswoman pulled the mic back to her mouth. "Why him specifically?"

"Our wiretapping, in conjunction with the FBI, has led us to believe Arkady was behind the explosion in Mississauga."

"Can you tell us more about what happened at the warehouse in Mississauga and why there's a publication ban?"

"All I can say is that the RCMP and the FBI are working together to catch as many of the Bratva as we can and process them through the system. We will deport them, jail them, and, or press charges that will stick. This has to stop."

"Are there more raids scheduled to take place?"

"Yes, but where and when won't be released."

"Last question, Inspector. The media has talked about a Canadian man named Darwin Kostas, also known as The Blade. Lately, he has led his own crusade against the mafia. Rumor has it that Kostas was in the warehouse when it was destroyed. Can you verify that for us? If not, can you tell us how he's involved?"

"I have no comment on the whereabouts of a private citizen.

Thank you." The inspector walked away from the screen.

"There you have it. This week's raid on two warehouses in Toronto and a shipping company in Quebec at the Port of Montreal, and now we have this strip club, The Mistress, as another Russian mafia establishment. Behind me, the raid is coming to an end as the female dancers are being escorted out to RCMP vans. My name is Juliet Lawrence—"

Yuri turned off the TV.

"What have you done, Arkady?" he whispered to himself.

After refilling his glass, he buzzed the front door and asked Sergei to come up to the den. Minutes later, there was a soft knock on the door.

"Enter."

Sergei Ivankov opened the door, slipped in, and closed it behind him. Dressed in his finest suit, as always, the barrel-chested Sergei had been a prizefighter in Russia for twelve years. Yuri had visited Russia seven years ago and offered Sergei a deal he couldn't refuse, flying him to Canada to act as his personal security. He became known on the streets as The Scythe.

"Come. Sit."

For a big man, Sergei walked lightly across the carpet and stood on the couch's far side. He crossed his arms and waited.

"Sit," Yuri insisted.

"Sir, I throw up at the smell of pirogue. I need to stand back here."

Yuri waved off his comment. "We have a problem."

Sergei waited.

"I need to find out if Darwin Kostas survived the explosion at the warehouse. If he is alive, we need to find him."

Sergei nodded. He wasn't much for words. Yuri sipped his

drink. That was one thing he loved about Sergei. He could explain everything he wanted without interruption. If Sergei needed more, he would ask at the end.

"I want you to arrange a sit-down with the Italians and the Chinese. We will have two meetings. The first is to be held at the golf course convention center. Have the address distributed through my restaurant on Queen Street. The second will be held three months from now. Let the Italians pick the spot for that one. Send word that I want Arkady there, too. Got it?"

"Yes, boss," Sergei said.

"Good. But before the first meeting, I need to know the whereabouts of Darwin Kostas. I want him brought to me alive. Understood?"

Sergei adjusted his suit and made a small nod of his head.

"Good. It is time to end all this fighting. This war can't continue." He looked up at Sergei as he downed the rest of the vodka. "I have a plan for Darwin that he won't resist."

He got up and headed over to refill his glass.

"Go, Sergei. We are out of time. Set up the meeting with the Italians and Chinese and find me Darwin Kostas."

44

THE EMOTIONAL SWAMP, THE absolutely desperate mental existence that had been Darwin Kostas's sleeping state, began to wake. He felt the air on his skin, the breath in his nose, and the pain, mostly the pain.

The nightmare came in snippets. The warehouse, the initiation rite, and the explosion. Arkady setting him up to have the Chinese angry at him and kill the hookers. Darwin jumped back inside the bus. The explosion, mostly the explosion, came to him. The fear, hoping he would survive to be with his wife again.

The horror came back, and he wanted the release that sleep offered. If only he could go back under. Stay under.

Thoughts of Rosina brought him up.

Moaning did nothing to ease the pain. It only brought on a flurry of movement around him. The presence of people moving to and fro close to him gave him a headache. He wanted to tell them to stop, but his mouth didn't work. He willed his eyes to open, but something held them closed.

"He's trying to wake up, Doctor." A female voice.

"Okay, that's good." A firm male voice. "Remove the tape from his eyes."

The tape was torn from his right eye, then his left.

"Dim the lights," the doctor said.

Darwin blinked. He opened his eyes to slits and waited.

"Take your time, Mr. Kostas. It's okay." Then, after a pause. "Nurse, remove the tube from his mouth."

Darwin closed his eyes and swam backward to avoid the pain, the harshness of being alive. It had felt so good to be under, so light. He had dreamt of holding his wife's hand and walking in fields of sunflowers basking in the sun.

He drifted back out and let the flow pull him down until he was gone.

***

Darwin opened his eyes slowly and scanned the hospital room. The night pressed against the window to his right, darkening the curtains. A single light on a table shined in the corner. Beside it sat a uniformed RCMP officer, a magazine in his hands. He hadn't looked up yet. Darwin took the chance to examine the room.

No flowers. A desolate hospital room with ugly blue walls, medical cabinets with glass doors, and supplies within. Nothing comforting. He looked down the length of his body and saw all the right parts where they were supposed to be.

The pain in his head had subsided since he tried to wake earlier. He moved his fingers and toes without hesitation. He rolled his head over the pillow. The cop stared up at him, the magazine on his lap now.

"I'll get the doctor," he said.

The cop walked to the door, opened it, whispered something to someone outside, and then closed it. He retook his seat and watched Darwin.

Darwin blinked and looked up at the ceiling tiles. Rosina wasn't in the room with him, and nothing revealed a feminine presence had been there recently.

The door opened, and a tall man in a white lab coat entered, followed by two nurses and two men in suits.

"Good evening, Darwin," the doctor said. Darwin recognized his voice from when he had partially woken before. "How're you feeling?"

Darwin nodded with a slight dip of his head as everyone filed in.

"I'm Doctor Jameson. You've had quite a traumatic experience. Can you talk?"

He opened his mouth and rolled his tongue around. "Water."

"Of course. Mary?"

The older blonde nurse grabbed a glass, brought it over, and lowered a straw to Darwin's mouth. He sipped slowly as instructed by the doctor.

After the nurse pulled the straw out, the doctor asked, "Is that better? Can you talk now?"

"Yes."

"Good. These men behind me are with the FBI, and the man in the corner is RCMP. The FBI has a few questions for you, but first, I'd like to explain what happened."

Darwin turned his head sideways and looked up at the doctor, waiting for him to continue.

"You hit your head pretty hard. I understand there was an

explosion of some kind. When you got here, it was touch and go. There was swelling in your brain. I had to induce a coma to get the swelling down, which has worked. But I have to say, you're quite the fighter."

"How so?" Darwin asked.

"You were in an induced coma, and you tried to wake from it. Yesterday morning, you almost opened your eyes, but then we lost you again."

The doctor moved closer and leaned against the bed. "The swelling centered on the brain stem, near the hypothalamus and the amygdala part of the brain. Are you aware of those areas?"

"No."

"The hypothalamus is one of the busiest parts of the brain as it regulates hunger, thirst, response to pain, anger, and aggression. When you asked for a drink, that tells me it's still working. Are you following?"

"Yes."

"Good. The hypothalamus also deals with breathing, blood pressure, and response to emotional situations. The amygdala is an area of the brain that deals with fear conditioning. Do you know what that is?"

"Please explain."

"Fear conditioning is phobias, really. It deals with the development of phobias. It also deals with positive conditioning, but mostly phobias." He leaned in closer still. "If you have any phobias, there may not be any change. On the flip side, they may have disappeared. Your aggression may have been altered, too. The swelling has gone down, but it's hard to tell if there was any damage to that area of your brain. You have to take it easy for a while." He stepped away from the bed and raised his voice.

"You're going to have to stay bedridden for a few more days without too much excitement so we can monitor your brain waves and—"

"Rosina?"

"Excuse me," the doctor said. "I'm sorry, I missed that."

"Rosina?"

"Who is Rosina?" the doctor asked.

"His wife," one of the two men in suits responded for Darwin. "You want to know where she is?"

Darwin nodded.

"So do we."

"That's what I'm talking about," the doctor interjected. "That kind of talk could upset my patient, and I won't allow it. He's been through a traumatic injury and intensive care for over a week, and he's now just waking from an induced coma. Your questions must be brief and not aggressive, or I'll have you escorted out of the building."

The suit raised his hands. "Take it easy, Doc. We're on the same page here. But you'll have to wait outside while we question Darwin."

The doctor moved back to Darwin's bedside. "Are you feeling up to it?"

Darwin nodded. "Yes."

"Okay, but I'll be just outside that door. If you need me for any reason, press this." The doctor slipped a button attached to a thick wire into Darwin's hand. "I'll come running." He turned to the men in suits. "If you upset him, that machine monitoring his blood pressure will alarm the nurses' station. Then I will have no choice but to have you removed until my patient is up and walking on his own."

None of the suits moved in any way to acknowledge what the doctor had said. He motioned for the nurses to follow him and exited the room without another word.

The suits moved closer, one on each side of the bed. The chair in the corner by the lamp was empty. He was alone with the FBI.

"Darwin Kostas, I'm Special Agent Kirk Williams. We need to discuss with you—"

"I'm sorry," Darwin cut him off. "About Greg Stinsen. He was," Darwin cleared his throat, "my friend. He helped me in Rome, Florida, and back here in Toronto."

Williams looked at his partner, then back at Darwin. "We're sorry, too." He gestured as he introduced the other man. "This is Agent Scott."

"Rosina? Can you tell me anything?"

"Let's exchange information, deal?"

"Deal."

"You tell me something I want to know, and I'll tell you what we have."

"Okay."

"What happened in that warehouse?"

Darwin told them as much as he could remember about how Arkady tried to trick him into believing he was joining the Bratva, the Russian mafia, how they had done the ritual ceremony and then driven him to that mall. He was meant to be killed there, but escaped and stole a city bus to go back to the warehouse, which was rigged to blow after Darwin answered the cell phone Arkady had left behind. While that was happening, Arkady's men in Florida were trying to locate and kill Darwin's wife.

"The last I remember was Arkady on the phone. He didn't have Rosina at the time. He said his men weren't far behind her."

Darwin cleared his dry throat again. "Now it's your turn."

"That was over a week ago," Williams said. "Agent Carson Dodge was shot three times and remains in a Florida hospital. Rosina and Arkady have disappeared. No one has seen either one. And the best part is everyone thinks you're dead."

"Everyone?"

"Everyone. Even Carson Dodge. Anyone who knew you or was close to you. We did that for your own safety."

"What happens if Rosina finds out? It'll crush her if she thinks I'm dead."

"As soon as we have her, we'll tell her the truth."

Darwin twisted away from the men to hide his grief. Rosina could be anywhere—dead in the Florida swamps, a captive of a maniacal killer, or starving and still on the run.

"Darwin, we're going to need a full statement."

He didn't look at the men. "Not right now. Tell me what else you have. How did the Russians find the safe house where Rosina was being kept? I understood it was highly classified because of what happened the last time." He rolled over and eyed Williams. He couldn't help but feel anger toward the FBI, who had repeatedly betrayed him. "Wasn't it only Carson and Greg who knew where she was?"

"That's what we understood."

"So, what went wrong?"

Williams looked at his partner for support. Agent Scott said, "We're looking into that."

"Well, fucking look harder," Darwin said. "There's a scared, lonely girl out there trying to stay alive while every fucking mafia boss in North America is after her." He leaned back on the pillow, his head throbbing.

"Maybe we should come back after you've slept more," Williams said. "We need a detailed statement and descriptions of all the people you came into contact with. You got a rare glimpse into their warehouse and what happens there." Williams adjusted his suit jacket. "We lost three RCMP officers from the emergency task force in that explosion. Inside the building, they found a Chinese man who appeared to be dead before the bomb went off and four female bodies we're still trying to identify. A couple of them fell under the bus you were driving. You need to rethink your position here, Darwin. We have enough to charge you on multiple counts of manslaughter, but until we get all the facts, we're willing to work with you. Do you understand what I've explained to you?"

Arkady killed those people. It was a miracle Darwin was still alive. How could they consider charging him with anything?

"Let's go," Williams said to his partner. Seconds later, the door opened, then closed.

The RCMP officer returned and walked up to his bedside.

"I gotta stick around in here," he said.

"Do what you have to do."

"Those guys are assholes, eh?" The cop seemed sincere. "I mean, you're a hero. How the hell did you get out of that warehouse?" He stopped talking, moved the chair, and cleared his throat. "But the best part is the media don't know shit."

"Why not?"

"There's a publication ban on what happened at the warehouse."

"A publication ban? Why?"

"The authorities have been conducting raids on warehouses, strip clubs, and all known hangouts of the Russian mafia looking for Arkady, but nothing has turned up. The higher-ups don't want anyone to find out you're still alive. I'm sure it's just a matter of time before they find Arkady, but if you ask me, he's fled the country."

Darwin's eyes were getting heavy.

"Listen," the cop continued. "I've got a friend in the Bureau down in Florida. Let me call him to see if they've discovered anything about Rosina, and I'll let you know when you wake up."

Darwin closed his eyes. "Thanks."

The hospital room door opened.

"You okay, Darwin?" the doctor asked.

"He's getting sleepy," the cop answered.

Darwin realized as he drifted off that he didn't get the cop's name.

The doctor's voice droned on as Darwin sunk lower. He wondered why he didn't react to the IV in his arm. He knew it was there. It was a sharp object—something he would've violently protested in the past but barely noticed now. When he first woke, only a single lamp was on in the corner by the cop. Otherwise, the room was pretty dark.

Could his phobias have been cured? If so, how come his temper flared so easily? Maybe it had something to do with what the doctor said about the aggression part of the brain being affected.

He drifted deeper.

In his mind's eye, he saw Rosina standing in the Rome airport and wished they could return to their innocence.

45

THE RCMP COP DARWIN had met the first day in the hospital was John Cavendish. He worked the night shift, guarding the inside of Darwin's room. That night, he looked into information regarding Rosina, but the FBI, Williams, and his buddies weren't relinquishing anything.

Darwin gave them a full statement after the stitches in his head were removed, and he was waiting to be discharged from the hospital. Doctor Jameson said Darwin had healed quickly. Special Agent Williams planned to place him in a hotel until they learned Arkady's whereabouts. When they found her, they considered flying him back to Florida to be close to Rosina.

Darwin settled back into bed, ate the bland hospital Jell-O and soup, and debated his next move. He was convinced Rosina was alive.

As soon as the authorities found Arkady, everything would end. With Darwin's testimony, Arkady would go away for a long time. Fuccini and Gambino were dead. With Arkady gone, Darwin and Rosina could move on as well.

He pushed the remains of his meal away and checked the bedside clock. The cop who worked the day shift didn't talk much. After dinner, the day cop got up, gathered his novel and magazine, his garbage from lunch, and left the room without a goodbye.

Five minutes later, Cavendish entered the room, a large smile pasted on his face. He nodded at Darwin and set his things by the chair in the corner. Cavendish glanced at the door and then walked up to Darwin's bedside.

"I've got good news for you."

Darwin pushed himself up in the bed, eager to hear John's news.

"Although you may not be happy."

"Just tell me, John."

"My source knows where Rosina will be—"

"What? Where?"

"Keep your voice down," John said. "She's here, in Toronto."

"Toronto? How's that?"

John shrugged. "No idea. Maybe Arkady's men picked her up in Florida, and that's how she made it here."

At the mention of Arkady's name, a weight pushed down on Darwin's stomach. "Is she hurt? Alive?"

"She's very alive. In fact, she's having dinner as Yuri Pavel's guest at his restaurant on Queen Street tonight in about," he checked his watch, "two hours."

Darwin frowned. "What the hell are you talking about?"

"Look, Darwin, I don't have all the details, so I will have to guess a bit here." John looked at the door again, then back at Darwin. "Arkady is reportedly working for Yuri. I'm going to guess that Arkady's men grabbed Rosina and brought her here like they did you."

Darwin grabbed the water glass beside the bed and took a drink to satiate his suddenly parched mouth.

"Then he handed *The Blade's*," he said Darwin's moniker with air quotes, "wife to Yuri as a goodwill gesture."

"Goodwill?" Darwin did not like where this was going.

"Yuri's pissed with all the raids taking place in his territory—"

"The raids you told me about?"

John nodded.

"Finally, something the RCMP and the FBI are doing that's working."

"They must know that Ontario's primary multi-force organized crime agency, Combined Forces Special Enforcement Unit, is being reorganized and possibly dismantled soon. Nothing would be getting done without the RCMP and the FBI working together on this."

Darwin gestured with a wave of his hand. "Let's get back to Rosina."

"My source said that Yuri's keeping her safe. But they still want you and won't risk coming here with this many cops watching over you. Since there's a publication ban on what happened at the warehouse and who died there, no one on the street has confirmation you're alive. As far as the street knows, you just disappeared."

Darwin dropped back onto the bed. Would it ever end?

"What's being done about it?" Darwin asked.

"What do you mean?"

Darwin glared at him. "How can he have her and no one arrest him?"

"As far as the law is concerned, she's with him willingly. She comes and goes without restraints, nor does she call out for help. Based on that, there's nothing we can do."

"But she doesn't want to be with him."

"I know that. You know that. Yuri has something on her to make her so compliant. Maybe she's waiting to see if you're dead. Then she'll decide what to do. Who knows?"

"You have no idea how fucked this is."

"True, but there's something you can do about it."

Darwin kicked his legs out from under the covers and slipped off the bed. He steadied himself before trying to stand.

"You want the crutches?"

"No."

He took a step. Then another, using the bed for support. At the end of the bed, he let go and, on unsteady legs, made it across the room to the closet without falling.

"Tell me what I can do about it while I get dressed."

"You can go get her."

"That's the plan."

"But you don't get discharged until later today or tomorrow," John said.

"I'm leaving now. My head's fine. My legs'll support me. I'm ready."

"What do you think you can do in your condition? You're unsteady. You can barely walk."

"I can go and get my wife," Darwin said as he let the hospital gown slip off his shoulders and hit the floor. "I will get Rosina, and we will leave North America. That's the only way for this madness to stop."

"Darwin, if you walk into Yuri's restaurant alone, he will kill you. Actually," John gestured with his hands, "if you walk in with backup, they will probably kill you and your backup."

Darwin slipped the T-shirt over his head and started on his jeans. "Then tell me what options I have. Seems like I'm all out of options."

"File a missing persons report for Rosina with the FBI. Explain that you have an unnamed source confirming Rosina is being held against her will with Yuri Pavel."

"And you think the FBI will help us? After all that's happened?"

Cavendish looked out the window, staring at nothing. "Right, sorry."

Darwin finished dressing and walked to the door. "What's the name of the restaurant?"

"Wait a second," John said as he approached Darwin. "You can't leave."

"Why not?"

"Because you're in protective custody."

"Protective custody? Have I been charged with a crime?"

"No."

"Then they can't hold me."

"True, but charges are pending."

"No, they're only holding them over my head until everything calms down. We know the Russian mafia attacked the safe house where Greg and Carson were holding my wife. At the same time that was happening, Arkady planned my execution. I got away, and Arkady blew up his warehouse. That's it in a nutshell. I'm a free man. Haven't Rosina and I been persecuted enough?"

"Look, I'm with you, man. But even if you walked out of this hospital and made it to the restaurant, Yuri would have you dead before sunrise. I can't have that on my conscience."

"John." Darwin put a hand on the cop's shoulder. "I'm leaving in the morning, or I'm leaving now. What's the difference? They can only hold me so long. I'm a Canadian citizen and can go freely." He let go of John's shoulder. "Is this source of yours reliable?"

"He is."

"I now have information on the whereabouts of my wife. Do you think I would just let it go?"

John shook his head.

"Exactly," Darwin said. "What's the name of the restaurant?"

"The Russian Quartet at Queen and Jarvis. He flies Russian singers in to entertain all the time. It's famous because it's one of the few Russian restaurants that has entertainment. I've lived here my whole life. Actually, I grew up off Jarvis Street, not five blocks from there."

"It's only a fifteen-minute walk from here. Maybe twenty minutes for me." Darwin waited, holding the door handle. He lowered his voice. "What will I expect when I walk by the cop outside this door?"

"Won't happen. He'll call it into the FBI, and they'll ask to detain you until they get here."

"Are you going to help me, or do I have to do this alone?"

They stared at each other for a long moment. John broke the silence.

"I'll get him to take a piss break. Then you walk out. When he returns, I'll ask if he saw you exercising your legs. All I know is you went out for a walk to circle the floor. Can you clear the area in the time it takes a man to piss?"

Darwin nodded. "Do it. And thanks."

John shrugged. "I have no idea what you're thinking of doing, but I can't see it working out for you."

"That's my concern. Just get that cop off my door."

John moved around Darwin to open the door and stopped. He pulled a piece of metal out of his back pocket.

"Here, take this."

Darwin took the proffered brass knuckles. "Why do you have these?"

"Don't worry about that. I took them off some punk yesterday. I've carried them around since and thought maybe you could use them. It might help if you get into trouble. Just make sure there are a lot of people wherever you are. Yuri won't shoot you in front of too many witnesses. Once you get Rosina, he'll send people to follow you. Lose them, and you're free."

They let one last look pass between them.

"I don't agree with this," John said. "But good luck."

John opened the door and stepped out. Darwin waited by bouncing from one foot to the other, getting his legs moving and ready for the walk. This was his chance. Rosina was close. He would walk in, get her from the restaurant, and walk out. If anyone stepped in his way, he would pull the fire alarm, call the police beforehand, or just wait until she left the table to go to the bathroom. Whatever happened, he was going to get his wife back.

The door opened, and John stepped back inside the room.

"He's on the phone. As soon as his call's done, he said I could cover him for a bathroom break."

"Okay."

"That gives me a chance to tell you about a case we had five years ago." He paused and cleared his throat. "A stupid man, who didn't realize what he was doing, threatened Yuri in front of his soldiers once."

"And?"

"They grabbed his wife at home and poured sulfuric acid on her face, burning her eyes out. The twenty-four-year-old model's face turned to a wrinkled, burned-up glob. As far as I know, she committed suicide a year later after plastic surgery failed to allow her to go out in public again."

"How is it men like Yuri aren't in prison or dead?"

"That's not all."

"What?"

"Part of the man was found in a field in Hamilton, and the other parts were found in his car's trunk."

"You mean they dismembered him?"

John's face hardened. "Not exactly."

"Then what?" Darwin stopped bouncing and sat in the chair.

"About thirty pounds of flesh was cut off the man while he was still alive. Before that, a blowtorch was applied to his face and his genitals. After burning his cock and balls off, they shoved them inside his burned mouth. He was suspended on the side of a barn with wire, where he was blinded by the blow torch and tortured for several days before they finally shot him fifty times. All that because he threatened Yuri." John leaned against the door, a hand on his stomach. "This is what they do."

"Then maybe I should walk into the restaurant and kill him. He deserves to die."

"Sure, but then you spend the rest of your life in prison."

"Might be better than spending the rest of my life looking over my shoulder."

"You won't survive prison. The mafia has the prison system sewn up. You get inside for offing Yuri, and you'll be knifed within the first week."

"Thanks for being so bleak. You're a pal."

There was a knock on the door.

"Coming," John said. To Darwin, he said, "Are you sure?"

"One thousand percent."

John slipped out the door. A moment later, Darwin heard John's knock.

He opened the door.

"You've got maybe four or five minutes. The staircase is over there." John pointed to the exit sign.

Darwin walked by him, hit the stairs, and reached the main floor without encountering anyone. He opened the stairwell door slowly and stepped out. The hallway was empty; the gift shop was already closed. He walked toward the exit sign where the emergency doors led outside.

Once outside, he fluffed his hair up, kept his head down, and sometimes limped south on University Avenue toward Queen Street.

He was quickly lost in downtown Toronto's evening foot traffic, but one thing kept nagging at him.

Why would RCMP Officer John Cavendish carry someone else's brass knuckles on him? Something told Darwin to be wary of Cavendish and the information he had just offered.

Did he really trust anyone anymore?

46

DARWIN PASSED YONGE STREET and continued along Queen, moving slower his right leg cramping. He leaned against a brick wall to rest. Then he hobbled over to a bus stop and sat on the bench, leaning his shoulder against the Plexiglas bus shelter.

The night air was almost still, a soft breeze rustling the leaves of the small city-planted trees lining the road. A horn honked somewhere. Someone with too much to drink hollered in the distance to his left. A tire squealed.

The sounds of the city.

He breathed slowly and focused on what he needed to do.

"I have no fucking idea what I'm going to do," he whispered to himself.

How could he walk into the Russian mafia's restaurant and take his wife, their guest, out with him? How many men would be guarding Yuri? How many men would be outside watching the door for law enforcement types? This was hopeless and useless.

But this was all he had.

Rosina was all he had.

Knowing she would be in the restaurant, half a block from him, he had no choice. Nothing could keep him from walking through that door.

He collected himself and got up. As he shuffled along the sidewalk, a young couple passed him, laughing to themselves. He longed for moments like that with Rosina. It had been a while since they shared a laugh together. Rome a few months ago? The safe house in Florida?

He remembered their wedding day and yearned to hold her like he did that night. A wave of anger coursed through him and caused goosebumps to rise on his arms.

"No more," he muttered under his breath as the restaurant came into view. The front window was lit up with bright lights from the inside, and an open neon sign shone in the window's top right corner. No one milled about the front door. He'd expected a Russian mafia type in an expensive suit standing guard.

He studied the area. Three people walked east along Queen Street, and one man strolled along on his side of the street. Other than that, the walking traffic had died down, and Darwin didn't see anyone else within a city block.

Cars drove by, but nothing looked out of the ordinary.

If John's source were accurate, which Darwin was willing to bet he was, Yuri would have no reason to expect Darwin. Which probably meant Yuri would treat tonight like any other night.

As Cavendish said, what could the cops do? The restaurant was probably legit. The guests inside would order food, eat, and leave. Everything looked as normal as it should be.

Darwin stopped across the street from the restaurant. Why would John say there was nothing the authorities could do? They were actively searching for Rosina. They'd want a statement from her after Stinsen was killed in Florida guarding her life. Unless Rosina wasn't at the restaurant, and this was all a ruse.

Did Cavendish sell me to the Russians?

Doubt stopped him. He touched the brass knuckles in his pocket for reassurance. It had been almost two weeks since he'd had to fight. He couldn't keep risking his life. It made him think of the stitches in his scalp, which had started to itch.

He slipped the brass knuckles onto his right hand. It felt good, bolstering his resolve. He was ready.

He stepped out of the shadows. Two Toronto police officers walked along Queen Street toward Yonge. They would pass the Russian restaurant before Darwin got there.

He waited.

They got closer. To his surprise, they stopped, opened the restaurant door, and walked inside The Russian Quartet.

"That's perfect."

No one would touch him with cops inside the joint.

He waited for vehicles to pass and hobbled across the road, his legs feeling much better. He just hoped he wasn't too early and Yuri wasn't there yet. One of Yuri's men might recognize Darwin. Would Yuri still show up with Rosina if that happened? Probably not.

What does Yuri Pavel look like anyway? He chastised himself for not asking Cavendish such a simple question.

He reached the window and stopped to peek in past the small white curtain on the inside. The place looked like any other restaurant. A waiter served an older couple halfway down by the end of the bar. Darwin counted ten people, plus the two cops and the waiter. Couples occupied three tables. Three other tables had single men ranging in age from early twenties to fifties. The one in his fifties faced the front of the restaurant, reading a newspaper. The bartender was talking to the police officers. They laughed about something.

Near the back of the restaurant was a small stage with speakers and a small drum set for the performers Cavendish mentioned.

Rosina was nowhere in sight.

She could be in the bathroom, but he doubted it. If Yuri was the man sitting alone reading the newspaper—he actually looked Russian—it was clear he hadn't come with any sort of security.

Everyone had a plate of food. The waiter walked through a door that led to the kitchen. Everything looked absolutely normal, although Darwin had no idea what a traditional Russian restaurant was supposed to look like.

He checked to see if anyone approached on the sidewalk. It was empty but for two men on the other side of the street walking away from him.

Back in the restaurant, one of the cops had disappeared.

Darwin decided to go in, walk toward the back, and sit in the corner near the rear door. He would order something small and wait. And watch.

If John's source was correct, Yuri Pavel would enter the restaurant with Rosina, and Darwin would make his move.

Whatever move that is.

The door chimed as Darwin entered the restaurant. The bartender looked his way and nodded, then turned back to the cop.

Darwin wondered if the cops were looking for him. Would Cavendish have told anyone where he was heading?

Too late now. He was already inside.

He moved through the tables, past the bar and the cop, making sure the brass knuckles remained hidden behind him and kept moving toward the back. One of the couples looked up at him as he passed, but no one's eyes lingered.

The old Russian-looking newspaper-reading man didn't stop reading.

At the back, he sat facing the front of the restaurant.

Before the waiter could come to his table, the other cop exited the bathroom, met his partner at the bar, and headed for the front door together.

At the front, the men moved apart. One of them turned off the sign and pulled down thick black shades over the window.

What the hell is this?

Everyone in the restaurant got up and walked toward the front. Darwin broke into a full-body sweat.

The couple closest to his table had left their plates piled high, beverages full.

Adrenaline flooded his system. His abdomen tightened, and his hands gripped into fists to calm the shaking. He clenched his already sweaty palm tighter on the brass knuckles.

The only person still sitting was the old Russian man, his back to Darwin. The fork clinked against the plate as he continued to eat.

When the shades were pulled down on all the windows, one of the cops locked the front door.

If he ran, Darwin couldn't make it past the dozen people congregated near the front. How much of this was planned? Did Cavendish call ahead? The feeling that John sold him out crept up again.

"It's a Darwinian world out there, isn't it?" The old man set his fork down. The man, who Darwin now assumed was Yuri, dabbed at his face with a napkin.

"Come, sit with me. It'll be easier to talk that way."

The crowd at the front dispersed. Most of them walked through the doors that Darwin assumed led into the kitchen. The two Toronto cops moved behind the bar, where they began to take their shirts off. Both of them are dressed in black turtlenecks.

"Darwin. Don't make me ask you again."

He scanned the back of the man's head. He had picked up his fork and dug into his food again.

Paralysis kept Darwin rooted to the chair. He didn't want to move until he saw Rosina. One of the fake cops walked out from behind the bar. As he did, he pulled a hairpiece off his head. His sleeves were rolled up, displaying an array of tattoos. Darwin recognized him instantly.

Miklos.

The man who attacked Darwin after Darwin had knocked out one of Arkady's soldiers that day in the warehouse. Miklos was Arkady's crazy bare-knuckle fighter. Where was Arkady, then?

Miklos approached. "Nice to see you again, Darwin." He cleared his throat. "Yuri never asks twice for anyone. That is going to cost you." He stepped closer and lowered his voice. "We didn't get to finish what we started in the warehouse."

Darwin stood and bumped the small table aside with his thigh. It moved a foot and then settled. Miklos stepped even closer, crowding Darwin. He was imposing, exuding violence. Miklos craned his neck sideways, cracked it, flexed his fingers, and cracked his knuckles. One hop from his left foot to right and back again.

Before Miklos could take the first punch, Darwin swung his arm up and connected with Miklos's cheek, the brass knuckles slamming home on solid bone.

The violence oozing off Miklos dropped by half as his skin split and squirted blood. He faltered backward and touched his cheek, his eyes wide in surprise. Darwin took a moment to advance and hit him again.

Miklos lost his balance and fell backward over a table. Darwin pounced, punching him repeatedly, letting all the pent-up rage out.

Arms grabbed Darwin from behind and lifted him off. He struggled, but they held firm. At least three men secured him and lifted him to his feet.

Miklos stayed still on the floor, his face a bloody mess of flesh and ruined bone. Darwin caught a glimpse before he was hauled away and thrust toward Yuri's table. The brass knuckles were ripped from his bloody hand as the men walked him around Yuri and then turned him to face the man.

Yuri lifted his gaze, still chewing. He set his newspaper on the table by his plate and gestured at the empty chair with his fork. The men pushed Darwin down and let go.

Darwin adjusted himself, righted his shirt, and settled into the chair. The three men moved behind the bar. The restaurant was empty now except for the three men behind the bar.

Yuri looked back at his plate of pasta and dug in as if he and Darwin were old pals catching up over a bite.

Darwin rubbed his knuckles. Everything was still intact. He touched the stitches in his head and was happy to discover they hadn't popped.

"We have business to discuss," Yuri said.

"No. We don't."

Yuri put his fork down, dabbed at his mouth with a white

napkin, and leaned back in his chair. He roamed his eyes over Darwin, checking out his shoulders and his arms, and then, finally, he met his eyes.

"I was expecting something a little different."

"Sorry to disappoint."

Yuri's mouth twitched. It looked like he wanted to smile but decided against it.

"You've created quite a name for yourself."

"How much did you pay Cavendish to sell me out like this? How much am I worth?"

"That's none of your concern. But what is of great fucking importance to you is Rosina."

"Where is she?" He placed his hands on the table.

The men behind the bar approached. Yuri waved them off.

"If you want to see Rosina alive, you'll remain calm and listen. Can you do that?"

Darwin removed his hands from the table and placed them at his sides.

"Good." Yuri moved his plate, setting it on the newspaper. "I have a proposition for you, but first, we talk."

"What kind of proposition?"

Yuri brought up his index finger. "First, we talk." He lowered his head and raised his eyebrows. "Understand?"

"Sure."

"You seem in a hurry. You have somewhere to go?"

"I haven't killed anyone in a few weeks. I'm getting the itch."

Yuri pulled out a small box and set it on the table. From inside the box, he lifted out a fat cigar. After lighting it, he dropped the box back inside his suit jacket pocket. He puffed the cigar to life and gazed at Darwin through the smoke. "Are you threatening me?"

"No. I'm threatening those three behind the bar. Miklos and I started a fight a few weeks back. I was trying to finish it before they interrupted."

"I know about that fight. That's why I brought Miklos here today. I needed to see it for myself. The rumors about you could be all lies."

"Don't believe all that you hear. I'm newly married and looking to spend a quiet life with my wife. It's you and your kind who keep getting in the way."

"That is too bad." Yuri dragged on the cigar and blew the smoke sideways. "Was it Cavendish who gave you the brass knuckles?"

"Yes. My turn. Where's my wife?"

"There are four weapons pointed at you at all times."

"Where's my wife?" Darwin asked again, this time louder.

"I have no idea. Probably with Arkady. He's skipped town."

Darwin wanted to dive across the table and jam the cigar into one of Yuri's eyeballs.

"Then who are you?" Darwin asked. "Why are we even talking? You're wasting my time."

"Because I'm the only one who can get you your wife back."

"How's that?"

"I want Arkady. Since I believe he has Rosina, and you want her, we have a mutual goal. Arkady won't kill her if he thinks he can still get to you. At the same time, he won't walk into a meeting with me. He knows I'll have him executed for what he's done to my town."

"Toronto's your town?"

"Toronto has always been a city that's too big for one family

—until now. Arkady was my last problem. He has hurt the Italians and now the Triads. Once he's gone, Toronto is mine."

"And you think I want to help you?"

Yuri tapped the ashes off his cigar. He gestured at one of the men by the bar. "Two vodkas."

His attention back on Darwin, he said, "Reason number one, you don't have a choice. Reason number two, Rosina."

Darwin waited. The small shot glasses of vodka appeared before them. The man set the bottle on the table close to Yuri.

"Drink."

Yuri picked his glass up and drank it all down.

Darwin glanced at the glass and decided to go for it. He needed a drink. When he was finished, he slammed the empty shot glass down as hard as Yuri did.

"Good," Yuri said. "Now we talk like men."

Yuri poured more into both glasses. He set the cigar down and steepled his fingers.

"I'm a patient man. It's a discipline. You learn it in prison. Patience allows you to think and strategize. Are you patient, Darwin?"

"Sometimes. But when it comes to Rosina, not often."

Yuri smiled this time. The tension in the room lifted. Darwin's pulse slowed, but he stayed alert, ready.

"When I grew up in Russia, we didn't have money. My father left, and my mother had to raise us. We had rats in our small one-bedroom apartment. I watched while my mother would strangle the rats with her bare hands to protect us."

Yuri took another swig from his glass. Darwin left his untouched. One was enough.

"Do you understand what I'm saying?" Yuri asked.

"Yes. You learned early to protect what's yours by strangling rats."

"Very good. In Toronto, I'm trying to build political and financial connections. I'm running a business. I can't do that with renegades like Arkady causing too much attention."

Darwin waited.

"The Gambino and Fuccini Families needed to be reduced or removed because they were directing subordinates to use intimidation and violence to collect a mob tax from me. I tasked Arkady to handle it. I understand you got in the way but ended up helping the cause. For that, we drink."

Darwin guessed that Yuri liked to hear himself talk.

"People asked who you work for. The FBI is stymied by you. The media call you The Blade, even though, as I understand it, you have a phobia of knives."

"Not anymore."

"How's that?"

Darwin turned his head far enough to show Yuri the stitches.

"They operated on you to remove a phobia?"

"No, I banged my head after Arkady tried to kill me. It caused swelling on the part of the brain that deals with phobias. Since then, they seem to have disappeared."

"Well, well, that's good news because I wouldn't know what to expect when I introduce you to The Scythe, my main executioner."

"The Scythe? And why would you introduce me to him?"

Yuri nodded while he poured more vodka. "He's back at the house. You'll meet him later."

"You don't travel with him?"

"No, he likes to stay hidden nowadays. He gets queasy around food."

"What? Queasy around food? Why?"

"He got shot a couple of times in the gut. Lost part of his stomach and his ability to eat certain foods. Half the time, he ends up in the hospital on an IV if he eats the wrong thing. Scy worked himself up so much about food that he can't even be near it anymore. He juices."

"Juices?"

"Yeah, fruits and vegetables in a juicer. That's how he gets his nutrients. Once in a while, there's the odd thing he will eat, but —"

"What does he eat?" Darwin asked, genuinely interested.

"I don't think we're here to talk about the eating habits of my employees."

The three men stood idly by, lingering behind the bar.

"What next?" Darwin asked.

Yuri addressed one of the men. "Go check if Miklos is still with us."

Darwin had forgotten about Miklos.

The tallest of the three men sauntered down the restaurant toward the back. He stopped and knelt by Miklos.

"Barely. His pulse is slow, but he'll make it."

"Finish him and clean it up."

The man pulled a long blade that glinted in the light. His arm stroked across the front of Miklos, near his neck, back and forth several times.

"He's gone, sir."

"Good. Clean it up." Yuri faced Darwin. "He worked for Arkady. I only brought him under my fold as your first test."

"Thanks for thinking of me."

"As soon as they clean up the body, we'll leave."

"Where're we going?"

"You will be a guest in my home until word reaches me of Arkady's location. Then you will set up a meeting with Arkady, and I will swoop in," he made a flying gesture with his hand, "and finish Arkady as my mother did to the rats."

"What if I refuse to help you?"

"You will die."

"That doesn't leave me many options."

"No, no, it doesn't."

The cigar had gone out due to lack of use. Yuri tried to light it again.

"You want to know the irony of my situation?" Yuri asked.

"Of course. Since I walked in tonight, that was second on my list of things I wanted to know."

Yuri stared at him. "Do you find the sarcasm keeps you alive?"

"I'm still here, aren't I?"

Yuri blinked. He drank and placed both hands on the table. "The American government paid for the flight that brought me here from Russia. Can you believe that?"

"Nope."

"I'm a *vor v zakonye,* which means *thief in law.*" He unbuttoned the top of his collar shirt and pulled it open. "See this giant eagle tattoo on my chest?" Yuri looked down, then back at Darwin. "This shows my status as a *vor.* We're sworn to abide by a code, or what we call Human Law. Never work a legitimate job or join the army. Never pay taxes and never help the police for any reason except to trick them. Back in the days of the gulag, the Russian prison system before the 1960s, *vors* had a secret language that even the authorities couldn't decipher."

"Impressive."

"Is that disrespect?"

"No. I'm serious. It really is impressive."

Two men lifted Miklos's body and carried him through the kitchen door.

"When I was twenty-two years old, the Soviet Union released me from prison, early, I might add, and stamped my passport, Jew. That allowed me to leave the USSR. I was flown to a transit camp near Rome, which the Hebrew Immigration Aid Society operated. After four months, in 1982, the American government paid for a flight for me to New York. Isn't that something?"

"Why tell me? How does this get my wife back?"

"I'm killing time. We don't open the front door until I am sure you weren't followed, and Miklos's blood has been cleaned up. Also, I'm telling you this, so you understand that it was the American government, along with the Canadians, that allowed us Russians to come here and flourish. I want you to know that the people you pay taxes to did this to you and your wife."

"Interesting rationale."

"In the Russian prison system, the authorities beat you before they interrogate you. They put dirt in a sock and whack your kidneys until you urinate blood for days. Once a man has done time on the Arctic Circle, what can the spineless North American legal system do to us? The Russian mafia now operates in more than fifty nations. We're smart, we're organized, and we don't care what the fuck happens." He gulped the remaining vodka and slammed his glass on the tabletop again.

The effects of the little vodka Darwin had were seeping into his consciousness.

"You see what I'm saying to you?" Yuri asked.

"This isn't a job interview."

Yuri frowned. "What?"

"You gave me an impressive résumé, but I'm not hiring. I work alone."

"What are you talking about?"

A man stepped up to Yuri and whispered in his ear. Yuri nodded.

"Stand up, Darwin."

"Where're we going?"

Yuri rose from his chair. "Do I always have to ask you things twice?"

"This is *my* second time. Where're we going?"

Yuri waved his arm. "Get him to his feet. I'm tired of talking to him."

Two men moved behind Darwin and grabbed his arms to lift him up. The other man was mopping the floor where Miklos had once been.

Before Darwin knew what they were doing, his arms were wrenched behind him, and some kind of twist ties were wrapped around his wrists.

"Hey, what the—"

He was shoved down onto the table, his face almost connecting with the plate and leftover pasta. An odd thought struck him about how he thought the Italians were the ones who ate pasta and not the Russians.

A black cloth hood came down over his head.

"I can't fucking see," he shouted.

"You won't need to see where we're going," Yuri said.

It was dark in the hood, and he wasn't panicking. This was the first time since he could remember that the darkness didn't cause him to become violently angry. But it was that anger that saved his life in the past.

They pulled him to a standing position.

"Are you going to be quiet while we walk you out the back door?" Yuri asked.

"I don't have ESP."

"ESP?"

"It means I can't tell the future—"

Something hit him in the back of the head so hard that his eyes rolled back in his head.

47

WHEN DARWIN WOKE, THE hood over his head had been removed, and his hands were untied. As far as he could tell, he was in the basement of a house. Vents hummed, pumping air into the room. The walls were see-through, made of glass or thick plastic. A toilet sat in one corner. The sun shone through a window high on the wall.

He lifted up onto his elbow and examined his wrists. Small chafe marks were left behind from the zip ties. The back of his head was sore, but at least whatever hit him missed the stitches area.

He rolled off the small mattress—a padded mat—and planted his feet on the floor. His head throbbed, but not as bad as when he first woke in the hospital.

The four walls of the square prison appeared to be the same length. A small vent the length of an average ruler was situated in the top corner of the wall above his mattress. There was no door in evidence.

He stood and walked the length of the closest wall, running

his hand along its surface. Then, the next wall. No indents or hinges where a door could be found.

On the other side of the glass, a set of stairs led up and out of the darkness. The only light came from the small rectangular window at the top of the far wall of the house, on the other side of his glass prison.

A wave of lightheadedness hit him, and he walked back to the mattress and sat down. After a moment, he lay down.

A door opened in the other room. Light spilled down the staircase. Someone descended the steps. A large man in a suit two sizes too small stopped at the bottom.

"Good morning," he said, the voice metallic through the walls. Somehow, the room amplified the man's voice from the outside. "How are you feeling?"

Darwin remained quiet.

The man disappeared behind a wall. When he returned, he had a white sock in his hand. He stopped on the other side of the glass and peered in at Darwin.

The basement door opened again. This time, two men came down the steps. After a moment, all three stood outside the glass wall, staring in at Darwin as if he were a caged animal in a zoo.

The first man pushed a button, and the wall before them began sliding sideways.

So there's the door.

The big guy eased out of his suit jacket and stepped inside the glass cell. The two men pulled large guns and cocked them.

"What's this?" Darwin asked.

"Your first day. Get up."

Darwin hesitated, then rolled off the padded mat and stood.

"Turn around. Face the glass."

"Why?"

The two guns rose in unison.

"I get it," Darwin said. "What're your orders?"

"Our orders are to teach you what life is about."

"And you're an authority on that?"

"In this house, I am. These men have orders to wound you if you try to fight back. Now turn around."

Darwin met the gaze of all three men. Then he slowly turned around and waited.

He couldn't believe how painful the first blow was. The sock felt like it was filled with coal as it came down repeatedly on each side of his spine. He yelled out like a house cat being tortured and dropped to the floor as his knees caved under the pain. He received a couple of more hits on the ground, writhing, and then the assault stopped.

When they were done, the men retreated and slid the glass wall back into place, leaving Darwin face down on the cold floor. His heart raced, lungs expanding and contracting. He was afraid to move in case something was broken.

Then, he had a sudden urge to urinate. He waited, tried to calm his breathing, and checked his bladder. He would go when his heart rate calmed and his breathing was more controlled.

He had to get away from these people. When that glass door opened again, he had to do whatever he could to escape.

He pushed up slowly and tried to get high enough off the mattress to stand. Pain flared in his back when he moved, but if he didn't get to the toilet soon, his bladder would release on the bed, and he'd be stuck sleeping in it for however long he was their prisoner.

He gritted his teeth and made it to a standing position. Four slow steps later, he undid his jeans and urinated. As he suspected, it was a bright red.

When finished, he zipped up and returned to the bed, where he lay down on his stomach.

The door opened at the top of the stairs. He didn't bother to look at who was coming this time. If they were coming to beat him again, he could do nothing about it.

After a moment, Yuri's metallic voice entered the glass cell.

"How do you feel?"

"Lovely," he said, his voice muffled by the pillow.

"You have no idea how many beatings I endured at the hands of someone who had power and control over me. Since we'll be working together, I thought you would need to get to know me more intimately."

"Okay, you've achieved that. I know enough now. Thanks. It fucking hurts."

"That's the point, Darwin. Only the strong survive, though, as your name suggests."

Darwin moaned, tired of remarks about his name. He moved his head enough to look at Yuri, who stood up against the glass by the part that was the door. He wore a different suit than when they met at the restaurant.

Darwin asked, "What's the point of that beating?"

"There's an old Russian proverb that goes, 'Revenge is the sweetest form of passion.' I want you to hate the people who put you in this position."

"Okay, well, you put me here. So I hate you."

"You have so much to learn. Arkady's trickery knows no bounds. He even tricked me. He has virtually ruined you. He has taken your innocent life away, and now, as far as we can tell, he has your wife. I want you to hate him with everything in your soul. Once you get to that place, I won't be anything to you except a means to an end. I will cease to be your enemy. Instead, I will be an ally, someone you can use to get to Arkady. On that day, we can work together."

"Okay, makes sense. I get it. I'm there now. I'm with you. Now let me out, and we'll have vodka together and discuss this further upstairs. Once we find out where he is, we'll kill him together. No more beatings. Let's be friends."

Yuri chuckled. "Under other circumstances, I could really get to like you."

"I'm serious. There's no need to make me more revengeful. I'm good." He turned more to face Yuri. The man was shaking his head.

"No, I don't think so. I have broken many men in my life. When you break, I will be able to tell by the look in your eyes. It takes weeks, sometimes months, but you will break, Darwin. I assure you of that. In the meantime, I will have my men beat you every day until then. When you are on your knees begging me to stop it and kill you, then I will have you where I want you."

"You're serious, aren't you?"

"Absolutely."

"What about dinner?"

"Excuse me."

"You're going to feed me, right? I mean, beat me, hold me prisoner, but you have to feed me. You can't take me out like this and expect me to give it up without a meal first."

"You're always trying to be humorous. I like that." Yuri waved a finger back and forth. "No, I don't think you need any food. You're better to me in a weakened state. You have water in the toilet. You will get a small bowl of soup once every four days if I remember to send it down, of course."

"You're joking, right? This is Russian humor?"

"No, I'm not joking. And because of your attitude and disrespectful ways, you just forfeited your first meal." Yuri looked at his watch. "Today's the eighth. That means I will bring you a little to eat on the sixteenth of the month." He met Darwin's gaze. "Maybe. Perhaps."

"You're fucked," was all Darwin could think to say.

"See, it's already working. I can feel the hate oozing off you." He turned away. "Goodbye, Darwin. I leave in an hour for Florida to look for Arkady. When I get back, we'll talk more." Yuri walked toward the stairs.

"Why're you doing this?"

"I told you. Start hating Arkady."

"I already hate the fucking guy."

At the stairs, Yuri paused. "Not enough, I'm afraid."

"You don't have to do this. I can work with you. We'll end this together."

"Darwin," Yuri turned to look at him. "I enjoy torturing people. Think of it as a pastime for me. One of the two true teachers in this world is suffering and pain. Only through real suffering can you learn life's lessons."

"What's the other one?" Darwin wanted to keep him talking. "You said there were two."

"Think about it. You might get it on your own." He turned away.

"How long do you plan on leaving me down here? You know the FBI will be looking for me. I walked out of that hospital without telling anyone."

Yuri started up the steps.

"How long?" Darwin shouted.

"As long as it takes. Three months, maybe four. We have to let Arkady feel that the heat is off him. He needs to get comfortable again, so he'll make a mistake." On the stairs, Yuri's feet were all Darwin could see now. "Even after I find him, I will wait, I will have patience, then I will take him out, and the Italians and the Triads will be there to witness the execution."

The door opened, and Yuri stepped away. The door closed, and the upstairs light cut off.

48

The basement fell into absolute darkness when the sun descended for another day. Darwin slept fitfully, dreaming of Rosina and what could've been. He stayed on his stomach to avoid adding pressure to his aching back, and he peed in the dark, listening to the urine hit the water, knowing it was still red.

Throughout the night, he didn't feel a single twinge of phobia. Nothing of his old habits surfaced. Just three weeks ago, he would've banged on the glass until his hands were bloody stumps and probably lost his mind to rage.

When light seeped through the basement window in the morning, he paced his small prison, examining options on how to extricate himself from the situation. There was really nothing he could do. The man with the dirt-filled sock was huge, more than double Darwin's size. The next time he came to visit Darwin, it would be to add more pain to his day.

It was survival of the fittest, after all. With two hired gunmen brought in to back the big guy up, there was no leverage, no hope.

He stopped pacing and stared through the glass walls. The

basement was empty. There was nothing on the floors, nothing stashed in the corners, nothing suspended from the ceiling. It wasn't a regular household basement filled with scattered furniture or junk. On the far wall was a door that looked like it could lead to a wine cellar or a cold room.

He had nothing he could use as a weapon inside the cell. The mattress was a very thin piece of foam without springs. The toilet had no seat and no working back. It was simply a porcelain circle with a button on the backside by the pipe that flushed the water. It reminded him of toilets he'd seen in Italy.

No tools, no weapons, no hope.

"What the fuck am I going to do?" he whispered in frustration.

No one answered. He watched the sunrise by the brightness in the basement and guessed the hours as they passed. All he had was time to think, which wasn't going too well.

It broke his heart to think of Rosina dead, but he needed to rationalize his reality. If she were alive, then Darwin getting beaten, starved, and deprived of freedom for months, only to be used as bait for Arkady, would not help her.

The only way to get back to her was to not be in this prison.

But how could he get out?

He had to try something or stay and rot in Yuri's personal gulag, which would eventually kill him. He was at the strongest he would be right now before they starved him and beat him further. His escape attempt had to be the next time anyone opened that glass door. Waiting longer was fruitless as he would be weaker and sorer.

Now that he had the time arranged, he needed to figure out the method.

"I've got the will," he muttered. "All I need is the how."

It took him over an hour to figure out the how, and even then, it was a slippery proposition, but he had nothing else to work with.

Now, to wait for someone to open the glass door.

The sun peaked, then headed farther west. After a time, it dipped. The light in the basement dimmed. Then it was black again.

He used his hands to feel along the wall to the toilet. Once there, he knelt and lowered his head. After cupping the water, he drank. Then drank more.

Once his thirst was sated, he stood and urinated. He thought about breaking the toilet off its mounts, but four large bolts at the back were secured tighter than his fingers could manage to undo.

After urinating, he flushed the toilet.

Maybe he could flush the toilet continuously. Or plug it with his shirt and fill the room with water.

What would happen if he was unsuccessful? His mattress would be soaked, and his shirt would stink. Yuri would be pissed and probably kill him as soon as light another cigar.

But it was worth a try. Wasn't it?

Maybe the water would short out the electrical in the house, thereby releasing the magnetized glass door to his prison.

Worst case scenario was he caused Yuri's home to be damaged before Yuri killed him. In the best case, he escaped while everyone was away for a week.

There hadn't been a single noise from anywhere in the house all day, and Yuri said he was going to Florida.

He removed his shirt and balled it up. After feeling his way to the bottom of the toilet, he jammed the shirt in the small hole and placed his thumb on the flush button.

One more drink from the non-contaminated water, and he was ready to go. Maybe only freshwater would pour over the rim, but he wasn't taking any chances.

He pushed the button. The water rushing into the bowl had nowhere to go. He waited, then flushed again.

The bowl filled and seeped over the edge.

He flushed again.

Then, the unexpected happened. Due to the increased weight of the water and the force of the pump on the inside of the toilet bowl, his shirt got sucked through the hole and disappeared. He felt the water level in the bowl as it left the inside of the toilet rapidly. Only a little had made it over the edge, where he sat on the floor.

"For fuck's sake."

He got up and slid out of his jeans. In his socks and Uomo underwear from Italy, Darwin balled his jeans up and jammed them into the bottom of the toilet.

He flushed the toilet, feeling the bowl fill. He flushed again. Then again. Soon, water filled the floor around him. He flushed and flushed. After every three or four flushes, he felt the jeans to ensure they weren't moving. Then he flushed again and again.

Renewed energy coursed through him. Tears rolled over his eyes. Adrenaline filled his muscles. He was escaping. He felt it and drank it in. Whatever happened after this, he was leaving the Russian mafia's basement, whether walking out on his own power or in a body bag.

Any other option was too depressing.

It would seem he was flushing for hours before the water collected to a couple of inches on his underwear, where he sat against the glass wall by the toilet.

He flushed one more time and then felt his way to the door.

As far as he could tell in the dark, the water seeped under the door and through cracks around the base.

He slapped the glass. "Damn."

It would take days to fill the prison and weeks to fill the basement. Water needed to get as high as the electrical panel. Usually, basements had drains for water-heater leaks or laundry rooms. Even if the water started filling the basement, it would drain out.

Nothing he had done was working. He'd lost his shirt, and his jeans were soaked.

The toilet stopped after his last flush.

The silence was intense after spending over an hour constantly flushing the toilet.

He had nothing else to go on, nothing left to do. No one was there. All he had was the toilet to keep him company. The sound of hunger pains twisted his stomach.

He felt his way along the wall to the toilet and sat down beside it.

He flushed it.

"So that's how you feel, eh?"

The toilet answered with gurgling noises.

"Do you think I can survive this?"

He flushed.

"That does not sound promising."

He flushed.

"Will Arkady die soon?"

He flushed.

"Now we're talking. Thank you. How about Yuri? Is he

coming up for execution?"

The toilet responded with a luxurious flush.

"Will everyone die?"

The toilet flushed twice.

"I like talking to you because you have all the right answers."

The flushing continued, the toilet not willing to offer more than that.

Water pooled around him.

Darwin fell asleep on the floor, lost in despair, blood from his wounded kidneys coloring his underwear as he contemplated what death would feel like and what was on the other side of that celestial wall.

49

Darwin woke with a sore neck. His back cried out where he was whacked with the sock the day before, and his head throbbed.

Last night came back to him in a rush. He looked around in the dim sunlight coming through the basement window. A lot of the water had moved to the lower parts of the uneven floor and pooled there. His underwear and socks were damp.

He got to his feet and stretched, moaning as his tight muscles protested. He needed to urinate but didn't want to use the full toilet as it was still jammed up with his jeans. He walked over to the door and pissed on it, yawning.

When he was done, he stopped and listened. The house was silent.

The mattress was darker on the underside, moist from the water it had lain in. He folded it in half, then placed it beside the toilet like a beanbag-futon chair, sat down, and set his arm on the toilet.

He flushed the toilet.

Then he flushed it again.

"Imagine that my life has been reduced to flushing a toilet in the hopes that something will come of it to gain my freedom. Fucking pathetic."

He flushed.

His thoughts turned to Rosina. He needed to think outside the box—the glass box.

He continued flushing as the water seeped across the floor in rivers and out the cracks at the bottom of the door.

"You're in for one hell of a water bill, Mr. Gangster."

He decided to cup water in his hands and take it to the door, searching for the electrical section that powered the opening, but the water slipped through his fingers.

A small silver rectangular block touched the door on the other side. That must be the magnet that keeps the glass door closed. It would prove impossible for him to get water to that area.

Dejected, he walked back to the mattress and sat down to put his face in his hands.

"There has to be a way," he mumbled in frustration.

Something banged outside the walls of his prison. It came to him with its metal tinny sound.

Someone was home.

He waited, hiding behind the toilet bowl in his underwear.

After a minute, he heard another noise.

The basement door opened. Light spilled down the stairs.

The moment had come. This was his UFC time in the spotlight. If he succeeded, he would win his freedom and get the girl.

Only one other person followed the giant Russian down this time. They stopped at the bottom and flicked on the lights.

"What the hell is this?" the giant asked gruffly. "What have you done?"

He followed the water trail to the glass prison.

"It got plugged," Darwin said, shrugging. "I didn't have a mop."

"It didn't get plugged. You jammed your clothes down there. That's why you're naked."

"That's good. Are all of you that smart?"

He didn't know how far he could push this large Russian without getting shot for his trouble. He recalled hearing the Russian's name—The Scythe. Yuri had talked about him at the restaurant. He called him Scy for short.

Scy walked around the glass walls until he reached the wooden cellar door in the far wall. He opened it and stepped inside. The man who had followed Scy down the stairs leaned against the wall and picked at something in his teeth.

"I bet you like to bugger little boys," Darwin said to the man.

"Fuck you. Talk all you want. You're the one who's dead when this is over. I'll still be drinking vodka, fucking the whores, and killing idiots like you for years to come."

"Not if I have anything to do with it," Darwin whispered.

"What was that?" the man asked as he pushed off the wall and stepped closer to the glass.

"I said, not if I have anything to do with it. If I had it my way, I would put you on the ground right here in front of me and step on your face. How would you like that? Can I step on your fucking face? Bust your teeth in, collapse your skull?"

"Oh, you little—"

"Don't talk to him," Scy yelled from the back room.

The man pulled out his gun and clicked off the safety.

"If I get the chance," he said, his voice low, "I will use this."

He shook the gun for emphasis. "I will put holes in your body for hours, keeping you alive long enough to go for a record. Would you like a new hole in your ass? Maybe you want a new hole in your balls?"

"What, so you can fuck me like the women you never get? No thanks. A bullet in the forehead will do me just fine."

The man slapped the glass. "I will kill you for that."

"You know, they say homophobia is produced in men who have gay tendencies. You must be attracted to cock and want one up your ass. But you think it's wrong and fight that side of you. I say go for it. Let yourself be free. Fuck all the men you want. You look the type."

The man smiled on the other side of the glass. "All you got is your mouth."

"I took my clothes off for you," Darwin said. "Come and get it. I'll let you take my underwear off. Come on."

"When Scythe opens this door in a minute, I'm coming in, and I'm going to put a bullet in your face."

"I said no talking," Scy yelled. He stepped back into view, exiting the little room. "And you will not shoot him. Those aren't our orders."

"You should hear the shit he's talking."

"I don't fucking care what he says. Don't worry, he'll get his. Now shut the fuck up."

Scy disappeared into the little room again.

"See, I proved my point," Darwin said.

The man stepped away from the glass, clearly agitated. He fidgeted with the gun, slipped it away, pulled it back out, and fidgeted with it some more.

"You're the woman here," Darwin continued. "Taking orders

from your husband. What, you can't stand up to him?" Darwin waited, then added. "Fucking pussy."

Scy stepped out, this time pulling a cart of some kind. Wires and netting stood at least six feet tall and had a small square table attached to its side. It looked like the inside of a mattress with all the cloth material missing. As Scy dragged it closer, Darwin saw the control box on the table with a large single dial.

An electrocution grid of some kind.

Two rings for the wrists were bolted into the top two corners. The base of the wire wall had a bowl to which Scythe had added water.

They're going to electrocute me.

Darwin flushed the toilet. Water seeped over the edge. He flushed again.

"Stop doing that," Scythe yelled through the glass. "We'll all fry if there's fucking water everywhere."

Darwin flushed again.

"You little punk."

Scythe pulled a small plastic fob out of his pocket and pushed a button. The glass door began moving on its rollers, opening slowly. He set the fob on the little table by the wire grid.

Darwin sat on the mattress by the toilet. He flushed one more time. He took a deep breath and tried to remain calm despite shaking all over.

"When I'm dead, what will Yuri say?"

"We're not going to kill you." Scythe stepped into the cell, followed by his accomplice, who still held the gun. "Just hurt you real bad."

Darwin pointed past Scythe. "He said he was going to shoot me. You heard him. Something about someone I killed being in his family."

Scythe stopped halfway across the cell and turned around.

"That true?" Scythe asked.

"No, he's just fucking with you."

"You heard him yourself," Darwin pleaded.

Scythe stepped closer to Darwin. "Stand up."

He flushed the toilet. "Fuck you. I stand up, and this guy will shoot me."

"No, he won't," Scythe said, grabbing Darwin's wrist and yanking him to his feet. Then he slapped Darwin across the face so fast he didn't see it coming. His face stung, and he saw stars at the corners of his eyes.

He couldn't get tied to that electrical unit and fried. He looked past Scythe's shoulder. Then he ducked back and yelled, "No! Don't shoot."

Reflex made Scythe lower his head and turn to look at the gunman.

Before he saw there was no threat and turned back, Darwin had raised his knee into The Scythe's stomach, where Yuri had told him The Scythe had been shot. As Scy bent over, Darwin threw fist after fist at Scy's face but only connected once.

Scythe returned with a fast uppercut that rocked Darwin's mouth, slamming his teeth together. If his tongue had been in the way, it would've been sliced off. He wondered in that brief second if his jaw could be broken.

His knees gave out, and he crumpled to the floor. If it wasn't for the cold water that his face hit, he might have passed out.

"You fucking prick," Scy yelled.

The Scythe grabbed his biceps and lifted him up fast. Darwin kicked and punched, but nothing connected. Scythe tossed him backward into the glass wall, and Darwin slipped down until he hit the floor, his kidneys on fire. He was losing this fight fast.

When Scythe came in again, Darwin neared exhaustion. All he had left was his mouth and a full set of strong teeth.

Scythe grabbed his shoulders, and Darwin turned into The Scythe's hand and bit down so hard he felt something crack. His mouth filled with blood instantly as if he bit into a juicy orange.

He dug deeper with his teeth and pulled like a wild dog would on a carcass in the wild.

Scythe screamed and dropped to his knees. Darwin bit again, this time deeper, energized by the win. A moan escaped his throat as he dug in the second time and locked his jaw in place.

Blows rained down on his head, but he knew unless they knocked him out, he wouldn't let go of Scythe's flesh. He blocked as many punches as possible, but The Scythe managed to get through his feeble attempt at defense.

Scythe got his other hand on Darwin's head and brought his fingers down to the top of Darwin's eyes. Then he pushed inward. Darwin wanted to scream at the pain, but his mouth would open if he did. Instead, he moaned louder, a roar coming out of his throat as he twisted away from the pressure on his face.

Scythe's fingers dug deeper still. The pain intensified. It was enough that Darwin had to let his mouth go and back away from the pressure on his eyes.

When he did, he wrapped a hand around the back of The Scythe's neck and pulled down hard, ramming Scythe's forehead into the edge of the toilet bowl.

Scythe's skin split, and blood shot out in a small torrent. He tried to pull away, but Darwin yanked again, putting more weight behind it and driving Scythe's forehead into the bowl repeatedly until Scythe crumpled to the floor on the other side of the bowl.

The whole time, the other man jumped from foot to foot, watching the fight over Scythe's shoulder, no doubt wondering how to help in the confined space.

Darwin reached inside the toilet bowl and snatched his sopping wet jeans out of the hole, then got to his feet, his eyes having trouble focusing after all the pressure on them.

The man leveled the gun at Darwin's face. "Stay where you are."

"What, you're going to shoot me? When Yuri gets home, he will cut you up for killing me. No, I don't think you're going to shoot me. We fight."

The man turned and ran out of the prison. He got to the wire grid and grabbed the fob to push the button for the glass door to close it. Darwin bolted after him as the door shut, his wet jeans in his hand. He slipped out in time and dove at the man, knocking into him like he was tackling a quarterback.

They hit the floor and rolled. The gun was lost under the cart.

Darwin wailed as he pummeled the man, pain shooting through his back like it was on fire. The man fought back, landing a few punches and two solid kicks that knocked the wind out of Darwin.

One solid knee connected with Darwin's solar plexus. His lungs emptied, and he rolled into a ball, trying to catch his breath. The man stood up, and a moment later, the room hissed with a buzzing sound.

The wire grid had been turned on.

"You are going to fry for what you've done here." The man sounded like he had a lisp as he spoke through broken teeth.

He stepped up to Darwin and kicked him in the back. Darwin

yelped, hoping he wouldn't pass out. The room spun, and his eyelids fluttered.

Blood seeped from sections of skin pulled back over his knuckles where they had made contact with the man's teeth. He brought his fist up to his mouth, closed his eyes, and bit down on the open wound. It hurt so bad he immediately yanked his fist out, but he was fully awake again.

The wet jeans were beside him. He grabbed them and rubbed his face in the cooled water that seeped from the denim. He rolled to his hands and knees, holding the wet jeans. The room buzzed with electricity.

"Good, get up," the man yelled.

Darwin brought his feet under him. The man stood between him and the wire grid. Once Darwin was fully standing, the man tried to grab him. Darwin tossed the soaked jeans at the man's face. The pant legs wrapped around the man's shoulders before he could stop them.

The second Darwin tossed the jeans, he shoved the man toward the grid and then jumped out of the way, stumbling toward a dry part of the floor.

The man fell backward, the wet jeans still wrapped around his neck and landed on the lower half of the live-wire grid.

It sizzled and crackled upon contact. The lights above Darwin dimmed. The man screamed and vibrated violently as he fried. Smoke oozed off his skin. A nasty odor hit Darwin's nostrils.

Sparks flew from the small box on the table. Then, it was over as fast as it had started. The grid shut off, and the lights in the basement normalized. The man slipped off the grid and dropped to the floor, smoke coming off his skin.

"Holy shit!" Darwin shouted. "How high did you have that

thing? Are you fucking crazy?"

He crawled away backward until he could see inside the small room where Scythe had pulled the grid from. Two tables were littered with boxes and tools. The back wall had shelves covered in canning jars. He couldn't tell what food was in the jars, but it looked like peaches and jams. There were various colors—oranges, tans, reds, and blacks.

He lay on the concrete floor, too sore to stand just yet. There could be more men upstairs, and he was in no mood to fight anyone else.

He closed his eyes to rest a moment and catch his breath.

Then, something hit him so hard that he felt as if his face broke. Before he could open his eyes, he was hit again.

He raised his hands to protect his face and tried to roll into a ball, but it was useless. He got hit three more times before he saw who was hitting him.

Scythe stood over him, blood covering his face from the wound the toilet bowl gave him. His eyes were wide, his mouth a smile.

"Now you die."

"Hey."

"You are no longer live bait."

"No?"

Scythe shook his head, blood falling from his chin. "You are dead. Yuri will understand. He underestimated you."

"Everyone seems to do that. Even you."

The pain in his cheeks made him talk as if his mouth was paralyzed.

"You're right. Even me." Scythe brought a gun up. "If you're religious, say a prayer."

"Wait," Darwin raised his hands. "Aren't you The Scythe?"

"Yeah. So?"

"Then why the gun? Where's your scythe? If this was a movie, wouldn't you have to kill me with your scythe?"

"This isn't a movie, and I will not leave you alone long enough to go and get my scythe." He clicked something on the gun. "I'm going to enjoy this."

Darwin lifted his foot into The Scythe's crotch. As Scythe bent over, Darwin rolled into the cold room. The gun went off, the bullet chipping the concrete beside his head. It went off again. A searing pain ran through his calf muscle. He rolled a few more times in case another bullet was headed his way until he bumped into the wall under the canned food shelves.

Scythe filled the doorway, his broad shoulders almost touching the door frame on each side. One hand held his crotch, and the other, the gun.

"I like the fight you have," Scythe said.

Darwin looked around for a weapon. Nothing was close but the canning jars. He reached above his head and snatched one off the shelf.

Peaches.

"What are you going to do with that?" Scythe asked. "Feed me to death?"

Darwin tossed the jar high in the air. It landed on the concrete floor between him and the door where Scythe stood. He grabbed another, then another, and lobbed them at Scythe. Each one broke, spreading peaches across the floor.

"Stop," Scythe yelled. He raised the gun, but his hand shook. "Stop it."

Darwin got on his knees and reached to a higher shelf.

Jams.

He threw them harder at the doorway, closer to Scythe's feet.

The gun fired. Darwin ducked. It fired again. A jar shattered beside Darwin's head.

He threw a smaller jar of pickles right at Scythe. It shattered the doorframe beside him, spewing green pickles and juice all over Scythe's chest and face.

Scythe fired his gun one more time and then dropped it. The last bullet broke one of the shelf supports an inch above Darwin's face. A dozen jars dropped, a couple hitting Darwin, the rest falling harmlessly beside him.

Darwin dropped to the floor. Peach juice and chunks of red jam filled the room with an intense strawberry smell.

Scythe had retreated from the door, retching around the corner.

Then Darwin remembered what Yuri had said about The Scythe.

Half the time, he ends up in the hospital on an IV if he eats the wrong thing. Scy worked himself up so much about food that he can't even be near it anymore. He juices.

That's why he wasn't at the restaurant that day.

Still in socks and underwear, Darwin got to his feet. He couldn't believe a body could be so wracked with pain. His back screamed, his face ached, and he was afraid to look at the damage to his hands after all the abuse he'd rained down on them, even though his vision was clearing.

On the verge of exhaustion, his stamina was all but gone. But he had to get out of the house and recuperate away from this madhouse.

In his sock feet, he tried to step around the shards of glass but picked a couple up on the way to the door. Jam dripped off his chest and belly. Peaches clung to his white underwear, making the blood stains look like an abstract collage of colors painted on him.

Scythe was on the floor near the stairs, vomit covering his chin and neck, clumps of it resting on his chest. It was a liquid-green mess. He slowly rose to glare at Darwin.

Darwin leaned against the wall. His legs threatened to not support him. One last kick, one more hit.

Darwin reared back and kicked Scythe in the head like a goalie kicking a soccer ball back into play. Scythe keeled over and didn't move again.

Darwin retrieved the gun and hobbled toward the stairs. On his way past the wire grid, he realized soaking his jeans in the toilet had helped him fry the man to the grid. It was one thing to be electrocuted, but quite something else to be electrocuted with sopping wet denim wrapped around your neck.

After checking the safety, Darwin aimed the gun at Scythe's forehead from one foot away.

Then he pulled the trigger.

Nothing happened. He pulled again. Nothing.

There was no energy left in him to search for more bullets. If he didn't leave now, he would pass out.

The stairs were like walking up the side of a mountain. He collected himself at the top, breathed deeply, and waited for his heartbeat to calm.

He pushed the door open and stepped into the hallway. This part of the house was empty.

Darwin strode to the front door of the house, leaving bloody footsteps behind him from the glass wounds. Chunks of peaches and jams slipped off his body and mixed with the blood.

He opened the door, and the sun hit his skin, warming him. He walked outside and started across the grass.

Yuri's house was on the end of a cul-de-sac with no other houses on either side. It was like he bought the whole block and then built his home there.

Someone yelled behind him. Darwin turned on his heels and almost lost his balance. He couldn't take anymore.

Behind Yuri's house was an expanse of green.

A golf course.

The man who had yelled slapped another's hand in the air and dropped a club into a golf bag on the back of a golf cart. The other man stepped up to the tee, took two practice swings, and then tried to murder the ball. He cursed and slammed his club into the ground at his feet.

Darwin started toward them. He raised a hand and tried to shout.

The men dropped into their cart and sped off without seeing him.

Darwin made it to the edge of the golf course grounds and headed toward the tee box. He stumbled halfway there, fell to his hands, and dropped to his knees. He couldn't walk any farther, so he crawled. With each lift of his knee, each foot he crawled, he expected to pass out.

The tee box marker came into view below him.

He stopped, fell to his side, and rolled onto his back. The sun warmed his thighs, his stomach, and his face. The scent of the wet peach and jam covering his body filled the air. He breathed it in and thought about his wife.

A golf cart engine revved from somewhere to his left.

"Hey!" a man shouted. "You okay?"

Darwin didn't want to move. He didn't want to talk.

"Hey?" the man asked louder.

Sleep felt wonderful. The idea of going under for a couple of days was what Darwin needed.

The voices were closer. His eyes were closed, but he felt two men standing over him, their shadows crossing his eyelids.

"Yeah, hello? Emergency services?" A pause. "Ambulance." Another pause. "There's a guy passed out in his underwear on the golf course, covered in some kind of fruit paste. He's bleeding all over, and he's been beaten up pretty badly. What? Yeah, in his underwear."

One of the men leaned in close. "Hey, you awake?"

"No, ma'am. He's not responding. Hurry."

Darwin lost consciousness.

50

HE OPENED HIS EYES and tried to bring his hands up to rub them. Bandages covered his right forearm, wrists, and knuckles. He blinked to clear his eyes.

Another hospital room.

"How was your sleep?"

A man in a white lab coat stepped up to his bed.

"Where am I?"

"In a hospital in Barrie about an hour north of Toronto. Do you know how you got here?"

Darwin rested his head on the pillow. No cop sat in the corner, no guard at the door. That meant the doctor didn't know who he was, and no one on the outside knew where he was. It also meant the mafia had lost him.

"I have no idea … about anything."

"You were found in your underwear on a golf course off of Highway 93. Do you recall anything that happened?"

Darwin looked up at the ceiling tiles and waited several moments. He turned back to the doctor and stared through him.

"Doc, I'm scared. What's my name? I can't remember who I am."

The doctor frowned as he pushed his glasses up his nose. He looked down at a clipboard in his hand.

"Can you remember anything, like who did this to you?"

Darwin glanced at the window in the room. Sunshine poured in.

How long have I slept?

"What happened?" Darwin mumbled. He forced a tear and looked back at the doctor. "What happened to me?"

"You're pretty beat up. Damaged kidneys, bruises all over your body. In half a dozen different places, you've been cut by glass. We had to pull a few pieces out when you arrived. I'm surprised your cheekbones didn't break. Whatever hit you actually bruised the bone."

You should see the other guy. Knocked him out cold with food.

The doctor flipped a paper on the clipboard. "It looked like a bullet grazed your lower leg, but I couldn't be sure. At least whoever beat you got some of it back. Your hands were a mess, but we've cleaned most of it up. Someone actually bit your knuckles. You had teeth marks in the open wounds."

"Why can't I remember anything?"

"You were found in your underwear covered in jams and the smell of peaches and other fruit, and you say you can't remember any of it?" The doctor stared at him, a look of disbelief on his face. "Very strange. But that's not the worst of it."

Darwin rolled his tongue around his mouth and found all his teeth were still intact.

"You had stitches in the back of your head from some kind of wound that looks to be about two weeks old. Any idea what that's from?"

Darwin shrugged, and pain accompanied it. *Shit.* "Maybe that's why I can't remember anything. Maybe I had a brain injury."

"Maybe," the doctor said. "We should know who you are soon enough, though."

Shit, shit. "Good. Did I have any ID on me?"

"No, just underwear and socks."

"Then how can you help me remember who I am?"

"We took your prints and photo and sent them this morning. We would have done it yesterday when you got in, but the emergency department was full. There was a large bus accident out on the highway. Two tour buses collided right outside our door. Fifty people showed up in emerg twenty minutes after you rolled in. We cleaned you up and left you to sleep." The doctor moved to the door.

"How long before they get back to you with who I am? I mean, what if I have a wife and kids? They could be worried about me."

From the doctor's expression, he clearly wasn't buying it. "I'll hear back from them later this afternoon or tomorrow morning."

"Thank you."

"I've got rounds to do. If you think of anything, buzz the nurse. She'll page me. When I know more, I'll come back and see you."

Darwin nodded.

The doctor stepped out of the room and closed the door behind him. He didn't lock it.

Darwin was free to go.

Yeah, if I can walk.

He tried to get up but lay back down as pain shot through his abdomen.

"Fuck, didn't they give me any Demerol or morphine?"

He tried again, gritting his teeth against the pain. Once he was sitting on the side of the bed, his head spun. He closed his eyes and waited for it to go away. He slid off the bed and touched his feet down gingerly, in case he was stepping onto wounds from the glass.

He was no longer the pudgy Canadian boy the mafia first encountered on that side road out by the abandoned airplane hangar so long ago. He was a man now. His innocence had been torn from him, and the void was filled with determination and anger. He was pissed off with what they had done to him and his wife, and he was determined to hunt them down until this nightmare was over.

Nothing would stop him now.

Bolstered by his escape from the glass prison in Yuri's basement, he realized that nothing *could* stop him.

Yuri was in Florida because he thought Arkady was down there. That meant Darwin needed to get down to Florida as soon as possible.

Maybe he could locate Carson Dodge and enlist him to use his resources to help find the Russians. But first, he needed to get out of the hospital. Then, he would figure out a way to get to Florida.

He walked across the floor, favoring the pain with a limp. It wasn't too bad once he got up and moving about.

He found a pair of track pants and a T-shirt in the closet.

They probably snatched it out of lost and found.

The pants were a little tight, but they fit okay.

Shoes? They have to have shoes.

He couldn't find any.

He used the bathroom, splashed water on his face, and wet his hair, styling it a little. The bruises on his cheeks were dark purple and made his cheeks puff up like a twisted clown's idea of macabre makeup.

Disguise wouldn't work. Nothing he could do would cover the condition his face was in. He turned slightly and saw the stitches at the back of his head had been removed.

Thanks, Doc.

He moved to the door, trying to walk as normally as possible. It felt good to be out, to be free.

Maybe when this was all over, he would write his memoirs.

This kind of stuff never happens to anybody, he thought. *It's stranger than fiction.*

Dressed in blue track pants and a white T-shirt with nothing on his feet—they must have discarded his ruined socks—Darwin opened the door and walked out into the corridor as if he had just been here visiting someone. Although the bruises and bandages that covered his hands would give him away.

No one tried to stop him as he headed down the hall. He went through a door that led to the stairwell, descended a floor, and walked down that corridor.

At each room, he slowed enough to look inside. Finally, he found what he was looking for, and it was far enough from the nurses' station that no one would see him enter.

He moved inside the room quietly. The bed was occupied by a man snoring softly. He picked up the shoes he had spied from the hallway. Black dress shoes.

Darwin checked the size. They were perfect. He slipped them on, tied them up, and tested the fit. Satisfied, he walked by the old man and almost got to the door when he noticed the old man watching him.

"Hi," Darwin said. He stopped, smiled, and waved. "I'm the night janitor. Had last night off because I was attacked in a back alley." He gestured at his face. "Anyway, thought I forgot something in here. Sorry to wake you."

The man smiled, and Darwin slipped into the hallway. His feet felt better with the protection of the shoes.

At the elevator, he pressed the down button. It came a few seconds later. No one tried to stop him, but he knew it was only a matter of time.

On the ground floor, he walked out toward the front, passed the gift shop on the left, and kept walking. Moments later, he stepped out into the sun and started down the sidewalk.

The air was clean and warm, the afternoon sun heating up the city of Barrie. He had no money, ID, or idea of how he would get to Florida.

But he had his freedom, and he had hope. And no one knew where he was.

Darwin walked on, not missing a step.

51

Darwin headed south toward the lake and west through downtown Barrie until he found a soup kitchen. With his bruised face and bandages, wearing track pants and a T-shirt, he was exactly what they would expect to walk in and ask for food.

He paused at the open door. The tables were half empty. Disheveled men in various states of dress were eating. They all had facial hair and smelled so bad he could barely detect the scent of the soup.

He walked past the tables to the counter. No one bothered to ask him if he qualified for the free offerings. The young volunteer behind the counter looked Darwin up and down, grabbed a bowl, filled it with soup, and handed it to him.

Darwin reached for a spoon. Beside the utensil container sat a pad and pen where someone had written a list of supplies. A few inches from the pad sat an iPhone.

As Darwin grabbed a spoon, the male volunteer turned to his associate in the back to whisper something, no doubt to discuss Darwin's appearance.

While the man's attention was diverted, Darwin grabbed the phone and the spoon and turned away. He slipped it into the pocket of the track pants and sat at the table closest to the door, where he ate quickly before the cell phone owner discovered it was missing.

A man wearing a long blanket over his shoulders got up from his table and shuffled toward the door. The cell phone in Darwin's pocket rang as he got close to Darwin. On the second ring, the female volunteer from the back ran up to the counter where the pad of paper still sat.

"Where's my phone?" she asked out loud.

It rang again.

Darwin got up and fell in behind the man in the blanket.

"Hey!" the girl shouted.

Then Darwin was outside. The man turned left, Darwin right. At the corner, the ringing stopped. He ran half a block and ducked behind a wall. The running was painful for his back, but he needed the phone. After a moment, he edged out, crossed the street, and started north.

Once alone and not being pursued, he called information and asked for the Jacksonville Bureau of the FBI. When they connected him, he asked to speak to Carson Dodge.

It wasn't so long ago that Darwin had saved Carson's life in front of Gambino's sprawling mansion in Florida, an exploit that involved a World War Two German tank and a gun armed with rubber bullets.

Carson Dodge owed Darwin.

Actually, you owe me your life.

"I'm sorry, sir," the receptionist said. "But Special Agent Dodge is unavailable at this time. Can I direct your call to someone else?"

"My name is Darwin Kostas. Locate Carson. I will call back in ten minutes. I will only talk to Carson."

Darwin clicked off. He kept walking north toward the highway. He had no immediate plan and no idea what to do next. Without his passport, how would he ever get back into the States? Hitchhike? Stowaway on a ship crossing Lake Ontario into New York?

The phone rang in his hand. Local number. He ignored it.

At the next corner, he checked the time on the phone. It had been at least eight minutes. The owner of the cell phone could easily call their service provider and have the phone shut down at any second. He couldn't risk that, so he called the FBI back a few minutes early.

The same woman answered.

"Darwin Kostas calling for Carson Dodge."

"Please hold."

There was a moment of silence. Darwin waited at a streetlight with a couple of teenagers. The light changed, and he crossed amid the constant stares at his bruised cheeks.

"Carson here. Who's calling?"

"Darwin."

"Bullshit."

"Fuck you."

"Darwin's dead. He died in an explosion in Toronto."

"Wrong."

"Even if he made it out of that building, he'd be scarred, and all fucked up, skin grafted a thousand times. But that doesn't matter because Darwin is dead. My own Bureau told me that, and I was the lead on his case."

"I'm scarred all right."

There was a moment of silence.

"Prove it," Carson said. "Make me believe I'm talking to Darwin."

"I saved your life at Gambino's."

"Anybody involved in the case would know that. Don't tell me the facts. Tell me something only I would know."

"You're an asshole. I'm sure you know that."

"If Darwin is alive, he's a ghost come to haunt me. Prove you're him, or I hang up."

"How?"

"Text me a picture of you."

"To what number?"

Carson gave him a cell number.

"Hold on while I take the pic and send it."

Darwin pulled the phone away, took a picture of himself, then hit the share button and, once in iMessage, typed in the phone number he'd memorized from Carson. After hitting send, he brought the phone back to his ear.

"Got it?"

"Hold on a sec."

Darwin waited.

"Holy shit." There was another pause. "What happened to you?"

"Too much."

"Where are you? They said you died." Almost to himself, he added, "Why would they lie to me?"

"I'm in Canada."

"Can you be more specific? That's the second largest country in the world."

"First, we talk."

"About what?"

"How are you doing?" Darwin asked. "They told me you were in the hospital."

"Idiots who attacked us shot me in the eye I don't use, adding to its ability to never be used."

"You okay, though?"

"Yeah, got a bullet in the hand that's missing a thumb, making that hand even less useful. It was like they wanted to maim me lightly by shooting me where I already had a deficiency."

"Weird."

"Yeah, weird."

There was a moment of silence.

"What can you tell me about Rosina?"

"The last I heard, she was with Arkady—"

"I heard that, too. And Yuri Pavel is on his way to locate Arkady."

"Yuri? You know about Yuri Pavel? How?"

"I just spent the last few days as his honored guest in his basement. A man he calls The Scythe kept me company, as evidenced by my face."

"Holy shit. What the hell kind of trouble did you get yourself into?" He gulped. "Are you sure it was The Scythe?"

"That's what they called him. Why?"

"The Scythe was rumored to be dead after a gun battle a few years back. Gut shot, something awful. No one's seen him since."

"Must be the same guy. He has food issues now. He'd be dead if his gun had held one more bullet."

"How the hell did you get away from Pavel and Scythe? That's impossible. When men meet The Scythe, they only leave in pieces."

"Food helped me escape."

"Food?"

"Yeah, Scy can't handle food—some kind of phobia after being gut shot. On a golf course, they found me covered in peaches, strawberry jam, and pickles. That's how I got away."

"You call him Scy? You guys that close?"

"Look, Carson, I need to be picked up. Get someone you trust and have them pick me up. Bring me in. I need clothes and food. Then we'll go get Rosina together wherever she is."

"Where are you?"

"I'm in Barrie, Ontario, just north of Toronto."

"Okay. The best bet is to get to a helipad at the main hospital. I'll have a chopper come pick you up."

"Wow, you've got some clout."

"Just be there. But I won't be taking you to Florida."

Someone shouted behind Darwin. He turned and saw the iPhone owner from the soup kitchen following him with two friends.

"Hey, you," the girl shouted. "I want my phone back, or I will call the police."

"Why not Florida?"

"Because our sources confirmed yesterday morning that Arkady is hiding in Toronto, and he has Rosina there."

Darwin watched his pursuers over his shoulder. "Bullshit. Yuri had his own people on the streets trying to find Arkady. He told me a few days ago that he was heading to Florida to find Arkady."

"Yuri never crossed the border. I've been following the case from down here. Yuri is still in Toronto. Apparently, there's a huge sit-down happening in two days between Yuri, the Italians, and the Triads. Arkady will be in the shadows, and Rosina won't be far behind."

"Why would Rosina be there?"

The iPhone owner and her friends were getting closer. Darwin kept pace, walking in the other direction.

"Only Yuri knows you're alive. The rest of them think Rosina is the last of the Kostases' troubles and want her present as an offering of peace."

"You mean a sacrifice."

"The authorities in Canada have every intention of stopping that."

"I have every intention of stopping that. Look, Carson, I gotta go." Darwin ran as the girl and her friends were only twenty feet away now. "Pick me up at the helipad. When are you coming?"

"I was leaving the hospital today but don't know when I can get away. I'll see what I can do from down here."

"Okay, talk soon."

Darwin hung up and stopped running. He set the phone on the ground and backed away from it. He matched their steps one by one as they neared the phone.

At the next block, he turned and disappeared down an alley. After ten minutes with no one chasing him, he came out and started toward the hospital.

Rosina in Toronto, after all? A meeting of rival mafia families?

All their troubles had started at a mafia meeting with Darwin as the guest. And now it had come full circle with his wife as their *guest*.

That meant the end was near. Maybe it was survival of the fittest after all.

52

It took an hour to make it back to the road that led to the hospital. Darwin took a break on a bus stop bench. This had been the most he'd walked in weeks, and he felt it.

The ultimate physiotherapy is running for your life.

It would take Carson more than an hour to arrange to have Darwin picked up in Barrie by helicopter anyway, so there was enough time to rest.

The mafia, whether Italian or Russian, were never going to just leave him alone. Killing a few of them wasn't deterring their efforts. Maybe he had to kill them all or as many as he could. Perhaps it was time to go on the offense, chase them, and have them fearing for their lives.

Then, an idea occurred to him. Something Carson said. The more he thought about it, the more he liked it.

Offer a man two cards to play, and each is a losing hand. When there's no hope of ever coming out of this with his marriage together, his wife unharmed, and his sanity intact, what did he have left to lose? Fuck the cards and the chips. Fall where they may. It was time to stop playing poker or chess or whatever the fuck his enemies were dishing out. It was time to play Darwin's game of war, and he had the ace of spades.

With a plan forming in his head, he got up from the bench and continued lurching toward the helipad at the Barrie hospital.

A four-door black Crown Victoria pulled up beside him. The back window lowered, and a familiar face smiled out at him.

"Get in," Special Agent Kirk Williams said.

Darwin remembered him from the Toronto hospital. He was Carson Dodge's replacement while Carson recuperated in a Florida hospital. At least that's what he was told.

The car pulled ahead of Darwin and then stopped abruptly. Williams jumped out, his jacket flaring open in the breeze. Darwin caught sight of his weapon resting in its holster.

"Get in," Williams said again, gesturing at the open door.

"How'd you know I was here?"

"You called Carson, no? You asked to be picked up. Now get in."

"He's sending a helicopter."

"We were close. This was the better option. Economically, it's better as well. Now, get in."

Darwin got into the back seat. Beside the driver sat another man in the front passenger seat. Darwin slid over to give enough room for Williams. When he did, he caught the profile of the passenger. Agent Scott is the man who questioned Darwin in the hospital with Williams.

Williams slammed the door. The driver performed a U-turn and got on the highway heading south toward Toronto. Once on the highway, Williams opened a briefcase on the floor and pulled out a thick manila folder. He bent over again, pulled a small bag from a fast-food restaurant, and placed it beside Darwin.

"Here, eat. Then we can talk."

Darwin opened the bag, grabbed the burger, unwrapped it, and ate as if he hadn't eaten in days.

"Talk while I eat," he said between mouthfuls. "Tell me you've arrested that asshole cop Cavendish."

"What did Cavendish do?" Williams asked.

"He fed me to the sharks."

"Explain it to us. What sharks?"

Darwin took another bite and wondered if the food was drugged. He was so hungry he had just bit right in without thinking of the consequences.

"You first. I'm eating."

Williams and Scott exchanged glances. Williams sat back in the leather seat and opened the manila folder. On the top of a pile of papers, Yuri Pavel's face stared back.

Williams held it up. "This is Yuri Pavel."

"Met him."

Williams raised his eyebrows. "Really?"

"That's who Cavendish fed me to." He chewed faster. He had no idea when the next time food would be this easily available. "Go on."

"We want you to go through this file on your own. Examine the pictures, read the rap sheets, and see who you know. We're looking for names, locations, and details about the people listed here. Anything you can tell us about the Russian mafia."

Darwin finished the last bite. "You got any more food?"

Williams shook his head.

"Gimme the file then."

Williams handed it over. Darwin flipped through the first few pages, recognizing some people from the Russian restaurant where he met Yuri that night on Queen Street. Then he thumbed through the rest of the pages and realized he had hit the jackpot. In his lap was the accumulation of the RCMP and the FBI's homework on the Russian mafia in Toronto. Every name, known address, business, and associate they had a file on.

In Darwin's hands, this became his map of executions. With the information within the file, he could systematically murder all of them.

Someone, contained on the pages in his lap, had his wife or knew where she was, and the only way to get to her was to wage war on the people within the borders of the manila folder in his hand.

"Brief us on what happened after you walked out of the hospital in Toronto," Williams said.

Darwin closed the file but kept it in his lap. He explained what Yuri did. He felt no reason to hold anything back, especially knowing Scythe was alive and well.

"You're kidding?" Williams asked.

Darwin shook his head. "He did this." He pointed at his face.

"Are you sure you're not embellishing some of the story?" Williams asked. "You have to be. The Scythe is dead. He was the Russian mafia's most ruthless executioner. As soon as anyone saw The Scythe, they knew it was game over. We'd hunted him for years. Our intel says he died in a shootout, and yet you claim to've met him. I don't believe it. No one has seen him in years. None of our informants or undercover agents."

"You think I care what you may or may not believe? You assholes constantly prove that we're not on the same team. I'm thrown back into the lion's den whenever I trust the authorities.

Let me out here. I'll catch a cab to the local mafia hangout. Got a date with the wife."

Williams asked, "Why're you still alive if you met The Scythe?"

Darwin detailed the fight in Yuri's basement.

Williams grinned. "Jars of canned fruit? Oh man, how the hell did you know to do that?"

They were placating him. "I didn't *know*. It was luck."

"You really do have a horseshoe up your ass. I read what Carson wrote in his report about how you singlehandedly stormed Gambino's house with a German tank and shot Greg Stinsen and your wife with rubber bullets to make Gambino think you'd lost your mind and were killing them." Williams shook his head. "Insane, for sure. But then there's that lucky horseshoe—"

"So now what?" Darwin broke in. "Tell me your genius plan. How do we stop them and get my wife back?"

Williams and Scott exchanged another glance.

"What?" Darwin asked. "What aren't you telling me?"

"We won't be *stopping* them."

A silence descended upon the vehicle. Darwin looked out the window and controlled his breathing. Then he met Kirk's gaze.

"I'm not sure I heard you right," Darwin said. "Say it again because I thought you said we *won't* stop them."

Williams nodded. "You heard me right."

"Why the fuck not? You're the FBI, for hell's sake."

"Because too many powerful people will be at that meeting in two days. The RCMP picked up the location on wiretaps of known associates of Yuri. It's like the G8 summit for the mafia, and it's happening right here in Toronto. If we do anything right now, we jeopardize the chance of that meeting ever taking place."

"And what about Rosina? Just leave her with those dogs?"

"We have no idea where she is at the moment."

"Is that true? Or do you know where she is, and you can't tell me because you have to let the mafia G8 meeting take place?" Darwin wiped his brow and took a deep breath. "I think you know where she is, or you at least have a good idea. I think she'll be a part of that meeting, but I don't think she'll be a willing guest. What're your thoughts on the subject?" he asked, sarcasm on each word.

"Look, Darwin, you may have trust issues, but we will do everything we can to get Rosina out safe. You have to understand something. The meeting about to take place is the result of years of surveillance, years of economic resources, and endless manpower hours staking out buildings, monitoring phone lines, and asking judges for search warrants. To have the leaders of three warring families coming together for one meeting is like hitting the jackpot. We have to let the meeting take place, hear what they're meeting about, and then take appropriate action. We must do it right so charges will stick in court, or all our efforts are wasted. If we rock the boat before the meeting, who knows who'll show up? It could all get wasted."

Darwin stared out the window. A sign said they were passing an exit to Newmarket. The top of Toronto would be coming up within minutes.

"Darwin, listen," Williams said. "In North America alone, the Red Mafia operates in almost twenty major cities. There are over thirty Russian crime syndicates in those cities." He cleared his throat. "Did you know that in all American history, the largest jewelry heist and insurance scams were perpetrated by the Russian mafia? The amount stolen has been estimated at over one billion dollars. They're involved in politics, businesses, financial markets, and even professional sports. The Russians didn't come here to be a part of the pursuit of happiness. They came to steal it. That's why my superiors won't consider one woman's welfare when three bosses of rival families are meeting in one place. I'm sorry, but that's the way the chips fall. I do have the green light if we see her and they intend to harm her. We'll have snipers watching from every direction."

"Where's the meeting taking place?" Darwin asked.

"You know I can't tell you that."

"It's okay. I already think I know."

He watched the traffic pass on the opposing lanes. No one said anything for a while. He rolled his thumb along the back of his other hand and tapped his foot. He knew what he had to do, and he knew he could. He just hoped none of the agents in this car got killed.

After fifteen minutes, no one had said another word. Canada's Wonderland had passed by on the left several minutes before as they entered the northern part of Toronto. The Finch Avenue bridge passed over them as they continued south.

He turned to Williams. "Ordinarily, I would completely understand and think you have it right."

Williams studied him from across the seat. "Have what right?"

Darwin ignored him and continued. "But they have my wife, and I've been causing the Italians hell for a few months. Now the Russians are involved, and Arkady killed a member of the Triads at that warehouse and tried to blame it on me. When they meet in two days, Yuri or Arkady, or both of them, will offer Rosina's sacrifice as a peace offering. I can't let that happen. She won't walk out of that meeting without intervention. My wife is not bait.

I don't care how many prison sentences you get or don't get in a court of law for these mafia guys. I'm only interested in securing my wife's safety."

Williams adjusted his suit jacket, glanced up at Scott, and then back at Darwin. "I understand how you feel. I really do. But the best thing for you is to let us do our jobs. We're the FBI. We're trained for this."

"Right, and it was the FBI who manned the safe house my wife and I lived in. It was the FBI who protected Rosina when she was taken the second time. It was the FBI who guarded my hospital room when I was fed false information that Yuri had Rosina when, in fact, he didn't. Arkady did. Yuri just wanted me so the Russians would have both of us. How am I supposed to trust you? Because you're the good guys?"

"You're supposed to trust us, Darwin. I'm afraid you don't have any other choice. To keep you out of the mix, we can lock you up until it's over."

"You could try." A wave of beautiful rage coursed through his body. He looked out the window and waited until traffic had thinned. The Crown Vic was doing at least 120 km on the 400 highway, still heading south. He slipped the manila folder beside him between the seat and the door. His knuckles ached from the abuse in Yuri's basement. He had no idea how he could punch, so he decided to use the lower part of the palm of his hand.

"Darwin, I know you're angry," Williams said. "Trust us, this is the only way. We will have the meeting covered by hundreds of agents. It's a combined task force. If Rosina gets into trouble, we'll be there."

Darwin breathed in slowly, mentally preparing himself.

"Darwin, are you listening?"

"I don't believe you," he said as he shot across the back seat and whacked Williams hard on the side of the throat. He wouldn't get a second chance, so he ensured the hit would count. Williams tried to defend himself, but Darwin already had his other hand coming around. He hit him again near the front of Kirk's throat, causing him to crumple back in the seat, gagging for breath.

Scott was lurching in his seat, already reaching over into the back.

Darwin slipped his hand inside Kirk's jacket, wrapped his fingers around the butt of his weapon, and pulled just as Scott's arm circled Darwin's neck. He was yanked back and away from Williams, but the gun came up with him. Scott's powerful arm cut off his breath instantly, and his vision blurred.

The driver screamed for them to calm down, and the car swerved, then righted.

Normally, Darwin would bring his hands up to pull on the offending arm around his throat. Instead, he flipped the safety off the weapon, aimed the gun, and fired a bullet out the side window beside Kirk's purpling face.

The wind swirled around the back seat, tossing Kirk's hair askew. The pressure from Scott's arm around his throat didn't decrease. His consciousness wavered, his chance at freedom diminishing.

He turned the gun and pointed it at Scott's elbow, making sure if he had to fire the bullet, it would go clean through and not hit him in the shoulder. His vision darkened at the edges, and his lungs screamed for air. Before his strength left him completely, he pulled the trigger.

Scott screamed in his ear, and the arm dropped from around his throat. He took a huge breath as his eyes watered and regained their clarity. Williams was breathing again but in short gasps. His lips were purple, but his face was coloring.

Darwin tried to tell the driver to pull over, but his voice broke when he opened his mouth. He pointed to the side of the road with the weapon's tip. The driver understood.

Scott had fallen backward onto the glovebox, where he cradled his arm, trying to hold the blood in. He moaned like a child with a skinned knee.

The Crown Vic slowed and pulled onto the shoulder near the Sheppard Avenue exit.

"Now," Darwin said and then cleared his throat. "Get out and leave your guns on the floor." His voice was hoarse. He turned to the driver. "You too. Gun on the floor and leave the keys in the ignition."

He leaned back to cover both of them.

"Exit the vehicle on the passenger side only," he said. "Do not piss me off today. It's not a good day to fuck with Darwin."

He lunged across Williams and pushed open the door on Kirk's side. Then he shoved Kirk's shoulder until he fell out sideways, the whole time watching as Scott exited the vehicle, still holding his arm. The driver got out and stood by the back door.

"Can I help Williams?" the driver asked.

"Get him to the grass over there," Darwin said.

He rested the gun on the back of the seat as the driver put a hand under Kirk's shoulders and dragged him away from the car.

Scott's face had gone white.

"You're going to be okay," Darwin shouted at him over the noise from the traffic racing by. "Tell the driver that I want Kirk's jacket, and everyone empty their wallets of cash."

Scott didn't move.

At any moment, the Ontario Provincial Police highway patrol could pull up. He had no patience for Scott. He turned the weapon, aimed it at Scott's foot, and pulled the trigger. The bullet kicked up dirt, not an inch from Scott's toes.

"Shit, I missed."

Scott jumped and started to run away.

"I will shoot you in the back." Scott stopped running and nearly fell. "Get me Williams's jacket, and I want the cash."

Darwin kept the gun trained on them as he closed the back door. Then he crawled over the seat and dropped down into the front. Scott had made it to the driver and Williams, who was already looking better. The driver helped him out of his jacket and collected cash from all three wallets.

Then, he took a few steps toward the vehicle.

"You aren't going to shoot me, too, are you?"

"Do you want to be shot?" Darwin asked.

He shook his head violently. "I'm just the driver."

"Bullshit. FBI doesn't have *drivers*. You're one of them. Just give me everything I've asked for, then step back."

He moved closer. He extended his arm at the open passenger door, set the cash down on the seat in a pile, and tossed the jacket in. It rolled off the seat and dropped onto the floor.

"I need a cell phone, too."

"In the glove box. We have extras."

"Step away from the car. Go back to them and call an ambulance."

Darwin dropped the car in gear and slammed his foot on the accelerator. He pulled away so fast that the passenger door shut on its own.

He hit the Sheppard Avenue exit, turned left, and raced east. Five blocks down, he turned onto a side road, parked, and collected the cash from the seat. He eased into the suit jacket, slipped a gun into each pocket, and got out of the car, the keys in his hand. He walked around to the passenger side and opened the glove box, where he found two cell phones. Then he changed his mind. They could probably trace him wherever he went. He reached across the back seat and snatched up the manila folder.

After shutting the door, he waited a minute to let his heart rate slow down. Then he crossed the street and approached two young men loitering by a tattoo parlor.

"Here. Take these." He tossed the car keys at the bigger guy. "It's yours." He pointed at the Crown Victoria he just walked away from.

"Is it hot?" the guy asked as he passed them.

"Not at all. I'm moving to Europe and don't need it." He turned around to face them and continued walking backward. "I didn't have time to sell it, so it's yours. Have fun."

He mixed in with the crowd of pedestrians and disappeared on the streets of Toronto.

<h1 style="text-align:center">53</h1>

Darwin spent the day shopping, picking up new clothes, and discarding the old ones. As soon as he looked completely different in jeans and a hoodie sweater, he grabbed a cab to Woodbridge and, five minutes later, took a cab to Brampton. After a ten-minute wait, he took a taxi to downtown Toronto, making sure always to use a different cab company. He needed it to be virtually impossible for the authorities to follow him. He had a full meal at a chicken restaurant downtown, courtesy of the FBI cash.

During the early evening, he kept his head down, watched his back, and searched out a knife shop on Yonge Street. As the sun dipped behind the skyscrapers and the beginnings of dusk fell upon the streets, Darwin entered a large knife shop that sold almost every type of weapon he'd ever seen. Samurai swords hung suspended behind the counter. Cases displayed Swiss army knives and hunting knives.

He could never have entered a store like this three weeks ago, not with his phobia of sharp and pointy things. Being around knives, seeing them this close, would've driven him into a rage. But now, after the swelling and induced coma, his phobias seemed to have disappeared.

"Can I help you?" a clerk asked.

A young man wearing a collared shirt and a tie stepped up to him. He was clean-shaven and wore glasses.

"You work here?" Darwin asked.

"Yeah. Were you expecting someone else?"

"No, you just don't look the type."

"The type? Should I have tattoos, a nose ring, a shirt with cutoff sleeves?" he said, his sense of humor coming out. Then he narrowed his eyes, smiled, and pointed at Darwin in a friendly gesture. "Are you stereotyping me?"

"No, I just—"

"It's okay. I get that all the time. This is my shop. What're you looking for?"

"A scythe."

"A scythe? What're you thinking of cutting with it?"

"Why do you need to know that?" Darwin snapped before he could stop himself.

"It'll help to determine the size and kind of blade."

"Oh, ahh, grass. I need it for grass."

"Come with me."

Darwin followed the clerk through the store. Under the counter were small, handheld scythes. Larger ones sat behind the counter, some as tall as Darwin with a long wooden handle.

"We've got a variety of scythes, from sixteen-inch blades to fifty-inch. It all depends on your needs."

"I need something small for close contact, I mean, culling closely spaced saplings." He thought that part sounded good.

"In that case, you might want to go with an eighteen-inch ditch blade or a sixteen-inch."

For what Darwin wanted, he couldn't buy the large ones with long wooden staffs. They would see him coming a mile away. He had to go with the smallest blade attached to a handle the length of a hammer with a little finger-grip piece on the handle.

"I'll take two of these."

"You'll need a whetstone and a whetstone holder."

"What's that?"

The clerk showed him the holder, how it clipped onto his belt, and what to do with the whetstone.

"You could go one step further and get a small anvil and peening hammer so it's easier to dress the blade in the field. Got to keep it sharp, you know."

"No, that's okay. The whetstone will be enough."

After he paid, the clerk threw in two blade covers.

Darwin walked back onto Yonge Street with his new assault weapons tucked under his arm. He had over a hundred bucks left from the cash but wouldn't need any of it until later. He had bought what he needed for the next step and had a destination in mind.

On the way to kill some Russians, he stopped for an extra-large coffee and drank it back as fast as he could without burning his mouth.

It was going to be a long night.

54

DARWIN KEPT TO THE shadows across the street from the Russian restaurant on Queen Street, where he'd met Yuri. He studied the faces of everyone entering or leaving.

Mentally, he had crossed a line. He no longer feared them or was angry at his enemies. They were enemies and needed to be treated as such. The mafia, whether it was the Italians or the Russians, were at war with his family. The FBI was doing nothing about it. No one was arrested, and no one was questioned. The mafia had kidnapped his wife, shot Carson Dodge, and decapitated Greg Stinsen, and the FBI was sitting on their collective hands while Rosina was still in danger.

If the Red Mafia could do whatever they wanted and still walk the streets, then so could Darwin. If the FBI weren't prepared to do anything about this mess, then *he* would.

It was time to set things right. Time to send a message. All the addresses of known clubs, bars, and restaurants owned by or affiliated with the Russian mafia in the Toronto area had been in the folder Special Agent Williams had provided him. Along with that were dozens of photos of mafia men and associates. All those photos and addresses were folded neatly in Darwin's back pockets. As he dealt with them, he would pull out their pictures, rip them up, and discard them.

He couldn't just walk into the restaurant, pull the scythes out, and not expect a bullet. He would need to use Williams's and Scott's guns. Then, he would use the scythes.

He stepped from the shadows. After crossing Queen Street, he walked up to the restaurant window and, just like on his first visit, peeked past a little white curtain. Only five people were inside. Four men sat at one table halfway down, and the bartender stood behind the bar. They all looked Russian.

Darwin moved to the door, pulled out William's gun, concealed it beside his leg, and opened the door. He slipped inside and pulled the door closed, latching the thumb lock.

He took a couple of deep breaths through his open mouth, lifted the hoodie over his head, and turned into the main part of the restaurant, his gun hand behind him. The four men turned to see who had entered.

The bartender had been wiping glasses behind the bar. Darwin stopped ten feet from him and set down the glass in his hand.

"You look for someone?" the bartender asked in a heavy Russian accent.

Darwin figured the four men would be armed, but he had forgotten that bartenders always had a weapon behind the bar. Once the shooting started, he would have to duck down somewhere and find shelter.

But where?

He moved sideways toward the table where Yuri had eaten the night he was there.

"Hey, he ask you question," one of the four men at the table said, his accent also heavy. "Why your hand behind your back?"

He was in too far. There was no other choice now. There was no way he could walk backward out of the restaurant. At any second, one of the four men would demand to know what he was doing in their establishment if he didn't act more like a customer.

He stood beside Yuri's table now. The bartender had moved closer to the bar, no doubt getting closer to a weapon.

"I'm looking for Yuri Pavel," Darwin said.

"He ain't here. We'll tell him you were by."

"How about Arkady?"

The men looked at each other. Then, the speaker stood up. "How you know Arkady? Who are you? Pull that hoodie off."

A weapon fired from somewhere behind him, and everyone jumped. Darwin's legs were already weak and shaking. He slipped to the floor when the gunshot startled him. Glass from the front window cascaded down in a high-pitched tinkling sound.

He spun around to see a man outside on the sidewalk aiming a gun at him through the broken glass of the restaurant window.

Darwin fired William's gun. The bullet hit the man in the left cheek. A squirt of blood shot out, and the man's face disappeared from the window.

Another loud bang, this time from inside the restaurant. Chunks of wood broke off the table beside Darwin's head, a couple lodging in his face.

He turned in time to see the bartender cocking a shotgun. Darwin aimed and emptied Kirk's gun in the bartender's direction, screaming as each bullet left the barrel. The gun clicked on empty. He tossed it aside and dropped down flat as more bullets whizzed by him.

The foursome were shooting now.

He brought up Scott's gun and peeked through a small hole in the table. The four men had scattered. Two were behind an upturned table, just as Darwin was. The other two were behind pillars near the back. He applied the gun to the hole in the table, aimed it as best as he could, and emptied it in the direction of the two men by the pillars.

One of them shouted and cursed and didn't stop cursing for a few seconds. Darwin snuck a peek around the edge of the table while he pulled the driver's gun out.

One gun left.

The man by the back pillar now lay sprawled across a table, blood seeping out of his arm and chest. He had stopped shouting as blood bubbled out of his mouth. One of the men from behind the table was half exposed as a random bullet hit him in the forehead. Shooting Scott's gun wild had luckily got both men.

A man stepped out from behind the support beam. From that distance, his bullets went wild, only one hitting the table Darwin hunkered behind. Then his partner tried, with one hitting the floor two inches from Darwin's hand.

He looked around the table again and understood what they were doing. While one fired at him, the other moved closer.

A moment later, one of them started shooting again, which meant the other was on the move. Darwin pushed his gun hand around the edge of the table and sprayed all the bullets he had in the direction he thought the man advancing would be.

There was a grunt and a gasp of surprise, then a solid thud. Now, it was just the two of them left.

But Darwin was out of bullets. He only had the two scythes. With all the gunfire and a man lying out front of the restaurant shot in the cheek, it was sure to draw a crowd fast. He had to get out before the cops showed up. If the police had taken him now, he would never have been able to help Rosina.

"Are you a smart man?" Darwin shouted.

After a moment, the guy shouted back, "Fuck you."

"I guess you're not that smart."

"What you talking about?"

"I work for Yuri. I'm here with a message about the meeting that's taking place in two days. Are you aware of the meeting?"

He didn't get an answer. For a second, he feared the man was approaching him.

He peeked around the edge of the table. The restaurant appeared empty. At the broken window, a young couple looked inside. Darwin gestured with his gun hand for them to get away.

Fucking idiots. What's wrong with people these days?

"Are you still with me? I work for Yuri."

"Then why did you walk in here shooting?"

"I didn't. The man in the window shot at me first. Then I had to kill the bartender because he had a fucking shotgun aimed at me. You would've done the same."

"Now what?"

"Now I'm going to stand up, toss my gun to you, and let you take me to Yuri. He'll confirm my story. He'll reward you for doing the right thing. It's either that or I will have to kill you like I did the others."

He waited.

"We haven't much time," Darwin said. "The cops'll be along shortly, and neither one of us wants to be here when that happens."

"How do I know you're not lying?"

"I will throw you my weapon. Once you talk to Yuri, if I'm lying, kill me then. Do we have an understanding? You won't shoot until you talk to Yuri?"

"Yeah, okay, but come up with hands empty."

"Okay, standing now."

Darwin threw the empty gun over the edge of the table and raised his hands. He lifted his head enough to see over the edge of the table. The Russian had stepped out from behind the pillar.

"Stand up and step away from the table," the Russian said.

Darwin stood to his full height. People were talking louder outside. Someone said they had already called the cops and an ambulance was coming.

Darwin's heart raced. At any second, he could get a bullet in the face.

"You can't shoot me because what would happen to you when Yuri finds out you all attacked me in his restaurant? If I'm wrong, you know I'm dead anyway."

"How come I've never seen you before?"

"When was the last time you saw The Scythe?"

"He's dead. Everyone knows that."

"No, he's not. But that's another story." Darwin swallowed involuntarily. "When someone sees The Scythe, what happens to them?"

"Execution."

Darwin stepped closer. "How many people do you know of that can claim to have met The Scythe and lived?"

"None."

"That's why you haven't met me."

"Huh?"

"If you had, you would be dead by now."

They were four feet apart. The man held his gun in a two-handed stance aimed at him. Darwin had his hands up, about as high as his ears.

"Do you have Yuri's cell phone number?" Darwin asked.

The man nodded.

"Good. Call him. Tell him who I am and that I have information about the meeting in two days. He will be pissed that you guys shot at me but happy that you were the smart one."

The Russian let go of his gun with one hand and pulled out a cell phone without taking his eyes off Darwin. He handed it to Darwin.

"You dial. I won't take my eyes off you."

Darwin moved slowly and took the phone from him.

"Number?"

After typing it in, he smiled and nodded at the Russian.

It rang twice, and then Yuri answered in a gruff voice.

"Hello, Yuri?"

"Yeah, what is it?"

Darwin waited a moment. He wanted to choose the right words. Then he said, "This is The Blade, and I'm coming for you."

He threw the phone toward the Russian's face and, at that same moment, ducked left. The Russian blinked and ducked but fired his gun over and over.

Darwin reached inside his hoodie and pulled out one of the brand-new handheld scythes. Before the Russian could recover and aim his weapon properly, Darwin sliced down hard across the Russian's wrists, cutting clean through. Both hands dropped to the floor, the gun still gripped to the right.

He brought the scythe up and cut along the man's neckline,

slicing through to the spine. Blood squirted across Darwin's face. He stepped back as the man's eyes widened, his mouth agape. Then his head dropped back, and as his wrists spewed blood like a small fountain, he fell to the floor, convulsing as he died.

Darwin cleaned the scythe on the man's shirt, pocketed the cell phone with Yuri's number, and grabbed the Russian's gun. He checked to see that each man was dead, pocketed two of their guns, and stepped behind the bar.

The bartender lay sprawled on the floor, bleeding from his head. He breathed in pants and gasps, and sweat had beaded on his shocked face. It was a miracle he was still alive, as a chunk of his skull was missing on the top left.

He wouldn't be long for this world, though. Darwin knew it, and so did the bartender.

"Shitty luck," Darwin said. "I can help you along." He showed him the scythe. "But I need to know why there was a *fucking* guy outside. How come I didn't see him standing by the door?"

"There's always," he said, then gulped air in. "There's always a guy watching the door."

"Why didn't I see him?"

"Can't make it—" his eyes closed.

Darwin thought he lost him. Then the bartender's eyes popped open, and Darwin jumped back a bit.

"Can't make it obvious. Bad for business."

"I'll remember that."

Emergency sirens roared in the distance.

"Where's Yuri?"

"Will you?" the bartender asked, looking at the scythe, then back at Darwin.

"Of course."

"He's at the club."

"The club?"

"His—" he paused and swallowed, "strip club."

"Misty's Retreat?"

It looked like the bartender nodded, but it was only a subtle head movement as the last breath escaped the bartender's mouth. Darwin checked for a pulse but couldn't find one.

He slid the scythe inside the hoodie, which was heavier with the added weight of the Russian's guns and moved away from the bar. He pulled out one of the guns, checked that the safety was off, and slowly opened the kitchen door. If the waiter had been there, he was gone now.

The back door to the restaurant swung open in the breeze. Darwin ran for it and stopped in the doorframe. He edged around the corner, the weapon ready.

With no one close or posing a threat, he jumped out and was lost in the shadows of the garbage bins in the back.

It took him fifteen minutes to get a few blocks south, where he jumped on a city bus. He had used a van's passenger mirror to wipe the blood from his face and hands, but he couldn't do anything about the splatter marks that were crisscrossed on his hoodie. Downtown Toronto was littered with eccentric people. He only hoped he would fit in and not get too much attention.

The bus would take him to within three blocks of the strip club. That worked perfectly as it would allow him to approach on foot and scout out the area for the men watching the doors in less obvious places. He wouldn't make that mistake again, and he wouldn't come in all nicely-nice again, either.

These people played dirty. They would gladly kill him for no other reason than the sport of it. He would address them on their terms from now on.

He was energized, liberated, and ready to kill as many as he could to remove the threat on his family.

Instead of being hunted, he was now the hunter.

55

DARWIN APPROACHED THE STRIP club from three different points and only saw two men, who could be Yuri's guys, smoking by the back entrance to the club.

Convinced that wasn't all of them, he stayed behind a tree without moving for almost a half hour, mentally preparing for what he had to do.

None of the cars in the parking lot appeared to have any occupants watching the building. Maybe they only had two men standing by the back door.

He had no idea if Yuri was still inside the club or not, but he suspected as much with the two Russian goons loitering outside a few steps from the door. The club would close soon as it was near midnight.

He was ready. With a gun in each pocket, it was easy to grab and shoot. The scythes were inside his hoodie in their sheaths and easily pulled out quickly.

He strode across the road between the streetlights and made it halfway through the parking lot before the two large men in suits saw him. They studied him too long. Both men looked like they had the night off from pro football.

Maybe they'd heard about the restaurant shootout. Perhaps Yuri warned them to be extra vigilant.

He kept walking.

The suited men moved to flank each side of it. Darwin nodded at them as he drew nearer.

"Pull the hood back," the guard on the right said. "No one gets inside without seeing the face."

Darwin halted. "I don't want my wife or any of my friends to see me going inside." He deepened his voice. "I come looking for discretion. You understand, yes?"

"There's no one out here. Look around. Hood off or no entry."

Darwin showed his hands. He raised them up to show he posed no threat, then reached inside his hoodie. He gripped the handles of the scythes, then yanked them out and sliced across the closest man's chest in one fluid motion. A quick step to the left and another swipe dropped the second man.

He wiped the blades on his own hoodie and stepped back to assess if either man would remain a threat as they crawled away, wounded and moaning.

Both men were cut deep, bleeding from their chest wounds. They weren't fatal wounds but would leave a nasty scar.

One man fumbled with a cell phone. Darwin kicked the phone out of the man's hand. It clattered away, bouncing on the concrete parking lot.

He seemed calm after attacking the two bouncers. Violence was getting easier, and that scared him. He never wanted it this way and would give anything to go back in time.

Darwin replaced the scythes in his hoodie and stepped inside the club. The music was so loud it could be measured on the Richter scale.

At any second, someone would discover the men at the back door. Darwin wasn't strong enough to haul both of them away in time. All he could do was get inside the club, find Yuri, and get Rosina's location before he had to kill him and then leave before the authorities showed up.

He ran through the back, turned toward the front, and almost bumped into two more large Russians in Hugo Boss suits.

"Are all you guys built at the same factory?" he asked. "How come you're all so big?"

The Russian looked down at the fresh blood on the front of Darwin's hoodie and grabbed Darwin's right arm. They locked eyes. Darwin snatched the gun on his left, leveled it at the Russian, and fired from one foot away three times in quick succession.

Three holes formed on the front of the man's dress shirt. Dark red blood seeped out. He looked down and then back up at Darwin, a scowl on his face. He hadn't let go of Darwin's arm yet. The grip tightened. The other man had stepped back at the show of violence.

Darwin raised the weapon, aimed carefully, and fired once more. A hole formed under the Russian's chin. A small spray of liquid shot out of the top of the Russian's head. His facial expression changed to a more subtle one of surprise. He tried to look at the man beside him for help, but his legs gave out, and he dropped hard enough to shake the floor over the vibration of the music.

Darwin turned the gun to the other man, who had watched everything in stunned immobility. He had stepped back another two feet and turned to run. Darwin let him go, pocketed the gun, and moved through the alcove into the main part of the club. He needed to find Yuri before his bodyguards ushered him out of the building and whisked him away in his car.

He scanned the crowd in the dark as best he could but couldn't see Yuri. Half-naked dancers paraded around the club looking for lap dance potential. Others were already sitting on men's laps, and two girls performed on stage, oblivious of the three dead men on the premises. Luckily, no one had picked up on the gun going off a moment ago.

He moved farther inside, squeezed past four businessmen in suits standing around drinking, and walked briskly to the far back of the club, where the lights were dimmer. He kept his hands in his pockets, gripping the butts of the two guns.

When he reached the back, a woman screamed from the area where the Hugo Boss guy had died. Another person screamed.

He ignored it and scanned the faces of everyone sitting along the back wall. He recognized no one. Then he started looking for bodyguards sitting with Yuri but saw nothing.

The music stopped. The two girls on stage were kneeling, their tops off. Both of them got up and covered their breasts. They gestured at the DJ booth.

"Ladies and gentlemen." The DJ came over the speakers. "May I have your attention?"

The VIP sign was lit five feet from Darwin beside a darkened door. He headed that way as the DJ asked everyone to remain calm as an incident was reported to him and emergency services had been called.

Another dancer screamed as she saw the dead Russian.

Darwin entered the VIP section and turned a corner.

Fully nude dancers moved up and down on men in booths separated by partitions. Two dancers handled one man in a booth on Darwin's left.

He pulled a gun and brought one of the scythes out of his hoodie. Then he stepped up to the first booth, bumped the naked girl aside, and looked at the man.

A stranger.

It struck him as odd that none of the VIP dancers had stopped after the DJ's announcement. No music played.

He went from booth to booth until he reached one where a man sat alone, no dancer present. The man's head was back, his eyes closed. Cyrillic letters were tattooed on each finger, telling Darwin this guy was part of the Russian mafia. Yuri must be in the next booth.

Darwin stepped up close and pushed the scythe against the man's neck. The man opened his eyes, saw Darwin, and went to move, but all he did was fall on Darwin's blade.

Darwin sat on the man, locking his arms in, and covered his mouth to mask any sounds he made as he died. The girl in the next booth kept dancing for her customer, unaware of the man dying beside her.

When the Russian stopped moving, Darwin got up and stepped behind the dancer. She faced her customer, blocking his view of Darwin.

After a quick look at the VIP door to ensure no one was coming, Darwin tapped the girl on the shoulder.

She turned her head around. "I'm busy here?"

"Fuck off," Darwin said. "Now." He showed her his gun.

She yelped like a little terrier and scuttled away, her arms over her breasts.

The man sitting in the booth wasn't Yuri.

It was Arkady.

He wore a smile, and a gun rested in his hand as if it came out of nowhere. Before either man said a word, they both aimed and fired their weapons.

Darwin felt a punch in his lower abdomen. He fired his weapon over and over, but only two bullets came out as he'd already used the others. He frantically reached in for the gun on his right side. Arkady had dropped his and was slumped to one side.

Darwin took the chance to kick Arkady's weapon out of the way and moved in on him. He set the tip of the barrel at the base of Arkady's mouth and held it firmly against the skin.

"Where's my wife?"

"Fuck you. I die first."

Darwin pulled out the scythe with his left hand and sliced along the top of Arkady's legs. Arkady screamed and writhed under the blade.

"You will burn for this," Arkady yelled. "I will have every Russian in the continent after you."

"And I will kill them all. Where's Rosina?"

"I have no idea," he shouted.

"Yes, you do."

He kept cutting. In seconds, Arkady's legs were unusable chunks of red meat. He made sure to stay away from major arteries and not to go too deep. Arkady bounced around in his seat in a vain attempt to escape the blade of the scythe but couldn't.

"Where is she?" Darwin screamed at him, grabbing his hair and yanking Arkady's face up to his.

"With Yuri," Arkady panted, the color leaving his face.

"That's all I know."

Something banged to his left. Darwin looked up at the door and saw a crowd of men watching him. The dancer he'd told off was with them. He raised his gun to scare them and fired wild into the ceiling tiles.

He turned his attention back on Arkady.

"I told you I'd be back. You fucked with the wrong man, Arkady. After what I did to the Fuccini Family and the Gambinos, how'd you think you were above that?"

"Wait," Arkady shouted. "I'll tell you where Yuri has her. But you walk away. No more cutting."

"Of course." Darwin smiled. "No problem. That's all I want."

"He's got her at the Park Road Hotel. It's about ten blocks from here. Room 456."

His side ached where Arkady had shot him.

"How do I know you're not lying?" Darwin asked.

"Because I don't want to die."

Amid the pain, Darwin detected a look of relief pass over Arkady's face as he leaned back off him.

Before Arkady knew what was happening, Darwin ran the scythe across Arkady's neck. He wiped the bloody blade on the man's silk shirt and stepped away as Arkady grasped at his neck, trying to keep the flow of blood in and not finding much success.

"Rot in hell, asshole."

The VIP room had emptied. The people at the entrance had disappeared. There were no windows or back doors to escape. The door he had entered through was the only way out.

Should he exit guns blazing, hitting anything in his way, and hope he made it? Or should he negotiate his way out? The police would arrive at any minute.

Pain crept into his heightened consciousness. He looked down and saw a red stain forming on the lower part of his hoodie jacket.

"Shit."

He lifted the hoodie and looked. A bullet had gone in just at the edge of his side and exited clean on the other side, missing his kidney. He lowered the jacket and moved to the door.

"I'm coming out," he shouted.

No one answered him. It was absolutely quiet outside the VIP room.

He edged around the corner. The lights of the club had been raised enough to see everything. It was nearly empty except for five men standing around in random places. They were all watching the VIP door. None of them had weapons in view.

"What's going on?" Darwin asked. No one answered. "Where is everybody?"

Someone cleared their throat through the speakers and said, "The dancers and customers have exited the building for their own safety."

"Who are all of you?" Darwin asked. "Why haven't you left?"

"Are you part of the mafia war?"

Darwin wondered what the right answer was. Then he decided on the truth.

"Yes. This is a war."

"Please leave before the police get here."

"You're just going to let me walk out?" Darwin asked.

"Is Arkady alive?"

"No."

"Then yes. Just leave."

"I could walk out and get gunned down."

"Arkady has been coming here for a year, causing all the girls trouble. We've had three dancers disappear in that time. The mafia has ruined the reputation of this club. When you walked in tonight and killed only the Russians who have been causing us trouble, we figured it out and want you to leave now. This is between you and them."

"Why wasn't there more security?" Darwin asked, still unsure if he was being told the truth, even though it sounded good.

"Some big boss was here earlier meeting with Arkady. When he left, they left with him. When Arkady is around, we just have normal bouncers, and Arkady has his one bodyguard with him, who I assume is also dead, right?"

"Yeah."

Silence fell between them while Darwin debated what to do. The five men scattered around the club retreated in a non-threatening gesture. Two of them put their hands on the bar.

"Please leave. The authorities will be here shortly."

The pain in his side throbbed, intensifying. If he stayed, it was over. If he left, he could get to his wife.

Darwin stepped out with a scythe in one hand and a gun in his other. He moved the gun around, waiting to see if he needed to use it. He kept his hoodie over his head and stayed close to the back wall, making his way to an exit door.

"When the police ask who did this, you tell them The Scythe did it."

"The Scythe?"

"Yeah, The Scythe. That's my name."

He reached the exit and hesitated. None of the men had moved. He heard scuffling behind the door but thought that was just the people who had exited the club minutes before.

Using his good side, he bumped open the door's bar handle

and stepped outside. As he did, he lowered the gun out of sight and slid the scythe back inside his hoodie jacket.

Dancers stood around with suit jackets over their shoulders, borrowed from caring customers. The parking lot had half emptied. The people milling about kept away from the two men bleeding on the ground by the back entrance door.

No one noticed him as he slinked along the building in the shadows and crossed the street.

He slipped the gun into his pocket and continued moving up the street, blood seeping from his abdominal wound with each step.

56

Darwin had to rest on a park bench after three blocks. He didn't want to look but knew he had to.

The lower hem of his hoodie jacket now had a large, dark red stain. He lifted it gingerly and examined the wound. The blood had slowed, but it still seeped. He had no idea how to help it stop other than to apply pressure. He could be bleeding internally, too.

He lowered the jacket and held his hand over the wound, adding as much pressure as he could without causing too much pain. He didn't want to pass out. His wife was seven blocks away. All he had left to do was go get her. Then he could go to a hospital.

No one would take her again. He wouldn't let her out of his sight. And he would stay armed at all times.

He got up from the bench but found standing too difficult. He wavered on his feet, head spinning, and dropped back down hard. Pain shot through his abdomen.

Lying down and sleeping for an hour sounded like a great idea.

Cars passed him on the street a dozen feet away. The sidewalk was closer. He couldn't sleep here, even though it was semi-concealed in darkness.

He scanned the park behind him and saw a pond with park benches in a semi-circle around it.

Resting there would offer shelter from the street and enough darkness.

With the adrenaline worn off and the pain in his side increasing, he gripped the back of the bench and forced himself to his feet. After a moment to make sure he wouldn't pass out, he walked around the bench and started across the dark terrain of the park. With each step, he grimaced with the pain.

Halfway to the pond, blood slithered down his leg, filling his shoe. He looked down and almost lost his balance, grabbing a passing tree for support.

Bent over, leaning into the tree, he focused on his breathing. In through the mouth, out through the nose. The ground trembled as his equilibrium gave out.

Darwin dropped and sprawled on the dirt floor under the tree, the exit wound in his back pressing directly on a piece of the tree's root sticking up. He yelped in pain, dropped his hand on top of the wound, and pressed.

Then he passed out.

57

A COOL MORNING BREEZE crossed his face. He opened his eyes, and panic stirred him. A sick dread twisted in his stomach.

Where am I? What happened?

It all came back to him in a rush. Arkady, the strip club, getting shot, passing out under the tree.

He hadn't moved all night. The sun was high enough to be at least nine in the morning.

He rolled his head sideways. On the other side of the pond, an old man tossed something at pigeons gathered near his feet. A young woman jogged by on the sidewalk twenty feet away. It would be hard for anyone to see him in the slight recess where Darwin lay. Toronto was up and awake, and no one cared about the bum with blood seeping out of him in the public park.

He leaned up to look at the wound. The bleeding had stopped. Getting to his feet could reopen the wound, but he couldn't stay under the tree all day. What if Yuri checked out of that hotel and chose another one before tomorrow's big meeting? Then what? He'd have no lead on Rosina. He needed to get up, buy another hoodie so he could get rid of the bloodstained one he wore, buy painkillers, and eat. Then, he needed to break into Yuri's hotel room and liberate Rosina.

He rolled onto his good side slowly, easing down onto his stomach. The dirt under him was stained with blood. A sharp pain made him stop moving. He knew it would get tolerable as soon as he was up and walking around. After two deep breaths, he brought his legs up and lifted onto his elbows. After a small struggle, Darwin got to his feet and leaned against the tree. He waited for the lightheadedness to abate. Besides the pain and how he looked, he felt better than expected.

The two guns were still with him, and both scythes were tucked snugly inside his jacket.

After his first step, he stopped, clutching the tree. Then he took another and let go of the tree. Once he stopped losing blood sometime during the night, he must have rested well, recuperating after a harrowing day.

Fully rested now, he knew how to deal with Yuri.

Darwin headed down the street, amid the stares of everyone passing by, and walked inside a clothing store. He gingerly tried on a hoodie his size, transferred the scythes and guns into the new one in the privacy of the change room, walked out with his old hoodie wrapped up in a ball, and got the clerk to throw it out for him.

Then, he bought over-the-counter painkillers and a pair of sunglasses with a beautiful case at a pharmacy.

He was ready for Yuri.

After consuming two large sandwiches from a convenience store and two energy drinks, he walked up opposite the street facing the Park Hotel. No visible security guards were standing around outside. Staring up at the front of the ten-story hotel, he imagined his wife inside somewhere.

When the traffic subsided, Darwin crossed the street, walking with only a slight limp as the painkillers set in. He'd opened his wound twice since he woke that morning. Once when he first got to his feet and the other time when he bought his new hoodie. But it had closed fast, oozing only a minute amount of blood. It was healing, and he felt great, ready to take on Yuri Pavel and finish this.

His mind was clear, his objective sound. He knew what he had to do and who he had to kill.

He entered the lobby of the hotel with the hood over his head. He kept one hand on his gun and the other free to grab a scythe.

The sun shone through the large front windows of the hotel, heating the lobby. Air conditioners worked tirelessly to control the temperature but failed as the sun proved relentless.

He walked to the side of the lobby and pulled out the sunglasses case. Then he folded his last fifty-dollar bill and slipped it inside the case. He closed and snapped the lid shut.

When the counter was free of customers, he walked over. A man in his early twenties, wearing a nametag that said Oleg, asked if he could help him.

"I'm staying with some friends on the fourth floor and wondered if you could put this in their slot for them when they come down."

"Absolutely. Can I have the room number?"

"It's room 456. Oh, and when's your shift change? I'm in meetings at the youth fellowship all day and don't want your relief to make a mistake with this. Those glasses are Mr. Pavel's personal property." He made a gesture with his hands. "Very expensive."

"I was supposed to be relieved an hour ago. She's late. When she gets here, I'll make sure she knows that the glasses belong to Mr. Pavel in room 456. I would take them up myself, but his room has a note on file to not disturb for any reason."

"Thank you. Enjoy your day." Darwin turned and walked out of the lobby. As soon as he stepped away from the counter, a couple in their forties stepped up with luggage and handed Oleg their room key.

Oleg asked how their stay was, and then Darwin opened the door and stepped outside into the blazing summer sun.

He headed across the street and ordered a coffee in a small café. In a seat near the front window, he watched the hotel's main entrance. No sign of Yuri or any of his Russian-looking bodyguards. Halfway through his coffee, Oleg exited the hotel, walked down the steps, and turned south.

His shift was over.

He took one more sip of his coffee and left the café. When he entered the hotel, a young girl was at the counter talking to two men who were checking out. She couldn't be more than eighteen.

The lobby was almost empty except for the men at the counter and an old man with graying hair sitting alone in a plush chair beside his luggage. Darwin waited. After a minute, the two men thanked the woman and stepped away from the counter.

Darwin walked up. "Good morning," he said, sounding cheery and bright.

"How can I help you this morning?" the girl asked.

Darwin looked down at her nametag. "Jessica, my friend and I are staying in room 456. I understand he left something for me."

"Let me look."

She turned away from the counter and checked a row of small boxes.

"It should be a sunglasses case," Darwin added. "I have a note on room 456 to not be disturbed."

"Yes, here it is."

She turned around with the case in her hand.

"Great, thanks." Darwin took the case.

"And your name was?" the girl asked as she typed on the computer.

"I'm with the Yuri Pavel party in 456. And if I'm right, he left me a fifty-dollar bill inside this case along with my shades. At least that's what he said he would do."

Jessica looked over and watched as Darwin opened the case. The money popped up when he did.

"Perfect. Just like he said he would." He glanced up at her. "I told him I forgot my wallet at home, and he said he'd put the money in the case so I could pick it up at the counter on my way back to the room." He stepped away. "I'll just head back up—" he patted his pockets and stopped walking. "Oh, damn. My key card was in my wallet, too. Can you give me a replacement?"

"Of course," Jessica said. She typed on the computer for a moment. "Check-out is eleven this morning, and the room was only booked for one night."

"Has Mr. Pavel already come down to check out?"

"Not yet, but sometimes guests just leave the key in the room and leave the hotel. Housekeeping confirms to us down here that they've vacated the room. I haven't got confirmation yet, but," she checked her watch, "you've got twenty more minutes until eleven."

Could he be too late?

"Well, as I said, I've forgotten a few things up there. The rest of my things are in the room. I'll come down and give you the key back within fifteen minutes, so we're out on time."

He smiled, showing teeth, trying for an innocent look.

"Of course," she said, smiling back at him.

At this time, he assumed most of the guests would've checked out by now. He hoped Yuri hadn't. Losing him now would be a catastrophe. If sleeping in the park meant he lost the trail, he would go insane with fury.

Jessica handed him the key card.

"Thank you so much," Darwin said. "Have a fine day."

At the elevators, Darwin pressed the button. He waited until the doors opened and then stepped on, hitting the fourth floor and the close-door button at the same time.

When the door closed, he exhaled the breath he'd been holding.

The elevator crept to the fourth floor. As it slowed, he tightened the grip on the weapon's barrel. His heart raced, and his pulse pounded in his ears. He was close to Rosina, as close to her as he'd been in weeks. Sweat lined the inside of his hand on the weapon. His grip slipped, so he let go of the gun, wiped his hand on the outside of his new hoodie, and re-gripped it.

The door slid open.

He waited inside the elevator in case a Russian bodyguard watched all access to the floor. Darwin placed his free hand between them when the doors began to close. They clunked to a stop and slowly reopened.

He listened but heard nothing. No soft patter of feet on the carpet, no whispered warnings.

He stuck his head out. The hallway was empty. With his gun

low and hidden in his left hand, he walked into the foyer of the fourth floor.

The sign on the wall directly in front of the elevator told him room 456 was to the right. The hotel was constructed in an L-shape, with the hall on the right going south and the hall on the left going east. He only had to watch his back as far as he walked toward room 456, not the other hallway's length.

Each corridor had cleaning carts topped with toilet paper, pads, pens, and garbage bags as the hotel's maids cleaned various rooms. As he drew close to room 456, the door was closed, and the nearest cleaning cart was one door down.

If Yuri had vacated, the maid would see that soon enough. Darwin put his back to the wall beside the room and waited, listening for anything inside the room. Maybe it was a distant voice, a slammed door, or a TV, but there was nothing. He couldn't wait long. At any second, a maid would see him and question his intentions.

He knocked on the door, stepped back three feet, and brought the gun up. The time to be discreet was over. If Rosina were inside the room, he would shoot the thug who opened the door and barge in with one less man on their team. If a maid saw him with the gun, she could call downstairs, but Darwin would have Rosina by then, and even if the police showed up and took them into custody, it would be better than leaving Rosina with the Russian mafia.

But no one answered the door.

A maid stepped out of the room next door. He lowered the gun beside him just as she looked up.

She smiled.

He smiled back.

He raised the key in his hand, twisted it back and forth in the air, and nodded at her. She returned the nod, gathered a small pile of towels, and disappeared backward into the room she had been cleaning.

He inserted the key into the slot on the door, pulled it back out, and watched the light turn green. Then he pulled on the handle and opened it with most of his body hidden behind the wall.

"Housekeeping," he said into the open door.

After getting no response, he stepped inside and closed the door behind him. The room was a mess, the three beds unmade. The room came with two doubles. A cot had been brought in to handle an extra person.

He checked the bathroom and the hall closet, but it was clear Yuri had left the hotel.

"Damn," he slammed his open palm against the bathroom door.

How would he find his wife now?

He had at least ten minutes. That was enough time to search the room. Maybe they left something useful behind.

He started in the bathroom but found nothing in the garbage besides a spent razor and used Q-Tips.

The main room had two empty Vodka bottles and two cigars doused in an ashtray. The window sat open. Otherwise, he would've detected the residual cigar smell right away.

There was nothing else in the room other than messy beds. No other garbage or notes or business cards. He was at a dead end.

To lose Rosina when he was so close was maddening. His eyes watered. He had no idea where to go next.

Then he remembered the papers in his back pocket that Agent

Williams had given him in the Crown Victoria after picking him up in Barrie. He pulled them out, unfolded them, and placed them flat on the room's desk.

He crumpled up the papers on Arkady and his bodyguard as they had been taken care of. He flipped through the rest, discarding the ones he didn't need and putting into a separate pile the ones of the faces and locations he didn't recognize.

He had thinned the file considerably. Under the paperwork that showed known businesses associated with the Russian mafia, the FBI had listed the restaurant on Queen Street that Yuri owned. It also listed an adult store in North York on Finch Avenue.

He stopped browsing and snapped his fingers.

The Italians run a store in Mississauga.

The entire nightmare had started in an adult store in Mississauga when Darwin had been given the address of an abandoned airplane hangar. He had been in the store to purchase a bottle of mint tree for Rosina—she loved the stuff. But Darwin got an address that day to a meeting where he thought he could work on his phobias in a group setting.

How ironic.

That day started his foray into the mafia world, but he'd come out the other side with his phobias healed.

There was a knock on the door. Then, a soft voice said, "Housekeeping."

"I'm still here," he said.

The door opened anyway.

The woman cleaning next door stepped inside, towels in her hands.

"Oh, I'm sorry," she said. "I didn't hear you."

"I'll be done in a moment."

Darwin gathered up the papers and folded them together. He stuffed all of them in his pocket as the maid moved farther into the room.

"Excuse me," Darwin turned to her. "I haven't checked out yet."

The towels dropped away from the woman's hand, and a gun popped up as the door behind her closed. The petite woman ordered him to sit.

Darwin was too far away to swat at her and not stupid enough to reach for his own gun.

He backed up and sat in the chair by the desk.

"It's past check-out time," the woman said. "Time for you to go."

"Interesting way for the hotel to ask their guests to check out."

She two-handed the gun and slipped her finger inside the trigger guard.

Darwin closed his eyes and braced for the bullet.

58

THE BULLET DIDN'T COME. He opened his eyes. The woman sat on the corner of the bed, the gun still up. More than eight feet separated them.

"Who are you?" Darwin asked. "Who do you work for?"

"No talking. We wait. When my backup arrives, you can tell your story."

If she was a cop, why didn't she identify herself right away?

"You're wasting valuable time," he said.

"Shut up."

"I will have your job when this is over."

"I said, shut up."

"Why the delay with the backup? They busy cleaning up all the bodies left behind by The Scythe?"

Her eyes flickered.

Got you.

She met his gaze. This time, she didn't tell him to shut up. Her silence was enough to let him know she was listening.

Darwin continued. "My search led me from the catastrophe at

the restaurant on Queen Street last night to the aftermath at the strip club. My sources told me Yuri Pavel would be in this hotel with a hostage. I'm trying to locate The Scythe before he continues his spree."

"What?"

"I know, I know. My name is Special Agent Kirk Williams."

If she had met Williams, his gambit was over. If not, he was on a tangent.

"You look young to be—"

"So do you," Darwin cut in.

"What happened to your face?"

"Didn't you hear what happened to us yesterday in Barrie? Our car was stolen on the way into town?"

"Yes, we had to send another car to the agents stranded on the highway. They were pretty pissed Darwin got away."

"Darwin Kostas is almost as bad as the mafia."

"I've heard he's some kind of hero throughout our ranks."

She lowered her gun to rest it on her leg.

Darwin raised his hand slowly so as not to cause alarm. Then he circled his face. "Darwin did this. That's why I'm dressed this way. I'm looking for him."

"Are you armed?"

"Of course. I'm surprised with your training that you're just asking me that now."

Sirens outside the building were loud enough to hear through the thick walls.

"Can I show you something?" Darwin asked.

She hesitated.

"It's in my back pocket."

"Slowly," she said.

Without any sudden movements, Darwin twisted in his chair, pulled the pile of papers that he didn't need, and unfolded them.

"Here, look at these."

He tossed them on the bed closest to him. The woman walked over and picked them up. She scanned through the pile while the sirens pulled up out front and turned off.

"These are confidential FBI releases from their files," she said. "At least that's what it looks like to me. How is it you have these?"

"How would I have them if I wasn't FBI?"

"Do you have ID?"

"Have you ever worked undercover? Not just dressed as a maid, I mean deep cover?"

She shook her head.

"If I were searched at the strip club, that would've been it for me. Now, I'm running out of time. I'm going to leave." He stood from the chair. "Your team can sweep this room, but you won't find much. In our experience, Yuri never leaves prints behind. I'm just pissed that I was an hour too late."

"Last question."

"How did you get in here?"

"This key card." He held it up. "The front desk gave it to me. We'd called it in an hour before I got here. You'd be surprised at the access we can get."

She lowered her weapon. He walked up to her and held out his hand. She shook it.

"Pleasure to work with you, Agent …'?"

"Shelly Paulson. I'm not an agent. I'm an Inspector with the RCMP. Although I'm pretty new at it."

"Brave of you to do what you did, but you were too late. The

Russians have left the building. I'll favor you in my report."

He stepped past her and walked to the door.

"Wait," she called.

He grabbed the door and waited, knowing each second counted.

"Don't you want these files? Aren't they confidential?"

"Shred them. Those are the files of the Russians who are dead now."

As he opened the door and stepped out, the elevator pinged. He turned away from it, walked as fast as he could to the next door in the hallway, and stood by it briefly. He watched the end of the hall toward the elevator.

Then, five men filled the entrance, briskly heading his way.

He turned away from the five men and walked without purpose, slowly making his way along the hallway, acting as if he didn't have a care in the world. He listened to everything behind him, trying to determine if they were closing in on him.

The men reached the door to room 456 and knocked. Shelly opened it. Their voices traveled down the empty, quiet corridor.

Three doors away from the end, Darwin picked up his pace.

"Shelly Paulson, we're with the FBI. This is Special Agent Scott, and my name is Special Agent Williams."

"What?" Shelly said.

Darwin half-jogged the last bit.

"ID, please," Shelly demanded.

As he hit the door to the stairwell, he heard Shelly say, "There was a guy in here who said he was you. His face was bruised up —"

"Darwin!" Darwin heard Williams shout through the stairwell door as it closed behind him.

He dropped down the four flights of stairs quickly, the wound in his side screaming at him to slow down. He passed the exit door on the first floor and continued down to the basement parking level even as footsteps pounded from above. He ripped open the door at the basement and ran for the sunlight pouring down the exit ramp. A lone vehicle turned the last corner and started toward the parking attendant behind a little glass-enclosed booth.

Darwin hopped between two cars, ran by a concrete pillar, and then jumped out in front of the brown Impala a dozen yards from the exit.

The driver hit the brakes and raised both hands in a what's-up gesture.

Darwin pulled out his gun, aimed it at the windshield, and motioned for the driver to get out as he moved to the driver's door.

But the hardened Toronto driver shook his head, defiant.

"What the hell?" Darwin shouted. "I've got a gun."

"Hey, what're you doing?"

Darwin turned to see the parking attendant had stepped out of his little glass booth. He brought the gun up and fired a bullet into the glass hut the parking attendant had just vacated, shattering the glass on both sides. The attendant ducked so fast that he stumbled and fell to the ground.

The stairwell door burst open.

Darwin tapped the glass on the driver's side window of the stopped Impala and aimed the weapon at the driver's face.

"Okay, okay," the man shouted, his voice muffled through the window.

The door clicked, and the driver started getting out of his car.

"Darwin, stop running," Williams yelled. "We can help."

"Fuck you!" Darwin shouted back.

He yanked the driver out of the way, dropped down behind the wheel, and gunned the engine. Luckily, the parking attendant had already gotten off his ass because Darwin came close to the booth as he rounded the corner and squealed the tires on his way into the sunlight of a bright Toronto day.

He hit the brakes so hard that the car slid several feet to the chagrin of pedestrians walking by. The sidewalk was jammed with businesspeople out for lunch. He waited for it to clear while studying the rearview mirror.

Williams showed up at the bottom of the ramp.

There was no end in sight of people walking back and forth in front of him.

Williams ran up the ramp toward the car, so Darwin edged forward, nudging people out of the way. He honked the horn and kept moving forward.

Someone shouted at him. Someone else slapped the passenger side window.

Then Williams jumped on the trunk and banged the back window.

Darwin made it through the people but had to wait for two taxis to pass before jumping out into traffic.

Williams slid off the trunk and jumped up beside the driver's side window. He smacked it with the butt of his weapon as Darwin hit the gas, bunny-hopping into the lane, where he sped away.

"The door was unlocked, asshole," he said to himself.

59

Darwin headed deeper into the city. Getting on a highway would be a mistake. The authorities would be watching for him and were probably sending the information about this car to every available unit in the area at that moment.

He sped north on Mount Pleasant Road, continuing until he hit Lawrence Avenue. Then he turned left and hit Yonge Street, where he headed north again. He needed to get as far away from downtown as possible by staying on side streets, but Yonge would get him above Highway 401 and nearer the Russian adult store on Finch.

Without interruption, he made it to the corner of Yonge and Finch, drove by the adult store, and continued for two more blocks. After pulling onto a residential side street, he turned off the car and sat listening to the ticking of the Impala's engine.

He wiped his face with his hands and took a couple of deep breaths. It was time. He checked his weapons and then got out of the stolen vehicle.

On the walk back to the adult store, he crossed the street and bought a coffee at one of the nationwide chains. He took it to go.

Red lights flashed in the windows where mannequins in lingerie stood in various poses. A couple of adult games and lotions were also on display.

He opened the door and stepped inside. A young, pretty girl sat behind the counter. She looked up and greeted him. He sipped his coffee, acted nervous as he passed the counter like it was his first time, and walked down to the section where the wall was covered with dildos.

After a moment, he moved to the counter.

"Is there something you're looking for?" the clerk asked, her accent clearly Russian.

"I'm here to pick up my paper for tomorrow's meeting."

She frowned, confused. "I don't understand. We have no meeting here."

"Not here? Yuri would've left notes on where the meeting would be. This is how they did it the last time. I was told to come here, and you would tell me where the meeting would be tomorrow." It was dumb and amateur, but he had nothing else to go on.

"I don't know this man, *Yuri*. I'm sorry."

Something moved behind him. He spun around just as a curtain at the back of the store dropped in place.

"Who's in the back?"

"None of your business," the girl said. "I think you should leave now."

Darwin set his coffee on the counter, turned, and started for the curtain.

"Hello back there," he said.

"Excuse me," the girl raised her voice behind him.

Darwin kept walking. At the curtain, he stood to the side, pulled out his gun, and placed a finger over his lips for the girl to be quiet. He showed her the gun.

After parting the curtain, he jumped through it, his back to the wall.

Someone banged through the back door ahead of him. It slammed against the outer wall and came lazily around.

He ran for the door and jumped outside. The man had a head start and was at least twenty yards away. Darwin couldn't run that fast with the hole in his side, so he carefully aimed. The back of the strip mall was empty except for garbage bins and a couple of cars.

He eyed the man and squeezed the trigger twice. Then he squeezed again and again. The girl in the store screamed behind him. On the last bullet, the man fell like he tripped over something.

Darwin started after him, walking briskly. Running earlier in the underground parking lot of the hotel had hurt like a bitch. He had felt it when he'd settled into the car. Only now was it subsiding.

He recognized the man from when he entered Yuri's restaurant. The defiant fake cop.

Darwin leveled the empty gun and made sure the tip was pointed at the man's crotch.

"Castration?" he asked.

"What? No!"

Blood trickled out of a small wound on the man's ankle. From that distance, Darwin was surprised he'd hit him at all.

"Where's the meeting taking place tomorrow?"

"Fuck you. I tell you that I'm dead."

"You *don't* tell me that, and you're dead."

"Then kill me because I will not snitch. Ya nechevo ne znayu!"

"What does that mean? Speak English."

"It means I don't know anything. I'm not a *stukatch*, a snitch."

At the girl's voice, he turned to check that she wasn't going to shoot him in the back or club him over the head. The weapon she held was a cell phone. She was calling the police.

"You will sing when I finish with you," Darwin said.

"Fuck you." He spat at Darwin, missing.

Darwin tossed the empty gun away and brought out both scythes in a smooth motion.

Behind him, the female clerk screamed for Darwin to stop.

The man pushed with his one good foot, trying to edge away, but Darwin cut the man's flesh by the bullet wound and then again on the man's other leg.

He howled and rolled onto his stomach to avoid the blades.

This was a high-traffic area of North York, but the back parking lot was still empty except for the Russian store clerk standing ten feet away, phone in hand, crying and shouting for Darwin to stop.

He brought his attention back to the man on the ground.

"You're losing a lot of blood," Darwin shouted to be heard over the clerk and the man's own wailing. "Tell me what I want to know, and it's over. I'll walk away. They will never know it was you."

"I will never tell you," he shouted as he rolled over onto his back again.

Darwin brought a scythe up close to his face and held it there.

"Last chance. I'm done fucking around with you lot."

The crazy man spit again. The store clerk screamed.

Darwin sliced through the man's cheek, gouging the scythe across and out at the edge where his upper and lower lip connected, giving him half a Glasgow smile. For a brief moment, before the blood started to flow, Darwin got a peek at the side of the man's dirty teeth. His stomach tumbled, and he almost let go, but he steeled his resolve and got ready to cut again if needed.

"Where are they meeting?" he shouted.

"You're too late," the store clerk yelled beside him, her face a mask of tears, her nose running. "You're too late."

The man clutched at the side of his face as blood poured out and around Darwin's knee.

"Why am I too late? The meeting is planned for tomorrow."

The clerk shook her head.

"Tell me what you know."

"Don't," the man under Darwin tried to say. "Don't tell him nothing."

Darwin smacked him. "Shut up. She's trying to save your life." Then he turned to the clerk, who hopped from one foot to the other. "Just please don't hurt him anymore, okay?"

"Fine. Tell me about the meeting."

"It's set for today," she said. "They're about to meet right now."

"Why did they move the meeting up?" Darwin asked.

"They moved it up because of you."

"What? Me? Why?"

"We don't get told everything."

"Shut up!" the man below Darwin shouted. The corner of his mouth flapped when he talked, challenging Darwin's stomach to stay calm.

"I'm The Scythe, and I'm pissed. Don't interrupt us again."

"You're not The Scythe," the man said.

The girl's eyes widened. She looked at the blades in Darwin's hands and then at his face.

"It's true …" she stammered.

"Tell me where the meeting is being held. I need the location." Darwin placed one of the scythes against the man's neck and applied pressure.

"They're meeting at the golf course," the clerk said.

"What golf course?"

"It doesn't matter." The man adjusted his hands, trying to keep the blood on his face. "You're too late."

"It's a sunny day in July," Darwin said. "Any golf course in this area would be filled with golfers. How could they have a private meeting with that much attention? Stop lying to me."

Darwin was beginning to hate the sound of police sirens. Every time he was dealing with something, they showed up and tried to thwart him. The sirens squealed in the distance, creeping closer.

"Tell me the truth," he said to the clerk. "What golf course?"

"They are meeting at High Hills Golf Club in the convention center. It's a private facility."

"You're not shitting me?"

"No, seriously," she said. "Just don't cut him anymore."

"It doesn't matter," the man said. "You show up, the lookouts will see you a mile away. You'll be dead on the first tee box." He spit blood. "There'll be eighteen holes, all right—eighteen holes in your face."

A cop car rounded the corner in front of the complex, announcing its arrival with a long squeal of tires.

"If you're lying," he said to the clerk, "I will come back and burn this complex to the fucking ground with you tied up inside."

"I'm not lying," she pleaded. "Just go. Leave us."

"Goodbye, asshole," Darwin said. He moved to get up but slipped on the blood. The scythe wasn't more than a foot away from the man's throat when he fell back down, the scythe dropping to where it was a moment before. Only this time, it cut into the Russian's neck as Darwin's weight fell back on it. He couldn't stop its downward angle until he caught his balance, but it was too late. The scythe came to rest on the man's spine.

"Damn, that's sharp," Darwin said.

The clerk went hysterical, screaming and running for the back of the store.

"The world is a better place without him. Sorry, though, I was actually going to walk away."

Darwin got up and jumped behind a dumpster. Just as he suspected, the police car came around the corner of the strip mall and raced toward the back of the building. The cop parked right in front of the garbage bin, got out, and ran to the dead Russian.

Behind Darwin was an eight-foot fence. Too high to climb without being seen, and it would tear open his wound.

The cop was radioing in for backup from his lapel radio. The Russian girl from the adult store came out the back door and motioned for him.

"He was just here a minute ago," she yelled at the cop, Kleenex in hand.

"We'll get him, ma'am. He can't be far. I have backup en route."

He was trapped. He couldn't move, yet staying there meant they would discover him shortly.

The girl went back to the store. The cop knelt by the body.

Darwin waited until the cop talked into his lapel mic again. It was his only chance. Otherwise, he would have to hurt a cop to escape, and he wasn't about to spend time in prison for injuring a cop, too. Any jury would sympathize with him about the Russian mafia, but not a cop.

The tinny sound of someone talking to the cop was loud enough for Darwin to hear a man say he was three minutes out.

Darwin jumped from behind the garbage bin, stayed hunched over, and ran around the back of the idling cruiser. How far could he run if he didn't have a car? How would he get up Highway 50 and make it to High Hills Golf Club if he didn't have a car?

The decision took no time at all. He jumped inside the cruiser just as another siren could be heard in the distance. Without shutting the door, he dropped it into reverse, hit the gas, and drove backward, trying to get as much distance from the cop as he could before the cop decided to use his sidearm.

With his eyes barely over the seat, watching where he was going, he was pretty shielded when the first bullet hit the windshield.

Then another hit.

Darwin spun the wheel hard and almost got tossed out the open door. He held the steering wheel to stay inside, tearing at the wound on his abdomen.

He screamed and waited for the car to stop spinning. When it did, he was aimed at the street, the passenger side facing the cop who stood with both hands on his gun, legs wide.

Darwin dropped the car into gear and hit the gas as a bullet entered the passenger window in the back seat. Then, he was past the building and free of the cop.

The radio in the car picked up non-stop chatter. He heard something about a stolen police car, but then he was on Finch Avenue and heading toward Highway 400.

He searched the dash until he found the button for the lights and siren. It was challenging to see through the windshield as the cop's bullets had caused two holes and concentric lines throughout.

He slowed at red lights but kept his speed up to eighty miles an hour until he hit the north highway that would take him to the golf course. He knew exactly where it was. He'd golfed there many times.

The sun beat down on his side of the car, warming his arm. Air rushed through the holes in the windshield with a high-pitched whistle that could be heard over the rushing air coming through the broken back window.

He swerved around slower-moving vehicles, making good time with hell on his tail.

Yet he never felt so free.

60

HE COULDN'T PULL UP in a police cruiser, expecting everyone to lay down their arms and send Rosina out. The FBI was sure the meeting was taking place tomorrow. There would be no backup, and no one knew where he was.

But he kept driving, nonetheless. There was nothing else he could do.

The bullet wound was bleeding again. It seeped through his new hoodie, darkening the front with a small stain. A minor amount, but it concerned him.

After turning off Highway 400, he drove along a concession road to Highway 50, which would put him on the outskirts of the High Hills Golf Course property.

He cut the siren and the lights and slowed to the speed limit. The wind and whistle inside the car dimmed with the speed, but the police radio kept up its chatter. As far as he could tell, they had no idea where their stolen police car was yet. He had also picked up that the domestic disturbance at the adult store on Finch had led to one deceased male, Caucasian.

He slowed the cruiser and pulled off the road a few hundred meters from the fence line of the course. A long driveway led down to a farmhouse. He started down it, pulled in between two trees, and drove the cop car off the lane and into the brush as far as he could go.

He turned the car off and popped the trunk. No noises came from the house. In the distance, he heard the sound of a golf cart.

Inside the trunk was a case of water and a small box of protein bars. Grateful, Darwin grabbed a protein bar, ripped it open, and took a large bite. He drank two bottles of water while eating the bars.

In the middle of the trunk sat a long metal gun box. He searched the car for keys to the gun box but couldn't find them anywhere.

He ate another bar and shoved two more into his pockets, plus a bottle of water.

Then he walked away from the car. He still had both scythes on him and one gun from the Russians, even though it was empty.

He headed through the brush to the farmhouse's driveway, then followed it to the road. A couple of cars passed him as he headed to the side of the golf course, but no one paid him any attention.

At the fence, he tossed the last protein bar wrapper away and jumped over. He pushed through the thick shrubs and came out slowly on the other side. He didn't want to be seen by any golfers close by.

The green of one of the holes backed onto the wooded area he hid behind. It had to be a par five. He couldn't see where the golfers would tee off from.

It was over five minutes before he saw his first party of four.

They took their shots, hopped in golf carts, and drove closer. Then they shot again from the edge of the green and prepared to putt out.

All four men were discussing something that happened last weekend. Darwin tuned them out, stayed low in the bush, and waited for the twosome behind them to approach.

He checked his wound. It had stopped bleeding again.

He lay down slowly to avoid breaking a twig or making any noise, trying to find a more comfortable position to wait in. The foursome was still putting, which started to work on his nerves.

He thought about the intel the FBI had. What if the meeting really is set for tomorrow, and the girl lied to him? If that was the case, then Darwin was shit out of luck. He was about to storm a golf course pro shop and convention center with his limited weapons to find an empty building and probably end up in jail.

The foursome finished up. Two of them high-fived each other as they walked to their cart.

They forgot to put the flag back in. One of the twosome standing a hundred yards back from the green yelled at them.

The heaviest of the four turned and saw the flag on the green, ran back over, and plunked it back in place.

"Sorry," he yelled and waved.

One of the twosome took a couple of practice swings and then stepped up to his ball.

The green was at a lower elevation. He misjudged the shot. The ball bounced once and then shot into the bush, landing ten feet in front of Darwin.

When the twosome got up to the green, the man who shot into the bush grabbed his putter and an extra ball and headed toward Darwin.

Once inside the woods, the man kicked at pine needles and rummaged around, looking for his ball.

"I can't find it," he shouted to his playing partner.

"Just use another ball. You don't have to take the penalty for it. Who knew the green would be back so far?"

The man muttered something under his breath and turned away.

Darwin eased out of hiding, hopped behind the man, and tripped him. He fell hard, but as soon as he did, the man flipped over and looked up at his attacker.

He recoiled at Darwin's appearance.

"What happened to you?" the man asked.

"What are you doing in there, Bob?" the other guy asked. "Come on, we gotta move to the next hole."

"Just a sec," the man shouted back.

"Take your golf shirt off."

"What?"

Darwin pulled both scythes out, blood still coating the tips.

"Now," he said.

"Why?"

"Just do it."

"And what'll I tell John?"

"After I cut your throat with these blades, I'm not sure you'll be able to tell John anything. Now, take off the shirt."

The man slipped out of it and tossed it at Darwin.

"What's taking so long?" John asked. "The other group is waiting on the ridge."

"Coming."

Bob was much bigger than Darwin, so he slipped the golf shirt over his hoodie and tucked the hood in the back. Perfect fit. Then he walked away.

The golfing partner's face lit up when Darwin stepped out of the woods wearing his friend's shirt. Darwin had already put the scythes away.

"Where's Bob?" the man asked.

Darwin hitched a thumb over his shoulder. "In there. I don't think he wants to come out. He's embarrassed."

John started for the trees.

Darwin walked across the green, got in the golf cart, and sped away. Both the golfers' cell phones were in the drink holders of the cart.

He followed the signs to the next tee box and continued driving the length of that fairway en route to the next tee box, and so on, until he got back to the clubhouse. Along the way, there had only been a couple of golfers angry enough to shout something as he passed them with no regard for who was hitting a ball or where they were.

The clubhouse came into view. Golfers on the first tee watched as he approached, waiting for him to get out of the way. He drove around the tee box, up a little concrete path just big enough for the cart, and parked out front of the pro shop.

He gazed at all the faces, trying to see someone he recognized. Nothing unusual stood out, which could be good or bad. A dozen golfers stood in groups, waiting to tee up, but none looked like the Russian mafia.

Without trying to draw attention to himself, Darwin walked away from the golf cart and around the building until he faced the convention center. The double doors were closed with a dark curtain over the window. He started for them.

The doors were locked. A sign on the wall beside the door said the way in was through the pro shop.

He headed for the pro shop. This made sense to him. With the kind of meeting that was taking place, the powerful people present, they wouldn't have these double doors unattended.

At the front, he stepped inside the pro shop, which was filled with golf supplies and equipment. Where was the security? If three rival mafia families were really meeting here right now, then it didn't look like it to Darwin.

Or maybe that was the idea.

They would have the meeting when it was a normal day at the golf course with the public buying green fees and driving golf carts around, and no one would be the wiser.

"Can I help you?" the clerk asked.

One golfer stood near the back, eyeing up a new driver.

"Looking for the entrance to the convention center. The sign said it was through the pro shop."

"You here for the meeting?"

He wondered what the right answer was and decided to just say, "Yeah."

"Name?"

"Dar—" he almost said his own name. "The Scythe."

The clerk's eyebrows raised, and he looked Darwin up and down.

"Really?"

Darwin pulled the handles of the scythes up high enough to show the clerk and then slipped them back.

"Yes. Really," Darwin said.

"Holy shit," the clerk whispered. Then louder, "I've heard of you."

"The convention center?" He arched his eyebrows.

The clerk pointed toward the back of the pro shop. "Back there. Go ahead. They've already started."

Darwin walked by the counter and headed for the back. The golfer with the driver in his hand stayed where he was, a blank expression on his face. The clerk was still behind the counter, shaking his head back and forth.

At the back, two doors opened to a hallway. At the end of the hall, his stomach in knots, he tried the double doors and found them unlocked. He paused, breathing in and out like a locomotive. When he opened these, the Russians could be waiting. They would probably have guns and shoot him down.

It was hopeless, and he knew it. But what else was there? They would live together or die together. One thing was for sure. If he didn't walk through these doors, his wife *would* die.

He pulled a scythe out and held it in his left hand. He took a deep breath and exhaled slowly. Then he took another breath and opened the door to the convention center.

No one stood on either side. There were no armed guards. Only a long wooden table on the other side of the cavernous room with four men sitting at it, their backs to him.

He took in the room as the door behind him clicked shut. Nothing threatening, nothing untoward.

He looked at the four men. To cross the distance to the table would take half a minute as they were at the wall on the far side.

All four men turned and then stood up at the same time. They adjusted their jackets. One fixed his eyeglasses. Darwin's heart pounded as he thought he would've seen Rosina by now. Whatever state she was in, he had to accept, but not seeing her brought his spirits down.

This nightmare seemed far from over.

"Good afternoon, Mr. Kostas. Glad you could join us."

Yuri stepped away from the others.

"Where is she?" Darwin asked.

Yuri smiled. "There are times when I wish you worked for me."

"Fat chance. Where is she?" Darwin pulled the other scythe out. Now, both hands gripped the comforting handles.

"You've come a long way," Yuri said, wiping at something on his chin.

"I'm not here to talk about me."

"You're holding blades. A month ago, you would've killed the person who got that close to you with those. Rosina told me all about you and your phobias."

At that moment, he felt no amount of bullets would stop him if he decided to cover the waxed wooden floor with Yuri's blood.

"It's over, Yuri. Tell me where she is."

"Before I bring her in here, I wanted to tell you how predictable you are."

Darwin rubbed the blades against each other and took a step toward Yuri. The metallic sound of the blades echoed throughout the large room.

"You fell face-first into my trap," Yuri said. "I want to thank you for that."

Darwin took another step.

"Of course, my bartender would tell you I'm at the strip club where Arkady is. I wanted to offer you the pleasure of killing that asshole for me. He was too uncontrollable. I made sure everyone thought I was staying at the Park Hotel. I even joked with Arkady that he could give you the room number if he saw you. What a fool he was that he didn't see the big picture."

Darwin continued to move closer to the four men.

"I was surprised when you connected me to the adult store in North York, and I didn't think you would kill my man in the back parking lot, but that's okay. I understand. You're angry."

Darwin's face flushed with heat. The nails of his fingers wrapped around the handles of the scythes so tight they dug into his palm.

"I sent word out on the street that if The Scythe—I love that you took on that particular moniker—came asking about me, tell him to come here." He laughed. "A stolen police car? Really?"

Darwin stood twenty feet away now.

"Stop where you are." Yuri's face tightened, his eyes hardening. "You will have a bullet in each leg with one more step."

Darwin stopped, not willing to test Yuri. None of the men had pulled weapons out, though. He could run and leap on Yuri, cut the life out of his throat in seconds, and be done with it, but still, he halted.

A red beam, like a laser light, flashed across his eyes. He looked up toward the ceiling. Seven men hung suspended in various poses. All of them had weapons pointed at Darwin.

When he looked down at his chest, red lights moved below his neck where the snipers had taken careful aim.

"Place the scythes on the floor," Yuri said.

Rosina wasn't here. She wasn't in this room, and they hadn't shot him yet. He took a step back. No one fired. He took another step and then turned and walked to the double doors, every second waiting for a bullet.

At the door, he yanked on the handle, but nothing happened.

"I said, drop the scythes, or they will be taken from you."

He put his shoulder into the door. It was like body-checking solid steel. He gazed across the room. Four men from the upper beams were shimmying down ropes. When they landed, weapons came up and aimed at Darwin. They moved forward while the other men used their own ropes to descend.

Unless the FBI was about to storm the convention center a day earlier than what their intel suggested, Darwin realized that he was probably dead.

Yuri motioned some kind of silent order with his hand.

A gun went off, and the scythe in Darwin's right hand was torn away. Another shot, and the left one zinged into the wall behind him. The vibration resonated through his hand and arm, but he didn't cry out.

A moment later, he was surrounded by four armed men. The nightmarish ride had taken its toll on him.

His luck had run out.

"Bring him to the office," Yuri ordered as he walked away. "He can wait with his wife." Yuri stopped and turned back. "On second thought, string him up with all fourteen hooks for his wife to see when she wakes. He's the walking dead anyway, so it won't matter much, but I'll enjoy it."

61

Since being in Florida, which seemed a lifetime ago, Darwin finally got to see his wife. They brought him to a room in the back of the convention center that would normally serve as an office but was large enough to be the size of two standard hotel rooms.

Inside, chains hung suspended from the beams in the ceiling. More chains dangled from wall mounts behind a square chunk of plastic taped to the floor. A metal table off to the side held a variety of implements that looked like something only a Nazi doctor could love. What lay on the table would get his blood flowing from a lot more places than just his bladder.

Rosina was spread out on a makeshift bed. Her hands were cuffed to a chain attached to a steel necklace at least an inch thick.

When he called out to her, she didn't budge.

"Is she alive?" he asked the men who pushed him inside the office.

"Drugged sleep."

They stood him over a square piece of plastic and cuffed his ankles and then his hands. The whole time, he stared at his woman, tears filling his eyes, lower lip quivering. He didn't resist as the men secured him.

After a few moments, his hands were bound behind his back and attached to a chain lodged to the wall. His feet couldn't move more than an inch as the ankle restraints were fastened to a chain that was also bolted to the wall.

In one quick movement, his stolen golf shirt was ripped from his body. Then, one of the men produced a large knife and sliced off the hoodie, careful not to touch Darwin. He almost thanked the man for his tenderness, then thought better.

He may not have a phobia of knives anymore, but he still didn't want one slicing through his skin. His neurosis had evolved to only a natural fear of knives.

They started on his pants.

"What the fuck are you doing?" he asked.

He didn't even get a grunt for an answer. A moment later, his pants were removed, and he stood in his underwear, the manacles already chaffing his skin.

Outside, the summer air was super-heated. Inside, air conditioners cooled the room, producing goosebumps on his flesh. He shivered and glanced over at Rosina. She looked so good, resting. He remembered watching her rest when they were first together, a lifetime ago. They had had such great times together.

He stared at her through tear-covered eyes and pledged to do whatever he could to get them out of this mess and make things right. They would deal with the trauma on their own time, tilling their garden, sipping wine in the evenings, eating pasta as the sun dropped over Italy. Their day would come, he was sure of it, even though the odds were completely against them.

A pain he had never felt pierced his consciousness as it tore into his skin. He yanked away from it, but the cuffs that held him only gave an inch.

He screamed and looked at the Russian to see what he was doing. The idiot had stuck a large fishhook with a barbed tip into the skin of Darwin's right triceps.

"What the fuck did you do that for?" he shouted. "I'm already tied up."

"Did not you hear the boss?"

"No, I *did not* hear the boss."

"He said no handcuffs."

"Then take these off, asshole. Untie me."

"We will. In time."

The man brought another fishhook up from a metal container on the floor and eased it into the skin of the other triceps.

Darwin pulled against the chains that held him, but there was no use. He couldn't get his arm away from the hook.

He panted, his breathing shallow as his face flushed and sweat beaded up all over his body.

"Okay, okay, that's enough. You don't need to do it anymore. You've made your point."

Blood trickled from each wound. The man used a long piece of wood, like a chopstick, to dab at the blood, applying a clear liquid on the wounded flesh. A moment later, the blood clotted and stopped flowing.

"Super Glue," the Russian said, holding it up.

"Are you done having fun yet?"

The man shook his head.

"Why do this? You've already got me secured."

"The boss, he says all the hooks." He turned to look in the

box, then smiled at Darwin. "I have too many to count. But it's okay, soon you sleep. Once you are all hooked up, I take off the handcuffs and ankle cuffs. Trust me, you won't move or try to escape. If you do, your skin comes off."

"I will kill you. Trust me, you will be the first to die."

He wagged his finger in Darwin's face. "You die first."

Darwin watched him gather another hook, unaware of how the man kept smiling. They were for a large ocean fish of some kind. The size of a rounded coat hanger, except these had a pointy tip with a barbed end. Trying to dislodge them would rip and tear and do more damage than when they entered the flesh.

Darwin shouted until his voice was hoarse as the man forced the hooks into his flesh, slowly easing through the skin, smiling with each one as if this was his whiskey after a hard day at the office. Then, the man sealed the wound with Super Glue.

The sentry at the door had lowered his weapon and watched with amusement. Rosina slept on the mattress, oblivious to what was happening to her husband five feet away.

The pain of the small hooks entering his skin became unbearable as the Russians did one after another. Soon, his shoulder blades and lower back were punctured and bound. His stomach gave out. The protein bars came up as he vomited on the floor, splashing his feet. The second bout flowed from his mouth as he almost passed out, leaving trails of bile down his chest and underwear.

The Russian didn't seem to notice the vomit. He stepped in it and continued his insane violation of Darwin's flesh. The sentry brought a wooden stool over and set it under Darwin's knees to help support his weight when he collapsed.

As a hook entered his cheek, the sharp tip probed the inside of his teeth.

That was the end for Darwin.

He passed out and dropped twelve inches, as far as the chains would allow, his knees stopping on the wooden stool.

62

WATER SPLASHED ACROSS HIS face. He snapped his eyes open and gasped in agony, his body locked up, holding still. Instead of screaming, he moaned. With a hook piercing each cheek, it would be too painful to scream with an open mouth.

They had hooked him up everywhere. The pain seemed to be what his body had become.

As he adjusted his weight, Yuri kicked the wooden stool out from under his knees. The chains snapped behind him as they took all his weight. From how he had been suspended, dangling in the cuffs and chains for so long, his toes had fallen asleep. Now, as blood coursed through them, they ached, pins and needles tingling and making him want to move them. The plastic crinkled under his feet.

He closed his eyes and focused on staying conscious. They must have set a hook in his skin every six inches. At least, that's what it felt like. There was a certain numbness where the hooks were embedded.

He opened his eyes and tried to assess the damage they had

caused but couldn't turn his head far enough.

"I was afraid you were going back under."

Two men flanked Yuri. One of them sported a buzz cut, tattoos on his arms, and a large bird tattoo on his chest. The other had a long, hard nose that had been broken several times. Both men looked like something he would see entering a boxing ring—a bare-knuckle ring.

"We're going to take the cuffs off now," Yuri said. "We need you awake for that."

Darwin moaned. Sounds from his throat were involuntary now.

Something moved behind him. He wanted to tell them to get out of there. Don't bump into him.

Then, a piece of metal clicked, and a slight pressure was added to the hooks in his back. There were more clicks.

Yuri pulled out a small mirror from a pocket.

"Let me show you what we're doing," he said.

He held the mirror up. The Russian who had impaled him with the hooks applied chains to the end of the hooks in his back. Darwin watched in horror as six chains were clipped into place, two at his shoulder blades, two near the middle of his back, and two at the small of his back. He had two smaller chains added to his triceps hooks. Yuri lowered the mirror and allowed Darwin to watch as four more chains were connected to the hooks in the hamstring and calf muscle areas. Twelve hooks embedded in his flesh, connected to twelve chains, locking him to the wall.

"There," Yuri said. "I think that should do it."

The man walked out from behind Darwin and unlocked the handcuffs. When he pulled them off, his weight adjusted again, and his pain threshold increased to the red zone. His sanity slipped a notch, and he understood then that he would never be the same. He would be a changed man if he walked away from this.

His ankle cuffs were unlocked, and he was pulled away.

He stood on his own two feet, which were almost fully awake again, held only by the chains clipped to the hooks. If Darwin were to step forward and walk, all twelve hooks would shred his flesh.

Yuri turned to one of his guards. "Call Sven and have two double coffins prepared for our guests."

The guard nodded and stepped out of the office.

"What's … a double coffin?" Darwin asked, keeping his mouth closed for the most part. He struggled to hold himself upright on weak limbs, knowing if his knees gave out, he would fall and rip out large chunks of meat.

"It's one of my most used means of disposal."

Yuri stepped to the side. Darwin followed his movement slowly until Rosina came into view. She was still asleep but had moved since he'd last seen her.

"A man out of Buffalo is credited with designing the double coffin," Yuri said. "When he has a client at the funeral home, they are buried in what appears to be a normal-looking coffin. Underneath is a cavern where I can bury my enemies without suspicion. There's actually a legit funeral and everything." Yuri pulled a cigar out of his jacket pocket. His remaining bodyguard leaned in with a lighter. After he lit it, he held it aloft, blew smoke out of his mouth, and looked down at Rosina's sleeping form. "You two will be buried in the bottom of two different double coffins, and Mrs. Smith or John Doe, or whoever's funeral it is, will be none the wiser."

He puffed hard on the cigar.

"No one will ever find your body," Yuri added. "What would make the authorities exhume a coffin of a man or woman who has no affiliation with us?"

The pain became a constant, like a strong toothache that just wouldn't go away. It came in waves and only increased when he moved, which was frequently to adjust his weight from leg to leg.

"There's a Russian saying that says, 'The house is burning, and the clock is ticking.' Do you know what this means?"

Darwin didn't reply.

"It means you have to keep making money every minute. As we speak, I have people making money for me. The clock is always ticking, and the house is always burning. It's hustle, hustle, hustle."

He puffed on his cigar until the tip glowed.

"I got my start robbing jewelers." He moved to Rosina and sat on her mattress. "We would dress up as ultra-orthodox Jews. The fake beards, side curls, black hats, and coats, you know, the whole thing. We'd get the retailer to pull out expensive jewels while we chatted away in Yiddish. One of us would distract the jeweler while the other would switch the jewels with fakes. After an excuse to leave, we'd walk out with thousands in jewels and no way for them to identify us. It was brilliant."

Darwin shifted to the other foot. A wave of nausea passed over him. His stomach twisted and tightened. Dizziness followed.

"I remember the day we got caught," Yuri continued. "It was stupid of us, really." He had a faraway look on his face as he thought back. "We had taken the train to another part of New York to hit a pack of jewelers we'd never seen before. On the way back to the train station, as we were getting ready to board, a police officer stopped us." His clouded eyes focused, and he turned to Darwin. "Do you know why?"

"Because you're an asshole," Darwin mumbled through the hooks.

Yuri smiled. "I like you, I really do." He puffed on the cigar. "I'm going to miss you. I've never met anyone like you, Darwin." He blew the smoke out. Rosina continued to sleep in her drug-induced slumber beside him. "They caught us because it was Yom Kippur, the holiest day of the Jewish calendar. Observant Jews are strictly forbidden to travel. The security guard was Jewish and asked if we were, now get this, *Observant Jews.* Can you believe it?"

"No."

"There was a gunfight. I spent time in jail. I stopped robbing jewelers when I got out. Started thinking bigger. And here I am."

"Impressive."

Yuri eyed him sideways. "You're being sarcastic again."

"Why tell me all this shit?"

"I'm stalling. Waiting for the meeting to start. I always want the man I'm going to kill to know who killed him. Since I'm not gay, this is as intimate as we're going to get."

"But you've got it wrong."

"How so?"

"It's me who is going to kill you."

Yuri laughed, a hand on his stomach. He got up and stepped in front of Darwin. "Damn, I wish I had an ounce of your tenacity in my men. Even in this state of constant agony, hooked up to the wall like a side of beef, you threaten me. Wow. If I didn't get so much pleasure out of killing you, I would hire you to work for me. I truly would."

"But I would never work for you."

"I know. That is why you have to die. This world cannot have the both of us."

"I agree."

Darwin's leg slipped as it weakened. He hopped onto the other and almost fainted. The room spun, then came back. The pain soared from the hooks in his legs. The crazy Russian who had hooked him up moved behind him with the wooden stick to apply Super Glue, where the bleeding had started again on his legs. Darwin felt it trickling down his ankle.

"That was close," Yuri said. "You almost came undone. Not long now. The meeting will start in fifteen minutes. Then, a bullet will enter your skull at close range near the hairline behind the right ear. Your wife goes first, though, since you're currently tied up." He chuckled.

The Russian behind Darwin got to his feet and laughed, too.

Yuri walked to the door and then turned to talk to the Russian torturer. "When I call, wake her with smelling salts and walk her out here," he pointed. "Then walk Darwin out. The execution will go as planned."

"Yuri?" Darwin said.

The large Russian had stepped out the door. He stopped but didn't turn around.

"What?"

"How long was I out?"

"All night. We drugged you. It's been nearly twenty-four hours since you snuck onto the golf course. Why?"

"You're having a meeting with the Chinese and the Italians?"

Yuri turned and faced Darwin. He pulled the cigar out of his mouth. "That's right. I almost forgot. Thanks for the documents you had in your pants. The ones the FBI gave you. It's good to know what they have on us."

"They're on their way."

"No, they're not."

"They told me they knew about this meeting."

"Sure they do. It's true. They just don't know where it's being held. They think we are meeting fifty miles from here at a restaurant in Chinatown. I even have a couple of Russians and Italians meeting for lunch there so the FBI can listen to them discuss whores. No," he wagged his finger, "they will not be here. They will not swoop in and save you. Darwin, there will be no heroics this time."

"The police car I drove here in. They will track it."

"Already covered. After you got here yesterday, the police car was taken away. Investigators were raising it from the bottom of Lake Simcoe near Barrie, last I heard, looking for the body of the man who stole it, The Scythe. They think he hightailed it out of Toronto and lost control near the lake."

"The Scythe?"

"Yeah, you told the adult store clerk and the strip club guys that you were The Scythe. That's what the authorities are working with. No one knows where Darwin ended up." He tapped ashes off the end of his cigar, then puffed on it. "And no one ever will." He looked at his watch. "You and your lovely wife have about ten minutes to live. Enjoy them."

"I'm sorry, baby," he whispered to her. "I tried." Tears streaked down his face. "We never really had a chance, did we?"

Rosina stirred in her stupor. The Russian walked over to her and checked her pulse.

"She's waking," he said. He looked at his watch. "Good

timing." He smiled wide, the kind of smile a kid wears when he's about to have ice cream and waffle cakes.

He wanted to say a thousand things to Rosina, but she would never hear them. They would just disappear. No one would ever see them again. They would be buried in that double coffin thing and would remain on a missing person's list eternally.

If there were anything he could do, he would. The despair held weight, an uncanny pressure on his psyche that made him feel he couldn't stand anymore. He tugged on the hooks until the chains pulled taut from the wall, and the pain increased. His skin lifted tent-like from his back and legs.

There was nothing he could do except ripping himself off the hooks. Even if he could successfully remove himself from the chains and hooks, everyone in the next room was armed. What chance did they have?

He slumped back, allowing the chains to slacken. At least the torment would be over soon. His failure as a man to save his wife, to protect her, colored his heart a dark gray.

If only things were different.

Yuri called from the other room.

It was time to die.

The Russian pulled a key out of his pocket and unlocked Rosina's restraints. Then he tossed them aside and put the key away. His hand came back up with something else, which he waved back and forth in front of Rosina's nose. She gasped and jolted awake, coughing.

Her eyes wide, she took in the room, settling on Darwin.

He tried to smile, but all he could do was wince. This was the last time she would see him. He looked away. The sadness in her eyes was too much to bear.

"Darwin?"

Their eyes met as the Russian hauled Rosina to her feet.

"Darwin?" Her voice grew stronger, louder. "*Darwin!*"

The Russian manhandled her to the door and shoved it open.

Rage, an intense fury, filled Darwin whole. It came on like a tsunami of molten lava. It covered him in its wake, pulsing every muscle into action, the pain welcoming and stirring instead of debilitating.

"Rosina," he shouted, his voice a growl, the hooks in his cheeks sliding along his teeth, cutting his gums. Then he roared her name, vibrating the chains that held him.

He ripped his right arm up in a vain attempt to grab the Russian, but the man had stepped out the door. He had pulled too hard. The hook in the skin over his triceps tore through the flesh. The chain slapped harmlessly into the wall behind him, useless now. Blood seeped down his elbow, but his arm was free. The pain added to his will to survive and to get to his wife.

Through the open door, Yuri held a small silver gun. He watched the Russian walk Rosina across the floor toward Yuri. Three men watched: Chinese, Italian, and Yuri's bodyguard. Other men lingered by the double doors on the far side.

"Rosina," he yelled. "*Rosina!*"

He pulled against the chains. He couldn't move again for fear of passing out, but he had to do something. They were about to shoot his wife.

The Russian handed Rosina to Yuri and started back toward him.

Rosina screamed as Yuri kicked her legs out from under her and dropped to her knees.

"Kneel bitch," Yuri yelled at her.

"I will kill you again and again, Yuri," Darwin shouted.

Yuri looked over his shoulder at Darwin. He grinned like a mischievous feline and brought the gun to the back of Rosina's bowed head. The Russian torturer got to the door and slammed it shut, blocking Darwin's view.

He shouted an inhuman growl and pulled against the hooks.

"Wait," he bellowed, his voice hoarse.

Then, he gave up on the pain and the resistance. There was nothing left to live for without Rosina. They were in a nightmare not of their making, but he could change things—he could make it worse. One thing he could not do was hear the gun that blew his wife's head open.

He clenched his teeth, allowed the rage to fuel him, grunted deep in his throat, and stepped one leg forward, hard and firm.

The hooks ripped out and dropped to the plastic, the chain part rattling against the wall. He stepped his other leg forward, knowing the damage he was causing, but he needed to get to Rosina. Without her, the damage to his flesh was nothing.

The Russian hadn't turned around yet. He must have assumed Darwin was only jerking around, rattling the chains. The Russian stood in the corner by the table that held the torture implements, his back to Darwin. As Darwin struggled, the man's head twitched, and he looked over his shoulder. When he saw what Darwin had done, his eyes widened.

Patches of flesh and meat still clung to each hook. The pain of what was happening to Rosina was a thousand times worse than the pain from the hooks.

Darwin pushed with all the willpower of a possessed man and ripped the rest of the hooks out of his back, tearing flesh and meat with them, blood spurting from each wound.

Wearing only his underwear, Darwin moved toward the torture table and the man who impaled him with the hooks.

The Russian grabbed a hammer off the table. He brought it up fast, but Darwin was filled with such a rage that his focus was clear, his strength that of a dozen men. In his mind, the Russian was already dead.

Darwin shoved the hammer's handle back, twisted it in the Russian's hand, and pushed the claw end toward the Russian's face. A struggle of raw strength ensued until the hammer entered the man's mouth. Darwin yanked downward. With a crack and a snapping sound, the lower section of the man's face dislocated.

The wail emanating from his mouth sounded inhuman as Darwin ripped the hammer from the man's hands and flipped it around. He brought it down again. The scream stopped as the claw end gouged into the Russian's right eye and sunk a couple of inches deep inside the orbital bone.

The Russian's mouth sagged open at an odd angle. He slipped to the floor in a pool of his own blood, mixed with some of Darwin's.

He tore the hammer out of the Russian's face with a sickening twist and a wet, mushy sound. At the door, he sucked in a couple of breaths and said, "I'm coming, baby."

He gripped the knob.

A gun fired in the other room.

Darwin screamed and ripped open the door.

63

MORE WEAPONS WERE FIRED. He kept his head low and his eyes on Rosina. Men fell around him, and bullets were fired in a chaotic mess. He couldn't tell who was shooting at whom.

Still by the door of the office, he waited because a couple of Yuri's men were still alive, shooting at an unknown enemy. Moving out of the office would make him a target.

Yuri and his men moved toward the doors that led out of the convention center with Rosina clutched in their arms, under fire from someone out of Darwin's sight range.

Darwin moved into the cavernous room. Both bodyguards turned to him as their backs hit the exit doors. They leveled their weapons. Pockets of blood popped out of the cheek of one man. The forehead of the other imploded at the same time. Neither one got a shot off at Darwin.

He ran toward them, slipping in his own blood, a struggle to stay on his feet. Yuri opened the door and yanked Rosina through after him. The door closed before Darwin got halfway across the room.

He shouted after them, a raw animal sound. When he was five feet from the door, it opened, and men in fatigues barged in, almost colliding with Darwin. He tried to slow in time, but his feet slipped. He fell on his butt and slid with a squeak.

Before he could get back up, arms restrained him.

"It's okay," someone shouted into his ear. "We got them."

Darwin stayed on the floor, nearly hyperventilating with blood loss and pain. His vision blurred for a moment as he tried to get his breathing under control. As everything came back into focus, he took in the room. Men dressed in emergency task force gear circled the area. Doors opened and closed. Men came and went, toting assault rifles.

"Where"—Darwin swallowed—"is my wife?"

"One sec," a man said, his hand raised. He listened momentarily, nodded to himself, and spoke into a microphone on his collar. "The area is secure?" He waited. "Copy that. Bring the injured to the ambulances. I got Darwin Kostas. In emergency need of medical care, though. Darwin's cut to shit."

"Where did you come from?" Darwin managed to ask.

The man tore off his mask.

Agent Williams. Relief washed over Darwin.

"I told you we knew about this meeting and that we would swoop in before they killed Rosina."

"Is Rosina okay?"

Williams nodded. "My men told me all combatants are dealt with and hostages released. Yuri didn't have a chance."

"But how?" Darwin asked. He sat up and tried to stand. "How did you know about the meeting?"

"Stay down. You're bleeding everywhere. Paramedics are outside. They're coming in now." Williams stared at the hooks still embedded in Darwin's cheeks. They were the only two that had no chains attached to them. "That's got to hurt."

"Not half as bad as the ones I tore out of my backside." Darwin balled a fist and pressed it to his lips to hold in the pain. "Yuri said he'd tricked the FBI." Darwin had to know.

"He didn't trick anybody." Williams spoke into a microphone and then looked back at Darwin. "We had a man on the inside." He turned and pointed up at the rafters. "One of Yuri's snipers was ours. He was instructed to start shooting if they were going to kill any innocents."

"You had someone on the inside?" Darwin asked. "Why didn't you tell me?"

Kirk's face grew stern. "And jeopardize a three-year operation to reassure you? You're a loose fucking cannon, my friend. Telling you would've put a man's life in danger. Darwin, we're the professionals here. We got this. I told you I would handle it. This cowboy stuff you pulled is going to get somebody killed—namely you. Just look at you. You're all fucked up."

Williams turned around as the door banged open, and paramedics rushed in with a gurney.

"Over here," he said to them. "Stop this guy's bleeding. He lost enough."

They set the stretcher on the floor and, on the count of three, hoisted Darwin onto it. Williams touched the arm of a medic as they were about to wheel Darwin away.

"Guess what else," Williams whispered.

Darwin nudged his head up. "What?"

"You were right about The Scythe. He cut a swath through Toronto yesterday, stole a police car to get to this meeting, and left it parked by a farm out on hole number twelve. Left Russians cut up at Yuri's Queen Street restaurant and attacked one of his businesses in North York. Two hours ago, detectives found his body in Lake Simcoe. His throat was cut, and his teeth were stomped out. Both hands and feet were missing."

"Nasty," was all Darwin could say. He was overjoyed that The Scythe was dead.

The medics tried to pull him away, but Williams held them back again.

"I found something odd, though." Williams stepped around and stared into Darwin's eyes. "A couple of the descriptions from witnesses didn't fit with The Scythe's body shape and mass. Everyone at the strip club where he killed Arkady—"

"Arkady's dead?" Darwin interrupted. He knew where Williams was going and didn't want to go there.

"A female adult store clerk described someone closer to you than The Scythe. I called Carson Dodge in Florida and asked if you could run around Toronto using The Scythe's name and cutting people up with a blade. You know what he said?"

Darwin shook his head, not trusting what his mouth would say. The last thing he wanted was a long court process and possibly jail after finally being liberated from the mafia attacks on his family.

"He said he could see you killing people. You're that determined to end this, but never with scythes or blades of any sort. 'There is no court this side of heaven that would convict Darwin Kostas for killing anyone with a blade,' is what he said. Can you believe that? He's not even here, and he's vouching for you."

"Agent Williams, you have your case. You have people saying it was The Scythe. I have a phobia of sharp or pointy things—"

"Didn't the doctor tell you something about your induced coma and the swelling on your brain the day we met? Aren't your phobias cured?"

"You have all you need. What more do you want?" Darwin looked up at the medics who were listening intently. "I'm bleeding to death. Can you guys do something about that?"

They pushed him away, leaving Williams to stand alone in the convention center, donning a sly grin.

"Hey, Darwin."

"Yeah," he called as they pushed him through the double doors.

"I don't believe in vigilantism."

"Me neither."

"But I'll give you a free pass." The doors closed, but through them, Williams yelled two more words. "This time."

64

Darwin sat in the back of the ambulance while they patched the open cuts and exposed flesh. They explained that a doctor at the hospital would take the hooks out of his face. He was supposed to be on his way already but refused to go until he saw his wife. He wouldn't leave without seeing her.

An FBI agent said he would find Agent Williams and ask where Rosina was taken. It had been less than five minutes since he had been wheeled out of the convention center, and no one had told him where Rosina was yet.

"What the fuck's going on?" Darwin said to no one in particular.

The paramedics worked behind him, dabbing here and there, pasting white stretchy bandages in places. He winced, gasped at times, and waited.

Williams exited the building, met Darwin's gaze, and shrugged.

"What does that mean?" Darwin shouted, the hooks in his cheeks clanking against his teeth.

The medics stopped what they were doing and faced the FBI agent.

Williams raised a finger for him to wait. He talked into his lapel but was too far away for Darwin to hear anything.

Darwin edged off the stretcher, hopped off the back of the ambulance, and dropped to one knee as pain shot up from his legs. He refused to look at the damage caused by tearing the hooks from his flesh. That was something to be dealt with another day. Today, he needed to guarantee Rosina's safety before he could succumb to any injuries of any sort.

It took effort, but he stood and faced Williams as he approached.

"They can't find her." He shook his head. "I'm sorry."

"What?"

"I don't know what happened. They said everything was secure. All hostages were safe. And now no one knows where Rosina is."

Darwin scanned the golf course in the immediate area. "You've got to be kidding me."

"I'm sorry, Darwin. She'll turn up. There's no way anything could've happened to her. We have fifty men here."

Darwin turned back to Williams. "Ask Yuri. He'll know where she is. He was the last one with her."

Williams shook his head and grimaced, a dark expression on his face. "He's missing, too."

The horror had restarted.

Just like that, Darwin felt Rosina slipping away from him yet again. The incompetence of the authorities was going to cost him his wife.

He'd come too far to let that happen.

Darwin spun on his bare feet in the grass, walked to the front of the ambulance, and hopped in the driver's seat. The keys were in the ignition. He turned it on and dropped it into gear as Williams approached the window.

"Hey, Darwin, what're you doing?"

He hit the gas. Both paramedics in the back jumped out as the vehicle lurched forward.

He ground the tires into the perfectly tailored grass of the golf course, drove over the first tee box to get around all the other emergency vehicles, and squealed the tires as he fled the High Hills Golf Course.

A siren screamed behind him, but he didn't care. It would only add to the entourage as far as the public was concerned.

He hit the two-lane highway and turned east toward Highway 400. How much of a head start did they have? What kind of vehicle would they be in? Once he hit Highway 400, which ran north to Barrie or south to Toronto, which way would Yuri have gone?

Some of his bandages curled at the edges, and some tore off. Blood ran down his back like sweat. He could spend the rest of his life healing. He couldn't spend the rest of his life without Rosina.

Highway 400 was coming up fast. In the mirror, he saw five police cruisers on his tail, taking up both lanes of the two-lane highway when no one was coming from the other way.

North? South? North? South?

He picked north. Yuri would head toward home. He wouldn't go to Toronto, where everyone was looking for him. He would go to the quieter city of Barrie, where he owned a house on Highway 93 by a golf course. The same course where Darwin was found covered in peaches.

He slowed at the ramp. For a brief moment, the ambulance tipped up on two wheels. Then the ramp ended, Darwin straightened the wheel, and the vehicle dropped onto all fours. He jammed the pedal down and checked the mirror.

All five cruisers were right behind him. He stared forward and watched the vehicles ahead for any sign of evasive action. With this much noise and lights, Yuri would accelerate away or get off the highway fast if he were up there.

Darwin had no illusions about the head start Yuri had. How he got past all of Kirk's men baffled him, though. He would've had to slink away quietly. Otherwise, someone would've seen him.

But how did he do that with Rosina? How did he keep her quiet?

He pounded the dash and drove on.

The sign for Canal Road got closer. He was on an open stretch of the 400, surrounded by farmland.

An erratic car up ahead caught his eye, and his hope rose that Rosina was in that car. The black Mercedes tore across three lanes and made a small zigzag as it snaked its way down the exit to Canal Road.

Darwin steered the ambulance into the slow lane to get ready to exit but had to go around a slow truck that had pulled onto the shoulder to make room for the emergency vehicles.

After passing the rig, he hung a hard right and exited the highway. It was easy to see the Mercedes just over five hundred yards ahead. Darwin turned east on Canal Road and chased the Mercedes, silently wishing Rosina was in that car and that she was still okay.

The pain in his hamstrings had become almost unbearable

from sitting and jostling with the violence of the wild ride. He wiped the sweat out of his eyes and checked the mirrors again. The cop cars were still there, like faithful dogs following their master.

He hadn't thought to flick on the ambulance's sirens with all the noise from the cruisers behind him.

After a full minute of chasing the Mercedes, he wasn't getting any closer. The vehicle ahead was moving away from him.

He checked his speed and pushed the accelerator harder, even though it was already on the floor.

His vision wavered. Would he pass out? He was in no condition to be driving. The face looking back at him in the mirror was pale white, eyes bloodshot.

He slapped his face twice to bring himself around, but the drowsiness persisted.

A howl escaped his lips at the injustice. He was frustrated that the Russian was getting away with Rosina as a hostage while five police officers and an ambulance chased them.

Up ahead, the Mercedes swerved, then righted itself.

It swerved again. Rosina was fighting back.

Then he watched in horror as the Mercedes left the road and went airborne. It headed for the canal that lined the left side of Canal Road. The grill hit first, shooting a white spray of canal water high into the air. The back settled, and the vehicle began to sink.

Darwin kept the ambulance barreling toward them. If Rosina needed medical treatment, he had brought the perfect vehicle.

When he squealed to a stop, only part of the Mercedes's trunk and bumper were still visible. He jumped out and ran to the water's edge on legs that almost couldn't carry him. He stumbled at the edge and fell, skinning his knee and nearly passing out again. The sharpness of the pain all over his body woke him enough for a moment of clarity.

The muffled sound of a gun ripped through the air around him. What looked like an invisible spear shot out of the water from the passenger side of the Mercedes. Then, another shot rang out, cutting a white line through the water.

Someone was firing a gun from inside the submerged car.

The police cruisers screamed to a stop behind him. Before he passed out, his head spinning from the pain and his stomach clenching like he was going to be sick, Darwin rolled to the edge of the water and slipped in.

The cold of the canal shocked him awake. He opened his eyes, but it was too murky to see much of anything. The water played with the hooks in his cheeks, moving them to and fro. It seeped past the holes, slowly filling his mouth. He expelled it but held his breath.

The Mercedes had slipped below the surface, but Darwin knew roughly where it was. He pushed hard, the pain in his arms and legs tempered by the cold water. It was a hot pain like a curling iron pressed against his skin while an air conditioner blew cold air on the wound.

The Mercedes popped into view when he was a foot away from it. He followed the trunk to the passenger side but then had to leave the slowly descending car for air as his lungs screamed at him to surface.

He dropped back under after a couple of large mouthfuls of blessed air. The officers on the side of the road had shouted something at him, but he couldn't discern what they had said.

At the trunk, he worked his way up the length of the vehicle and tried to open the door.

It was locked.

The glass in the front passenger window was broken.

Must've been the bullet.

He reached inside the broken window. The water was so dark at this level that he couldn't see more than ten inches in front of him. Already underwater for over half a minute and losing time fast, he felt for the lock release, popped it, and opened the door slowly. The canal's water had already filled the car's interior, so the door opened, but with great effort.

Someone was in the passenger seat. He unclipped the seatbelt and felt the person's face.

Rosina.

In a panic, his lungs willing to kill him for the urge of a single breath, he yanked Rosina out of her seat, pushed off the rim of the open door, and headed for the surface.

It felt too long. Suspended as they were, floating upward, the sky's light so far away as it rolled lazily along where the water stopped and the air began.

He thrust with his legs. He twisted his body and arched it any way he could, but they just weren't rising fast enough.

Rosina was heavy, her clothes water-laden. The surface was an impossible distance.

Inside, he cried for his wife, limp in his arms. He wailed that they had gotten so close to freedom, and in the end, it was water in a canal that would kill them and not a bullet or a knife.

Bubbles raced past his face and tickled their way up his forehead as Darwin opened his mouth to scream. Then his lungs won the battle, and he sucked water in. He would not let go of Rosina. Even to swim to the surface on his own.

He held her closer as they began to sink again, his ability to breathe gone. He took her lovely face in both hands and said he was sorry as his chest filled and his vision clouded.

Then he kissed her lips and shut his eyes. A last thought crossed his mind as he let go of consciousness.

I'll always love you ...

65

AGENT WILLIAMS SAT IN the office the RCMP had given him during his time in Toronto, aiding in their cases against the Russian mafia.

It had been four days since the raid at High Hills Golf Course. He was tired and ready to return to the States and his life.

But there was one more call he had to make. A call he dreaded.

His desk was cleared off. The sun had dropped, and he had a trip to the airport to make, but first, he had the call.

He dialed, and after a minute of transfers, Carson Dodge answered.

"Agent Dodge here. Williams?"

"Yeah."

"You doing okay?" Carson asked.

"I guess."

"It wasn't your fault. I hear you guys did a stellar job."

"Not good enough, though, eh?"

"Canada rubbing off on you?"

Williams appreciated Carson's attempt at keeping things light. He rose from his desk and faced the window.

"I guess you heard?"

"I'm unclear on a few things, but I think I got most of it."

"What're you unclear on?"

"How, after everything was secured, did Yuri get away with Rosina without someone seeing them?"

"We're still trying to figure that one out. I'm convinced one of the men on our team helped Yuri, but I have nothing to go on, definitely nothing I can prove."

"But you were there. I understand Darwin stole an ambulance and chased Yuri."

"There was an exit door by the entrance to the convention center. As far as we can tell, Yuri snuck Rosina in there and hid the two of them in a portable cabinet, almost the size of a bedroom closet. Then, when the coast was clear, we're guessing he walked her out the back door where his car was parked and drove off. That was how Darwin and the cops who followed Darwin were able to catch him so fast on the highway. Yuri only had a one-minute head start."

"Tell me what happened to Darwin and his wife."

"Well, you know about the stolen ambulance. When Yuri saw the convoy of cops on his tail, he pulled off the highway. All that we can gather, and we're guessing here, was Rosina fought Yuri for control of the steering wheel. He lost control and veered into the canal. Darwin stopped the ambulance, ran to the water's edge, and dove in after her."

"That's it?"

"No."

"Tell me the rest."

"You sure? Weren't you close to Darwin and his wife?"

"We only met here in Florida, but he saved my life. It was my fault Rosina was taken again. I owe him. The least I can do is hear what happened."

Williams cleared his throat. "This comes from the report of the officers who followed Darwin in the ambulance. He dove into the canal and only surfaced once for air. After that, he didn't come back up."

"And no one tried to help."

"Of course, they did. The second they stopped, two of them tore off their gun belts, kicked off their shoes, and even yelled at Darwin when he surfaced that they were coming in. Once underwater, our guys couldn't see anything. It took them some time to locate the car. Yuri still sat behind the wheel, but Darwin and Rosina were missing."

"And they found them," Carson cut in, "at the bottom of the canal beside the car."

Williams bowed his head. "Yes. Darwin had somehow opened the door enough to pull Rosina out and start to bring her to the surface, but we figured he ran out of energy, and they sank to the bottom. He was pretty banged up. They fucking tied him to a wall with meat hooks. He ripped himself off the wall to get to his wife." He smacked the window for effect. "Sorry, it's hard to deal with. I'm happy Yuri's dead. Darwin and his wife ended up a few feet from the car. That was why it took an extra fifteen minutes to find them. By then, it was too late."

"I heard the Russians really worked Darwin over."

"They did. Poor guy. You should've seen him. Whole patches of flesh were torn out of his back and the backs of his legs." He paused and rubbed his forehead. "At least the nightmare is all over for them."

"Yeah, there's that," Carson said. "To come so close, though."

"What still rattles me was the diver said Darwin and Rosina were found locked in each other's arms. It looked like they were kissing as they died. That'll haunt me for the rest of my life. This fucker really loved that woman and would take down as many mafia men as he needed to get to her. Too bad that kind of badass doesn't work for us."

"We could never have someone like that. Too much bad press."

"Yeah, but we could send him underground, off the radar."

"Wouldn't work. His love for Rosina fueled his rage. Without that, he'd be useless."

"You're probably right."

Williams knew the small talk was a diversion from the grief they both needed to work through. At least, that's what Carson needed to feel.

"Look, Carson, I'm done here. I'm leaving for the airport, but I thought I'd call you myself and fill you in."

"I appreciate that."

"This truly saddens me."

"Me too, man. Darwin Kostas will go down in my books as one hell of a man. The kind I'd be honored to call a brother. Much respect."

"Much respect."

Williams clicked off and turned around. He set the phone down and met the gaze of his visitors.

"There," Williams said. "It's done."

"Thank you."

"He was the last one that needed to be told, and it was more believable coming from me."

"We agree. That's why we suggested it."

"You two ready?" Williams asked. "Feeling up to it?"

Darwin touched his wife's cheek. "Baby, you ready for one more plane ride?"

"I'll go anywhere with you, Darwin."

The Kostases stood at the same time.

"Take us to the airport, Williams. I want the fuck out of this country."

Ten minutes later, after exiting the back of the RCMP building with jackets over their heads and armed security flanking their every move, Darwin and Rosina sat in the back seat of a three-vehicle convoy en route for a military plane leaving the Toronto airport for Rome under heavy security.

The two most-wanted people in the world had multiple contracts on their heads from the Italian mafia and the Russians as far away as Moscow. A Russian boss in jail was even credited with offering a hundred thousand for Darwin or Rosina.

The world thought they were dead. Only seven people outside of the Kostases knew the truth. Agent Williams, his boss who authorized their travel plans and covered the expenses, and the five officers who followed Darwin in the ambulance.

They had located Darwin in the canal's murky water from the bubbles of his final scream as he started to sink back down with Rosina in his arms. Both of them were yanked from the water and revived immediately. Rosina took a little longer to recover and only got out of the hospital the previous evening under tight security—military tight.

Darwin and Rosina hadn't talked much yet, but they held hands and hugged continuously. Their lives would never be the same, but both were willing to start anew.

Darwin's body was scarred up, but the holes in his cheeks had closed and would leave behind small circular scars. Nothing he cared about or was bothered by.

A house awaited them in the green hills of Umbria in a small city called Spoleto. Enough cash was deposited into an American account under their new names. It was electronically accessible from Italy, allowing them to live comfortably for over twenty years. They were told that the house had a large garden, a car, and a wonderful view of the sunset. A vineyard backed onto the property where the aging owner offered Montepulciano wine from an old Badia at five euros for five liters.

They thought it was perfect.

With Yuri's death came a flood of anger and Russian retaliation. The Italians had been calmer, but the Triads warned of war after their representative had been detained at the meeting at the golf course.

None of that mattered for Darwin or Rosina anymore.

The world thought they were dead, and both of them intended to keep it that way.

At the airport, Williams was flying back to the States, which explained his presence. The three of them followed the lead vehicle in silence, with nothing left to arrange and nothing left to say.

Then Kirk's phone rang.

He picked it up. "Yeah?" After a pause, he said, "Okay."

He touched the phone and then set it down.

"You're on speakerphone. Go ahead."

"It's Carson Dodge," Carson's voice boomed from the car's speakers.

"I know who you are," Williams said. "I'm on my way to the airport. You asked to be put on speaker. What's up?"

"I just wanted to have whoever is in the car with you—"

"I'm alone," Williams interrupted.

"Don't cut me off," Carson shouted. "I just wanted to say safe travels to those in the car. I will keep my ear to the ground, and if I hear of anything, well, let's just say I owe you my life. If the day comes, it's the least I can do for you, my friend. Take care of her as I know only you can."

Carson hung up.

"How the hell?" Williams said out loud.

"Carson's no fool," Darwin said. "But we can trust him." He peered out the window at the passing cars. "Having Carson on the team makes me feel better."

"Me too," Rosina said. "He almost died protecting me at that safe house."

Williams watched them in the rearview mirror.

"Then it works for me, too."

66

DARWIN AND ROSINA SETTLED into their new lifestyle in a little village in Italy, far from the city. Their house was comfortable with plush chairs, a large kitchen with an island, and a loft bedroom that looked out over the garden.

Being around each other again after so long on the run had been ecstasy for both of them. It allowed them to open up about what they had gone through individually.

Rosina predicted the nightmares and waking in a cold sweat would be with them for some time. Darwin countered that as long as they had each other, they would learn to live with it. Maybe not get past all of it, but live with it.

It was late September, the sun setting off the mountainous hills of Umbria. The air was still. The olive tree, ten feet from Darwin's chair, motionless. A car's engine revved in the distance down the hill somewhere. He estimated it to be a mile away as he tried to find it among the cypresses that lined the road leading into town.

"Keeping an eye on things?" Rosina asked.

"Always, baby, always."

Rosina brought the rest of the dinner out to the pergola, set it on the table, and sat beside her husband. She sipped from her wine.

"Will we ever just be normal people?" Rosina asked.

Darwin set his wine glass on the table and turned to her. He took her free hand and stared into her eyes.

"Honey, we are normal people. Our neighbor, Angelo, if you were to ask him, wouldn't he say we are normal?"

Rosina nodded. "You know what I mean."

"We've been through a lot, but I'm grateful for every day I get with you. It's one more than I thought I would get."

She set her glass down. "I agree. There are no conditions on us. We will choose to be happy and grateful. We made it out of a murderous situation and are better for it."

"Don't know if I would go that far," Darwin said, leaning back, a smile playing across his lips.

"You know what I mean. You can use a fork and a knife at dinner now. I can get you to cut the turkey at Thanksgiving. We can also turn all the lights off when we go to bed. I love the new Darwin."

He leaned close and kissed her.

"It's real, isn't it?" Darwin asked.

"What?"

"You sitting here with me. Neither one of us is tied up or having to wonder if we'll live to see tomorrow. We're in our own home, alone, living the life."

"It's real, honey. That's all that matters. But there's one thing that still bothers me."

"What's that?" Darwin picked up his wine and cradled it in his lap.

"We have no security here. This isn't a safe house. No guards are roaming the property, just us." She tapped her leg with her fingers. "Do you feel this is the safest solution?"

"Absolutely. People can be bought. Hundreds of thousands of dollars is a huge temptation for any man. All he has to do is drop a piece of paper to someone, get paid, and move to Argentina. Then, our lives are over. No." Darwin shook his head. "It's better that we are the only ones who know where we live."

"Then how did that letter get to us?"

Darwin looked at the letter on the table beside the leftover pasta. It had arrived earlier in the afternoon when Rosina was in the garden, her iPhone earplugs in her ears blasting Dean Martin singing about Roma. She hadn't heard from the delivery man and didn't know about the letter until just before dinner. They planned on opening it after dinner, together, and then decided what to do with what was inside.

"It came from Florida. It's probably from Carson Dodge. He knows how to find us."

"That's my point. If he can find us, so can anyone else." She gulped the rest of her wine back and set down the empty glass. "And maybe Italy isn't the best idea, either. I mean, this is the home of the Cosa Nostra, the Italian mafia."

"I know. That's why it's perfect. They would never expect us to live here." He drank the rest of his wine and set his glass beside hers. "You've heard me talk about the media playing up The Blade and then The Scythe. Rumor on the street, from what I can find online, is if I'm alive, then everyone wants me dead because they're afraid of me and what I can do. None of them wants to meet me in person unless they have a small army to back them up.

You and I both know how silly that is, but rumors get blown out of proportion."

"It's not rumors, Darwin." She moved closer to him. "You're my hero, even with all the scars."

She always teased him about that.

"Gee, thanks, hun."

They kissed, the moment of passion welcomed by a soft breeze wafting up the valley. When they pulled apart, Darwin picked up the envelope and opened the top.

"Time to see what news comes from the States."

Rosina nodded. "Read it to yourself first. Then summarize for me. I don't want to hear it word for word if it's bad news."

Her eyes expressed a sadness he hadn't seen in months.

"Of course. Give me a sec."

Darwin finished the short letter, folded it, and stood from the table. He walked to the edge of the fieldstone patio and scanned the horizon as the sun's light dimmed behind the hills.

"Well?" Rosina said.

He turned back to her.

"It's not good news. But for us, I think it's okay."

"Tell me."

"Remember there were five police officers who followed me in the ambulance that night?"

"Yeah." Rosina moved to the edge of her seat.

"They pulled us from the canal. They knew we made it."

"Go on."

"All five were killed within two weeks of the time we flew to Italy. A bullet was placed behind their right ear, execution style."

"What does that mean for us?"

"Someone wanted to know where we are. Since none of those

men knew we had gone to Italy, they were executed. Our whereabouts are still protected, but someone's searching."

Rosina's hands cupped her open mouth. "Those men, their families …"

"I know. Tragic."

"Anything else?"

"Williams was killed a month ago on a raid that proved to be a hoax. They were set up. The investigators concluded that Williams was the target."

"How could they know something like that?"

"He was tortured. They found a pen and a pad of paper beside his body. Our names were on it, and the names of two cities."

"Two cities?"

"They concluded he was making up names to stop the torture because even he didn't know where that military plane was taking us the night he dropped us off at the Toronto airport."

A tear slipped down her face. "You said this might be good for us. What'd you mean by that? It doesn't sound very good so far."

"The only people that saw us alive and know about us are dead except Carson. No one on earth knows we're alive. They only suspect it."

"And Carson wrote the letter?"

Darwin nodded. "He sent it to tell us that everything was finished. Our secret location and our new names are still safe. His informants say that the mafia has moved on. They're tired of the war with The Blade. They couldn't find any new information on us after three months, and now they're convinced we're dead." He wiped a tear of his own off his cheek. "It is actually over, baby."

He walked over, lifted his wife to her feet, and hugged her. They said a prayer for the lives of the good men lost in their name, and he guided her inside their home.

He picked her up at the stairs and carried her to the bedroom in the loft.

They made love and fell asleep.

Neither one dreamed.

The nightmare was over.

Afterword

Dear Reader,

Many years ago, a UPS driver accidentally hit and killed a child who had run out into the street. Sometime later—I don't remember how long—that UPS driver was found dead, murdered. The media reported that the child was connected to a crime family in New York. The UPS driver's killer was never found.

There was an undercurrent of darkness to this story—an ominous feeling that at any moment, you could fall victim to an organized crime group by accident, as was the case above.

A decade later, while I was at the Fiumicino Airport in Rome waiting for my flight to Greece, where I would live for the next year, I was hit with some inspiration. While waiting to board the flight, the first scene of *The Kill* came to me. Darwin would find a way to get Rosina on the plane as they were heading to Greece so he could get her to safety as the mafia were after him for killing one of theirs with his car.

And the rest is history.

While writing *The Kill*, I used many of the places in Rome I'd visited. The hotel they stayed in with the little balcony was the exact room I had. The train station, Roma Termini, was written as close to detail as possible. Even down to the pay phone, Darwin used to call Greg Stinsen in the States—I actually used that phone once, too.

I enjoyed a cappuccino in the restaurant on the second floor overlooking the north access to the train station. I used this as the location for the scene when Darwin held a pencil to the gangster's neck.

After leaving Rome, the locations got easier as I grew up in Toronto.

For this novel, I researched torture (I'm sure you could tell). My goal was to have an innocent enough kid (Darwin), even though he's in his early twenties, fall into the hands of an ultra-violent underworld boss and find a way to survive and get out alive with all his fingers and toes intact.

To do that, I gave my main character two phobias: aichmophobia, an irrational fear of sharp and pointed objects, and achluophobia, a fear of the dark. When presented with these fears, he would lose his mind, attack when he normally wouldn't, and generally go insane, causing the mafia to not only fear his motivations as they die one by one but also need to kill him to remove the problem he's become.

By writing the second part of the book, they had been unsuccessful. Even burying him alive didn't work. When the Russians get involved, Darwin is surely done. They're smarter, stronger, and more ruthless—the most dangerous criminal organization on the planet. When I began researching *The Kill*, I decided to keep this series to the Italian mafia—the Russians seemed too dangerous. (La Cosa Nostra—you guys are great as villains, but the Russians are more frightening, which is better for fiction).

In the end, I decided to use the bratva for part three. What a way to end the novel, I thought. They would become the craziest villain that Darwin would have to face.

Both golf courses I used in the novel are ones I've golfed at but shall remain nameless (lawsuit avoiding here). No High Hills Golf Course is on Highway 50 in Toronto or the surrounding area. (I know. I looked it up).

The Russians are into strip clubs and restaurants, and Toronto is indeed too large a territory for one family, but fiction is what I do, so most of what you read was made up.

I used the Barrie Hospital because it opened to the public on September 22, 1997. My firstborn daughter was delivered there a week after it opened on September 29, 1997. I will often respect past events and locations in this unique way. They have a highly visible Helipad right by the highway. Although it's mentioned in the story, it remained unused by my characters.

Barrie is a nice city (I lived there for a few years), but Toronto is my hometown. Hence, numerous novels of mine are set there.

In the meantime, I must say goodbye to Darwin and Rosina— for now. May they enjoy their time in Italy, sipping wine, making love, and looking over their shoulder.

Happy reading,

Jonas Saul

P.S. Darwin and Rosina make their first appearance in the Sarah Roberts Series, book eight, *The Rogue*. Darwin is still going strong with the Sarah books, which total over forty in the series.

Hope you enjoy them!

About Jonas Saul

Jonas Saul is the bestselling author of the Sarah Roberts Series—more than two million sold!—and has written and published over sixty thrillers. After acquiring an agent, he signed several deals in Los Angeles, with MadRiver Pictures optioning his Sarah Roberts Series—over forty books!—(currently in development).

Jonas has often outranked Stephen King and Dean Koontz on Amazon over the past decade. He's regularly invited to be a guest speaker, teacher, or workshop presenter at international writing conferences and film festivals worldwide. He hosts an annual writer's retreat in Greece, where he currently lives. He focuses his teaching on how to get tension and emotion in every scene, on every page, how he made it as a creator/writer, the path to success in this business, and the pitfalls to avoid. He also hosts a reading retreat in Greece with guest authors, yoga retreats, and hiking retreats. Visit the Imagine Greece Retreats website at www.imaginegreeceretreats.com, or email him directly to discuss an opportunity to join one of the retreats at jonas@imaginegreeceretreats.com.

Jonas is also a professional freelance editor. He works for several publishers and does private editing for clients, with many testimonials on his website at www.imaginepress.org, which details each author's response to Jonas's editing skills. Email Jonas directly for an editing quote at editor@imaginepress.org.

To book Jonas for a speaking engagement at a writer's conference/festival, to have him on your jury at a film festival, or even to say hello, email Jonas directly at jonassaul@icloud.com.

For updates on releases, hit the "Follow" button on Amazon or Bookbub, and join Jonas on Facebook, where he's most active.

Contact Jonas Saul

Linktree: Find me here

Email: jonassaul@icloud.com